O9-BTJ-498

THE ALLIGATOR MAN

ALSO BY JAMES SHEEHAN

The Lawyer's Lawyer
The Mayor of Lexington Avenue
The Law of Second Chances

THE ALLIGATOR MAN

JAMES SHEEHAN

CENTER STREET

New York Boston Nashville

This book is a work of fiction. Names, characters, places, and incidents are the product of the author's imagination or are used fictitiously. Any resemblance to actual events, locales, or persons, living or dead, is coincidental.

Center Street
Hachette Book Group
237 Park Avenue
New York, NY 10017

www.CenterStreet.com

Printed in the United States of America

RRD-C

First edition: October 2013
10 9 8 7 6 5 4 3 2 1

Center Street is a division of Hachette Book Group, Inc.
The Center Street name and logo are trademarks of Hachette Book Group, Inc.

The Hachette Speakers Bureau provides a wide range of authors for speaking events. To find out more, go to www.HachetteSpeakersBureau.com or call (866) 376-6591.

The publisher is not responsible for websites (or their content) that are not owned by the publisher.

Library of Congress Control Number: 2013939107

ISBN 978-1-4555-0864-8

For John, Justin, and Sarah
You have made this journey all it was meant to be

THE ALLIGATOR MAN

PROLOGUE

Billy Fuller had spent his whole adult life as an employee of Dynatron, a major energy company located in northwest Florida, until the company folded and he lost everything. He had two recurrent nightmares that left him constantly tired and on edge and haunted him during the daylight hours as well. This night he was dreaming about his wife, Laurie. It was always the same dream.

He's sitting in the chair by Laurie's bedside, watching her as she lies there with her eyes closed. Dark, hollow sockets harbor those eyes, her cheeks are gaunt, her body ravaged by disease.

Her eyes open. She turns as she always does to where he is sitting and smiles. At that moment, she is so beautiful to him. He wants to cut his wrists open and give her every drop of the good, clean, healthy blood that flows through his veins.

"Come here," she says, and Billy comes to her and kisses her on the lips.

"I love you," he says.

"I love you too, honey."

He sees a faint twinkle in those deep-set eyes. He wants to reach in, pull it out, and make it light up her whole body. He wants his life and his wife back. This time he wants a happy ending.

She raises those thin arms, arms that are black-and-blue from the

IVs. They are part of her beauty too. She puts her hands on Billy's shoulders.

"My body's tired, Billy. I'm going to have to leave it soon. I can't fight anymore," she says. "I need you to be strong for the kids."

"Don't say that, honey. There's still time. There's still hope. I need you. I can't do this alone."

"Yes, you can. I'll help you. Part of me will always be with you."

"I don't know."

"You'll have to trust me on this one, sweetheart," she says, closing her eyes. "I'm so tired."

Billy puts his hands to his face then and weeps. No, *he says to himself.* No.

The sound of his own voice shouting those words wakes him up.

His other dream was about his best friend, Jimmy Lennox. Jimmy had stood with him through Laurie's hospitalization despite his own personal setbacks. He'd been Billy's lifeline.

Billy is sleeping. The phone rings in the middle of the night. He doesn't want to answer it. He knows. But he is compelled to get out of bed and pick up the phone.

"Hello."

"Billy."

"Hi, Jimmy."

"Billy, I just want to tell you how much I appreciate your friendship and all you've done for me."

"What are you talking about, Jimmy? It's me who should be thanking you."

"Billy, I can't take it anymore."

"Take what? What are you talking about? We can take anything, you and me."

"I'm sorry, Billy. I really am."

"Jimmy, Jimmy, don't hang up. I'll come over. I'll be there in a minute. We'll talk this out."

He hears the click.

He runs out of the house. Calls 911 on his cell phone as he jumps in his car and races over to Jimmy's house. "Come on, faster," he yells at the car as he presses the accelerator to the floor. Finally, he reaches Jimmy's apartment. The door is unlocked. He walks in and sees Jimmy on the living room floor, his arms and legs splayed out, the phone in one hand, a revolver in the other. Blood oozes from his right temple. His left leg is twitching.

"Oh my God! Oh my God. Hang on, Jimmy."

He kneels down, opens Jimmy's mouth, breathes into it, presses down on his chest. Does it again. And again... until the police and paramedics arrive and pull him off.

"No. No," he yells as they drag him away.

Then he wakes up in a sweat.

CHAPTER ONE

Sunday, April 10, 2005

Gazillionaire Roy Johnson was, among other things, a lush. Every night somewhere between ten and eleven, Mighty Roy would get a bottle of red wine from his wine room, walk outside into his enormous backyard garden, and sniff his various, expensive tropical flowers. Then he'd sit in his overstuffed chair, drinking by himself until the bottle was empty and he'd have to get up and get another one.

He'd screwed a lot of people over to get to that position in life.

Johnson had been the CEO of Dynatron, a major energy company in the United States and overseas that employed over twenty thousand people. In his heyday he'd dined with kings and queens and heads of state, including the president. A little over a year ago, over a period of three months, Dynatron stock fell from seventy-five dollars a share to fifty cents and then to nothing as the company slipped into bankruptcy.

Roy was not around for that debacle, however. He'd long ago cashed out to the tune of a hundred million dollars.

His employees were there, though—to the bitter end. Their pension savings had all been converted to Dynatron stock before the collapse, and the fund had been frozen so they could not transfer their assets to other securities.

No word or combination of words could capture the collective havoc inflicted on those people. In addition to their jobs, every employee lost his or her retirement and health insurance. Some lost the ability to hope; some lost their spouses and families; others took their own lives.

None of that seemed to bother Johnson as he sat in his garden chair gazing at the stars. When he was good and soused, Mighty Roy and his bottle would take a walk on Gladestown Road, a two-lane road that was the only entry and exit into Gladestown, the little town where Roy had chosen to build his kingdom.

After Dynatron collapsed, the feds determined it had inflated the value of its stock for several years through a series of sophisticated accounting procedures. The chief accountant pled out to a three-year sentence. Mighty Roy claimed no knowledge of wrongdoing, and so far there was no evidence linking the slimy bastard to anything. That was it. Millions of investors screwed, twenty thousand employees decimated, or worse, and one guy got a three-year sentence. Case closed.

Or maybe not…

He was walking down the road with his bottle in his hand. He loved this sleepy, little town with its clear moonlit skies. There were no lights on the road, no traffic, and no other signs of civilization. The only sound was the croaking of the gators who resided in the swamps that surrounded the narrow asphalt strip. There were hundreds of them down there, he knew, and they could smell him for sure as he walked along. It was such a narrow, artificial line between safety and danger, life and death. He laughed out loud as the thought struck him.

A gator could shoot out of the swamp at any time and grab him.

Hell, they crossed the road all the time. Others had disappeared. Maybe it was him, the smell of him, that kept them at bay. Fear. Irrational fear. He loved it.

He turned and started back toward home, staying in the middle of the road, mindful of the fact that if he slipped by the shoulder and fell, he would have crossed the line. There would be no hesitation then. They would be on him in a heartbeat, and to them he would become just another piece of meat.

He heard the engine behind him, saw the road light up from the headlights, and moved to the left side of the road, paying careful attention to where the asphalt ended and the swamp began. It was a little strange for a car to be out here at this hour of the evening, but he wasn't worried about it. There was plenty of road for the car. His fuzzy brain didn't detect the sound of the engine increasing speed, didn't notice until it was too late that the headlights were focused dead center on him. The car hit him without attempting to stop, propelling him into the murky darkness. There was a splash as his body hit the water, immediately followed by a thousand other little splashes as the creatures of the night raced each other for a piece of the unexpected evening meal.

CHAPTER TWO

Carlisle Buchanan was the sheriff's man in Gladestown, an insignificant, old Florida town with a population of three hundred fifty people. Situated at the southwestern tip of the state on the western edge of the Everglades and surrounded on two sides by swamp and the third side by Florida Bay, Gladestown didn't even have its own police force. It was under the jurisdiction of the Forrest County Sheriff's Department. The sheriff occupied a tiny A-frame at the intersection of Highway 41 and Gladestown Road.

Carlisle was a native. When Sheriff Frank Cousins decided he could not commit an officer to the little hamlet because of its distance from his main headquarters in Verona some sixty miles away, he decided to hire somebody local to keep an eye on things at a much lower pay rate than a sheriff's deputy. Carlisle was far and away the best candidate. He was twenty-seven years old, stood six feet two inches tall, was strong as an ox, and knew everything about Gladestown and the surrounding waters. Even though he was not required to carry a gun for the auxiliary job, Carlisle was an avid outdoorsman, well versed in all kinds of weaponry.

Carlisle hadn't wanted the job. He didn't even apply. Office work was simply too confining. But Sheriff Cousins had stopped at Rosie's Café one day and found out about him from Rosie. After that, the sheriff wouldn't let go until he had his man.

"Just open up in the morning, Carlisle, and stick around for a couple of hours. After that, as long as you have your phone on, you can patrol the town, the surrounding waters, the woods—wherever you want to go.

"I just want you to be my eyes and ears out here. If there's any trouble, you just contact headquarters."

The job paid better than what he was doing at the time, so Carlisle finally relented. It had turned out to be a good decision so far. In the two years since he'd started, Carlisle had little occasion to even call headquarters.

Things were about to change.

On Monday morning at eight thirty-five, he was puttering around the office—sweeping, cleaning desktops, anything to stay busy. Carlisle didn't like just sitting around unless, of course, he was out on the water and he had a fishing rod in his hands.

He was putting the broom and dustpan away when a woman walked in. It was such a rare event that Carlisle was startled for a moment.

"Can I help you?" he asked politely as he walked toward the counter.

"I'd like to report a missing person," the woman said. She had that well-heeled look: tan and toned in a plain white summer dress with plenty of accoutrements—earrings, necklace, watch, bracelet, two diamond rings, and a white gold wedding band. Her skin was smooth and her seemingly natural golden blonde hair was tied in a ponytail.

"A missing person," Carlisle said. "And who would that be?"

"My husband, Roy Johnson." She waited for the look of

recognition on Carlisle's face when she uttered the name of the most famous part-time resident of Gladestown.

"When was the last time you saw your husband?" Carlisle continued in a professional manner, grabbing a legal pad to document the conversation.

"Last night around ten or eleven o'clock. He went out in his garden as he usually does. I went to bed as I usually do. When I woke up this morning, he wasn't there."

"So you just noticed him missing this morning?"

"Yes."

"Have you checked around town or called his business associates or friends?"

"My husband doesn't frequent any places in town, and he has no friends or business associates around here."

Carlisle was not all that concerned. Missing husbands were not uncommon in Gladestown. Usually they were out all night on their boat or at a buddy's house. Sometimes, they went to Verona, the big city down the road, for the night. He had never filled out a missing person's report, and they always showed up either the next day or, in rare cases, the day after. A guy with resources like Roy Johnson could be anywhere. Carlisle remembered the whole town talking about the time a helicopter landed on Roy's front lawn to pick him up.

"Doesn't your husband have bodyguards?"

"How did you know about them?"

"I ran into them one time."

Carlisle had walked to the office late one night from his home, a distance of a little over a mile. On the way back, he decided on a whim to look around the great Johnson mansion. It was set back off Gladestown Road right on the water where the canal opened out onto Florida Bay—a lovely spot. There was no gate or fencing. Set amid the serenity of the swamp, the tall pines, the cypress and cedars, it stuck out like a canker sore.

Carlisle had been down by the dock looking at the yachts when two men came out of the dark with guns in hand and made him lie on the ground facedown with his arms and legs spread apart. They only let him go after they found his wallet and saw his identification as an auxiliary police officer. Carlisle was angry at himself over that incident. He vowed that he would never let anybody catch him off guard like that again.

"They don't know where he is either." Sylvia Johnson brought him back to the present.

That *was* strange. It seemed like a man with bodyguards would at least let them know if he was disappearing on the wife for a while. And from what he'd heard about Roy Johnson, there were a lot of people who would like to see him disappear forever.

"Ma'am, I'll report this to my superiors right away."

CHAPTER THREE

"Have I told you how sexy you look when you eat slow?" Susan asked him as the shovel he called his right hand was funneling the puttanesca al something-or-other into his mouth. It took him a moment to swallow it all.

"I am eating slow," Kevin replied.

"Maybe if you were an anteater. Look, honey, once again we are out at a nice restaurant, all dressed up, and in a moment I'm going to be eating by myself. Is it too much to ask you to give it a rest when we go out to dinner?" They were eating in an upscale Italian restaurant in South Beach called Bella Noche.

"Okay, I'll slow down," he said as he reached across the table for a slice of Italian bread.

"Thank you, sweetheart," she said. Feeling the need to pump him up again, she added, "You look very handsome tonight." She meant every word of it. He had a soft Roman face, his nose curving gently, his lips slightly thick, and his eyes hidden in their own individual caverns. He was dressed in a short-sleeve blue silk shirt, black slacks, and loafers without socks, his brown hair wavy and somewhat unruly.

"You don't have to say that."

"I know. I wanted to. Can't you just accept a compliment?"

Kevin Wylie and Susan Bishop were semiregulars in South

Beach. They knew to arrive early on a Saturday night if they wanted a table with a view of the sidewalk and the street where the fancy cars paraded by. It was always a spectacular show. People of every persuasion, the beautiful and not so beautiful—the fine-figured model who posed for millions and the drunk who walked down the strip pouring leftover drinks in his glass as he made the perfect kamikaze. Some were dressed to the nines, others almost not at all.

"We could live here, you know."

"Susan, don't go there," he replied. "Let me just enjoy the sexy feeling of eating slow. Don't ruin it."

"You don't want to talk about it because it's about money. You can't afford it."

"It's not about money. I just don't want to live here."

"This is the home of the rich and famous. Who would not want to live here?"

"This is the home of the wacky and the wackier. It's a fun diversion on a Saturday night, but as a daily menu it would make me want to stick pins in my eyeballs."

"I'm not talking about living on the strip. I'm talking about living on the beach. You know exactly what I'm talking about."

She could be relentless at times. At thirty-two, she was in line to take over her father's insurance business in a few short years. She wanted a partner who was just as successful.

Kevin had been working for a prominent criminal lawyer named Bernie Stang for the last seven years. He made good money but from Susan's perspective it was a dead-end job. His seeming complacency irritated her and she was constantly nudging him to move on. The house on the beach was part of the prodding.

"I've been looking at office space," he told her, hoping to get off the subject of residential relocation.

"That's great," she said. "When are you going to give Bernie the news?"

"I figure I'll be ready to leave in six months."

"Six months! What are you waiting six months for?"

"Well, I have to rent space. I have to buy furniture and computers. I have to establish a client base."

"Kevin, you can rent space and buy furniture and computers in a day. And how do criminal lawyers establish a client base? Do criminals keep you on retainer?"

"Very funny. But you know we do have regular clients. And people come to us based on Bernie's reputation."

"As long as you work for Bernie, they'll be coming to the office based on Bernie's reputation. Kevin, in the last five years you have tried as many cases as Bernie. You told me so yourself. Bernie cherry-picks the high-profile cases so only his reputation is enhanced. There is only one way to stop that. There is only one way to establish your own client base."

"I'm just not ready to walk out the door."

"When will you be? You've been talking about office space for the last year. I think you just mention it to appease me."

"I need money. You don't just open the doors without money. You have to have some staying power."

"Get a letter of credit from the bank."

"You've got all the answers, don't you?"

"No, honey. I just want you to succeed. I think you are one of the finest criminal lawyers in Miami." She knew when to quit. "C'mon, let's join the show."

They paid their bill, descended the steps of Bella Noche, and blended into the Saturday night crowd.

CHAPTER FOUR

Sylvia Johnson was back at the sheriff's office at 8:00 a.m. on Tuesday waiting for Carlisle to arrive. This time her anxiety was palpable. She was dressed in khaki shorts and a white top, and she wasn't wearing any jewelry or makeup.

"Have you heard anything?" she asked Carlisle as he approached the door to the A-frame.

"No, I haven't," Carlisle calmly replied. "Maybe there'll be a message from headquarters this morning. However, if they had heard or found out anything they probably would have called me at home." It was all a ruse. He'd made his report but the department wouldn't put out a BOLO (Be on the Lookout) until Roy Johnson had been missing for forty-eight hours. Carlisle couldn't give her that news.

"I haven't heard a thing from him." She almost whispered the words.

"Please calm down, ma'am. If your husband has gone somewhere, we'll find out where. If something has happened to him, and I wouldn't assume that at this point, we'll find that out as well. Now do you have somebody who can come and stay with you?" He motioned her to come around the counter and sit in the chair next to his desk.

"Aida, our maid, is at home with me."

"I'd like to get a little more information if I could. Do you and Mr. Johnson have any children?"

"No, not yet. We've only been married for two years. He has grown children from his first marriage."

"Have you contacted them?"

"No. We don't speak."

"I'm going to need their names and addresses."

"Fine. They don't know anything. They don't speak to *him* either."

"I understand. It's just routine police procedure," Carlisle told her. "You mentioned yesterday that the last time you saw your husband he was going out to the garden like he usually does, and you went to bed like you usually do, is that right?"

Carlisle had his pad out again.

"Yes."

"Is there anything else your husband does at night besides going out into his garden?"

"He sometimes takes a walk on the road."

"You mean Gladestown Road?"

"Yes. It goes right past our house. He told me he likes to walk on it at night."

"How late at night are we talking about?"

She shrugged. "I don't know, eleven, maybe a little earlier or later. I'm not sure."

"Did your husband drink at all when he went out into his garden or when he took a walk down the road?"

"I don't know. I'm always in bed."

"Well, I think you said you've seen him walk out into the garden. Was he drinking then?"

"He'd have a little wine maybe."

"How much wine?"

"He'd usually open a bottle."

"Did he finish it?"

"I don't know. Why are you asking these questions?"

"Just trying to cover all possibilities, ma'am."

"Do you think he could have fallen into the swamp?" she asked. "Do you think the gators could have gotten him?" She was rubbing her left arm up and down with her right hand, probably not realizing she was doing it.

"Your husband grew up in these parts, ma'am. It's not likely he'd slip and fall in the swamp."

"You knew my husband?"

"No, ma'am. My father did, though. Many years ago."

"Will you take a look anyway, just to be sure?"

"Yes, ma'am."

Carlisle was thinking of another scenario not totally unrelated to what Sylvia Johnson had suggested. There was a migrant community that lived farther down Gladestown Road closer to town. They'd been there for years, and the men sometimes got drunk and walked the road. Gators crossed that road all the time. There were stories over the years of men getting snatched from the pavement and pulled into the swamp. It was unusual but it happened. Since the migrants were illegal no police reports were ever made and no investigation ever took place. The men simply vanished into thin air.

"Ma'am, do you recall what your husband was wearing when you saw him last?"

"Yes, he had on a short-sleeve cream-colored silk shirt, black shorts, and sandals."

"How about identification? Did he have any identification with him?"

"I believe he did. He always carried his wallet with him, and I have been unable to locate it." She started to cry. "He always put it on the nightstand before coming to bed."

CHAPTER FIVE

Carlisle typed up his report immediately after Sylvia Johnson left the office and faxed it to headquarters. He followed the written report with a telephone call. He was referred to a Sergeant Anderson.

"Sergeant, I know this is a little early to be stirring things up over a missing person, but this is Roy Johnson we're talking about. His wife doesn't know where he is."

"I'll bring it to the attention of the sheriff," Sergeant Anderson told him.

After placing the call, Carlisle headed to Rosie's Café for breakfast.

Rosie's was a little wooden building situated right on the bay in town. There was an outside porch on the waterside that fit three tables and had a great view. There was no benefit to sitting inside unless you were a tourist and wanted to look at the eight-foot stuffed alligator hanging from the wall, or the mahi mahi, or the grouper, or the fishing nets and hats and countless other pieces of crap that cluttered the place. Rosie, a sixty-year-old widow and a native of Gladestown, had run the place for the last twenty years. Carlisle loved eating there because the food was down-home and plentiful and because he loved Rosie.

"Mornin', Rosie," he yelled as he plopped down at a spot on the porch. The place was empty.

"Mornin', Sheriff Buchanan," Rosie replied as she exited the kitchen and came to take his order. She was a bit of a thing with short black hair, constantly in motion. Rosie wasn't kidding about the title either. In her mind Carlisle was the sheriff of Gladestown. "The other guy don't care about us," she'd tell him, referring to the real sheriff. "We won't see him again until the next election when he'll blow through for about five minutes. You're it, Carlisle. And I for one wouldn't want anybody else at the helm."

Rosie meant every word, but she didn't make the statement too often. She knew it embarrassed Carlisle.

"I'll have the corned beef hash, Rosie, with three eggs and some grits."

It was a slow morning so Rosie delivered Carlisle's meal and sat down for a chat.

"So what's new with Gladestown's finest?" she asked. When he was younger, Rosie would reach over and tousle his thick blond hair. He was too big for that now, although she was still tempted.

Carlisle had already decided before he entered Rosie's that he was going to tell her about Roy Johnson. If there was scuttlebutt about Roy stepping out on his wife or something of that nature, Rosie was the person to talk to.

"Roy Johnson is missing. He hasn't come home for two nights. His wife is frantic."

"I'd be frantic if I were her too," Rosie replied. "Nobody wants to lose their golden goose."

"Now, Rosie, be nice. I know she's a lot younger than him and he's got a lot of money, but she seems genuinely concerned. She cries all the time."

"That's you, Carlisle. You see the best in everybody and that's why I love you. That woman could probably cry at the drop of a hat if she needed to."

"Have you heard anything?" Carlisle asked, ignoring the compliment.

"No. This is the first I heard of it. You got any ideas?"

"Well, she said he was walking down Gladestown Road late at night and he was drinking."

"Do you really give credence to the stories about gators snatching those migrants off of Gladestown Road?"

"Absolutely. I'm sure they're true," Carlisle replied.

"Well, you have more knowledge about the subject than anybody."

"Gators don't usually mess with people," Carlisle told her. "A dog maybe or a little kid, but not a full-grown man. Anything is possible after this drought, though. They're starving and it's mating season so they're very aggressive as well."

"But snatching people off the road? I could understand it if he fell in."

"A couple of years ago there was a drought like this one, and three people in Florida were killed in a week. One woman, a jogger, was snatched off the road. And those incidents are documented. You know, more people are killed by alligators in Florida than by sharks."

When it came to the water, the animals, and the delicate ecosystems of the Everglades, Carlisle was a human encyclopedia.

"Well, I'll be," Rosie replied. "So what are you going to do about this other than report it to those people down the road who never come here?"

"I think I'll take the airboat out and look around. I promised her I would."

"You promised her you would? You watch out for that woman, Carlisle. I wouldn't trust her as far as I could throw her."

"Come on, Rosie. Give her a break. She's worried about her husband."

Carlisle lived with his mother in the family home on the water. It was like most houses in Gladestown (other than Roy Johnson's), a small two-bedroom wooden structure with a tin roof and a large screened-in porch. Carlisle pulled up in the driveway and headed straight for the dock behind the house to ready the airboat for his trip. He checked the gas and the equipment before stopping in to see his mother. Then he was off.

There were two boats in the dock, a thirty-two-foot-long Grady-White that Carlisle used to fish on the open water and the airboat. He'd inherited both from his father. The airboat was made for the shallow swamps. A regular motorboat with its propeller dipping below the surface could not operate in the Everglades where the water barely covered the surface in many places and sometimes not at all when there was a drought. The powerful airboat engine was situated atop the boat and above the water with a huge fan five feet or more in diameter. The velocity of the fan against the air allowed the boat to move over very shallow water or even dry land, although it was a very loud process and required the operator and any passengers to wear ear guards to muffle the sound.

Carlisle had one more thing to deal with before he started the airboat and headed out into the swamp. There was a great blue heron standing in the water right in front of the canal that Carlisle needed to pass through.

"Mornin', Scotch," he said to the bird, a daily ritual. "I've got to go out and do some police work this morning. I'll try and bring you back some food if I get a chance. Now, I need you to let me by."

He started up the engine and the magnificent bird immediately started flapping its wings, tucked its skinny, sticklike legs under its body, and flew off.

CHAPTER SIX

Carlisle Buchanan's knowledge of the Everglades ecosystem was only surpassed by his ability to maneuver his airboat through the saw grass prairies and the mangrove corridors. He didn't need a compass, although he always carried one. He knew exactly where he was at all times.

Once he was out of the canal and into the saw grass, the devastation wrought by the winter drought was visible everywhere. Land that was normally submerged under two or three feet of water was bone-dry in spots. One could actually see the cracks. It was as if the earth was opening its mouth and crying out for water.

Carlisle was used to the scene. As someone who spent a lot of time on the water, he accepted it all as part of the ebb and flow of nature. He knew that the rains would eventually come and restore the balance, although it was April and they were long overdue.

Carlisle passed through the saw grass to the mazes created by the red mangroves. The mangroves grew in such a way that there was a path through them, their roots protruding from the sea like the legs of the great blue heron. The water was deeper here and Carlisle upped his speed. The path, however, was not always straight and at times became very narrow with the tops of the mangroves meeting to create a cylinder-like corridor with roots coming out of the water and branches closing in from the sides and the top. Carlisle flew along like a bat out of hell, slowing and turning on a dime, then speeding up until the next turn, which was visible only to someone who knew the terrain.

He went to the west side of Gladestown Road first. The trip took about fifteen minutes. There was a canal right next to the road and the water was at its deepest there, reaching five, seven, sometimes ten feet deep in spots. The mangroves were thick and especially close together and movement was slow and hazardous, even for Carlisle who was totally in his element.

Some egrets and herons were wading in the shallows. Others were perched on branches that reached out over the water, oblivious to the sound of the engine and so close it seemed as if Carlisle could have reached out and touched any one of them if he had a mind to. Their attention was totally focused on the water, searching intently for a fish or a stray insect while at the same time warily watching for the predatory gator.

Carlisle was searching too, in the water and the thicket, for a sign of Roy Johnson, *or any part of him*. It took an hour and a half to cover the west side, and by the time he reached the east side, which involved retracing his initial route and going around the southern tip of the town, the sun was up and it was hot, although it was only April and the blistering humidity of the summer had not yet arrived. Carlisle didn't seem to notice. He was on a mission.

It was well past the third hour when he spotted it, a large piece of black cloth hanging on a mangrove root close to the water. He grabbed it from the branch and cut the engine so he could inspect it. None of the edges were smooth and it appeared to have been ripped on all sides. Carlisle stepped out of the boat and, after wedging it between two bushes, started climbing along the roots of the mangroves, diligently searching for any other piece of evidence that might exist. He was a hundred and fifty yards away from the boat when he saw something white in the water. It was a much bigger piece of cloth.

The white cloth had the same rough edges as the black one. It appeared to be the front quarter of a man's shirt with the pocket still in place. And the material was *silk*.

CHAPTER SEVEN

Bernie Stang was a salesman and a fixer in the business of criminal law. His clients were men and they were mostly drug dealers. Bernie had a suite that took up the twenty-first floor of an office building in downtown Miami, but that's where the similarity to his business neighbors ended. The reception area was overstated and gaudy, with dark mahogany paneling on the walls, thick gold lettering on the door, and a huge crystal chandelier in the entryway. It also came with Rhonda Hamilton, the receptionist with a bedroom voice, a provocative smile, and a body that made grown men salivate.

Bernie's inner office was also over the top—complete with an American flag, the Florida state flag, a thick blue rug with the state seal in the middle, and pictures of Bernie center stage with presidents and senators. It was impossible to tell from the décor that Bernie represented lawbreakers.

"This is a man with a monumental ego and no taste," Susan told Kevin the first time he brought her into Bernie's office. Kevin just laughed.

"I think the pictures are all fake too," she added. "I can't see presidents, senators, and movie stars all lining up to have their picture taken with Bernie."

"You're probably right about most of them," Kevin replied.

One picture in particular struck her. Bernie was standing with his arm around a man dressed in a white suit with a full head of thick white hair. "Who's that?" she asked.

"Funny you should ask," Kevin said. "His name is Franklin Rutledge and he is one of the most prominent criminal trial lawyers in the country. He lives here in Miami. He and Bernie are friends, although I think Bernie envies Rutledge's reputation, which far overshadows his own."

"Why did you say, 'Funny you should ask'?"

"Well, Rutledge once told me that his white suit is his trademark. He always wears it into court because it stands out so much and people remember it. I never really bought into that theory until now. Out of all these pictures on Bernie's wall, the only one you asked about was Franklin Rutledge."

The rest of the place was pedestrian. Individual attorney offices were situated on both sides of a long hallway. Outside each office was a secretarial station. The walls were white and the carpet was commercial-grade gray.

Kevin, who was easygoing and cool in the courtroom, co-counseled with Bernie on many of his high-profile cases and, next to him, was considered the best trial lawyer in the firm. Still he was given no special treatment when it came to office space.

His office, like those of the other nine attorneys, was a box with room for a desk, two client chairs, and nothing else. The wall behind Kevin's desk was filled with various diplomas, licenses, memberships, and awards—one of Bernie's requirements, like Rhonda's dresses, to impress the criminals. There were two pictures of fruit on the other walls and a small picture of Susan on Kevin's desk, and that was it.

Kevin's undoing at the Stang law firm started with a simple phone call from a client named Bob Dunning, a drug dealer.

"What's up, Bob?"

"Kevin, I can't get a hold of Bernie and I need a hundred grand today to close this deal I've got going. Can you authorize that for me in Bernie's absence?"

"I'm not sure I understand what you're asking me to do, Bob."

"It's very simple. I need the money. You're Bernie's right-hand man. Get me the money."

"We're your lawyers, Bob, not your bankers."

"That's news to me and it'll be news to your fuckin' boss too. You playin' a game with me? I need this money now. If I don't make this deal, there'll be hell to pay."

"I'm not playing any games and I don't know what you're talking about."

Kevin heard the phone click dead on the other end of the line. He immediately tried to get Bernie on his cell phone to no avail. He left a message on Bernie's phone that he needed to talk to him, and he left the same message with Rhonda and Bernie's secretary, Mary.

Mary didn't call him back until the next morning.

"He wants to see you right away," she told him. Kevin went directly to Bernie's office.

Bernie was sitting at his desk as Kevin walked in the door. He had his chair turned sideways so he was looking at his wall of plaques and awards rather than at Kevin.

"Sit down," Bernie said before Kevin could even mention the call from Bob Dunning. "My sources tell me you're looking at office space." Bernie continued to look at the wall as he spoke. "Are you considering making a move?"

"Nothing gets by you, does it?" Kevin replied.

"Nope."

"I've been checking out space just to get a feel for what the market is out there. I don't plan on making a move in the near future."

Bernie was feeding himself grapes as he leaned back in his power chair still facing the wall. "But you do plan on making a move eventually?"

"Yeah. I'd like to start my own practice eventually."

"Doing what, criminal defense work?"

"That's what I do."

"And you plan on taking some clients with you?"

"I don't plan on it, but I imagine some of the people I've represented will come to me in the future."

"And send their friends to you?"

"And send their friends to me—yes. That's how it works, isn't it?"

Bernie ignored the question. "So you plan on competing against me?"

"In the sense that I'll be doing the same type of work like hundreds of other criminal lawyers in this town. My going out on my own is not going to affect your operation at all. Do you have a problem with me eventually starting my own business?"

"I have a problem with you working for me and looking for office space behind my back."

"I wasn't doing anything behind your back. I was checking out the real estate market. If I make a decision to go, you'll be the first to know." Kevin stood up and walked around. He was mad and he wanted to leave, but he had a feeling Bernie wasn't through yet.

Bernie didn't respond right away. He kept looking at the wall and eating his grapes. "That's nice of you to let me know and all. However, it's not enough. I don't mind you going back to the state attorney's office or over to the public defender. I don't mind you practicing civil law and making a fortune. I just don't want you doing criminal defense work and competing against me."

Kevin couldn't believe his ears. "Is that right? You don't want me stepping out from under your thumb? In case you haven't noticed, that is an American flag next to you. You know, the land of the free—capitalism, competition, the American dream, and all that shit. I'm going to do everything aboveboard, but when I leave I'm going to practice criminal law in this town and I'm going to compete against you, so get used to it."

It was Bernie's turn to stand up. Although he was fifty-plus, Bernie was still in good shape. He was a tall man with a barrel chest and thick arms. He had a few scars on his cheeks from teenage acne and a thick black mustache.

He walked over to where Kevin was standing. Inches separated the two men. Kevin was a little over six feet himself but Bernie was taller.

"I read in the paper a couple of weeks ago that Charlie Willis was killed during a robbery. They said he had an accomplice with him who got away. Charlie and your buddy Sal were inseparable, weren't they?"

Kevin didn't move even though Bernie was literally in his face. Sal Trivigno was the closest thing to a regular client Kevin had. He was a small-time hood who couldn't seem to get his act together and go straight no matter how hard he tried. Sal was not part of the Charlie Willis robbery and murder but he was a suspect, and Kevin had talked to him and met with the state attorney on his behalf.

"What are you driving at, Bernie?"

Bernie turned his back to Kevin and began to walk away. "I figured Sal would be calling you if he was involved. You have to anticipate business when you run your own show, Kevin. Then I hear from my sources downtown that you are representing Sal and that you even went to a meeting with him and the state attorney. I checked your billing records and Sal wasn't on there. So I asked myself, *Has Kevin started his own business already while I'm still paying his salary?*"

"You know that's bullshit, Bernie. I don't operate like that."

"Really? You had to meet with Sal. Knowing Sal like I do, that was at least two hours. You probably had some conversations with the state attorney's office and at least one other meeting with Sal before appearing with him downtown."

"What's your point?" Kevin interrupted.

"My point is I'm already out thousands of dollars and that's just the beginning of your little game of stealing business from me."

"Look, Sal didn't have any money, that's all. It had nothing to do with me looking for office space."

"So besides leaving me, you decide you're going to run a charitable organization without my knowledge."

"It's one client for Christ's sake. The bar requires us to do pro bono work anyway."

"That's my decision, not yours."

"Fine. But don't accuse me of pilfering your clients or running my own operation behind your back."

"I won't be accusing you of anything anymore. You're out of here as of right now."

Bernie walked back to his desk casually, sat in his chair, and took out a big Cuban cigar from a wooden box on his desk. He clipped the tip and lit it up.

"What the hell are you doing, Bernie?" Kevin asked. He wasn't talking about the cigar.

"I'm just quitting you before you quit me."

Kevin was really angry now. He started pacing back and forth in front of Bernie's desk. *Calm down*, he told himself. *Think about what's really going on here and what you're going to say next.*

"This isn't about me looking for office space or me representing Sal, is it? It's about that phone call I received yesterday from Bob Dunning."

"What phone call?"

"Come on, Bernie. I've been here for seven years. I'm your best trial lawyer. You're not just going to up and fire me because I was looking for office space. I heard something yesterday that I wasn't supposed to hear, didn't I?"

It was Bernie's turn to get a little fired up. "You know, Kevin, I never liked that holier-than-thou attitude that you have. You're a damn good lawyer but you don't get the big picture. We're *criminal* lawyers. The big cases that come in this firm are drug cases. They support this business of ours. We support their business by keeping them out of jail. It is what it is."

"Where are you going with this, Bernie?"

"Nowhere."

"Nowhere?"

"That's right. I was just being polite, explaining something to you. The explanation is over. It's time for you to go."

"That's it? Just like that I'm out the door? And you expect me not to compete with you after you do this?"

"Perhaps you didn't understand me, Kevin. I didn't *ask* you not to compete with me, I *told* you."

"Are you threatening me?"

"I wouldn't call it that."

"And what happens if I ignore you?"

Bernie stood up and smiled with the big Cuban still in his mouth. He walked around his desk toward Kevin once again.

"That's where it would get interesting."

"What does that mean?"

"Let's just say that after your conversation yesterday with Bob Dunning some people are not happy with you. An opportunity was missed. Hundreds of thousands of dollars in profit was lost. I negotiated on your behalf—and I guess you could say on my behalf as well—and this is what we all agreed on. We'll just let you go quietly into the night."

"I'm not afraid of you, Bernie," Kevin said as Bernie approached him.

"It's not me you should be thinking about. You know the people I represent. Hell, you've represented some of them yourself. They don't like mistakes, especially when it costs them money. You're a handsome man, Kevin. You wouldn't want that pretty face to get messed up—or even worse."

"Why would they care if I opened my own practice?"

"They don't. They'd rather do something to you right now. Since I negotiated on your behalf, I threw in a little something for myself."

"This is crazy."

"It's a crazy world."

"You're serious?"

Bernie took another puff of his Cuban and blew the smoke to the right side of Kevin's face.

"Dead serious. You're a good lawyer, Kevin—best lawyer I know other than myself. That's why I don't want you competing with me in this city. You'll have no problem becoming a civil trial lawyer or opening up a practice in bumfuck Egypt or some other place. I'd go as far away from these boys as I could if I were you."

They were standing in the middle of Bernie's office, toe-to-toe, Bernie still smoking the Cuban, Kevin barely able to breathe.

"So that's it," Kevin said.

"That's it."

Bernie walked over to his conference room door and opened

it. His driver and bodyguard, a huge man named Vic, walked into the room. He'd been waiting there all along.

"Vic, would you walk Mr. Wylie back to his office, wait for him to empty out his desk, and then escort him out of the building?" Bernie asked in his most pleasant tone.

Kevin turned to leave. There wasn't any upside to tangling with Vic at this point.

"Kevin," Bernie called to him as he reached the door. Kevin turned and looked back at Bernie's sarcastic smile. "Have a nice life."

CHAPTER EIGHT

Carlisle called headquarters immediately to report the discoveries he had made in the swamp. Early the next morning, Wednesday, he rang the front doorbell at the big mansion.

He knew that the sheriff's department had to contact the Florida Department of Environmental Protection and the National Park Service to notify them of the possibility of an alligator attack either within or bordering Everglades National Park. Once that happened the whole world would know that Roy Johnson was missing, assuming he was still missing. Government agencies were like badly leaking ships when it came to keeping information secret, and reporters were like leeches sucking up everything that seeped out.

Carlisle wanted to tell Sylvia Johnson what he had found as early as possible to soften the blow to the extent that he could before all hell broke loose. He hoped that Roy Johnson himself would answer the door and end the drama.

Aida the maid answered it instead. Mrs. Johnson was home, she told him, and ushered him into the living room to wait. Carlisle had never been in such a big, beautiful place. The carpet was white plush and so clean he was afraid to walk on it, or sit on the flowered couch, or look in the gigantic mirror over the fireplace.

Sylvia Johnson arrived right away. As usual, she looked lovely wearing shorts, a tank top, and sandals.

"Have you heard anything about my husband, Deputy Buchanan?" she asked.

"I'm not a deputy, ma'am. I'm just an auxiliary officer. I haven't heard anything specific. However, I did find some items in the swamp that I wanted to show you." Carlisle watched her grab her arms and brace herself. He saw the fear in her eyes as he reached into the brown paper bag that contained the two pieces of cloth.

"I went out on my boat to look around the waters in the vicinity of Gladestown Road like you asked me to. I found these two pieces of cloth."

Carlisle removed both the black cotton cloth and the white silk piece with the pocket still in place from the bag. He watched as Sylvia Johnson gasped in horror and began crying uncontrollably. That told him all he needed to know about the two pieces of evidence. Without thinking, he put his arm around her and tried to console her as best he could. Sylvia Johnson put her head on his shoulder and continued to sob.

When she had cried herself out, Carlisle tried to explain to her what was going to happen in the immediate future. "I anticipate this news is going to get out real soon," he told her. "Reporters are going to be all over the place, so you may want to think about leaving town for a few days."

"I can't leave with my husband missing, Officer Buchanan."

She looked so forlorn. Carlisle felt terrible for her.

"Ma'am, I don't know exactly how to put this, but these pieces of clothing do not mean anything. I can tell from your reaction that they resemble the clothes your husband was wearing the night he went missing, but it doesn't mean they're his. We haven't run any tests yet. And even if they are his, you don't have to assume the worst."

Sylvia Johnson sat there listening to his words, her hands covering her face. Carlisle watched her body shake. He couldn't take it anymore and stood up to leave.

"The reporters will be here later today or tomorrow, ma'am. I'd expect a full onslaught, so don't plan to go out much in these next few days. You have my number and you can call me for anything. In the meantime, I'll have those tests run immediately."

"Thank you, Officer Buchanan. You've been so kind."

CHAPTER NINE

He drove to Verona that afternoon and went directly to the property room with the intent to sign in the two pieces of evidence. As soon as Carlisle identified himself, the property room clerk alerted Detective Vern Fleming, who arrived in a heartbeat.

"Are you Carlisle Buchanan?"

"Yes, sir."

"Vern Fleming, homicide." Vern extended his hand. Carlisle shook it, looking the homicide detective up and down. Vern sure fit the part. He was a thin man, not too tall, maybe five nine or so. His brown hair was combed straight back and he sported some flyboy shades. Carlisle spied a pack of Marlboros in the chest pocket of his long-sleeve white button-down shirt. Like a true homicide cop, Vern had his sleeves rolled up to mid forearm. His collar was open but he had a thin tie slung around his neck.

"Nice to meet you, Vern."

"The sheriff asked me to talk to you. He said you've got a missing person problem."

"I guess you could say that."

"Why don't you come to my office and tell me about it?"

"Sure."

Carlisle followed Vern to his office, which was nothing more than a desk with a partition in a large room filled with desks and partitions. At Vern's insistence, Carlisle sat down in a chair next to the desk.

"Can I get you some coffee?" Vern asked.

"Sure."

Vern walked over to a table against the wall where there was a coffee machine and some Styrofoam cups. He poured two cups and came back to the desk.

"Why don't you start from the very beginning?" Vern suggested.

Carlisle told Vern all about Sylvia Johnson's visits to his office, especially the second one where she seemed kind of frantic. Finally, he told him about searching in the swamps for any sign of Roy Johnson.

"Let me get this straight," Vern said when Carlisle had finished. "This woman reports her husband missing twice within twenty-four hours, and you go out looking for him in the swamp, is that right?"

"That's about it."

"What made you think to do that? I mean, I was a cop for twenty years in Chicago and we had missing persons' reports all the time for husbands who didn't come home. The guy was usually sleeping it off with his mistress or a hooker, or he was out all night gambling—something that was usually explainable. We didn't do anything unless he was gone for forty-eight hours. Are you following me?"

"I am. And we have the same kind of stuff happen over in Gladestown as well. However, this wasn't just anybody. It was Roy Johnson. And she told me he walked down Gladestown Road at night after he'd been drinking. That road is surrounded by swamp and we have reports all the time about gators walking across it. There's been a drought this winter that's extended through the start of the spring and the gators are aggressive because it's mating season. He could have fallen into the swamp. The wife asked me to go out and look for him and I did."

Vern just shook his head. He didn't know shit about gators himself.

"Let's go see the sheriff," he said.

Sheriff Frank Cousins was waiting for them. Sheriff Cousins was a politician. He knew that the incident had to be reported to the state and the feds. He also knew this story was going to get out and probably be big news, even if Roy Johnson showed up tomorrow. He extended his hand to Carlisle.

"How are you, Carlisle?" he said, putting his left arm on Carlisle's shoulder like they were old friends.

"I'm fine, Sheriff."

Vern filled him in on the particulars.

"Did you bring those two pieces of evidence with you?" the sheriff asked.

"Yes, sir."

"Fine. I want you to sign them into the property room as soon as you leave my office. We'll send them to the FBI lab for testing immediately. I'd like a full written report on your investigation by the end of today. Can you do that?"

"Yes, sir. If you give me a computer, I can type it up while I'm here."

"Good, good. I'm assigning Vern to work with you on this case. I want you to report everything that happens in town to him. We are assuming the press might get a hold of this story in the near future, and I don't want you to talk to them. Refer everything to Vern or me, you got that?"

"Yes, sir."

"Good, good. You're an auxiliary officer and a good one, but we need trained personnel handling this investigation. You understand, don't you?"

"Yes, sir."

"You've done a tremendous job, Carlisle. You may end up a deputy yet when all this is over."

"Thank you, sir."

CHAPTER TEN

Susan was sitting in the living room waiting for Kevin to come home from work. It was not like him to be over an hour late and not call. She wasn't particularly alarmed or even upset. She was hungry. There was nothing in the house to eat, and she had made the decision earlier that they were going to go out rather than shop and cook. Kevin had five more minutes or she was going alone.

It was as if he had eavesdropped on her thoughts because five minutes later Kevin walked through the door. He kind of lurched in actually, his shoulders slumped, his tie loose, and his head hanging forward like a limp ostrich. As she approached him, Susan smelled the alcohol and the cigarettes.

"Kevin, you smell like a saloon. Where have you been?"

Kevin lifted his head and gave her a deranged smile. "Hi, honey, I love you too."

He lunged for her and she caught him, afraid that if she stepped out of the way he would hurl himself headfirst into the furniture. He was quite drunk, which was unusual since he was not much of a drinker. "You'll be happy to know I'm going out on my own immediately." He slurred the words as she struggled to hold him upright.

"When did you make that decision?"

"I didn't. The Rug made it for me. He even had his trusty bodyguard escort me out of the building."

The Rug was their nickname for Bernie who, unbeknownst to most, wore a very expensive toupee. He was going to replace the toupee with implants but he had not yet made the transition.

There was no sense talking about it now. Kevin was in no position to have a rational conversation. Susan led him toward their bedroom.

"You know what I think, sweetheart? I think you need a shower and a good massage. How does that sound?"

Kevin ignored her question for the moment. "Do you think I'm a good guy?"

"Of course I do. Why would you even ask that?"

"Well, I always thought I was a good guy too, even though I represent criminals. I was just providing them their constitutional right of representation." He was slurring his words badly. "But I guess that's not true. When you swim in shit, it's gonna get on you and you're gonna stink. I just found that out today. How stupid can a person be?"

"What are you talking about?"

"Bernie and me, we're knee-deep in shit. I didn't see that." All day he'd been talking to himself. He needed to say it to someone else. Get it out. When he was done, he looked at Susan and smiled. "Would you take a shower with me?"

"You don't think I'm letting you get in there alone, do you?" She set him down on the bed and started taking his shoes off.

"You're so good to me," Kevin replied as he laid back and closed his eyes.

"No, no, no. Don't go to sleep on me. Not yet." She had his pants and underwear off and was unbuttoning his shirt. "Come on. Sit up and put your arm over my shoulder. That's it." She slipped one side of the shirt off, switched arms and did the other side. "Okay. Both arms on my shoulders now, one, two, three, and up."

They sidled into the shower as if they were dancing a waltz very badly. Susan leaned him against the wall, stepped out, and turned on the cold water.

"Oooh!" Kevin bristled.

"Just stand there for a minute or two," she told him. "Don't adjust the knobs. I'll take care of it."

Five minutes later after giving the cold water time to do its job, Susan adjusted the knobs until the temperature was comfortable. She then entered the shower from behind the magic curtain.

Kevin always believed that if he was dead and Susan passed before his corpse naked, he would instantly come to life. To him, she had the most beautiful, sensuous body. Everything was symmetrical. Her breasts were not large but they were firm and erect and fit perfectly with the rest. He especially loved the curve of her hips.

Susan knew her power over him. After he placed his hands on her hips, she kissed him slowly, softly, holding his head in her hands. She then silently covered him in soap and began massaging his body like it was a work of art, moving her fingers back and forth. When she reached the choice spots, she paid them special attention, Kevin all the while struggling to keep his balance.

CHAPTER ELEVEN

He woke up the next morning to the smell of bacon and eggs. Susan was no longer next to him in the bed.

"Thought you might need a little grease this morning," she said as he walked into the kitchen. She had her white terry cloth bathrobe on and she flashed him just before she gave him a warm, wet kiss. He was momentarily tempted to forego the bacon and eggs but his body was screaming for grease. He wolfed them down in a matter of seconds while Susan waited patiently, rubbing his shoulders all the while, her white terry cloth robe temporarily taking up residence on the kitchen floor.

Two hours later, Kevin awoke from his midmorning nap to find Susan still lying next to him, smiling coyly.

"Do you know what time it is?" he asked.

"Yes, honey," she replied, playing with the few strands of hair on his chest.

"You're not going to work?"

"Nope. I'm staying home with you."

Since he had known her, Susan had never missed a day of work. He found out why she had chosen this day soon enough.

"Do you want to talk about what happened yesterday?" she asked.

Kevin did not want to tell Susan about his conversation with

Bob Dunning and the ramifications of that conversation on his employment situation, so he gave her the sanitized version of the events of the previous day.

"I'm not exactly sure what happened myself. Bernie found out I was looking at office space and I think that pissed him off. Being the weasel that he is, he didn't call me in to talk until he had something on me."

"What could he possibly have on you?'

"I did a favor for Sal Trivigno and Bernie found out about it."

"What did you do for Sal?"

"I represented him and I didn't charge him. Bernie blew it way out of proportion, made it seem like I was operating my own business while he was still paying my salary."

"That's ridiculous."

"That's what I said. Then he fired me and threatened to have his clients beat me up if I go into business and compete with him."

"That's insane. It sounds like the movies or something."

"Honey, I operate in a world where people do crazy shit every day that they're not supposed to do. It's a lot like the movies actually."

"Do you think Bernie's serious?"

"I'm afraid I do, crazy as it is."

"Are his clients capable of doing something like that?"

"In a heartbeat."

"So what are you going to do?"

"I don't know. I hate buckling under pressure but what's the alternative? I can go to the state attorney's office or the public defender, or I can get a job with an insurance defense firm and learn the civil side. I've got a lot of options."

"That's like starting over. I don't want you to do that."

"I'd move up the ladder pretty quick."

"What was that you were saying last night about you and Bernie being dirty? I didn't understand that at all."

"I was just drunk, that's all."

She leaned over on her left side in the bed and looked at him. "This is one of the problems we have," she said. "You don't talk to me."

Maybe she's right, Kevin thought. *Maybe that's why we can only get so close.* He didn't know if he could explain what he was feeling without telling her the whole story, including his conversation with Bob Dunning, but he owed it to her to at least make an attempt.

"Being a criminal lawyer has always been a bit of a mind game. You're representing criminals, but you figure if you're ethical and you do your job the way it's supposed to be done and let the chips fall where they may, then the system is working. Yesterday, the veil was lifted for me. We're representing drug dealers who are destroying people's lives. I saw Bernie in a different light yesterday and I saw myself as well. I don't want to do this anymore."

"Wait a minute. That's where all your training is. You don't want to give up all that experience."

"I'll still represent people in criminal proceedings. I just won't represent the people that I believe are guilty."

"You can't make a living doing that."

Kevin thought he'd heard her wrong for a second.

"I can do civil work as well as criminal work. I can do appellate work and make a living. There's plenty of opportunity."

Kevin had just finished the sentence when the phone rang. He picked it up. "Hello."

"Hello, is this Kevin Wylie?" It was a female voice.

"Yes, this is he."

"Kevin, my name is Kate Parker. You don't know me but—"

"I know who you are," Kevin rudely interrupted the woman. "Why are you calling me?"

"Your father is in the hospital. He has cancer. He's having surgery tomorrow morning and they don't know if he's going to make it."

"Why are you telling me this? I haven't heard from him in twenty-eight years."

"I just thought you should know," the woman said calmly. "He's at St. Albans Hospital, room 388."

Kevin slammed the receiver down, jumped out of bed, and started pacing the room.

"What was that all about?" Susan asked, stunned by Kevin's behavior.

"That was my father's girlfriend calling to tell me that he's dying of cancer and I'm supposed to give a shit."

Susan didn't know what to say. She knew little pieces of the story. Kevin's mother had left his father and moved to Miami when Kevin was eight. Kevin never spoke to his father after that. His mother later remarried a man named Stephen Linehart who had raised Kevin as his own son. That was all she knew. The rest was locked up in a little closet in Kevin's psyche. It was a taboo subject between them.

"Why is she calling now?" Susan asked.

"He's in the hospital. He's having surgery tomorrow morning and they don't know if he's going to make it. Don't ask me any more questions, okay?"

Kevin had already put on his running shorts and was tying his sneakers. He had decided he needed a long run to sort things out.

CHAPTER TWELVE

Carlisle finished his report in the late afternoon and headed back to Gladestown. He planned on having a nice quiet dinner at Rosie's but the circus had already arrived in town.

He first spotted a few reporters camped outside his office as he turned down Gladestown Road. As he drove closer to the Johnson mansion, he saw the TV trucks and the kiosks with the bright lights and the talking heads set up almost at the front door. He thought of poor Sylvia Johnson holed up inside. Then he drove over to Rosie's only to find that it was filled to capacity. *Reporters!* he said to himself and steered his beat-up old Honda in the direction of home.

Roy Johnson's disappearance, and the finding of pieces of his clothing in the swamp, was all over the Friday morning news shows and was front-page fodder for the papers, as was the speculation that he had been snatched by an alligator on Gladestown Road. They even had pictures of the two items of evidence. Carlisle could smell Sheriff Cousins's fingers on that one. Politicians never shied away from publicity, especially national publicity. If it was going to happen anyway, why not be the one to report it?

Vern Fleming was waiting for him at the office. He'd already let himself in.

"Mornin', Carlisle," he said way too cheerfully as he sat in Carlisle's chair with his feet up on Carlisle's desk. "The sheriff suggested I spend the next few days over here in Gladestown. Kind of manage things until the fire subsides."

Carlisle didn't know how to respond to Vern, who had his sunglasses on at eight o'clock in the morning.

"I guess you don't need me here," he finally said.

"Not right now. You can go back home and relax if you want. Later this afternoon I'd like to take a boat ride with you to see where you found the stuff."

"Sure. I'll come back around two and get you."

"That'll be fine."

It was a cool day for April, one of the rare days in south Florida when the sun did not peek through the clouds. The locals were again praying for rain. Vern was in uniform—white shirt rolled at the sleeves and dark slacks. He'd left the tie in the office and brought a jacket along. Carlisle wore shorts, a T-shirt, and docksiders. After introducing Vern to Scotch, the great blue heron, and asking Scotch to allow them access to the canal, Carlisle fired up the boat. As Scotch flew off, Vern started to wonder about Carlisle's sanity.

They headed for the swamp on the east side of Gladestown Road where Carlisle had made his initial discoveries. Vern Fleming had retired to Florida from Chicago for the sun and the beach before he decided to go back to work to get away from his wife. He wasn't a golfer or a fisherman. As soon as the boat left the dock, Vern, the tough city cop, was out of his element. He was a little skittish at the outset when Carlisle handed him the headset with ear cups. He became more frazzled by the sound of the airboat engine, although nobody could notice since his eyes were hidden behind the flyboy shades. And he stiffened up like a board holding on to the sides of the boat for dear life when Carlisle started weaving in and out of the mangrove corridors.

The turtles sunning on pine tree roots did not impress him, nor did the hawks and osprey circling the tree line above his head, and he definitely had his fill when Carlisle stopped the engine for a minute to get his bearings and a gator popped its head up a few feet away to ogle him.

"Is that what I think it is?" he said to nobody in particular.

"Sure is," Carlisle replied. "But don't worry, it won't hurt you." Carlisle was enjoying Vern's paranoia. *After all, look what happened to Roy Johnson.*

He started the boat again and didn't stop until he had arrived at the exact mangrove root where the black cloth was discovered. He again cut the motor.

"This is where I found the black cloth," he told Vern. And then he did something that made Vern cringe from his fingers to his toes. He stepped out of the boat and started walking on the mangrove roots deep into the swamp.

Vern saw a snake dart under some mangrove roots as Carlisle tried to get his attention. He held the side of the boat even tighter.

"I found the shirt piece down here," Carlisle yelled back to him, pointing farther into the swamp.

"I got it. Good," Vern replied. He wanted to be on dry land in the worst way.

"I'm going to take a look around, see if I can find something else."

Vern hung his head in utter despair.

It wasn't two minutes later that Carlisle shouted, "Oh my God!" and immersed himself completely underwater. Vern was sure he'd been attacked by something and wanted to cry out for help. Before he could find his voice, however, Carlisle reappeared holding an object.

"What is it? Vern yelled.

"A wallet."

After the discovery of Roy Johnson's wallet with his license and credit cards intact, even such luminaries as the well-known editorial writer from the *New York Times*, William Frishe, weighed in on his disappearance. With his article in the Sunday *Times*, Frishe gave Roy Johnson a moniker that would last forever.

Roy Johnson was the poster child for the new religion of greed and excess. He was an alligator, swallowing companies up whole and spitting out their remains. His rationale was that the free market was perfect like nature itself. The strong preyed on the weak, but in the end, everything would adjust and come back into balance. Riches eventually would abound for all, trickling down from the highest mountaintop to the lowest valley.

Roy and his ilk convinced those in power of the righteousness of their ways. In the end, a few succeeded in acquiring great wealth, Roy among them, while the country and many of its citizens fell by the wayside. Some shareholders lost fortunes, some their nest eggs. Some employees lost their jobs and pensions, others literally their lives.

Last week, nature corrected the imbalance that the market could not. Roy Johnson walked down a deserted road and an alligator rose from the depths of an Everglades swamp to greet him.

The Alligator Man has gone home.

CHAPTER THIRTEEN

It was four o'clock in the afternoon when Kevin finally jumped into his Jeep Wrangler and headed for St. Albans. He was still reeling somewhat from the argument he had had with Susan. It started as soon as he returned from his run.

"You're going, aren't you?" she said to him as he was taking his clothes off to jump in the shower. He didn't answer her directly.

"Did you ever feel that things were happening that were more than mere coincidence and you had no control over them?"

"That's just like you, Kevin," she yelled. "Trying to shift responsibility even when there is nobody else to shift it to."

"I'm serious." Kevin said the words slowly and calmly. "Is it just coincidence that on the day after I lose my job I get a call that my father is sick and I need to go to St. Albans?"

Susan wasn't buying Kevin's philosophical questions. "For twenty-eight years he hasn't needed you. Twenty-eight years! He hasn't called. He hasn't inquired about your health. Even after your mother's funeral he didn't contact you. You don't even know the man, Kevin. Your future is at stake here. You need to stay and take care of *your* business."

"Susan, he's my father. This *is* all about me and my future.

What if he dies and I never get to ask him why he abandoned me? Why did he not want me? If I don't get those questions answered, it may haunt me for the rest of my life. Do you understand that?"

"The only thing I understand is that you're running away from your problems here. You may be more like your father than you know."

"That's unfair and uncalled for, Susan. I don't know why you're acting like this. I'm only going to be gone a few days."

"I know, I know," she said as she sat down on the bed and started crying. "I don't know why I'm acting like this either. It's just a feeling I have that makes me very, very afraid."

"You have a feeling but you don't know why?" Kevin asked.

"Yes," she said.

"That's the same feeling I have, Susan. I have to go."

He hugged her and she hugged him back, the tears still in her eyes.

He drove north on Route 120 from Homestead and turned west on Highway 41. Kevin was very familiar with the route, having tried several cases in the city of Verona over the last few years. It was a fun drive. There were canals on both sides of the road and in the winter the alligators would be sunning themselves at the water's edge. This particular evening he had a panoramic view of the sunset and it was spectacular. The sky, in a matter of minutes, went from a brownish yellow to pink and then deep, deep purple before succumbing to the darkness. He could feel the pressure from his argument with Susan releasing itself like the steam from a boiling teakettle.

When he hit Interstate 75, he headed north to Ocala where he decided to pack it in for the night. St. Albans was located on the west coast of Florida southwest of Tallahassee and was still four hours away. He'd head out in the morning for the place of his birth—a city he had not been to in twenty-eight years.

He knew a little bit about St. Albans from the newspapers and from conversations over the years with people who had either lived or visited there. It was one of the oldest cities in America. The Old City, as it was called, had been pretty much preserved in its entirety and served as a tourist attraction. The modern part of the city, the business section, served as a corporate headquarters for small and midsized businesses.

It was also the home of his father, Tom Wylie.

Even though it had been twenty-eight years since they had seen each other, Tom Wylie was never far from his son's thoughts. He was a big man with enormous hands, as Kevin recalled, who always seemed to have a smile on his face. *What happened? Why did that smiling man leave me?*

Tom Wylie was a lawyer. Kevin had gleaned that much from listening to grown-up conversations that he was not supposed to hear. His mother never talked about him in her son's presence, nor did Steve Linehart, her husband and Kevin's stepfather. It was as if he had been erased from their memory in one swipe, like a name on a chalkboard.

Later, when he became a lawyer himself, Kevin learned that his father was very well thought of in the legal community. Just two years before, Tom Wylie had represented a prominent Miami lawyer in a very high-profile murder case, a case that Kevin had followed with great interest.

He also remembered his dog, a black-and-white English setter named Matty. Gone with his father in that same eraser swipe.

He had remained angry with his father over all the years. It was an anger that started as a small hurt in a little boy's heart, a little pitch fire. He'd stoked that fire at every event where his father failed to show—birthdays, Little League games, high school football, graduation, law school—until it became a raging, out-of-control blaze that he carried hidden behind a closed door.

Kevin counseled himself on the drive north to meet the man in a cool, unemotional way, not only for his own well-being but also because of the circumstances. His father was dying. Eventually, hopefully, they could get around to discussing what happened so long ago.

He hadn't pursued it with his mother, partly because he knew she didn't want to talk about it and partly because he'd had no desire to find out. He had his mother and Steve and the fire to sustain him. All that had changed.

Seven years ago, his mother, Carol, and his stepfather, Steve, had purchased a cabin in the mountains of North Carolina. Steve had been a pilot for years and owned a single-engine Cessna. The plan was for them to spend the weekends in the mountains during the summer months. One Friday night six years ago, they ran into a thunderstorm. Steve apparently lost control of the plane and it crashed, killing both of them on impact.

With his father's impending crisis, there was now an urgency to discover the answer to this important piece of the puzzle that was his life. There was a little boy still inside of him demanding answers.

CHAPTER FOURTEEN

Carlisle's world had changed drastically in the days since Roy Johnson's disappearance. Vern Fleming came to his office every day, sat at his desk, and acted like his boss. Carlisle wasn't one to take orders. Most of the time he simply ignored Vern but the man was getting on his nerves.

Every morning, Carlisle made it a point to check on Sylvia Johnson. He'd go up to the back door of the mansion, the one that led out to the garden, and give a special knock and Aida would let him in. Sylvia always came down when he showed up, and they had a cup of coffee and Carlisle filled her in on the investigation even though nothing was happening.

She'd had a minor breakdown when Carlisle told her about the discovery of Roy's wallet. He had stayed with her most of the day. He hadn't planned to, but he just couldn't bring himself to leave someone in that much distress alone. Ever since that day, there'd been something between them.

Things really started to heat up after the third week of the ordeal, when the search officially turned from rescue to recovery.

Sylvia began to cry upon hearing the news that the rescue effort was over and Carlisle comforted her, putting his arm around her as he usually did and stroking her head with his strong hands. On this day, however, she picked her head up off his shoulder, looked into his eyes, and kissed him. He kissed her back slowly, sweetly. After a few minutes, without saying a word, she took his hand and led him upstairs.

He stayed with her until almost two when he moseyed over to Rosie's. He was avoiding the office and Vern.

Things were starting to get back to normal in town as the recovery phase of the search started. The tourist business had pretty much petered out and the place was once again empty.

"Two more minutes and you woulda been outta luck," Rosie told him as she personally delivered a serving of gator fritters that he had never ordered. "I was about to empty the Frialator when you showed up."

"Timing is everything," Carlisle replied.

"Speaking of timing, a few of the high school kids were here for lunch. They do that sometimes—cut a class and sneak out. Anyway, I was cleaning up and kinda listening to their conversation. I do that so in case they're up to no good I can tell their parents or something."

Carlisle didn't believe a word of it. Rosie was just nosy, that's all. She listened in on everybody's conversations. He nodded like he understood just so she would tell him what she'd overheard. He wasn't averse to hearing gossip.

"Do you know Freddie Jenkins, Margie Jenkins's boy?"

"Yeah, I know him. He and his dad are real good fishermen."

"Well, he was telling his buddies that he was out neckin' with Becky Yates in the parking lot of the Chamber of Commerce, right next to the sheriff's office the night Roy Johnson went missin'. Said his truck was facing Gladestown Road with the lights out when he saw this car make the turn and head down the road. From the lights of the car, he saw a man on the road and he saw the car hit the man and the man went flyin' into the swamp."

"Are you sure you heard this right?" Carlisle asked.

"I've been listenin' in on kids' conversations for years, Carlisle. I know what I heard."

Carlisle's brain was churning. "That means old Roy Johnson didn't get snatched by a gator or fall into the swamp."

"Nope," Rosie replied, a serious frown on her face. "It sounds like a hit-and-run."

Just then Rosie witnessed an event she had never seen before. Carlisle Buchanan rose and walked out of the restaurant, leaving a half-dozen gator fritters still on his plate.

CHAPTER FIFTEEN

Kevin arrived at the hospital at eleven thirty the next morning and was told at the reception desk that Tom Wylie was in his room, which surprised him. He figured his father would still be in ICU.

Hospitals were not his thing. The indefinable smell and sight of the sick permeated every floor. As he emerged from the elevator, Kevin saw two patients lying on gurneys against the wall, their IVs in place, waiting to be taken somewhere. Others were walking up and down the halls half-naked in their hospital gowns as the nurses flitted from room to room.

Kevin checked the room numbers as he walked down the hallway. He had learned long ago never to ask for directions in a hospital. There would always be some rule he was breaking. Either he was too early or too late or the patient was not allowed to have visitors—something. His father's room was at the end of the hall. He took a deep breath and walked in.

It was a private room. Tom Wylie was lying in the bed with his eyes closed. His hair was grayer and he didn't appear to be the giant Kevin remembered from his youth. His face had a lean, healthy glow even though Kevin had been told that he was dying.

There were two other people in the room. One, a plump,

red-faced man with white hair, Kevin recognized right away, although he had no idea why Florida Supreme Court Justice Ray Blackwell was at his father's bedside. The other man was a complete mystery. Both of them looked at him as he walked in. Kevin addressed the face he recognized.

"Justice Blackwell?" he asked to be sure, extending his hand.

"Only at the office," the judge replied good-naturedly, shaking his hand. "And you are?"

"Kevin Wylie."

"Tom's son. Why, of course. I should have recognized you. You look just like your dad." Kevin bristled at the statement. He didn't see the resemblance at all.

The judge took the opportunity to introduce the other man in the room. "Kevin, this is Billy Fuller. He's an old friend of your dad's too."

Billy stood up and shook Kevin's hand. He was a tall, thin, balding man who had the look of an athlete and a strong handshake, although he had dark circles under his eyes and appeared to be very tired.

"I remember you, Kevin. We used to play catch at your dad's house when you were a little boy." Kevin had no memory of that and he wondered if Billy was mistaken. Billy saw the question on his face.

"I was a lot older than you," he said. "Your dad was kinda looking out for me at the time, so I was hanging out at your house."

It was coming back to Kevin slowly. There was an older boy lurking in his memory somewhere, and they did play catch and fish together out at the lake. He had never known before that moment whether those images in his mind were real or not. He smiled at Billy as he shook his hand.

"I remember," he said. "We used to go fishing together too."

"That's right. You always had to have Matty come along in the boat."

Kevin caught a brief glimpse of himself, Billy, and his dog, Matty, in an old rowboat out on the lake. "Wow, that was so long ago."

Just then, a woman walked into the room with a brown paper bag in her hands. She set the bag down on a table and looked at Tom Wylie lying motionless in the bed.

"Any change?" she asked Ray Blackwell.

"None," the judge replied. "The nurse said he should be waking up soon, though."

"Do you think we should call Alex?" she asked. Alex was Tom's doctor and, as Kevin would later find out, a close, personal friend for forty years.

"He just stuck his head in a few minutes ago. Said he had some rounds to make and he'd be back in a few minutes. Have you met our new visitor?"

Kevin had been standing to the side, watching the conversation between Judge Blackwell and this woman, wondering who she was. He couldn't find her anywhere in his memory. She was a tall woman with long brown hair streaked with gray. *Probably mid- to late forties,* Kevin surmised. She wore blue jeans and cowboy boots and a long-sleeved flannel shirt, and her healthy, well-tanned face was not obscured by any makeup.

"I'm Kate Parker," she said. "You must be Kevin."

Kevin was shocked. This woman looked nothing like the Jezebel he had created in his mind. And she looked so much younger than his father. His mother had made references to her several times over the years, always in a derogatory manner. Kevin had simply assumed she had something to do with the divorce and had hated her all his life. He had no choice under these circumstances but to be polite.

"That's me. Nice to meet you."

"I'm glad you decided to come," she said, politely shaking his hand. She then turned to her brown bag. "I brought an extra coffee in case you might be here. I've got milk and sugar and Sweet'N Low so you can all fix your own the way you like it."

Everybody took a few moments to prepare their drinks. Kevin was still reeling from the introduction and that she had thought to bring him coffee, especially after the way he had treated her on the phone the day before. He was holding on to his anger, though, not letting it go that easily.

"Kate, why don't you fill Kevin in on what has transpired over the last several hours?" the judge suggested. He seemed to have a sense of the anxiety permeating the room.

"Sure," Kate replied and focused her large brown eyes directly at Kevin. "Tom was scheduled to have surgery this morning, but after he was anesthetized, they took a look at his chest X-ray and discovered he had pneumonia and scrapped the surgery. Later, they realized they had reviewed the X-rays of another man.

"We're just concerned Tom might have an emotional letdown when he wakes up and finds out what happened."

Kate had barely finished the sentence when Tom's doctor, Alex Rivard, entered the room. He appeared to be a contemporary of Tom's in age, although he also had a healthy glow about him.

Must be the water up here, Kevin thought.

"Kate, may I have a word with you?" Alex asked.

The judge took the hint right away. "The rest of us will go down to the cafeteria and drink our coffee," he said, motioning to both Billy and Kevin.

"I'm gonna go home," Billy told them when they were in

the hallway, heading for the elevator. "I've got some things that have to get done today. I'll be back tonight. Kevin, how long are you in town?"

"I'm not sure."

"I'll see you both tonight anyway."

When they were seated in the cafeteria with their coffees in hand, Kevin started with his questions.

"Can I ask how you know my father, Judge?"

"Sure. I met your dad right out of law school. We worked at the same law firm and I reported to him. You might say he was my mentor. We've been friends ever since."

"Was he a good lawyer?"

The judge did not answer right away. Kevin could see that he was thinking about his response.

"He was the best at certain things. Your father was never a detail person. He was a big picture guy and he was great in the courtroom.

"Later, when he went out on his own, he took the cases nobody else would touch, simply because he believed in the people he was representing. I thought he was crazy but it's what I admired him for the most."

"He hasn't talked to me in twenty-eight years. Do you admire that?"

The judge seemed to be expecting Kevin's anger.

"I knew your mom very well," he said. "She was a wonderful person. I felt very sad when things went bad between the two of them. I still feel bad for you, Kevin, because you were the casualty of that war. I know there's still rage inside of you."

Kevin gave him a look that asked, *How the hell do you know what's inside of me?*

The judge read his eyes. "Kate told me about the phone call yesterday, how you treated her. She asked for my advice before she made that call and I encouraged her to do it. I still think it was the right thing to do."

Kevin was embarrassed that the judge knew about his conversation with Kate. "I didn't handle the call very well."

"Listen, son," the judge continued. "I presided over a number of divorces in my days on the bench, enough to understand that this is a totally emotional issue for you. You can't rely on the rational lawyer to evaluate the situation and react appropriately. You're here for some answers as you should be. My one suggestion to you is be patient. Bite your tongue if you have to. If you have some time, and if your father survives this surgery—a lot of ifs, but that's life—you'll eventually get your answers. You won't like them—they'll be painful—but I do believe that you need to hear them. Your father and I have been friends for a long time so I'm not totally impartial in this matter. However, I do know that as much as you need to learn the truth, he needs to tell it."

"I hear you, Judge. I don't know if I can hold it all together, but I hear you."

"I think you'll handle it and I think you'll get your answers. Everyone may not live happily ever after, but who knows?"

CHAPTER SIXTEEN

Freddie Jenkins was sitting in the back of Mr. Reese's history class, listening to him drone on about the Spanish-American War, when Della, the principal's secretary, came over the intercom and asked him to report to the office. Freddie didn't realize he was half-asleep until Della said his name, which caused him to jump and almost fall out of his chair.

"I'm glad somebody can get your attention, Mr. Jenkins," Mr. Reese said as Freddie tried to regain his composure. By that time, the whole class was laughing at Freddie.

He was relieved to get out of Mr. Reese's class no matter what the reason, but as he walked down the hallway, he started to wonder why the principal wanted to see him. He knew it couldn't be good.

Carlisle had left Rosie's and driven immediately to the high school. There was about an hour of school left and he wanted to catch Freddie Jenkins before the school day ended. He probably should have taken the information to Vern but there was no time. He'd report it to the sheriff after the interview was over.

He had some initial problems with Harvey Shay, the principal.

Mr. Shay had been the principal when Carlisle went to Gladestown High. It was a small school, and Mr. Shay remembered everything about Carlisle, including that he was a bright young man who didn't particularly like the classroom environment. Carlisle would rather be out on the water or in the woods with his father, one of the numerous ne'er-do-wells in Gladestown. He was reluctant to let Carlisle speak to one of his students, even if that student was Freddie Jenkins, who was of the same ilk and whom he disliked even more than Carlisle.

"You don't have the authority to interview one of my students, Mr. Buchanan, and I'm not going to allow it."

Carlisle was cool. He was getting a lot of practice maintaining his composure since he had to deal with Vern Fleming at some point every day. Mr. Shay didn't even come close to Vern.

"You watch television, don't you, Mr. Shay?"

"Very little."

"I'm sure. I'm also sure you haven't missed the worldwide publicity regarding the disappearance of Roy Johnson. We believe that Freddie Jenkins has some information regarding this matter. You can stop me from talking to him now, but at some point we are going to talk to him. Any delay in that conversation is going to cause problems, I can assure you. Do you want to accept responsibility for that delay and have your name plastered all over the news?"

Harvey Shay was a thin, little man with a loud voice. He stood there for the longest time with his hands on his hips, like he was modeling petulance. Carlisle didn't even look at him. He knew he had him.

"Della," Mr. Shay finally yelled to his secretary. "Get Freddie Jenkins down here." He then turned his attention back to Carlisle. "You've got fifteen minutes, Mr. Buchanan."

Carlisle knew he had as much time as he wanted, but he let Mr. Shay have his small victory.

When Freddie Jenkins arrived, Mr. Shay sat him down and did the introductions.

"Mr. Jenkins, Auxiliary Officer Buchanan here wants to ask you a few questions about the disappearance of Roy Johnson." Mr. Shay then turned to Carlisle. "You may proceed, Mr. Buchanan."

Carlisle sat in the chair across from Freddie Jenkins. "Mr. Jenkins, it's my understanding that you saw something out on Gladestown Road the night Roy Johnson went missing, is that correct?"

Freddie Jenkins had decided somewhere on the trip down the hallway to the principal's office that no matter what was asked, he wasn't admitting to anything. Now he was being asked direct questions about Roy Johnson, and Mr. Shay was standing over him, listening to every word.

"No, I don't know anything about that," he said, never taking his eyes off of Mr. Shay.

Carlisle saw that look of terror. He knew from experience what it was about. Mr. Shay, when he was angry, screamed in your face. He got so close, you could smell his breath as he ranted and raved. You were sure at any moment he was going to explode. If Carlisle was going to get anywhere with Freddie, Mr. Shay had to go.

"Mr. Shay, would you leave the room please?"

"I most certainly will not. This is my office."

"And this is my investigation."

Mr. Shay backed off. Carlisle had gotten under his skin with the threat of publicity.

"Della," he yelled to his secretary. "I'm going to take a walk around the school while these two talk. Page me when Mr. Buchanan is done. I don't want Mr. Jenkins going back to his class until I have had a word with him."

When Mr. Shay had left the room, Carlisle turned to Freddie.

"I don't want you to worry about Mr. Shay, Freddie. Let me handle him. This is a serious matter, though. Somebody died and he may have been killed. You need to tell me the truth right now. If you do, you're not going to get into any trouble. But if you lie to me you may go to jail. Do you understand?"

"Yes, sir."

"Good. Now, I was at Rosie's today a little bit after you left. Rosie said that she overheard you telling your friends that you saw someone get hit by a car out on Gladestown Road the night the Alligator Man went missing. Is that true?"

Freddie hesitated a minute. Carlisle figured he was weighing his options, thinking about whom he had told and whether they would lie for him.

"Yes, sir. It's true," Freddie finally said.

"And you were there with Becky Yates?"

"That part wasn't true. We go out there all the time. She called me to meet her there but she never showed up. Of course, now she claims she never called me."

"So, you were there by yourself?"

"Yeah. Just waiting."

"What did you see?"

"I saw this car turn down Gladestown Road heading for town. I watched because I was looking for Becky's car. The radio wasn't working. Then I saw this guy in the car's headlights. And then I saw the car hit him and he went right into the swamp. It all happened really fast."

"How far away were you?"

"I'm not sure—twenty or thirty yards. I could take you out there."

"What time did this happen?"

"I'm not sure. It was after eleven because I didn't leave my house until at least ten minutes after eleven. My parents go to bed at eleven. I have this beat-up, little pickup truck, and I had to sneak it out of the driveway and wait until I was down the road to turn the lights on."

"How long does it take you to get to the chamber parking lot?"

"Five minutes or so."

"And how long were you there before you saw this guy get hit?"

"Maybe another five minutes."

"Could you tell what the man was wearing—the man who was hit?"

"Like I said, Officer, it all happened so fast. I don't remember much. He had a light-colored shirt on and he had dark hair. That's all I remember."

"What about the car? What did the car do after it hit the man?"

"It just kept going. I never saw it again."

"Can you describe the car?"

"It was gray. I could see it when it stopped at the corner. There's a streetlight there. It was a Honda or something like that. It didn't look new."

"Anything else you recall?"

"No."

"Where was the guy walking before he was hit? I mean, was he in the middle of the road?"

"I don't think so. I think he was walking on the side of the road. And he was walking back toward town, facing traffic, but there wasn't any traffic coming toward him. Does that make any sense?"

"So, the car would have had to come all the way over to the opposite side of the road to hit him, is that what you're saying?"

"Yeah. That's what it looked like."

"Are you sure?"

"Pretty sure. I got that picture in my head, you know. It's one of those things you don't forget."

"But you don't remember what he was wearing?"

"No. I wasn't concentrating on that."

"Why did you tell your friends that Becky was with you when she wasn't?"

Freddie didn't answer right away and Carlisle could tell he was having a little trouble with the question.

"I was freaked when this happened, you know. I lit outta there right away. I had to drive down Gladestown Road, right past where that man went in the swamp because it's the only way home. I knew what was happening to him but I didn't stop. I was too afraid. I thought whoever it was who did this might come back for me.

"I didn't wanna tell anybody about what I saw but it's hard to keep those things in, you know. So I just said Becky was with me. If any of the guys asked why I didn't stop to help the man, I was gonna say Becky was freaked out. I guess I didn't think it through."

"I guess not."

It was a stupid kid's move but Carlisle could understand it. The kid was being honest now, Carlisle was sure of that. He could tell by the way Freddie was fidgeting. He was a good kid.

"Listen, Freddie, you're probably going to be asked about this again by another police officer or the state attorney, maybe more than once, and probably in a more formal way with a tape recorder, a court reporter, or a video recorder taking down what you say, so I want you to think about what you told me and when you go back to class write it down and make sure you say exactly the same thing every time, do you understand?"

"Yes, sir."

"I have to make a report about what you told me to the sheriff. Reports have a way of leaking out to the press, you know what I mean?"

"Yes, sir."

"The more people you talk to, the more problems you have, do you understand that?"

"Yes, sir."

"So don't talk to the press, no matter what."

"Yes, sir."

"Now go on back to class. I'll wait for Mr. Shay."

Della was a little upset when Carlisle told her he had sent Freddie back to class and asked her to page Mr. Shay. She hoped Mr. Shay didn't blame her for the violation of his orders. She was going to protest to Carlisle that he didn't have the authority to send Freddie back to his classroom, but she could see that it was no use. The boy was already on his way.

As he waited for Mr. Shay to come back to the office, Carlisle thought about Freddie's story. This was no longer just a hit-and-run.

Harvey Shay was livid when he found out Carlisle had countered his orders.

"I run this school, Mr. Buchanan. Della, get that boy back here."

"Don't do that just yet, Della," Carlisle told the woman. "Mr. Shay and I are going to have a discussion first."

Carlisle walked back into the principal's office and beckoned the principal to follow. Mr. Shay sheepishly walked behind him. When they were in the office out of the sight of Della, Carlisle got into Harvey Shay's space, where Shay could smell *his* breath.

"That boy is a witness in a criminal investigation. He is going to be under a great deal of pressure in the coming days and weeks. I want you to leave him alone. If you don't, the sheriff is going to hear about it and so will your superiors. I'll know because I will personally be talking to the boy."

Having said his piece, Carlisle turned and left, leaving Harvey Shay to ponder his words.

CHAPTER SEVENTEEN

When Tom Wylie regained consciousness, at first he didn't know where he was. He could hear voices but he couldn't move, not even to open his eyes. He recognized the voices as those of Kate, his love, and Alex, his longtime friend and doctor. Alex's was the first voice he heard.

"I know scrapping the surgery was a monumental screwup but it happens that X-rays sometimes get mixed up. It doesn't happen often."

Kate wasn't buying it. "That's crap, Alex, and you know it. What if you cut off the wrong person's leg instead of just reading the wrong X-rays? You have to have procedures in place to make sure that never happens again. But my immediate concern right now is Tom."

"We have to do this again tomorrow, Kate. It can't wait."

"I know, I know, I'm just worried. He'd never let on about it, but getting ready for this surgery was a huge emotional ordeal for Tom. Now he's going to wake up and have to do it all over again."

"Listen, Kate, I've known Tom for over forty years. He'll handle it fine."

Lying there, his brain still foggy from the anesthesia, Tom struggled to take in all that had been said. The surgery was canceled and he would have to do it tomorrow—that was clear. And Kate was worried.

A few minutes later, two other people entered the room and joined the conversation. Tom recognized one of the voices as that of Ray Blackwell. The other one was a mystery.

Everyone simultaneously realized that Tom had regained consciousness when, without thinking, he raised his arm to scratch his head. Tom could tell they'd noticed, even though his eyes were still closed, because all conversation abruptly ceased. They were waiting for his next move.

Even under the circumstances, Tom was coherent enough to work out a little skit to deal with all of their anxiety, especially Kate's. He opened his eyes, calmly looked at them, and smiled. Then he picked up the cover that was resting at chest level and peeked under it at his stomach where the bandages should have been.

"My, they did a lovely job," he said. "I can't even see a scar." He then looked back up at them with a sheepish grin on his face.

It took a moment, but his old friend Ray caught on first and started laughing, followed by Alex, and finally Kate. Kevin never did catch on because he did not know Tom Wylie and his sardonic humor. He stood there feeling awkward and unrelated.

"Alex, you shouldn't be laughing," Tom said. "You violated the cardinal rule: Never make a mistake with a lawyer as a patient."

There was more anxious, nervous laughter.

"How did you know?" Alex asked.

Tom looked at Ray Blackwell and winked. "And these guys think they are the gods."

The judge roared at the remark. So did Alex and Kate. Kevin was still the odd man out.

"And who is this young man?" Tom finally asked, looking at Kevin.

Kate brought Kevin around to the side of his father's bed. She knew what was coming.

"Tom," she said, "this is your son, Kevin."

It was Tom's turn to be surprised. The older man's eyes welled up and he began to shake slightly. His voice left him. He took Kevin's right hand in his and held it. His hands were huge, just as Kevin remembered, and they were gentle, and he suddenly remembered that too. The tears began to fall from Tom's eyes now as he continued to just look at his son, a smile on his face, unable to do or say anything else.

Once again, Kevin didn't know how to react. Part of him wanted to hug his father; part of him wanted to strangle him. He decided to simply return the smile.

Seeing Tom's emotions start to strain, Alex gave the two men a moment and then ushered everybody out of the room. In the hallway, he pulled Kate aside.

"Go in and say good-bye to him now because I want him to sleep for the rest of the day. He needs to be strong for tomorrow."

Kate gave him a worried look.

"Don't worry, Kate. I'll look in on him all day."

In the elevator, Kate invited the judge to spend the night out at the ranch.

"I'd love to, Kate," he replied. "But my Aunt Birdie already has my promise to spend the night."

She turned to Kevin next. "How about you, Kevin? The ranch is very relaxing and you've had a long day."

Kevin knew it had to take a lot to make the offer after the way he had treated her. Still, he was emotionally in knots. Things were happening way too fast.

"Thanks, but I've already got a room for the night. Maybe tomorrow."

CHAPTER EIGHTEEN

Only about five square miles in area, St. Albans's Old City was more like a small town. Because its origins extended all the way back to the early eighteenth century when the Spanish ruled Florida, it was a modern-day tourist attraction. All of the buildings were Spanish Colonial in style. The original structures—and there were still quite a few—were made of shale, a combination of shell and sand. The more modern ones were composed of concrete and stucco, and since they had to conform in every way to the original architecture, no building in town exceeded two stories.

Kevin chose to stay in the Old City because it had been his home as a young boy. He found a bed-and-breakfast close to the parking garage, checked in, deposited his bags in the room, splashed a little water on his face, and went out for a walk—stopping at the front desk to ask the charming woman who had signed him in if there was a locals' bar close by.

"Chico's on La Plaza, two blocks down on the right. Everybody goes there," she told him.

There was a cool wind blowing as Kevin walked the narrow, winding streets. It was dusk and he saw several couples snuggling close to each other as they walked. He wished that Susan was with him at that moment and that for once they could simply enjoy the romantic setting and forget about their troubles.

Although he looked for the better part of an hour, he couldn't find his father's house, the house where he had grown up. Nor could he retrieve that sense of belonging. It was a beautiful place, but it didn't feel like home. He was tired and ready for a drink when he finally arrived at Chico's.

Chico's was a dark, comfortable little joint and it was fairly busy although not full. Music was playing in the background at a level that allowed the customers to have a conversation with one another. Kevin found a spot at the bar and sat and ordered a bourbon and soda. It had been a tough day emotionally and he needed a good stiff drink. As he took his first sip, his eyes scanned the bar. That's when he noticed Billy sitting three seats down. At least he thought it was Billy. He couldn't tell for sure until Billy got up from his barstool and ambled over.

"So you found the neighborhood bar?"

"Yeah, I didn't want to drink with the tourists."

"I don't blame you. Hey, it's really good to see you after all these years. And I know your dad will be excited to know that you're here. I was just on my way back over there."

"I'll save you the trip. My father woke up this afternoon and Alex ushered us all out after that. He said he wanted Tom to sleep until tomorrow's surgery."

"Oh, so you got to see each other?"

"Yeah."

"How did that go?"

"It went."

"That good, huh? I'm sorry to hear that."

"It wasn't bad. It's just—what do you say after twenty-eight years? How are you supposed to feel?"

"I don't know."

"Neither do I, Billy."

"At least you're both still alive and maybe you can sort things out."

Kevin finished his drink and ordered another. "Billy, what are you drinking? Let me get you one?"

"Jack on the rocks. Thanks."

"No problem. So tell me what you do up here in St. Albans."

"Not a whole lot of anything. I work part-time at the supermarket. I help Kate out at the ranch some. There's not too much work around here since Dynatron went under two years ago."

"I read about that. That company screwed all its employees."

"Not that company—Roy Johnson. And Roy Johnson didn't just screw his employees, he killed some of them. My wife, Laurie, died of leukemia when our insurance was canceled and she lost her doctors. My best friend, Jimmy Lennox, committed suicide because he was in debt up to his fuckin' ears. And that's just my people."

Kevin realized that his problems with his father paled in comparison to what happened to Billy. The man had a gaping hole in his heart. He tried to say something upbeat.

"Well, Roy Johnson got his."

"Yeah. It's a small piece of justice. It doesn't bring people back. It doesn't put money in ordinary people's pockets. But it's something. They should line every one of those guys up and shoot 'em."

"Who?"

"You know. The CEOs who bilk their employees and shareholders out of everything and walk away with millions. They oughta be shot."

Kevin didn't disagree with the assessment but he knew it was time to change the subject. "Did you and Laurie have any kids?"

"Yeah, two. Thomas and Heather. Thomas just started high

school this year. Heather is in sixth grade. They're great kids. They just lost their mother when they needed her most."

Kevin thought Billy was going to cry but he didn't.

"They're with my sister tonight."

They drank in silence for a few minutes after that. Kevin was about to finish his drink and leave.

"Don't leave yet," Billy said. "Let me buy you a drink. And I'm sorry for being so morose. It's just a place I can't visit without getting upset."

"I understand. I'd feel the same way. Sure, I'll have another. I've only got to walk two blocks."

They kept it light after that, talking about sports. Billy was an avid sports fan, especially basketball. He had played in high school. Kevin started to relax and enjoy himself. Billy had an easygoing way about him when he was off the subject of Roy Johnson and the devastation that he had wreaked on his family and others. He was funny and he made Kevin laugh. They had a couple more drinks and left together walking down the street side by side.

CHAPTER NINETEEN

Sheriff Frank Cousins initially wanted to shoot somebody when he read Carlisle's report about his interview with Freddie Jenkins. That somebody was Vern Fleming, whom he had stationed in Gladestown to oversee the investigation. *Why the hell was he letting Carlisle do such an important interview?* But he read the report again and he realized that Carlisle had covered all the bases and then some. *Vern probably doesn't even know about Freddie Jenkins,* he mused. *Maybe this kid can be a deputy some day.* Then he called Vern anyway.

"While you're picking daisies over there or whatever the hell you're doing, Carlisle Buchanan has been investigating." Sheriff Cousins then filled Vern in on Freddie Jenkins and his eyewitness account of a murder. His hunch was right.

"Hell, I didn't even know about this kid," Vern blurted out without realizing the consequences of such an admission.

"I didn't think so," Frank Cousins replied. "Now I want you to go over to that school and pick this kid up and bring him over here. We'll put him under oath and do a video interview following Carlisle's script. He did a good job on this, but I want you on top of things over there from here on in. This isn't a missing persons case anymore. It's a murder investigation."

"Sure thing, Frank. I'm on it."

"I want you to talk to Carlisle about coordination and working as a team and all that stuff, but I don't want you to come down hard on him. He used initiative and he did a good job."

Yeah, and made me look like a fool! Vern thought. "Gotcha," he said to the sheriff.

Carlisle walked into the office fifteen minutes after Vern's conversation with Frank Cousins.

"What's new?" he asked.

Vern wanted to pile-drive him into the wall but he knew that wasn't an option, considering Carlisle's size and strength. Carlisle couldn't see the fire in his eyes underneath the flyboy shades.

"Nothing much. I just talked to the sheriff. He said you did a real good job with your interview of this Freddie kid. He was just a little concerned."

"About what?" Carlisle asked.

"About an auxiliary police officer investigating a possible murder without telling the homicide detective in charge." Vern said it as politely as he could, but Carlisle could see his clenched teeth.

"Oh, that. Yeah, I should have told you, but I thought getting Freddie's story right away was the most important thing. I knew Freddie would talk to me since I'm a local and all."

"Well, make sure it doesn't happen again or you might be looking for work. You got it?"

Carlisle didn't answer. He simply looked at Vern and smiled.

"You got it?" Vern asked again, this time in a little harsher tone.

"Let me tell you something, Vern. I'm not used to taking orders. My father raised me that way. That's kinda the way it is around here. Now I will listen to you because you know what you're doing. And I will follow your suggestions. But if you keep giving me orders, we're gonna have some problems."

Vern had no idea how to respond. Back in Chicago people just did what they were told no matter how big they were. There was a hierarchy. Rank meant something. Here he was out in the middle of nowhere with some redneck who could probably rip him in half and who had no respect. What the hell could he do?

"All right. I'll try not to tell you what to do. I'll try to make suggestions but I want you to listen to me. Now where the hell is this high school? I've gotta pick this kid up and take him to headquarters."

"I'll go with you."

"No. You stay here and hold down the fort. I mean, why don't you just stay here and hold down the fort? I'll handle this one by myself. Just give me the directions."

"Suit yourself."

CHAPTER TWENTY

The next day at the hospital was long and grueling. The day before, everyone knew Tom Wylie would be okay. They were simply concerned about his emotional stability when he woke up. Today, they were waiting to find out if he would ever wake up again.

Kevin was part of the group now, although he was the most ambivalent and confused member. He was still very angry and bitter toward his father but he didn't want him to die. He sat in the surgery waiting room between Billy and Ray Blackwell. Kate sat across from the men.

Alex Rivard broke the suspense when he walked into the room at a little after two o'clock in the afternoon. They all looked at him as if they were defendants in a murder trial and he was about to deliver the verdict.

"He's okay. He's resting comfortably," Alex began. Kevin saw Kate put her hands to her chest and let out a big sigh of relief, as did the others.

"We didn't get all the tumors," Alex continued. "Some were just too close to the main artery." Kevin noticed Alex's shoulders visibly slumping as he delivered the bad news. The man looked worn-out.

Kate hugged Alex for a long time. Kevin just stood there with the judge and Billy. Nobody asked any questions, which surprised him. He had a million of his own but he didn't want anybody to think he cared enough to ask.

"He won't be awake for at least another hour so you all ought to go get something to eat. Kevin, I'd like to see you in my office if I could."

"Sure," Kevin said and proceeded to follow the doctor out of the room.

"Why was everybody so silent in there?" he asked Alex when they were seated in his office.

"They've been through this before. They know the consequences of what I told them. You're the one who doesn't."

"I hope you're not treating me like the long-lost son who is so concerned about his dad."

"You are, aren't you?"

"I'm what?"

"Concerned."

"Look, I don't even know the man. He's my father and all, but we don't have a relationship. I'm just here to get some answers."

"Well then, here are the answers about your father's physical well-being. He originally had colon cancer that metastasized into his bloodstream and eventually showed up in his liver. There were a number of tumors in his liver and we tried to shrink them with chemotherapy but we were unsuccessful. The only other option was surgery. We were going to try and cut the tumors out. We can cut out up to eighty percent of the liver because it regenerates. The main thing we have to worry about is blood flow. We've got to be careful of the veins and arteries in there.

"We got everything we could. I almost lost him a couple of times. I had to close him up when I did."

The man looked defeated. Kevin could see it in his eyes.

"So what does the future hold?"

"His tumors will grow and they will eventually kill him."

"That's it? Isn't there anything that can be done?"

"I'm afraid not, Kevin. Medicine is a limited science. At this stage, cancer has the upper hand."

"How long does he have?"

"Three months, maybe six."

"And everybody else knows that?"

"Yeah. I've gone over all the options before with them."

"What will his life be like in the months ahead?"

"Well, he's got to recover from the surgery, which will take a while. But I expect his wounds to heal in a month or so, maybe sooner. He'll start walking here in the hospital in a couple of days. He's always going to be weak and he'll gradually get weaker as the tumors take over, but your father will recover quicker and better than most."

"Why do you say that?"

"I know him. He's a tough guy. He didn't even want to have this surgery. He did it for Kate."

The last two sentences caused an artery to burst in Kevin's brain. He stood up and leaned on Alex's desk. "What the hell is with you people? You act like the man is a saint. I can tell you firsthand, he's a far cry from sainthood. What do you know about him anyway? You're a doctor. He's a lawyer. What do you do, have drinks together at the country club?"

If he had thought about it, Kevin would never have laid into Alex Rivard at that moment. Alex wasn't a young man, and he had just spent seven hours in surgery and was physically and emotionally drained. But Kevin wasn't thinking straight. He hadn't been thinking straight since he'd arrived in St. Albans.

It was funny. The more worked up Kevin seemed to get, the more relaxed Alex Rivard became. He leaned back in his chair with a smile on his face, his hands behind his head, and waited for Kevin to finish.

"Are you done?" he asked when Kevin almost fell back in his chair. Kevin didn't answer.

"I'd like to tell you a story," Alex began. "It goes back to 1963. Your father and I were young hotshots back then. We were both going to save the world in our different professions.

"You probably don't know this, Kevin, but St. Albans was a flash point in the civil rights movement. In 1964, southern senators were filibustering against passage of the Civil Rights Act and had been doing so for months when some protesters, black and white, jumped into a pool at an all-white hotel here in St. Albans. The owner poured acid into the pool and somebody took a picture of him doing it. That picture was shown in newspapers around the world. It was a symbol of American bigotry. The filibuster ended right after that and the Civil Rights Act was passed.

"My story goes back to 1963, however. The Klan was real active here. Your father and I were part of the local movement. I was the doctor for the black community and your father was one of their lawyers.

"We got threats. One time they threw a brick through my office window. Another time they burned a cross on my front lawn." Kevin noticed that Alex's hands were no longer behind his head. His elbows were now resting on his knees and he was rubbing his hands together. He had a faraway look in his eyes like he was actually going back in time.

"We had a procedure that if I was called out on an emergency somebody would ride shotgun with me. Usually, it was your father because he and your mother lived right next door.

"One night I got a call. It was a setup but I obviously didn't know it at the time. I almost didn't contact your father because it was so late, but I decided to let the phone ring a couple of times. He answered it on the second ring and was standing outside my door, rifle in hand, in a matter of minutes. I don't remember where we were going, but I do know we turned down a side street to get there. Halfway down the street this car pulls out of an alley right in front of us.

"It's funny the things you remember. We were both laughing at the time because your father was telling me a hilarious story about this deposition he had that day, where the witness showed up dead-drunk. I didn't think anything of that car pulling out, but your dad—he immediately stopped talking, opened the passenger door, slid out, and disappeared.

"Two seconds later a dump truck full of men in hoods pulled up behind me. The driver of the first car stepped out. He stood in front of the streetlight so I could see him clearly. Besides his hood, he had a rope with a noose on it slung over his right shoulder, and I was sure that I was about to die. I forgot all about your father. I was just looking at that noose.

"That's when your father stepped out from behind an old oak tree not two feet from the man with the rope. His rifle was pointed right at the man's right temple. Everybody could see him as well because of the streetlamp.

"I'll never forget his words. 'Listen up, boys,' he said to the men in the truck in a calm but edgy tone. There were about eight of them huddled in there. 'I've been wanting to shoot one of you for quite some time now. Looks like I'm finally gonna get my chance. I see a hood move on that truck, I'm gonna blow this man's head off. He knows I'm going to do it too. He's had fair warning.'

"The guy with the noose was shaking as bad as I was. 'Listen to him, boys. He's a crazy fuck,' he yelled to the men in the truck.

"There was silence for what seemed like the longest time. Then your father spoke again, his voice as calm as could be. 'What'll it be, boys—do you wanna see your friend's brains splattered all over kingdom come or do you wanna just drive on outta here?' There was a second there when I didn't know what was going to happen. I was looking in my rearview mirror and nobody on that truck was moving a muscle. Then slowly the truck started backing down the street.

"I'll tell you that whole incident probably didn't last more than five minutes, but it's as indelible a part of my memory as the day my first child was born. So you see, your father and I are not the country-club set. When I tell you he's a tough guy, I'm speaking from experience."

Kevin ignored the point Alex was making—a point that shot down his accusation entirely—and focused for some reason on the minutiae.

"What did my father mean when he said that the man had fair warning?"

"A couple of months before this incident Tom had represented a black man, Reginald Porter—he still lives here in town—on a rape charge. It was a shit case. They had no evidence against Reginald except that he was black and he was in the neighborhood when the rape supposedly occurred. The woman never saw her assailant. Anyway, your father started getting the hate mail and the threatening telephone calls, all of which he ignored. Then one night they threw a brick through his living room window, almost hitting your mother.

"At the time everyone knew who the local leader of the Klan was. It was the worst-kept secret in town. The next day, Tom went to this guy's real estate office and, in front of the entire office, put a .357 Magnum to the man's head and told him that if anybody ever came to his house uninvited again, he was going to come back and blow his brains out.

"Tom somehow knew that the man with the noose was the real estate agent he had threatened, and every man out on the road that night knew about the history between the two of them. I don't think anyone else could have made them turn around and go home. They thought your dad was crazy."

Kevin had represented drug dealers and killers before so he was not easily surprised. He had never heard a story quite like the one Alex had just told him but it didn't matter. He had something else on his mind.

"Do you know what happened between my father and mother, and why he never contacted me all these years?"

"I'm probably the only person who does."

"Then why don't you tell me that story?"

"It's not my story to tell. I'll make a deal with you, though—if your father dies without telling you what happened, I promise you I will. Fair enough?"

"Fair enough."

CHAPTER TWENTY-ONE

Luck was no lady to Vern Fleming.

He ran into a firestorm by the name of Harvey Shay at the high school. Harvey was incensed when Vern showed up and wanted to take Freddie out of school.

"Carlisle Buchanan was here yesterday. He disrupted the whole school. It's not going to happen again." Harvey's face was fiery red and he whined and whined.

Vern gave him five minutes. Then he put on his shades and addressed Harvey like the little pissant that he was.

"If the kid isn't here, ready to go, in the next five minutes, I'm arresting you for obstruction of justice."

Harvey just stood there, looking at the flyboy shades in astonishment.

"Four minutes," Vern said, putting a toothpick in his mouth.

Harvey relented once again. He hoped this investigation was over soon. His ego couldn't take any more visits from the Forrest County Sheriff's Department.

Five minutes after his ultimatum, Vern left with Freddie in tow.

It had just been a bump in the road for Vern so far but that was about to change. He and Freddie reached Verona an hour later, having not said a word to each other. To Freddie, Vern was an alien with his shades and his smokes and his skinny black tie. He was a little freaked like he had been that night out on Gladestown Road. Even after he'd met the sheriff himself, Freddie refused to talk to anybody but Carlisle.

Two hours later, Freddie and Carlisle met again—this time in a small white room bare of all furniture and accoutrements except for a metal table, two chairs, and a big mirror inset on the side of the wall facing Freddie. Freddie had seen enough cop shows to know that there were people watching on the other side of that mirror.

Carlisle calmed him down by telling him everything.

"Now Freddie, our conversation is being videotaped and there are people watching, as you know." Those words pissed Vern off so bad he wanted to barge in the room right then and shoot Carlisle.

Carlisle proceeded to ask Freddie the exact questions he had asked the day before and Freddie, who had followed Carlisle's instructions and written down his story, gave the same answers. The interview took less than half an hour.

The sheriff just looked at Vern after the interview was over.

"What?" Vern finally asked.

"Nothing," the sheriff replied. "I'm just trying to calculate in my head the difference between your salary and Carlisle's."

CHAPTER TWENTY-TWO

Vern's "lucky" streak wasn't over by a long shot. Five days later, a Monday, he took off simply because he was sick and tired of driving over to Gladestown and sitting in that little office, staring into space. The reporters were back because someone had leaked Freddie's interview to the press and Vern was sick of them too.

"I've got nothing to tell you," he told six different newsmen on six different occasions after they had peppered him with a barrage of questions. Until they got a lead on the automobile, the investigation was at a standstill. He had Carlisle knocking on every door in town, inquiring about friends or family members who owned an old gray car.

"You're going to be doing real police work," he had told Carlisle as he sat in Carlisle's chair and put his feet up on Carlisle's desk. Carlisle didn't respond. His little talk with Vern hadn't worked. He had already decided that his days as an auxiliary officer were coming to an end. He would have quit already except he was sleeping with Sylvia Johnson and keeping her abreast of the investigation on a daily basis. He didn't want to screw that up.

When Vern took Monday off, Carlisle manned the office. He was sitting at his desk about to head to Rosie's for breakfast when the door opened and a burly man in his midforties or thereabouts with a full beard walked in. He was dressed in black slacks and a white short-sleeved shirt. His outfit looked a little like something Vern would wear without the tie.

"Is this the Gladestown sheriff's office?" he asked.

"It's the Forrest County sheriff's office," Carlisle replied. "There is no Gladestown sheriff's office."

"Well, I've been reading about that Alligator Man murder and I've got some information that I thought might be useful to you."

Carlisle shot up from his desk. "Why don't you come around the counter and sit down here, Mr.—?"

"Russo, George Russo."

"Good to meet you, Mr. Russo, I'm Auxiliary Officer Carlisle Buchanan. Now what's this information that you'd like to share with us?"

"I don't know if it's important or not. I'm a bartender down in Verona at a place called the Last Stop. It's kind of connected to the Verona Inn and most of our customers are guests at the inn. It's not a very upscale place. The week before the Alligator Man disappeared, this guy was coming in every night. He was drinking real heavy. As a bartender you can kinda tell when somebody's agitated about something, and this guy was real agitated.

"Anyway, he was in the night the Alligator Man supposedly went missing. He left sometime after eleven—I can't be sure of the time—but he was real agitated and real drunk. He mumbled something like, 'I'm gonna kill him tonight.' I'm not sure those were the exact words but that was the gist of it. I didn't pay him any mind. Drunks say a lot of stuff. Then I started reading the stories about the Alligator Man—and I thought maybe there's a connection."

"You obviously know that Verona is sixty miles from Gladestown because you drove here today, correct?"

"Yes, sir."

"Why would you think a drunk saying he was gonna kill somebody late at night in Verona, when he was totally wasted, had anything to do with the Alligator Man's disappearance?"

"That's just it, I didn't. Not until I read the kid's story the other day in the paper. That's when it hit me. This guy drove an old gray Toyota."

CHAPTER TWENTY-THREE

As soon as George Russo left his office, Carlisle typed up his interview and faxed it to headquarters. He then called Sheriff Cousins to fill him in.

"I made an appointment for Mr. Russo to come into head quarters tomorrow and give a sworn statement," Carlisle told the sheriff.

"Good work, Carlisle."

Sheriff Cousins immediately called the "sick" Vern Fleming to find out how he was doing and to give him the news. Vern was with his wife at the supermarket when the cell phone rang.

"Vern Fleming."

"How much a pound is the grouper?" Dottie Fleming asked the man at the fish counter at that exact moment. The sheriff couldn't help but hear it.

"Well, it sounds like you're feeling better."

Vern was caught red-handed and he knew it. There was nothing to do but go with the sheriff's suggestion. "Yes, I am. I decided to go to the store with the wife."

"Good. I'm happy for you. Carlisle Buchanan has just interviewed a bartender who thinks he can identify the murderer."

Shit! Vern said to himself. *That yokel is going to cost me my job.*

"I'm just going to drive the wife home. I'll be in shortly," he told the sheriff.

"That's probably a good decision."

Vern immediately read Carlisle's interview with George Russo when he got to the office. He didn't wait around for the sheriff to dress him down, however. He set out for the Verona Inn and sought out the manager.

"I want to see all your registrations for the first two weeks in April," he told the man after identifying himself.

"And if I don't want to show them to you?" the man asked. He was a slightly built Indian man and Vern wanted to just smack him across the face and say, *I'm the law, now get moving!* but you couldn't operate like that anymore. He thought of the principal back at Gladestown High and his attitude. *What the hell is it with people these days?*

"This is a murder investigation. Do you want to go to jail for obstruction of justice?"

It was the language of a new era but it worked even better than the slap to the head. Ten minutes later Vern was sitting in a room with a small stack of registration books in front of him. Initially, he was looking for people who paid with cash. If they weren't using a credit card, they did not have to use their real name. Of course, a criminal could use a fake ID, which would make things a little more complicated, but Vern's method was always to start with the simple scenario. He found what he was looking for in a little over an hour. A man named Tom Jones had stayed at the hotel from the third to the eleventh and paid in cash. Tom Jones was obviously a false name unless he was a Welshman who swiveled his hips and sang a mean ballad.

"I want to see this man's registration information," he told the manager, who pulled it up on the computer almost immediately.

Unfortunately, Tom Jones had not put down an address or a license plate number for his vehicle.

"Why don't your people make them fill out the entire card?" he asked.

"We're just a small hotel. People can go anywhere they want to spend the night. If they come here, we don't hassle them with little details like that."

"But it's a safety issue." Vern didn't know why the hell he was arguing with this man about hotel procedures. He was just frustrated. He had the murderer, he was sure of it, but then again he had nothing.

"We try to be safe," the manager told him. "When it's not busy, we usually have one of the desk people write down the license plate numbers in the parking lot. We do it twice a day. It gives us information on where our out-of-state customers are coming from, and we do match the information with what we have on file."

"What do you do with the information?"

"I'm not sure I understand what you're asking me."

"Well, if the license plate numbers don't match up with your guests, and obviously they won't if some of your guests don't even write down their license plate number on the registration card—what do you do?"

"Nothing."

Vern wanted to smack the man in the head again. *You make work for your desk people and then you don't use the information. It's idiocy.* But then he got an idea.

"Can you print out the license plate numbers collected by your desk people for the second week in April?"

"Sure."

"And you can give me a computer printout of all the guest registrations during that period as well?"

"Yes."

"Good."

It was a tedious task, but he could get the names of the vehicle owners from the Florida Department of Highway Safety and Motor Vehicles and match those names with the guest registrations to narrow down his search for the mysterious Tom Jones.

He was ready to go back to the office now and have his inevitable little chat with Sheriff Cousins.

CHAPTER TWENTY-FOUR

Tom Wylie woke up at four thirty on the afternoon of his surgery. Unlike the previous day, he was in a lot of pain and unable to focus on his audience. He squeezed Kate's hand and smiled at her and, eventually, at everybody else in the room. After a half hour or so, he drifted back off to sleep. One by one, his audience slipped away as well. Billy was the first to go, citing some odd jobs that needed to be completed. Ray Blackwell left for Tallahassee soon after that, leaving Kevin and Kate alone with the sleeping patient.

"Your father still has his house in town. Why don't you stay there while you're visiting?" Kate suggested. "There's nobody there and you can spread yourself out and relax. No sense paying for a hotel room."

Kevin was about to decline. He still didn't want to accept anything from this woman. But his father's home had once been his home. He could roam around exploring the nooks and crannies of his past. It was an opportunity he couldn't pass up.

"Maybe I'll do that," he said.

"Good. I'll drive you over. Tom's going to sleep for a while."

Tom's home in the Old City was a two-story Spanish Colonial set on one of the canals that led out to the Gulf of Mexico. Kate let Kevin in and gave him a brief tour of the place. It was a modest home with two bedrooms and two bathrooms upstairs, including the master, and one bedroom downstairs. Kevin vaguely remembered the house, although in his mind it had been much bigger. The downstairs bedroom had been his room.

There was a breakfast nook in the kitchen with an oversized window that looked out on the water. Kevin sat and lingered there for a minute.

"I loved to sit here when I was a little boy," he told Kate.

Kate smiled. "It's your father's favorite place too."

The centerpiece of the home was the living room with its massive fireplace buttressed on both sides, floor to ceiling, by bookshelves filled with books on a wide range of topics. The floors were hardwood with antique rugs and runners throughout. The furniture was old but comfortable.

"I could sleep on this couch," Kevin said as he plopped himself down.

"People have," Kate assured him, which raised another subject in Kevin's mind.

"You and my father don't live together?"

"In a way, we do. I've got my ranch and that's my space. This is your dad's—this and the lake house. I spend a couple of days a week here. He spends a couple of days a week with me at the ranch, although that will change while he is recuperating."

"I was wondering about the ranch when you invited me out yesterday. I thought maybe he had sold this place and moved."

"Not a chance. He'll never sell this place."

Kevin wondered why. There had to be bad memories here. "How did you and he meet?"

"We met at a coffee shop, actually. About a year after your mother and father split up and she moved to Miami. Your father was not doing very well back then." Kevin did not know what she meant by that remark but he did not interrupt her. "We frequented the same place most mornings. There was a common table where we used to sit with a group of people. One day we were the only ones at the table so we struck up a conversation. After that, we were friends and it went from there."

"How is it that you knew my mother?"

Kevin was probing like a surgeon looking for a stray bullet. Kate did not seem the least bit uncomfortable, however.

"I didn't. I mean we never met. In the early years, anytime there needed to be communication between them for any reason, I would be the one who talked to your mother. Your father either wouldn't or couldn't talk to her."

"Do you know why?"

"I knew it had to do with you."

"How did it have to do with me?"

"That I can't tell you. That's something you need to talk to your father about."

Kate departed soon after Kevin's interrogation, leaving him free to explore his childhood home. It only took him a few minutes to find what he was looking for. His father used the second bedroom upstairs as a den. He had a table set up in the middle of the room against the far wall containing small boxes of hooks and feathers and glue. This was obviously where he made his fishing lures. Next to the table was a small chest and on top of the chest were two eight-by-ten-inch pictures of a little boy. In one picture, the little boy was sitting on the grass, giggling, his face covered with chocolate. In the other, he was dressed in a light blue summer suit with short pants, sitting on a small bench, smiling. Behind the table on the wall was a bulletin board full of pictures of Kevin with his father. His mother was in a few; the rest were of just him and his dad. In all of them, they were smiling and laughing and appeared to be so happy.

There were a few of a black-and-white setter as well—Kevin's dog Matty. He felt a hollow feeling in his stomach for a moment as he looked at them. When he and his mother moved to Miami, they'd left Matty behind. He didn't have a say in the matter and he never saw his dog again.

Kevin sat in his father's den for a long time, taking it all in. He was thirty-six years old, a seasoned criminal lawyer. He knew from experience that the world was gray. Yet in his own life, in his own play, everything was black and white. He loved his mother, Carol, and his stepfather, Stephen. They had always been the good guys. And Tom Wylie and Kate Parker had always been the bad guys. Now he found out that Kate had not even met his father until a year after his mother left. And this room told him that his father had never forgotten about him. *What the hell happened? Why did I never hear from him again?*

CHAPTER TWENTY-FIVE

Vern handled the sworn videotaped interview at headquarters of the bartender, George Russo, and to his credit he stuck pretty much to the script Carlisle had provided. He wanted a more in-depth description of the angry, agitated bar patron, however.

"Can you describe this man?"

"Sure. He was tall, probably six two or thereabouts. I would say he was in his midforties, dark hair but thinning on top. He didn't have a beer gut or anything and he actually looked to be in pretty good shape. I know drinkers. I can spot them a mile away. This guy wasn't a drunk in my opinion."

"Any distinguishing characteristics, like a scar or something?"

"None that I noticed. You know the bar is kinda dark."

After that interview, Vern had his nose to the ground like a bloodhound. He heard back from the Department of Highway Safety and Motor Vehicles that very afternoon, and it only took him a few hours to go through his two lists and find his man. William Fuller owned a 2000 gray Toyota Corolla. His car had been identified in the parking lot of the Verona Inn from April seventh to the eleventh, the same days Tom Jones had stayed at the hotel and paid cash. There was no doubt that William Fuller was Tom Jones.

Vern immediately called the department back and had them fax a copy of William Fuller's driver's license. He then created a photo pack with William Fuller's picture in it and called George Russo back. At nine thirty the next morning, Russo identified Fuller. Vern had his man.

He took everything to Sheriff Cousins, who was both surprised and relieved that Vern had solved the case so quickly. He knew it wouldn't be long before the feds were breathing down his neck.

"Great job, Vern. I think Carlisle lit a fire under your ass. This just shows what a good homicide detective can do when he puts his mind to it."

Vern was sure there was a compliment in there somewhere.

"We need to get the state attorney up to speed right away. I want to get a search warrant issued for that car and I want to arrest that son of a bitch before he knows what hit him. Where does he live?"

"It says here, Twenty-nine Maple Court, St. Albans, Florida," Vern replied.

"What's that, eight hours from here? He didn't come this far to kill somebody for no reason."

"St. Albans was the corporate headquarters for Roy Johnson's company, Dynatron," Vern told him.

"He's probably a disgruntled employee or something like that. That's gotta be the connection."

"That's my guess. I'm gonna run that stuff down next."

The next morning, however, Vern was in Gladestown sitting in Carlisle's chair with his feet up on Carlisle's desk, chastising and gloating.

"Law enforcement is a paramilitary operation. You've got to follow the rules and you've got to be thorough. You don't follow the rules, Carlisle. You investigate what comes to you but you don't take it to the next level."

Vern's words didn't make Carlisle angry. On the contrary, they affirmed what he had been thinking since this investigation started. He didn't like following rules. He was somewhat like his dad in that way, although he wasn't a lawbreaker. And when he actually sat down and thought about it, he didn't care about finding Roy Johnson's killer. The man deserved to die. The only reason Carlisle had put up with Vern this long was Sylvia Johnson.

He was sure she would understand why he quit, although he wasn't going to tell her how he really felt about her deceased husband.

"You know, Vern, you're absolutely right," Carlisle said as he turned and walked out of the office.

"Hey, come back here. Where are you going?"

Carlisle ignored him. He got in his little white Honda and drove directly to Verona. He felt he owed it to Sheriff Cousins to give him the news personally.

"I'm resigning, sir," he told the sheriff when he was finally ushered into the man's office.

"What's the problem, Carlisle? Vern getting on your nerves? I know all about it. He gets on mine every day. Look, this investigation will be over soon and everything will be back to normal."

"I understand what you're saying, Sheriff, but I won't be back to normal. Things have changed in the way I see myself. I'm not cut out for this type of work."

"I could get you a raise if that would do it."

"No, sir. To tell you the truth, I don't want to find Roy Johnson's killer."

"I understand. What will you do?"

"I'll go back to giving airboat tours. And I'm a fishing and hunting guide. I'll make ends meet."

"I can't talk you out of this?"

"No, sir."

CHAPTER TWENTY-SIX

After he'd sat in his father's den alone for an hour or so and sorted nothing out in his mind, Kevin called Susan.

"Hi, honey, I've missed you," she said when she heard his voice.

"I've missed you too, honey."

"So what's going on?"

"Well, my father had his surgery and he survived, although he still has terminal cancer."

"Did you and he have your talk?"

"No. He's barely conscious. We haven't said anything to each other."

"Well, maybe tomorrow he'll be more alert."

"Maybe, but I don't think so. This whole situation is a little more complicated than I believed it to be. I'll probably be here for a little while."

"What's 'a little while'?"

"Two weeks or so."

"Two weeks! Kevin, do you realize you don't have an income anymore?"

"Stop it, Susan. Of course I do. It's not like I'm destitute. I've got plenty of money in the bank."

"That money is going to go quick with your mortgage and utilities and food..."

"I'm not worried about it, okay? I'm just not worried about it."

"You don't worry about anything, including me. I'm just supposed to sit here like the dutiful girlfriend and wait until you decide to come home. And I shouldn't say anything about you running off to St. Albans and spending all your savings and destroying all of our plans for the immediate future. I'm just supposed to put up with it."

Kevin had had enough. "It's always about money with you, isn't it? Well, I've got news for you. My life isn't a balance sheet." He hung up the phone.

She called back immediately but he didn't answer. He was already on his way to Chico's. He needed a drink.

Billy was at the bar in the same spot Kevin had seen him the night before. It was a little more crowded, but still very relaxed.

"Hey, Kev, right on time. Let me buy you a drink."

"Sure. I'll just have a light beer, any kind," he told the bartender.

"Draft or bottle?"

"Draft."

"You look a little down," Billy observed.

"Yeah, I just had an argument with my live-in girlfriend."

"She wants you home, right?"

"Yeah."

"Well, that's reasonable. She misses you."

"I've only been here a couple of days. And it's not like I've been on a golfing trip or something. She just can't let things be. She's got to press and press." He took a long sip of his draft, almost emptying it.

"Well, it'll all work out." It was the best Billy could come up with.

"Or it won't," Kevin replied, surprising himself with his

words. "By the way, Billy, while we're talking about relationships, how is it that you're so close to my father?"

"We go back a long ways. Your dad and my dad were friends, and then my dad died when I was seventeen. I was a little out of control after that. I don't know if my mother called your dad or not, but he just started showing up, taking me out to the lake with him and you—that kind of stuff. He never talked to me—you know, like play the substitute father with the sage advice and all that bullshit. I probably would have tuned him out completely if he did. Instead, he taught me how to fish and hang out and enjoy stuff just by doing it. Some days it was just you, me, and him, and we'd have a cookout at the lake and cook the fish we caught. I mean, it was great. We've been friends ever since.

"Getting through that time straightened me out. I finished school, got my two-year degree, and met Laurie, the love of my life. We had a great life. Of course, I've lost everything now."

"Not everything. You've still got the kids."

"Yeah, I probably wouldn't be around if I didn't have them. It's still hard to cope some days. That's why I find myself in here a lot more often than I should be. Listen, let's get off this subject. If you decide to stay in town for a while, I need to take you to a ball game. We've got a great Double-A baseball team here. It's a nice old ballpark, costs nothing to get in, and beers are a buck. My kids love to go too."

"It sounds like a great night out and I want to meet your kids." Kevin wasn't ready to leave the discussion they were having just yet. He had one more question to ask Billy.

"Were my father and I close back then?"

"Oh, man, you guys were inseparable."

CHAPTER TWENTY-SEVEN

Jeanette Truluc had been a prosecutor for almost ten years, eight of those years in Forrest County. She was the top prosecutor in the Forrest County state attorney's office and she usually tried all the high-profile cases. Frank Cousins was not surprised that she would be handling the Alligator Man case. Vern Fleming, however, didn't like her at all. The fact that Jeanette was a dark-skinned Jamaican woman who usually wore her hair in braids probably had something to do with his feelings.

"Can't they assign somebody else to this case?" he asked the sheriff.

"Who else would they assign? She's the most experienced."

"Well, I don't like her."

Sheriff Cousins knew that Vern's opinion of Jeanette had a lot to do with the color of her skin and her gender, although he also knew that Vern would never admit it.

"You don't have to like her. This isn't about you."

Jeanette Truluc came to the sheriff's department at Frank Cousins's request and reviewed the entire investigative file—including Carlisle's initial interview with Sylvia Johnson and the sworn testimony of George Russo and Freddie Jenkins. The DNA report regarding the pieces of clothing found in the swamp came back as well. No DNA samples were found.

When she concluded her review of the file, Jeanette left without discussing her thoughts and opinions with anybody.

When Frank Cousins heard that she had not talked to Vern at all, he smiled to himself. It was the smart thing to do.

She called him the next morning at nine o'clock sharp.

"I think that there is enough evidence to establish probable cause for a search warrant to be issued. However, the arrest issue is tenuous in my mind. While there arguably is probable cause to arrest, I'm not convinced there is enough evidence for a conviction."

Frank did not reply right away. He wanted to listen between the lines for a moment. "What's the problem?" he finally asked.

"There's no evidence of motive at this point. That has to be filled in. Without it, we have a guy from St. Albans, who has a gray Toyota, spending a week in Verona and a murder occurring in Gladestown at the end of that week, involving a gray car that might be a Honda or a Toyota, or a dozen other vehicle brands. Those two events are intriguing but they are not sufficiently tied together. The bartender's testimony that this guy said he was going to kill somebody gets you into the probable cause arena for arrest, but it's tentative."

"I see your point, Jeanette. Let's just get the search warrant for now, continue our investigation, and at least try and talk to the guy."

CHAPTER TWENTY-EIGHT

There was a patio on the south side of Tom Wylie's house bordered on the east side by a wall and on the west side by the Gulf. The wall was attached at the southern end to a two-story building, which served as a garage on the bottom floor. Kevin had no idea what the second floor was used for. He was having his coffee on the patio, looking out at the water, when he heard a car pull into the garage. When nobody emerged from the building, he decided to investigate and walked up the outside steps to the second floor. He startled a middle-aged woman who was scurrying around in what appeared to be an office.

"I'm sorry if I scared you," Kevin said when the woman grabbed her chest at the sight of him and let out a loud gasp.

"Well, I wasn't expecting anybody."

"I'm Tom's son, Kevin. I'm staying at the house." He extended his hand. The woman hesitated a moment before reciprocating.

"I'm Jan, Jan Meyers," she said. "I'm your father's secretary."

Kevin looked around. Jan was standing at her desk, which was obviously a secretarial station. There was a large office to his right. To his left there was another vacant secretarial station and a smaller office. "So this is his office?" Kevin asked, pointing to the bigger office on the right.

"Yeah," Jan replied. "This is it. It's been the same for the thirty years I've been here, although there's not a whole lot going on these days. Your dad's been phasing himself out for a while. He's only got a few appeals left. I just putter around mostly, answer the correspondence that I can, and put the rest aside for him when he gets back. There was a time, though. I can't tell you the cases your father has handled out of this little office."

"Who's in the other office?"

"Nobody. We've had some people in there for short periods from time to time but mostly it's been vacant."

Jan was an attractive woman, probably in her midfifties, Kevin surmised.

"Maybe I can help with the correspondence," he heard himself say. "I'm a lawyer."

"Just like your father. That's nice."

Kevin didn't reply. He didn't want to get into it with this woman.

"He's got an appeal that just got set for oral argument. Somebody needs to request an extension of time," she said.

"Sure. I'll need to talk to him about that, but why don't I take a look at the file?"

She hesitated for a minute. Kevin could see that she was going over things in her mind. Client files were confidential, but this was Tom's son. And he was a lawyer.

"You go in and sit in his office, and I'll bring the file to you," she finally said.

Kevin spent the next hour reading about Aurelio Hernandez, a cab driver in the business district who had been shot and paralyzed from the neck down by a robber. Hernandez had no medical insurance and received no workers' compensation or disability payments because he was classified as an independent contractor. Tom Wylie was arguing in the appeal that cab companies were abusing the system and denying cab drivers fundamental rights by calling them independent contractors rather than employees. The classification was an illusion. The company escaped the obligation to provide workers' compensation and Social Security benefits, and the driver had no protection whatsoever, which in the end left him crippled and destitute.

This is the kind of work I should be doing, Kevin thought to himself.

He didn't get to the hospital until after ten that morning but it didn't matter. His father was still pretty much out of it. He was in a great deal of pain and the hospital staff was keeping him medicated. Kate was there until Kevin convinced her to take the opportunity to run any errands that she had. It gave her a break and gave him an opportunity to be alone with his father, even though Tom Wylie was not in any shape to carry on a conversation. Tom smiled when he woke up and saw Kevin at his bedside. He held his son's hand as he had done on that first day.

The next day was pretty much the same. Kevin was there when Alex came in to check Tom's incision. He watched as the bandage was removed and Tom winced in pain. There was a long scar down the middle of his stomach, and Kevin could only imagine what had been cut and displaced to allow the doctors to get in there and remove 80 percent of his father's liver.

"You've got to start walking today, Tom," Alex told him. "Otherwise you'll get pneumonia." Tom just grunted. Kevin could not imagine his father getting up and walking in that condition.

That afternoon, two orderlies came in and assisted the poor

man as he stood up and attempted to walk down the hall. The expression on Tom's face as he tried to first sit up and then stand was so severe it made Kevin wince. Kate was next to him and she grabbed his arm to steady herself. His anger at his father seemed so small at that moment.

On the fourth day, Tom seemed even more alert. Ray Blackwell showed up that day, as did Billy, who had been sticking his head in for a few minutes every morning.

Billy and Kevin had been meeting almost every night at Chico's for a couple of drinks.

"I'm just allowing myself a couple now," Billy said. "Eventually, I have to get back to my old ways, exercising daily and having a few beers on the weekend. It's just hard right now."

"I hear you," Kevin said. "I'm struggling myself."

The two men were becoming fast friends. They had gone to the baseball game the night before and Kevin had met Billy's kids, Thomas and Heather. They were nice kids and Kevin couldn't help but notice how much they adored their father. It just didn't seem to be enough for Billy. He had lost too much.

"They get it all from their mother," Billy told him when Kevin complimented him on his children. "She loved them to death but she made them toe the line. They'd be fine even if I were gone tomorrow."

"I don't think so," Kevin told him. "I see a lot of you in those kids."

Alex came in when everybody was still there. As soon as he completed his examination and confirmed that Tom was coming along nicely, the ribbing started with Judge Blackwell leading the way.

"Kate, you're going to have to watch him when he gets out of here. He'll be pulling his shirt up and showing all the ladies his scar and telling them he's a war hero."

"He's been doing that with his appendix scar for years," Kate replied. "It's never gotten him anywhere."

"Don't make me laugh," Tom told them, smiling from the bed. "We don't want to ruin Alex's masterpiece."

Kevin enjoyed the moment with the rest of them, no longer feeling like an outsider.

CHAPTER TWENTY-NINE

It only took a few days for Jeanette Truluc to obtain a search warrant. In the interim, Vern Fleming continued his investigation and made plans to go to St. Albans. He started by calling an old friend in the police department whom he had met at a seminar.

"I'm working the Alligator Man homicide. I need the personnel records of a guy who worked for Dynatron to help my lame-ass prosecutor establish motive," Vern told his friend.

"The feds have the records, Vern. The local FBI agent in charge is a guy named Harvey Booth. You can use my name but I don't think it will help you."

Vern knew exactly what he meant. The local cops and the FBI sometimes didn't get along.

"I need access to the employee records of Dynatron," Vern told Booth when he got him on the phone. Vern had never learned the art of buttering up people.

"Can't get 'em," Booth replied.

"This is a murder investigation—the Alligator Man down here in Verona. I'm sure you've heard of it."

"Sorry. Can't help you."

You arrogant son of a bitch! Vern thought, although he kept that to himself. "What if I don't need the records, but just some specific information about an employee?"

"Sorry."

"Even if that employee is a suspect in a murder case?"

"Can't help you."

Vern slammed the phone down.

That afternoon Sheriff Cousins called Robert Morris, the St. Albans County state attorney. The two men knew each other. Sheriff Cousins told Morris about Vern's conversation with the FBI agent, Harvey Booth.

"Roy Johnson is dead and they convicted that chief accountant—what the hell are they keeping the records for?"

"I don't know," Morris replied. "But I'll check into it. Tell me exactly what you need. I've had my own war going with these guys. This was a state case to begin with but they took it over. The only way I've been able to get anything is if I have a very narrow and specific request."

"I need a certified copy of William Fuller's personnel file. To be honest with you, I don't even know if the guy worked there, but if he did, that file has to include the dates he worked there and the amount of money he had in his 401(k) before everything tanked. You know the Dynatron story—all the employees lost their retirement..."

"Like I told you," Morris interrupted, "I've been living with this disaster for two years. Crime, suicide, you name it—all because of Roy Johnson's company and its shenanigans. Call me tomorrow. I'll put as much pressure on Booth as I can."

Two days later, Vern was on Maple Court, the street where William Fuller lived, or, at least, where his driver's license said he lived. He was canvassing the neighborhood and had gotten very little information from the first four houses he visited. Vern had

Fuller's driver's license picture blown up and a few people recognized that but didn't know much about the man. He hit the jackpot with a hunched, elderly woman who lived by herself almost directly across the street from the Fullers at 32 Maple Court.

"A police officer?" she asked after Vern had just identified himself as a detective.

"A detective, ma'am," Vern corrected her.

"Well, come on in and have a seat on the couch. Would you like a cup of coffee?"

Vern knew to accept. By making himself comfortable, he would make the old woman, whose name was Anne Lyons, comfortable.

"I knew Billy and his wife, Laurie, and the kids very well," she told him when they both had their coffee and were seated in the living room, Vern on the couch right where Anne had told him to sit. "Sometimes I babysat the kids when they went to a movie. A lovely family. What a tragedy."

"What was the tragedy?" Vern asked.

"What was the tragedy?" Anne repeated. "You live in this town, don't you?"

"No, ma'am."

"The tragedy of this town was Dynatron. Billy had worked for Dynatron for twenty-something years. He lost everything including his health insurance when Dynatron went out of business. Then he lost Laurie. He sat right there on that couch where you are sitting and cried his eyes out the day she died. I never saw a man so devastated."

Anne had no idea that her story was a death sentence for Billy, giving the state all the motive it needed to convict him of first-degree murder.

The driveway across the street, Billy's driveway, was empty. "Do you know what time he gets home?" Vern asked.

"Who?"

"Mr. Fuller."

"Oh, Billy doesn't live there anymore. The bank foreclosed on the place. They moved out April first of this year. I remember the date because Billy came over with the kids to say good-bye and I asked him if this was an April Fools' joke. He just smiled at me. I honestly don't know how the man has held it together. Kids will do that for you, though. Keep you focused."

"Do you, by any chance, know where he moved to?"

"Not exactly. He moved back to the Old City. That's where he grew up. I think it's the Cordoba Street Apartments, but I have no idea what apartment number."

"Mrs. Lyons, if I picked you up tomorrow and drove you to the police station, would you come in and give us a sworn statement?"

"Sure. I'll do anything I can to help."

Vern just smiled. *You'll help all right.*

Vern called Sheriff Cousins that night and filled him in on his interview with Anne Lyons. He was sitting at a bar, nursing a scotch on the rocks at the time.

"The state attorney says he'll have Fuller's personnel file in a week. He confirmed his employment at Dynatron," Cousins told Vern.

"We're picking up his car tomorrow morning. I'm gonna have a conversation with Mr. Fuller if he's around."

"He probably won't talk to you," Sheriff Cousins replied. "But you may as well give it a shot."

CHAPTER THIRTY

Tom Wylie was alert and sitting up in his bed, talking with Kate, when Kevin arrived the morning of the sixth day after Tom's surgery. The two were laughing about something.

"Good morning," Kevin said to the both of them.

"Good morning, Kevin," Tom replied. Kate just looked at the two of them and smiled.

"I think I'll leave you two alone. I have some shopping to do," she said and made a quick exit.

"How are you feeling?" Kevin asked.

"Not too bad. I've actually been waiting for you."

"Really?"

"Yeah. Alex was in this morning. He says I've got to take a walk in the morning and the afternoon. I really liked the guy before I became his patient. I was wondering if you would take a walk with me—me and my pole here." Tom pointed to the thin pole next to his bed that held his IV fluids.

"Sure," Kevin replied, moving to the side of the bed as his father started to try to get up by himself.

"You've got to be careful, Tom. You'll rip those staples out."

"Yeah, I know," Tom replied.

Kevin sat on the bed and put his right arm loosely around

Tom's waist. "Okay, on the count of three we stand up slowly. One, two, three."

Tom pressed down hard on Kevin's shoulder with his left hand and stabilized himself on the right with his IV pole. Kevin tried to give him as much lift as he could with his right arm. There was a tense second or two as Tom's body shook and he winced in pain, but he managed to stand up.

"Okay," he said. "Hardest part is over. Kevin, slide those slippers over here, will you?"

Kevin not only slid the slippers over, but also knelt down and slipped them on his father's feet one at a time. He then stood up, and with his right hand, he held his father's left bicep to steady him. "Ready?" he asked.

"Ready as I'll ever be," Tom replied as they set out, slowly inching along out of the room and down the hallway. Kevin could see the pain on his father's face at every step.

Ten minutes later, they passed the nurses' station. Nurse Jones came out from behind her desk and stood in front of them, her hands on her hips, a scolding expression on her face. She was a short woman, probably in her midforties, a little top-heavy.

"Mr. Wylie, you're not supposed to be walking without an orderly accompanying you," she said in a very disturbed tone.

"That's okay," Tom replied. "I brought my own."

"I'm sorry, it's against regulations."

"I'm sorry too," Tom said as he started to move around her. "I was never one to follow the rules."

The nurse looked at Kevin for some assistance. He just smiled and shrugged his shoulders. "Me neither," he said.

The two men continued walking down the hallway, both with big smiles on their faces.

The next morning, Tom had another request of his son. Kate had again excused herself so it was just the two of them.

"I need to take a shower after our morning walk," he said. "It's been a week; the washcloth baths aren't doing the job, and I can't let Nurse Ratched have that much power over me. Will you help me?"

Kevin had to laugh at the remark. "Sure," he said.

They took the same walk. When they reached the nurse's station, Tom paused to smile at Nurse Jones, who scowled back.

"Wait until she finds out I'm taking a shower on my own," Tom said. "She'll probably call out the National Guard and have me arrested."

"And flogged," Kevin added.

When they arrived back at the room, Kevin helped Tom take off his hospital gown. As his father stood there naked, Kevin could see exactly how much of a toll the cancer and chemotherapy had taken on the man. He was almost a skeleton.

"There's a plastic wrap in the top drawer of the nightstand by my bed. Would you get it for me?" Tom asked.

"Sure," Kevin replied, quickly opening the drawer and finding the wrap.

"We have to put it over the dressing so it doesn't get wet."

Kevin helped him put the plastic wrap on and then walked him carefully to the bathroom and the shower. He worked the knobs until he found the right settings.

"Stick your hand in there and see if that's okay for you," he said to his father.

"I trust you," Tom replied. "Just help me in there."

Kevin walked him into the shower, oblivious to the fact that he was getting himself wet in the process. Tom took the soap and lathered up as much as he could, getting his arms and his face and his neck.

"The lower parts will just have to be satisfied with a little water," he said.

"I'll get them," Kevin instinctively replied. He grabbed the soap from the soap dish, dropped to his knees, and began to lather his father's legs without giving it a thought.

When they were done, Kevin helped Tom put his hospital gown on and get back into bed. They did not speak until Tom was comfortably ensconced under his covers. Using the controls on the side of the bed, Tom raised it until he was almost sitting up.

"It's time," Tom said.

Kevin had no idea what he was talking about. "What time?"

"It's time for us to talk, Kevin."

CHAPTER THIRTY-ONE

It was seven thirty in the morning when Billy got back from dropping the kids off at school. It was his favorite time of the day—getting the kids up, making their breakfast, and hustling them off to school. It made him feel useful, but it was more than that, and he was sure the kids felt it too, although nobody ever spoke about it. Mom was always there in the middle of it—at the breakfast table, in the car during the drive to school. She was as tangible as the fresh morning air.

Vern intercepted him between his car and the apartment complex. He was hiding behind his flyboy shades as usual.

"Are you William Fuller?"

"Yeah," Billy replied, wondering what bill it was that he hadn't paid.

Vern had his badge out and flashed it. "I'm Detective Vern Fleming, Forrest County Sheriff's Department. I've got a warrant here to search your vehicle." He handed Billy the warrant.

Vern noticed that Billy didn't ask why he wanted to search the vehicle and he didn't look surprised either. His expression was one of fear. Billy didn't say anything so Vern continued talking. "The tow truck will be here in a few minutes. You'll be without your car for a couple of days but that can't be helped. If you have anything in there that you need, you can remove it from the vehicle now as long as I have an opportunity to inspect it first."

Billy still didn't reply. He just stood there.

"Why don't we go up to your apartment?" Vern suggested. "I've got a couple of questions I need to ask you."

"What's this about?" Billy finally asked.

"We're investigating the murder of Roy Johnson. You remember him, don't you?"

"He's a hard man for any former Dynatron employee to forget. Am I a suspect?"

"Yes."

"Are you arresting me?"

"Not at this time."

"And I suppose I don't have to talk to you if I don't want to?"

"It might be in your best interests to help us out."

"And it might be in my best interests not to talk to you at all. I'll let my lawyer decide."

Vern was surprised. When he saw the initial fear on Billy's face, he thought he could get him to talk.

"Suit yourself," Vern replied. "I'll be seeing you soon."

CHAPTER THIRTY-TWO

"You're thirty-six now, aren't you?" Tom asked his son.

"Yeah."

"And you're a trial lawyer so you've seen enough to know that all of life is a gray area, haven't you?"

"I think so," Kevin replied.

"Nobody is ever right and nobody is ever totally wrong. We do what we need to do to get along. You get that, don't you?"

Kevin was getting a little perturbed with the amateur philosophy. "Look, Tom, if you've got something to say just say it."

"Yeah, I hear you. I just don't want you jumping to any conclusions."

"I won't. Just get on with it."

"All right. In 1977, I was in my early forties, not much older than you, and I was consumed with my work. I was a sole practitioner then and my office was downtown in the business district. I represented a young black man named Adrian Pierce who had been arrested and charged with the violent rape and murder of a beautiful blonde girl in her early twenties.

"By the way, Alex told me about his conversation with you concerning what had happened in the sixties. Well, the Klan was still around in 1977. It was underground, though, waiting to rear its ugly head at the first opportunity. The murder of Ellen Wells—that was the young girl's name—was the lightning rod that the Klan had been waiting for to resurrect the overt racism and hatred. People came out in droves to every hearing. There were signs and placards. It was vicious.

"You and your mother weren't spared. There were death threats and rocks through the window—all of that stuff. We'd been through it before.

"I was working until at least eight every night. Sometimes, if I had a hearing the next day, I'd stay at the office. I had a change of clothes there and a shower. I'd just call and let your mother know I wasn't coming home. I want you to know I didn't leave you totally unprotected. I tried to get your mother to go to her mother's for a month or two but she wouldn't hear of it. She had her own career at the bank. Alex lived next door, and if I wasn't coming home, I'd call him too so he would keep an eye out.

"This case went on for well over six months. I never saw what I was doing to my family. I just wasn't there. I was out saving the world. And it wasn't just for six months. It was who I was back then. I couldn't see the big picture. Oh, you, me, and Billy would go fishing out at the lake and stuff, but it was a few hours on the weekend. But that was for me as much as for you boys, and your mother wasn't involved. I had emotionally abandoned her.

"The whole time the Pierce case was going on, I carried a gun with me, a little .22 caliber pistol. And when I was at the office late at night, I wasn't above having a drink or two."

Kevin noticed that his father was starting to sweat a little and he was rubbing his hands together. He was already tired from the walk. "Are you sure you want to continue? We can do this another time."

"No, I'm fine. I don't want to do this ever again. Where was I? One night I called your mother and told her I was going to stay at the office. I had a hearing the next day. I worked and drank until I couldn't see the paper in front of me anymore. And then I decided to go home. It wasn't too late, probably eleven, but all the lights were out and everybody was in bed so I just slipped in.

"I went upstairs and opened the bedroom door, turned the light on, and there they were." He stopped talking for a moment. He seemed calm but his eyes were looking down like he was studying the weave of the sheets on his hospital bed, still rubbing his hands and sweating. "Your mother and Steve were in bed together."

"Steve, my stepfather?"

"Yeah. Anyway, I was drunk and I was tired and I had a gun in my pocket. I simply lost it. I took my gun out and I shot twice before, thank God, the damned thing jammed. I wanted to kill him but I hit your mother instead—once in the shoulder. I don't know what would have happened if the gun hadn't jammed. I might have killed the both of them.

"Alex was there in a heartbeat. To this day, I don't know how he managed to get there so quickly but he did. He took the gun away from me and took me in the other room and calmed me down. Then he went back in and took care of Carol's shoulder. It was just a superficial wound. He had his wife bring his medical bag over and he patched her up right there."

"Where was I?"

"You were asleep in the downstairs bedroom. I thanked God for many years that you never woke up and saw that mess."

"You mean I slept through the police and everything?"

"There were no police. And that's the other part of the story.

"It turns out your mother and Steve had been seeing each

other for a long time. I was oblivious to it because I was in my own world. And this is what I want you to understand. She had a right to want happiness and to want a decent companion. She wasn't getting that from me. She had a right to look elsewhere.

"I didn't come to that conclusion at that time. It took a lot of years for me to see things as they were—to see myself. You're old enough and experienced enough to know exactly what I'm talking about. That's why I asked you all those questions before we started. You can't blame your mother and Steve for falling in love."

"And ruining my life."

"They didn't ruin your life, Kevin. You had a pretty good life."

"Without you. Without my father."

"Yeah, well, I lost my father in the war. Billy lost his wife and his children lost their mother to cancer. Shit happens."

"It doesn't mean it couldn't have been prevented."

"No, it doesn't. But it's over. You can't change it. You gotta go on. I have to tell you this story because you're here and you want to know and you have a right to know. I just don't want you to feel differently about the people who loved you and brought you up and gave you everything they could."

Kevin was way beyond worrying about his father's health now. He was wallowing in his own stuff. He was starting to sweat and there were tears in his eyes. "You never would have called me, would you? I'm only here because Kate called."

"That's right."

"Why?"

"You had the memory of a loving family. You were successful. Was I supposed to come in at this late date because I was dying and tell you this story about your mother so I could have some peace? No. Kate did what she did and I won't hold it against her, but I wouldn't have done it."

"And that's why you didn't see me for twenty-eight years?"

"No. That's not why. I haven't finished.

"Steve was a smart guy, as you know—a very successful businessman. He had been trying to get your mother to leave me for some time and move to Miami but she wouldn't because of you. She knew I would never give you up voluntarily and I wouldn't let you go to Miami without a monumental custody battle.

"Steve saw his opportunity immediately—and I mean before Alex had finished bandaging Carol up. *He* made the decision not to call the police. *He* convinced Alex not to report the shooting. Alex was reluctant at first because he could lose his license. Steve convinced him that I would be charged with attempted murder if he made the call.

"So I went home with Alex that night and stayed there for a couple of days to let things cool down. That was Steve's suggestion too—one that Alex convinced me to agree to. A couple of days later, Steve's lawyer approached me at my office and offered me the deal: They would forget the whole matter. I would just have to agree to give up custody and never see you again. If I didn't, they would charge me with attempted murder. I would go to jail and both Alex and I would lose our licenses."

"And you agreed to give me up?"

"Only after I talked to your mother and she told me it was what she wanted. I had almost killed her in a fit of drunken rage. At that moment I truly believed you were better off without me.

"I had Alex to think about too, and I was two weeks away from a trial where a man's life depended on me."

"What about my life?"

"It was the worst decision I ever made, Kevin. I wanted to go back and change it a million times. But after a couple of years I knew it would do you more harm than good so I left it alone."

They both sat there in silence for several minutes. Finally, Kevin stood up to go.

"I've got some things to do. I'll stop in tomorrow."

"Sure. I'm a little tired anyway. I need a nap."

CHAPTER THIRTY-THREE

After his conversation with his father, Kevin headed straight for Chico's. It was a little after twelve and it was time for a good stiff drink. He was almost finished with his second bourbon when he decided to call Susan. He hadn't spoken to her since he hung up on her a few days before.

"Hey," he said when she answered, still at a loss for words.

"Hey yourself," she replied.

"Well, I finally had the conversation with my father."

"And?"

"It's complicated. I'll tell you when I see you."

"And when's that going to be?"

"I'm not sure. I want to see the lake house and I want to spend a little time with him—get to know him a little better."

"You're not sure. Let me make a suggestion—don't call me until you are sure. I think there is a lot more going on with you than even you know. I don't need these occasional phone calls so you can tell me you're not sure what you're doing. Do you understand?"

"I don't know why you're so upset. I haven't been gone that long."

"I'm not upset anymore. And it's not about money or any of

the other things we've been arguing about. Something's happening with you and you need to resolve it by yourself."

"I don't know what you're talking about."

"I can't explain it any more than I have. Call it woman's intuition. Ever since you left I have had the feeling that you're not coming back, that I've lost you."

"That's nonsense."

"Maybe so. But don't call me until you're on your way home."

This time Susan hung up on him.

He was going over the conversation in his head for the fourteenth time when Billy showed up.

"I thought I might find you here," Billy said. "I stopped at the hospital and Kate told me that you and Tom had talked."

"Yeah, well, it's one of the enigmas of my life—when I need clarity I head to the bar. Maybe I really want to stay confused."

Billy understood the sentiment. "I think we both have the same way of coping."

"You have good reasons. I'm not so sure I do."

"Hey, coming to see your dying father after twenty-eight years isn't exactly a walk in the park."

"I guess you're right. It was hard for him today, but he told me what happened and he didn't embellish it at all."

"That's Tom. He tells it like it is. Well, do you feel any better?"

"I don't know yet. It hasn't all sunk in."

"I have a legal matter I need to talk to you about. Maybe this is a bad time."

"Hell, no. It's the middle of the afternoon, we both have a full drink—at least we will have when I get the bartender's attention. What better time and place to discuss the law?"

Kevin was trying to make Billy feel at ease, thinking he had a collection problem or something of that nature and felt awkward about asking for advice. He had no idea what was coming.

"A cop came to my house today," Billy began. Kevin saw the same anxiousness in Billy when he started talking as he had witnessed in his father earlier in the day. "He had a search warrant for my car and he wanted to talk to me."

"About what?"

"You know that Alligator Man thing down in Gladestown?"

"You mean the hit-and-run murder?"

"Yeah."

"What about it?"

"They think I did it."

Kevin almost choked on the bourbon he was sipping. "You're kidding me."

"No, I'm not."

Kevin's first instinct was to look around the bar to make sure nobody was listening to the conversation. His second instinct was to ask the bartender for the entire bottle of bourbon. It had been a long day already and it was only half over.

"Did you tell Tom about this?"

"No. I didn't want to burden him. I called Kate and she suggested I talk to you."

"She did?"

"Yeah."

Kevin struggled to concentrate on the specifics of the case for a minute. "So they impounded your car this morning but they didn't arrest you?"

"That's right."

"You didn't talk to them, did you?"

"No."

"They probably want to see if they can get any evidence from the car and they obviously don't have enough to arrest you just yet. Listen, we can't talk about this in here. And I need to decide whether I can take your case or not. You don't have any money to speak of, do you?"

"None."

"All right. Why don't you plan on coming over to Tom's office tomorrow at nine? We can make some decisions then. In the meantime, don't talk to anybody, and I mean nobody. Got it?"

"Got it."

Kevin threw a twenty on the bar and left.

CHAPTER THIRTY-FOUR

Kate was at the hospital when Kevin arrived. She was sitting by the bed and laughing with Tom about something. In the brief time that he had observed them together, Kevin noticed that they had a loose, easy relationship.

Tom smiled when he saw Kevin walk in the door. "Kate told me about Billy," he said.

Kate stood up. "I'll leave you two alone," she said.

Kevin didn't want Kate to leave again. He no longer had any animosity toward her and she always seemed to be "leaving them alone."

"There's no reason for you to leave, Kate," he told her.

"I'll just go to the cafeteria and get a cup of coffee. Do you want one?"

"Sure," Kevin replied.

"Do you know anything about this?" Kevin asked his father when Kate left the room.

"No," Tom replied. "In a way I'm shocked. In another way I'm not so shocked."

"What do you mean by that?"

"I don't think Billy could kill somebody under any circumstances. On the other hand, one of those twenty thousand employees was going to take a shot at Roy Johnson eventually. He hurt Billy more than most. What did he tell you?"

"They impounded his car, which means there was enough evidence to get a search warrant but not enough for an arrest."

"Maybe, maybe not," Tom replied. "They could just be going slow."

"You're right. It is a high-profile case. They don't want to arrest the wrong man.

"I've got to make a decision. Billy wants me to represent him. Let's assume for a minute that he's guilty—and I know we don't have any facts—would you take his case?"

"Absolutely."

"Why?"

"For one thing, I know Billy. I know he's not a killer. If he killed Roy Johnson, something beyond himself drove him to do it."

"I don't think a temporary insanity defense would work a year after his wife died."

"It won't, but it doesn't mean that Billy wasn't temporarily insane."

"So, keeping the same assumption—that he's guilty—do you think I should take the case? I mean, if he were to be indicted?"

"That's up to you, son. You know Billy a little bit now and I think that's a plus. I could help you by doing some background investigation on the computer and even some legal research. I know you're with a firm in Miami and you need to charge him. I'll pay his legal fees. I don't want him going to a public defender."

"Do you know what Miami rates are for a murder case?"

"I can only imagine."

It was time for Kevin to be honest with his father. "I don't work for a firm in Miami anymore. I got fired just before I came up here."

"Well, then Bernie Stang made a big mistake."

"How did you know I worked for Bernie?"

"You think I didn't follow your career? Do you think I don't know about the high-profile cases that you tried? I know all about you, son. And I know this firing had to be a personality clash because it couldn't be about your competence as a lawyer."

Those words from his father certainly made him feel good.

"Thanks. It was a personal issue."

"You know, you could start your own law firm off with a bang if you had a case like this." Tom was selling it now. "It won't matter if you win or lose; you'll be in the paper every day in Miami and all over the state."

"I don't know if I want to go back to Miami, at least not right now." Kevin could not believe what he was saying. The words just came out.

"Really?"

"Really. I'm starting to feel at home up here. It's a much slower pace and I like that."

"Well, you can stay at the house for as long as you like. I'm going to be at the ranch when I get out of here and I don't think Kate is ever going to let me leave."

"I appreciate the offer and I'll think about it."

As he left his father's hospital room that day, Kevin remembered what Judge Blackwell had said about his father taking cases that nobody else would take.

This might be one of them.

CHAPTER THIRTY-FIVE

Kevin met with Billy the next morning at his father's office.

"Let me explain something to you, Billy," Kevin told him. "I don't want you to tell me anything that incriminates you because I can't ethically put on a defense that I know is false. What I want you to do is tell me facts that prove your innocence. For instance, this murder occurred on April tenth in Gladestown. If you were somewhere else and you can prove it, then I want to hear that. Do you have an alibi or anything like that?"

"An alibi—no. Do you want to know what happened?"

"Not now. Your kids couldn't testify that you were home on the night of April tenth?"

"No."

That pretty much told Kevin what he needed to know for the moment.

"I'm going to take your case and my father's going to work with me on it. After I look at the State's file, I may have some more specific questions for you."

Billy let out a sigh of relief. "Whew! You and I haven't known each other that long, Kev, but I feel a whole lot better with you handling my case rather than some public defender I don't know at all."

"Don't feel too good, Billy. Things can still go very badly for you. I'm going to contact the state attorney now and find out what they have."

"Won't it be hard for you and your dad to work together with you in Miami and him up here?"

"I'm not going to be in Miami. I'm going to be right here."

"Man, I don't want you to do that. Your livelihood is in Miami."

"Don't take offense, Billy, but it has nothing to do with you. I want to spend some time with my father while he's still here." Again, they were words he had never spoken before, even to himself.

Three days after his conversation with Kevin about Billy, Tom Wylie went home. Alex did not want to release him but Tom was relentless and Kate assured him that she could change Tom's bandages, make him take a walk twice a day, and watch him like a hawk.

"If he has any problems whatsoever, I want you to call me on my cell," Alex told her. "And I'm going to stop by every few days just to check on you," he told Tom.

"That's twenty miles out of your way, Alex. You don't have to do that. I'll just call you," Kate told him.

"All right. But I want to hear from you every day."

"That's a promise."

The weekend after his father went home, Kevin drove to Miami. He planned on calling Susan on the way, just to tell her he was coming, but she beat him to the punch. He was just east of Tallahassee when the phone rang.

"I've decided to move out," she told him. "I've been living in limbo with no word from you."

He was about to tell her once again that he hadn't been away that long but he caught himself. She was absolutely right. He had left her and he wasn't going back to stay anytime soon. The length of time he had been gone had absolutely nothing to do with that fact.

"I understand," he told her.

"No, you don't. You don't understand anything about me and I don't understand anything about you. I'm trying to think about the future and you've got your head in the clouds. I'm not criticizing you. I'm just stating facts."

Kevin had been dreading the confrontation that awaited him when he showed up to get more clothes. Still, he wanted her to be there. He wanted to see her and hold her. They had problems, but he knew that he loved her and she loved him. He didn't know what to say to make it all right.

"I'm on my way home. Maybe we can talk about the future. Work out a plan."

"You don't get it, do you? There is no future. I'm moving on."

He suddenly felt it in the pit of his stomach—the pain of losing someone he loved. He had been with Susan so long he took her for granted. Sure, she was difficult at times but she had been his family since his mother died.

"Don't say that. I understand you're moving out and I understand why. But I'm going to be back eventually and we can patch this up."

"I'm sorry, Kevin. It's over. We can talk about it from now until doomsday. It's not working and it hasn't been working for a long time."

CHAPTER THIRTY-SIX

Sheriff Cousins got Billy's personnel file from Robert Morris, the St. Albans County state attorney, and promptly shipped it over to Jeanette Truluc. It took Jeanette two weeks to get the case before the grand jury, but she presented it in an afternoon and got an indictment for first-degree murder.

Kevin had been in contact with Jeanette so she gave him a courtesy call to let him know that an arrest was imminent.

"Don't send anybody out to arrest him," he told her. "I'll drive him down tomorrow morning and he'll turn himself in. That way I can file my motion to set bail immediately."

"What time tomorrow?"

"We can be there around one, I guess."

"You need to be here exactly at one. If I am going to allow you to do this, I need to be very specific. I have people I have to answer to and this case is about as high-profile as you can get."

"I hear you. And I appreciate you allowing us to do this. We'll be there exactly at one tomorrow."

"Fine."

Kevin had been talking to Billy for a while about what would happen if he got indicted. Billy had to be prepared.

"If you're indicted for first-degree murder, they may not let you out on bail. I can file a motion, but it's up to the judge whether he lets you out or not."

"Well, what do you think?" Billy asked.

"I wouldn't count on it. I don't know all that the prosecution has yet, but they just need to show the judge they've got a decent case and he can deny bail."

"Really?"

"Really."

"I guess I need to tell the kids and make arrangements for my sister to keep them."

"That would be a good idea, Billy. They can only hold you for ninety days so they either have to try you within that time or let you out on bond. My sense is they will push for a quick trial. This is too high-profile a case to let it linger."

"Is that what we want to do—have a quick trial?"

"I'm not sure. I need to see their evidence."

"When will you see that?"

"If the indictment happens, I'll hear a summary of their case very soon afterward."

CHAPTER THIRTY-SEVEN

Kevin delivered Billy to the Forrest County Sheriff's Department on May 9, a Monday, at exactly one o'clock in the afternoon. Vern Fleming was there to witness the event along with Sheriff Frank Cousins and Jeanette Truluc. The sheriff was polite and shook Kevin's hand as he introduced himself. Jeanette did the same. Vern just stayed in the background with his flyboy shades on and a smirk pasted across his face. Two uniformed police officers took Billy to be processed.

After Billy had been taken away, Jeanette approached Kevin. "Why don't we go in one of the sheriff's rooms and sit down and talk about logistics for a few minutes?" Her demeanor was serious and businesslike. She was a tall woman with caramel-colored skin, high cheekbones, and braided hair that was pulled back off her face in a loose ponytail.

Kevin was mildly surprised by the offer. State attorneys didn't usually talk about logistics. You filed your motions, they filed theirs, and you met in the courtroom. The only discussions were about plea bargains. This was indeed surprising. Kevin was wary. The opponent always wanted something.

When he and Jeanette were seated in one of those white, ammonia-smelling rooms found in every police department in

America, complete with one table, two chairs, and absolutely nothing else, Jeanette opened the conversation.

"You mentioned that you were immediately going to file a motion to set bail."

"I am. I'm going straight to the courthouse from here."

"I will be filing a motion for pretrial detention today as well," she told him.

He smiled at her. He had expected the motion would be filed. He didn't expect that she would tell him about it beforehand. In capital cases, the court had discretion to deny bail upon request of the state. Jeanette's motion was that request. What followed was an *Arthur* hearing, so named after the case that established the proceeding, *State v. Arthur.* In that hearing, the state would have to prove that guilt was evident or the presumption of guilt was great, which basically meant that they had to outline their case for the judge. The hearing was required to take place within five days of the motion.

"I guess I'll be here for a few days," Kevin replied.

"If you want a continuance, I'll agree to it."

He didn't want to delay the hearing. It was the fastest and most efficient way for him to find out what the state's case was about.

"No, that's fine. I'm here. We may as well go ahead with it. Who is our judge, do you know?"

Jeanette smiled. "Phillip Thorpe."

Kevin understood why she smiled. Phillip Thorpe was a former federal prosecutor, a big, thick bear of a man. Kevin had tried a case with him in the past and it had not gone well. Thorpe was one of those judges who wanted the focus to be on him at all times, so he would randomly interrupt the lawyers, make his own objections, and do whatever it took to inject himself into the proceedings rather than oversee the process and make sure it went smoothly. He also had been a government man all his life and he believed in the swift, just arm of the law. This was not good news for Billy.

"I tried a case with him once," Kevin told her.

"Yeah, I heard about that." Jeanette smiled again. She had perfect, white teeth. She also had done her homework on him. "I heard that you and Judge Thorpe had quite a confrontation in the courtroom during that trial."

It was Kevin's turn to smile. "As I recall, we did. The judge did not appreciate my style of cross-examination and he let me know after every question. It seemed as if I was trying the case against him rather than the prosecution."

"That's what I heard."

"It won't happen in this case. Judge Thorpe and I worked through our differences." It wasn't a completely true statement. Judge Thorpe didn't work through anything but Kevin was a good trial lawyer. After a couple of days, he had learned what he could and couldn't do in Judge Thorpe's courtroom and made the appropriate changes. The problem that could arise in this case, however, was when he might *need* to do something to protect his client—something that the judge didn't agree with. Then the war could start all over again.

"Listen, since you are going to be here for a few days, I can make a copy of the file available for you so you can prepare for the *Arthur* hearing," Jeanette told him.

Again Kevin was surprised. No state attorney had ever given him any material before he filed a demand for discovery with the court.

"I appreciate that."

"I'll have my staff get started right away. Why don't I put this case on the docket for tomorrow morning? We can meet with the judge and get our scheduling taken care of, and I'll give you the file then as well."

"That's fine."

"It will be in courtroom C at nine a.m. sharp."

Kevin got that message. Judge Thorpe would like nothing better than to rip into him in front of a group of attorneys for being late on that very first morning.

CHAPTER THIRTY-EIGHT

Kevin was already sitting at counsel table in the courtroom the next morning when Judge Thorpe entered. Since there were a number of preliminary hearings that morning, there was a slew of state attorneys and public defenders and private attorneys present. Billy's case was third on the docket. When the court clerk called the case, Kevin and Jeanette both approached the podium. The judge was in a chipper mood.

"Mr. Wylie, you haven't graced us with your presence in quite some time."

"I apologize, Your Honor. I've been very anxious to get back here."

Jeanette could not stifle her smile nor could the other state attorneys in the courtroom who knew the history between the two men. Judge Thorpe took it well.

"Good, good. I expect we'll have a very uneventful trial. What do we need to do today?"

Jeanette answered that question. "Your Honor, Mr. Wylie has filed a motion to set bail and we have filed a motion for pretrial detention pursuant to rule 1.332. This is a capital case and I believe the next step is to set an evidentiary hearing pursuant to *State v. Arthur*."

"Do you agree with that assessment, Mr. Wylie?"

"Yes, Your Honor."

"Okay, how much time do you need, Ms. Truluc?"

"Half a day, Judge."

"Do you agree, Mr. Wylie?"

"Since I don't know what the state's case is about, Judge, I have no reason to disagree."

"I imagine you have an idea what it's about, Mr. Wylie." The judge looked at his calendar. "Okay, next Monday afternoon, sixteenth. We'll start at one o'clock. Any objections?"

"No, Your Honor."

"No, Your Honor."

"Next case."

As promised, Jeanette delivered a copy of her file to Kevin outside the courtroom after the hearing.

"It looks like you and Judge Thorpe picked up right where you left off."

"I can tell he still loves me."

"That's exactly what I was thinking. If you have any questions, my number is on the file. I'll see you Monday afternoon."

Kevin stopped at the jail to see Billy and let him know the timetable of events. Billy seemed to be doing okay and Kevin hated to dampen his spirits, but he had to.

"He will rule on Monday, but I wouldn't get your hopes up."

"I understand," Billy replied.

Kevin called Tom at Kate's house when he was in his hotel room and unpacked. He briefed his father on what transpired at the hearing that day.

"From what you tell me about this judge, if there's any basis to keep Billy locked up, he's not going to let him out. It's too high-profile a case. He lets him out and Billy skips, the press will eat him alive. We like to think it's about the law, son, but it's not."

"I hear you. How are you feeling?"

"Not bad. Kate's taking good care of me. It's nice to breathe the fresh air every day. That hospital can kill you."

CHAPTER THIRTY-NINE

On Friday afternoon Kevin went to the law library. He didn't need to go. He could have done everything on his computer at the hotel. There was something about law libraries, however, with their long tables and hard chairs, that made them conducive to spreading files out and studying them for hours.

He had already been through the file once. Now he wanted to pore over it in detail and plan his defense while trying to figure out the state's strategy.

He now knew the basic outline of their case. Billy had apparently been in Verona for five days. That fact had been established from the hotel records. The bartender had said he threatened to kill somebody the night Roy Johnson was killed. And a young man, Freddie Jenkins, had seen an old gray car similar to the one Billy owned turn down Gladestown Road coming from the direction of Verona and strike Roy Johnson. Kevin knew most of the story; he just hadn't known Billy's part.

An *Arthur* hearing was much more informal than an actual trial. Some witnesses would surely testify live at the hearing. Hearsay was allowed, so somebody from the sheriff's office could just tell the judge about the results of the investigation without the state having to call each witness. Transcriptions of sworn statements could be submitted into the record as well, and the state attorney could simply summarize the testimony for the judge.

In this case, the crucial testimony was from the kid, Freddie Jenkins, because he witnessed the murder. Jeanette would probably put him on the stand at the hearing. Kevin had to decide whether he wanted to cross-examine Freddie. Freddie had identified the car that hit Roy Johnson as a Honda when it was actually a Toyota. Kevin could make a little hay with that in front of a jury but it made no sense to bring it up on cross at the *Arthur* hearing. There was something else about Freddie Jenkins's testimony that bothered him, but he couldn't pinpoint it yet. He knew it would come to him eventually if he just left it alone to stew in his brain.

The bartender, George Russo, was pretty straightforward. Jeanette would probably just introduce his sworn testimony into evidence. She'd do the same with Roy Johnson's wife. Her testimony wasn't crucial; she would just identify the pieces of cloth as similar to what Roy was wearing that night. The emotional sway of the grieving widow would go nowhere with the judge.

Either Carlisle Buchanan, the auxiliary officer, or Vern Fleming, the homicide detective, would talk about the investigation. She wouldn't call both of them. Vern was the more likely candidate because he was an actual detective and he had wrapped up the investigation. Vern had actually done a good job, in Kevin's estimation. He'd established that Billy's car was in the hotel parking lot for a week and that Billy had signed into the hotel under a false name. Cross-examining him at the *Arthur* hearing would probably be a waste of time and he certainly didn't want to waste Judge Thorpe's time.

The State would surely present evidence through Vern or

maybe the neighbor, Anne Lyons, that Billy lost his job, his pension, his wife, and his best friend to establish motive. It was a tight case.

Billy wasn't going home anytime soon, Kevin was sure of that.

CHAPTER FORTY

The library closed at seven and the librarian had to ask Kevin to leave.

"Do you know a good restaurant around here where I can get a bite to eat?" he inquired as he gathered up his file.

"There's a steakhouse two blocks down. It's called PK's. It's a small joint, but the food is good and the prices are reasonable," the woman told him.

That was a good enough recommendation for Kevin.

PK's was indeed an intimate little spot, and it had a nice vibe to it and, most important, a bar. Kevin ordered a beer and took a sip as his eyes adjusted to the darker atmosphere. He planned on eating at the bar but he took a look around to soak in the place. There was a familiar face sitting alone in the corner of the room at a table for two.

"Is it okay for a defense lawyer to talk with the prosecutor over dinner? I promise I won't bite."

Jeanette Truluc looked up from her legal pad to see Kevin Wylie standing at her table, a beer in hand.

"I'm not sure I believe you." She smiled as she spoke. "In case you are tempted, however, I must tell you that I carry a gun."

"Really?" Kevin asked. "Prosecutors carry guns here in Verona?"

"We have our own big-time drug dealers, Mr. Wylie. You know that. You've defended some of them here before."

"I would hope that my clients would never resort to any type of violence."

"Unfortunately, I cannot rely on that hope. I have to carry a gun and I have to go to the firing range once a week to make sure I can use it accurately."

"And can you?"

"I can hit you in the chest ten out of ten times at thirty yards."

"Okay, I believe you. Can we talk about something else?"

"Anything you'd like," she said. "Have a seat."

Kevin slid into the seat across from her. The waiter arrived immediately with a menu.

"What would you recommend?" he asked Jeanette.

"All the steaks are good but I prefer the fillet."

"I'll have the fillet," Kevin told the waiter when the man came to take his order. "And another beer." He noticed that Jeanette was nursing a glass of white wine.

Jeanette's meal came first. She was having fish and broccoli.

"I thought you liked the fillet?" Kevin asked.

"I do, but I don't eat a lot of red meat so I only have it once in a while."

His fillet arrived soon after and it was as advertised.

"You're right. This is delicious," he told her after the first bite.

"Everything is good here. I'm a regular customer since it's so close to my office and the courthouse."

"Are you a Verona native?" he asked.

"No, I'm from your neck of the woods—Tallahassee."

"How did you know that's my neck of the woods? After all, I'm a Miami lawyer. Don't tell me you researched me back to my childhood."

Jeanette laughed. "Don't flatter yourself." In this setting, with her hair down and a smile on her face, the woman was very pretty. "Actually, I'm assuming you come from St. Albans because that's where your father lives."

"My father? How do you know my father?"

She had him totally confused and she was enjoying it. "I don't. My father knows your father."

"Really?"

"Yes. My dad is a professor at FSU law school. Your father has lectured there on several occasions at the invitation of my dad."

"Really? It is a small world. Why would your dad invite my father to talk at FSU?"

"My father has always been very interested in the history of the civil rights movement in Florida, particularly the legal history. Your father was part of that history, at least in the northwest area of the state. There was a case in 1977 that particularly interested my dad. You probably know about it."

"The rape and murder of Ellen Wells." Kevin surprised himself that he actually remembered the woman's name.

"That's it. That's the case. There are only a handful of people in the state of Florida who remember that case. It's very strange, under the circumstances, that you and I are two of them."

"Yes, it is," Kevin replied. He had no reason to tell her that he had just learned about Ellen Wells—or that the case of Ellen Wells was the backdrop for the disintegration of his family. He preferred to listen to her perspective.

"I was a third-year law student at the time. My father wanted me to attend the lecture so I did and it was very interesting. Your father talked so eloquently about the tension between the races in the sixties and how it was all still there, just below the surface in the late seventies. It only took a spark to ignite everything all over again."

"How did that case turn out?" Kevin asked. During his discussion with his father, Tom had never told him whether he had saved his client from conviction or not.

"The defendant was convicted, and of course, he got the death penalty, but he was exonerated years later when the only eyewitness recanted his testimony. Your father was still representing him. That's the part I think my father wanted me to remember—practicing law isn't just about making money."

Kevin felt like Jeanette was looking through him as she said the words. She had certainly learned the lesson from her father. She was working for the state. He, on the other hand, had spent his career working for a lowlife representing drug dealers for nothing but money.

While they were having a fairly pleasant conversation, Kevin decided to address the issue of a plea bargain, although he already had an idea what the answer would be. "I have read through your file and I appreciate your providing it to me so quickly. Is there any possibility that we could come to some kind of deal?"

Jeanette shook her head. "Normally, in a case like this, with the extenuating circumstances of what happened to your client and his family, I would say yes. But this one is out of my hands. I've already talked to my boss about not asking for the death penalty because of those reasons. He wouldn't even go for that.

"This is a high-profile case, probably the biggest case ever in Forrest County. My boss is a politician. If he backs off at all in the prosecution, his opponent in the next election will beat him over the head with that, calling him 'soft on crime' and a million other things. That's just how it works. I don't think we have a chance in hell of getting the death penalty, but I'm asking for it."

"Well, at least we know where we stand. I appreciate your candor."

"No problem.

They both finished their meal in silence.

CHAPTER FORTY-ONE

Carlisle liked to take out the big boat, the Grady-White, to go deep-sea fishing on the open water at least once a week. It helped him sort things out in his head.

He usually headed for the Dry Tortugas. It took him several hours, but it was a great trip and he always planned on staying a day or two. Like his father, he enjoyed the world out there that wasn't filled with people.

The waters around the Tortugas were mostly deserted except for the area immediately surrounding Fort Jefferson, the historical coastal fort, which was now a national park and tourist attraction. There were usually some commercial boats and some luxury boats fishing the waters, but that was it. The luxury boats were owned by wealthy weekend warriors who liked to get away for a few days to go after the big grouper and mullet snapper and then return to their fast-paced lives. There was no better place for that kind of fishing than the Tortugas.

Carlisle was particularly intrigued by one boat that he had seen over the course of a month. It was a sleek-looking Sea Ray about sixty feet in length and it was always moored in the same little cove. He wasn't usually attracted to the slick, modern boats, especially the big ones, but the lines on this one were beautiful. He'd seen it before but he couldn't remember where.

Sometime during each day that he was out there, he'd drive by and try to catch the attention of somebody on board so he could make small talk and maybe get an invitation to come aboard and look around, but he never saw anybody fishing. Eventually, he concluded that it wasn't a fishing boat at all so he kept his distance. There were still drug smugglers in the area and you didn't want to get too close to a drug smuggler's boat unannounced. It could be fatal.

He always brought fish back to Rosie so she could put it on special and Rosie was delighted.

"I'm going to tell everybody who comes in here what a good fisherman you are. Before long you'll have more work than you can imagine," she told him after he'd quit his job with the sheriff.

Carlisle just smiled.

Rosie couldn't let him go with just a compliment, though. She needed to know more. Perhaps it was her mothering instincts or maybe she was just nosy.

"You didn't bring Mrs. Johnson out there with you by any chance, did you?"

"No, Rosie. That's over. She dropped me like a hotcake after I told her I quit the sheriff."

"I'm sorry to hear that, Carlisle. I really am."

"Thanks, Rosie. I'm okay. She was just using me for information, that's all."

CHAPTER FORTY-TWO

Kevin called his father after his dinner with Jeanette to fill him in on what he had learned.

"Sounds like they have a pretty solid circumstantial evidence case," Tom replied. His voice was strong.

"Yeah. I'm not sure how to attack it yet."

"If you can't attack their facts, you've got to come up with another reasonable explanation for this murder. You don't have to prove it, though."

As soon as he said the words, Tom wanted to take them back. Kevin was an experienced criminal trial lawyer. He didn't need a lecture from his father on the basics. His son handled it well.

"Yeah, I know, Dad. Create a reasonable doubt. I'm going to go to Gladestown tomorrow and at least get started on that process."

Tom had to fight to retain his composure on the other end of the line. It was just a word in a conversation but it was a word Kevin had not used before—*Dad*.

"I've already started doing some things here. Roy Johnson had an estate lawyer here in town, Greg Harris. He's an old friend of mine. I checked with him just to find out if the young wife had anything to gain if Roy were removed from the picture. That looks like a dead end. She had a prenuptial that paid her a million dollars, which was already in a separate account in her name. Roy simply replenished it every month. She also got the house, but that's it.

"I asked about the adult children too. They all had trust funds set up for them and their children. I don't know what's in those trust funds and Greg said it's almost impossible to find out. However, all that money was already transferred before Johnson died so there doesn't seem to be any motive for the kids either. Greg says that because of all this planning there's no estate. It's confusing because there's no way to find out where all the money went."

"You've been busy."

"If I can't be in the trenches with you, I want to do as much as I can. I found some other interesting things about Gladestown that we can discuss when you get back."

"One other thing, if they keep Billy, they can only hold him for ninety days, which means they will probably want a quick trial. What are your thoughts about that?"

"I always want to push the State," Tom replied. "As a rule, the less time they have, the less prepared they are."

"I'm with you," Kevin replied.

CHAPTER FORTY-THREE

On Saturday morning, Kevin drove the sixty miles from Verona to Gladestown and stopped at Rosie's Café for breakfast since it was the only place in town. It was midmorning and Rosie was alone.

"Come on in and sit down," she said to Kevin, who was dressed in shorts, T-shirt, and sandals. "What can I get for you?"

"Well, I'd like a little coffee and some scrambled eggs and sausage and maybe a little conversation."

Rosie smiled at him. "You're my kind of man," she said. "I just wish I was a few years younger. Give me a minute."

It didn't take more than a few minutes for Rosie to cook his breakfast. She gave him a little time after that to eat, but after she freshened his coffee for the third time, she sat right down.

"So, where are you from?"

"Miami mostly. My name's Kevin, Kevin Wylie."

He extended his hand and Rosie shook it.

"My name's Rosie. As you can see, I run this place. I've heard your name mentioned recently," she said. "Can't remember where, though."

Kevin smiled. Rosie was funny and sweet. "I'm representing William Fuller, the man accused of killing Roy Johnson."

Rosie's sweet disposition changed at the mention of Roy Johnson.

"Well, if you ask me, your client did the world a favor. If anybody deserved to die, it was Roy Johnson."

Kevin wished he could sneak Rosie onto the jury pool. It didn't matter if she was selected as a juror or not. She'd turn the whole crowd against Roy Johnson in ten seconds. It was time to make his pitch.

"I'm looking for a guide. Somebody who can take me on the water and maybe give me a feel for what could have happened to Roy Johnson."

"I've got just the right person for you. His name's Carlisle Buchanan and he is a master guide."

"Now you've got me going. It seems like I've heard that name before."

"You have. Carlisle was the sheriff's man here in Gladestown. He did most of the initial investigation into Roy Johnson's disappearance. He quit the sheriff's department, though."

"What happened?"

"Well, for one thing, he's like me and most everybody else in this town. He thinks Roy Johnson deserved to die. He wasn't cut out for law enforcement anyway. I'm sure Scotch started rolling around in his grave the day Carlisle took the job."

"I'm not following you," Kevin told her.

"I'm sorry. Can I get you some more coffee?"

"No, I'm good. Tell me about Scotch."

"Don't tell me you never heard of Scotch Buchanan. Are you sure you're from Miami?"

"Yes. I think I've heard the name but I can't remember the details."

"Well, Scotch was Carlisle's father and one of the most remarkable characters you would ever meet. He's famous because he was probably the best hunter and fisherman ever to come out of these parts. Scotch was the original Alligator Man. He trapped them, hunted them, and when it became illegal, poached them. That's why he started rolling in his grave the day Carlisle went to work for the sheriff. He was quite the ladies' man too."

Kevin saw the smile come across Rosie's face when she said those words. She was a younger woman behind that smile. Perhaps she and Scotch Buchanan had been more than just friends.

"So I take it Carlisle is not like his dad?"

"He's as good on the water and in the woods as his dad. But Carlisle has stayed within the law so far and he doesn't have the rogue in him. At least not yet."

"What happened to Scotch?"

"He died two years ago. He'd gone out night fishing and they found him dead in the water. The coroner ruled it accidental, saying Scotch probably slipped in the boat, hit his head, and fell overboard and drowned. I've never said anything to Carlisle, but I don't believe that story for a minute. Scotch Buchanan would never die like that. Never."

She appeared a little upset and excused herself and headed to the kitchen. She was back in a few minutes with the coffeepot. There were still no new customers in the restaurant.

"Can I fill you up one more time, Counselor?"

"Sure. Do you think I could get Carlisle to take me out on the water today?"

"I could almost guarantee it. He needs the money. I'll call him for you."

She disappeared into the kitchen again but not for long.

"He'll be here in a few minutes. Said he'd take you out all day if you want. I'd say, give him a couple hundred dollars for the day." That was Rosie, looking out for her people.

CHAPTER FORTY-FOUR

Carlisle showed up fifteen minutes later, a smile on his face, raring to go. Rosie made the introductions.

"Carlisle, this is Kevin Wylie. He represents that man who is charged with killing Roy Johnson."

"Nice to meet you, Mr. Wylie."

"Kevin. Call me Kevin."

"Sure."

Rosie left them alone to talk business.

"Carlisle, do you have a problem taking me out on the water and showing me where you found the pieces of clothing? Before you answer, let me say this to you—you're going to be on that witness stand in this trial testifying for the State and I'm going to be cross-examining you. And I'll use anything I can to help my client."

Carlisle looked hard at Kevin. He had cold blue eyes to go with his brown hair. His tanned face was smooth and pleasant and strong like the rest of him.

"I don't have a problem, Kevin, because what I tell you and show you is exactly what I've told and showed the sheriff. Ain't no difference at all. The truth is the truth. Now when do you want to go?"

"Right now."

"Fine. You can follow me or we can just jump on my motorbike. I'll bring you back here when we're finished."

"Let's do that."

Down at the dock it was sunny and hot. There were two boats tied up alongside each other: the Grady-White, which Kevin estimated to be about thirty-five feet long, and the airboat. It took a little time for Carlisle to get the airboat set up.

Kevin was familiar with airboats. He had a friend in Homestead who had one and they would go out riding from time to time on Sunday mornings. He wasn't surprised when Carlisle handed him the ear cups. The ritual with Scotch, the great blue heron, was another matter, however.

"Mornin', Scotch," Carlisle said to the bird that stood in the middle of the entrance to the canal. "This is Kevin. I'm taking him out on the water today. We'll bring you back some food so let us pass, okay?"

He started up the boat and the big bird took off into the trees. Kevin figured it was the noise from the airboat engine that caused Scotch to take off, not Carlisle's words.

Kevin's friend in Homestead could not hold a torch to Carlisle as an airboat operator. The man was an artist, gliding over the dry areas and weaving through the mangrove corridors like a Jedi warrior. They rode south to the open water before turning east. There were numerous little islands out there before the open expanse of the Gulf of Mexico and Carlisle gave him a little tour. They even stopped at an out island that had a little cabin on it.

"This is where the freshwater of Florida Bay meets the salt water of the Gulf of Mexico," Carlisle told him. As Kevin would soon find out, it was the beginning of his Everglades tutorial with Professor Carlisle Buchanan.

After they left the island, Carlisle headed into the mangroves again and about a half hour later they arrived at their destination. Carlisle pulled the boat next to a cluster of bushes and cut the engine. For a moment, there was total silence—not one chirp. Then the background music started up again.

"This is where I found the black cloth," Carlisle said, pointing to the mangrove next to him. "Farther in there," he said, pointing deeper into the swamp, "is where I found the white silk cloth and, later, the wallet."

"Can we wade in there?"

"Sure. Let me just tie the boat here. Try and stay on or close to the roots. It can get deep in places."

They both stepped out of the boat and walked along the mangrove roots. They got soaked in the process but the water felt refreshing in the heat. Carlisle came to a stop.

"This is it. This is where I found the pieces of clothing and wallet."

Kevin studied the area intensely, not knowing what he was looking for.

"Do gators actually get in here?"

"Sure. It's not usually where you see them. They're usually in the canals but they can go anywhere. They own this part of the world."

As they stood there, Carlisle told him about the delicate ecosystem of the Everglades and the significant role the gator played in that ecosystem. Kevin had earlier marveled at this man's strength and ability to handle a boat. Now he was even more impressed by Carlisle the naturalist.

"During a drought, they dig these gator holes and that's where all the animals in the ecosystem feed."

"And you think that's where the remains of Roy Johnson are—in those gator holes?"

"Probably. And probably scattered far and wide."

"How would that work?"

"Well, you know we had a drought. In fact, it's still going on. They're all hungry, including the gators. It was probably a feeding frenzy. Every gator took a piece. They ripped his arms and legs off and scattered."

"Don't you think it's a little unusual that there is just one piece of black cloth hanging on a mangrove branch out there and then these other two items in here? I mean, the wallet was probably in his back pocket. Where's the rest of his pants?"

"It's all explainable. If one gator got the whole thigh, for instance, you might find these remains. The rest of his pants are just somewhere else."

They were so focused on the issue they were discussing, neither man was aware of the grotesque nature of the conversation.

"But there are no bones?"

"I don't think that's unusual either. There's something we haven't talked about."

"What's that?"

"The Burmese python. It's not native to the Everglades but there are thousands of them here now, maybe hundreds of thousands."

"I think I remember seeing that picture in the paper of the python swallowing the gator."

"Exactly. The python is like the vacuum cleaner of the Everglades. If an arm or a leg or even the torso of Roy Johnson surfaced, a python could swallow it whole. You're not likely to find any remains."

CHAPTER FORTY-FIVE

When they got back to the boat, Carlisle drove to a shady spot where the mangroves grew together, forming a cylindrical corridor. He stopped the boat, opened the cooler, and took out some sandwiches.

"I've got turkey and ham and cheese, bottled water, and Diet Coke."

"I'll have turkey and some water, thanks," Kevin told him. He was beginning to enjoy Carlisle's company. He had some more questions, though, and he figured this was the right time to get them answered.

"What's with the bird?"

"You mean Scotch?"

"Yeah."

"I don't tell too many people this but since you asked—my father died two years ago, April twentieth to be exact. We were really close.

"About a month after he was gone, Scotch showed up. I know it sounds crazy—that's why I don't tell too many people—I think Scotch is my father. He's come back to keep an eye on me."

It was a strange story, but for some reason, in this setting, it made sense. Kevin finished his sandwich and Carlisle tossed him another one without him even asking. Kevin stretched his legs out and took a swig of water.

"Carlisle, you know as much about this case as anyone since you did most of the investigation. I'm going to be honest with you—it's a pretty strong circumstantial evidence case. I'm going to try to attack it, but I also have to continue to investigate the possibility that somebody else committed this murder, that things may not be as they seem. I'm going to need somebody like you, who knows the area and the people and can help me connect the dots and see that bigger picture."

Carlisle just sat there looking around for a minute or two, not saying a word.

"I'm not a fan of Roy Johnson," he finally said. "He and my father didn't get along. But I don't think I can help you. I think your client's guilty. What does he say happened?"

"I haven't asked."

"I don't get that, Kevin. You haven't asked your client what happened but you want me to help you investigate some other possibility? That doesn't make sense."

"I can't ask because if I ask and he says he's guilty, then I can't put facts into evidence that I know are not true."

"And that's a problem because—*he's guilty?* Am I missing something here?"

Carlisle had a point. It had been Kevin's dilemma while working for Bernie. And it was what he told Susan he wasn't going to do anymore.

"I'll tell you what, Carlisle. I'll ask Billy what happened, and if he tells me he's not guilty, will you help me investigate other possibilities?"

"How will you know he's telling you the truth?"

"I won't know for sure, but if I don't believe him I'll tell you I don't believe him."

"How will I know you're telling me the truth?"

"You won't."

Carlisle gave Kevin the same steely glare as he had at Rosie's—the one that went past his eyes and into his person. He held it for a few seconds.

"Okay," he finally said. "I'm in. There's a reason I told you about Scotch. I'm supposed to trust you."

"By the way," Kevin asked, "you said something about your father not liking Roy Johnson. Did they know each other?"

"Oh yeah. Roy Johnson grew up in Gladestown. This is where he got his money to start Dynatron. He was a drug dealer back in the late seventies, early eighties."

"Really? I can see why your father didn't like that."

"Not for the reasons you might be thinking. My father wasn't all that much of a law-abiding man himself. But he told me that Roy Johnson's operation eventually would have destroyed Gladestown and our way of life. He didn't want that to happen."

"And it didn't?" Kevin asked.

"No. The feds busted everybody back in 1982. Roy, however, was long gone. That was the end of big-time smuggling in Gladestown. But there's still some small stuff going on."

"Did anybody go to prison?"

"Roy's two lieutenants, Randy Winters and Bobby Joe Sellers, got twenty-plus years. They were released recently. Rosie pointed them out to me not too long ago in the restaurant. I only knew them by reputation. Everybody else just got a little time."

It was an interesting story, and Kevin had no idea if it had anything to do with his case or not. If it did, however, he was certain he had the right man to help him navigate through that murky swamp. First, he had to have a "come to Jesus" conversation with Billy.

On the way back, Carlisle stopped at the marina for a bucket of pinfish.

"For Scotch," he told Kevin as he set the bucket down in the boat. "I promised him I'd bring him something."

CHAPTER FORTY-SIX

At four o'clock on Sunday afternoon, Kevin stopped in at the Last Stop, the bar where bartender George Russo worked. Russo had identified Billy as the agitated patron who came to the bar every night the week before Roy Johnson was killed. Kevin wanted to eyeball him and see if he could get Russo to talk. It was Sunday so he might not be there at all, and since Russo was the night bartender, it was probably a little early to catch him, but Kevin wanted to talk to the manager too.

He sat at the bar and ordered a beer. The place was dark and somewhat dingy, although it looked clean enough. There were two people at one end of the bar staring at their drinks.

"I'm looking for George Russo," Kevin told the bartender.

"Who?"

"George Russo."

"Never heard of him."

"Is your manager here?" The guy looked at Kevin as if to ask, *Do you think this place needs a bartender and a manager?*

"I'm the manager," he finally replied.

"My name is Kevin Wylie. I'm a lawyer and I represent William Fuller, the man accused of killing Roy Johnson over in Gladestown. A man named George Russo is a witness in that case and he said he worked here."

"Oh, that bum. Yeah, he worked here for about a month, enough to get his name in the papers. Then he up and quit."

"Really? Do you happen to know the dates that he worked here?"

"Off the top of my head—no."

"You must have a record somewhere."

"Listen, Mister, I'm running a bar here, not an information service."

Kevin pulled out a fifty-dollar bill. "I'm just asking for a little information and I'm willing to pay."

The manager stared at the fifty-dollar bill for a few seconds while he went over things in his mind. "Let me check my customers at the end of the bar, make sure they've got full drinks and everything, then I'll see if I can find what you're looking for."

"Thanks," Kevin said and rested the fifty on the bar next to his beer.

The manager checked on the catatonics down at the end: One pointed at his drink, indicating he wanted another. The other didn't say a word, just kept staring at his half-full drink. Then the manager disappeared, returning ten minutes later with a notebook in his hand.

"He started working April fifth and he was gone by May sixth—a month, give or take a day. No notice. Left me hanging."

"Did he fill out an employment application or anything?"

"I'm sure there's some paperwork around here somewhere, but I'm not going to be able to find it now. He had good references, as I recall. He could do the job and I'd been looking for somebody for months. That's all I can tell you."

Kevin had a picture of Billy with him. He showed it to the bartender. "Did you ever see this man in here?"

"No. But I didn't work nights at that time, Russo did. Now I got a real looker in here. We get a good crowd; you should come back."

"Thanks, maybe I will. Can I get a copy of that information you just gave me?"

"For another twenty bucks you can."

Kevin sneered at the man as he took out his wallet and made the payment.

He stopped at the Verona Inn after that, talking to the same manager Vern Fleming had grilled the month before. After identifying himself, Kevin showed the man Billy's picture.

"Did you ever see this man before?"

"I didn't," the man said. "However, the police were here last week, and they interviewed everybody at the hotel and one of our chambermaids did recognize this man. She said he stayed for a week and he was very nice. That's all I know."

Kevin tried to figure it all out on the ride back to the hotel. It was strange that George Russo showed up days before the murder and left his job almost immediately after talking to the police. Maybe he disappeared because there was something in his background that he didn't want to surface. Kevin wondered if he would show up for the trial. It didn't matter anyway with the chambermaid as a witness. She would put Billy in pretty much the same location as Russo did. She hadn't shown up in the state attorney's files yet, probably because the police were behind in their reports. Or maybe they were just hiding her for now.

CHAPTER FORTY-SEVEN

There were a few reporters and cameras outside the courthouse when Kevin arrived for the *Arthur* hearing. The major stations were probably waiting for the trial. Kevin usually did not like to talk to reporters or try his case in the press, but since part of his strategy was to put Roy Johnson on trial, it was never too early to start poisoning the well with the general public, from whose ranks the jury would eventually be chosen.

"My client is a family man who has never been in trouble," he told the group of reporters and cameramen. "He is charged with killing Roy Johnson simply because he, along with twenty thousand other people, lost everything—their jobs, their pensions—when Roy Johnson raped and plundered his own company. My client is innocent of all charges."

Having said his piece, he walked into the courthouse. Jeanette was already in the courtroom. Billy was brought in soon thereafter in prison garb and handcuffs. He sat down next to Kevin.

"How are you holding up?" Kevin asked him.

"Pretty good," Billy replied.

"Are you ready for this?"

"Yeah. I'm prepared for the worst."

"All rise!" the bailiff yelled as Judge Thorpe limped into the courtroom.

"Are we all set?" the judge asked.

"Yes, Your Honor," both lawyers answered.

"Ms. Truluc, you may proceed."

There were no surprises in Jeanette's presentation of her case. Vern Fleming took the stand first and summarized the investigation, starting with Sylvia Johnson's first visit to the office to report her husband missing. Vern told how Carlisle Buchanan took an airboat ride into the Everglades after learning that Roy Johnson may have taken a walk that night on Gladestown Road. Vern explained to the court that alligators crossed that road at night all the time, hence the reason for the excursion into the swamp. Jeanette then had Vern identify the two pieces of cloth and the wallet as items found on the two trips into the Glades.

She then switched gears and had Vern talk about motive, introducing through his testimony tidbits from Billy's personnel file and his personal life: The fact that he lost $750,000 in pension money, his health insurance, his job, his wife, and his home.

Kevin listened intently but had no cross-examination. It was a very effective presentation and Kevin knew it would work well with a jury.

Freddie Jenkins followed Vern Fleming to the stand. His testimony was short and to the point, and again, Kevin had no cross-examination.

When Jeanette was finished, the judge looked at Kevin, who had not said a word during the entire proceeding. "Would you like to add something before I rule, Mr. Wylie?"

"Only this, Judge. My client is not a risk to leave the state of Florida. He has children here. He has no criminal record. There is still a presumption of innocence. Counsel has presented a totally circumstantial case. There is no direct evidence linking my client to this crime. They examined his car—nothing. There is no eyewitness identification. There isn't even a body.

"This is within your discretion, Judge. However, the combination of no criminal record, no likelihood of flight because of his children, and no direct evidence of guilt should cause you to lean toward allowing Mr. Fuller to be released on bail."

To Kevin's surprise, the judge actually seemed to be listening and considering his argument. Maybe it was all a show but he reviewed his notes in detail before speaking.

"I believe the State has met its burden of showing a likelihood of success. However, it is within my discretion to set bail. Mr. Fuller is not a career criminal and his ties to the community in which he lives mitigate against him fleeing the jurisdiction of the court. But Mr. Fuller has never been charged with murder before. Mr. Fuller has never faced the possibility of death or life in prison before. That can make a man want to get up and go even when he's never wanted to get up and go before. Therefore, I believe the more prudent approach to this issue is to deny bail at this time and set the case for trial as soon as possible.

"So let's talk about a trial date. Mr. Wylie, do you have any depositions you want to take? Have you received all the discovery from the State?"

"I've received some discovery, Your Honor. I'm not sure I've received all of it. I'm also not sure if I want to take any depositions at this point. However, if the State will accommodate me and agree to produce witnesses within the next thirty days, I could be ready for trial in sixty days."

The judge looked at Jeanette, who was in no mood to compromise. "I'm not sure I can agree to that, Judge."

"Well, I'm sure," Judge Thorpe replied. "I'm ordering that Mr. Wylie receive the entire State file within the next ten days, that all depositions be set within the next thirty days, and that the State accommodate Mr. Wylie's schedule for those depositions. If any problems arise, I will be available to resolve them.

Now, take out your calendars and let's pick a week. From what I've heard here, this trial is not going to last more than that. How about the week of July eleventh?"

"That's fine with me, Judge," Kevin replied.

"That's acceptable, Your Honor," Jeanette said.

"Good. Trial is set for the week of July eleventh. Get yourselves ready, folks, because I won't grant a continuance unless there's a really good reason. Court is adjourned." Judge Thorpe stood up and hobbled out of the room.

CHAPTER FORTY-EIGHT

Jeanette was in his face before the judge was out of the room. "Why'd you tell the judge you didn't have all the discovery?"

"Because I don't."

"I personally handed it to you."

"And I personally talked to the manager of the Verona Inn, who told me that the police interviewed a chambermaid there last week. I don't have that interview. Who knows what else I don't have?"

"I didn't know about that interview."

"Well, I suggest that in the future you ask before you get in my face making accusations."

He turned away from her toward Billy, who thankfully had not yet been removed by the guards. "This is just the beginning. I want you to keep your spirits up. Tom and I will be working on this night and day."

Billy just nodded. He had told himself he was ready but he really wasn't. The reality that he might never see his kids again was beginning to take hold. He stood to leave but Kevin stopped him.

"Give us a minute," he said to the guards who were waiting to transport Billy back to the jail. "Billy, you asked me before if I wanted to know what happened and I put you off. Now I want you to tell me."

Billy turned and looked at the guards. "Here?" he asked.

"What better place? The guards can't hear us. Do you want to do it in your cell?"

"Hell, no."

"Well?"

"You're sure, Kev?"

"I'm sure, Billy. If we're going to get you out of here, I've got to know the truth."

"Okay. Here goes. I went down there to kill him. I felt I owed it to Laurie and to my friend Jimmy Lennox and everybody else that son of a bitch screwed. I went over there from Verona three nights in a row before that night, but I couldn't get it done. Every night I got a little more drunk, working up my courage."

Kevin could see Billy, all of a sudden, get that faraway look in his eyes like he was reliving the event.

"He went into his backyard every night. I saw him there, sitting in his chair, drinking his wine. The prick. I was going to shoot him right there. That fourth night I was really drunk. I can't believe I made it all the way to Gladestown and back. I mean, I was all over the road. I recall looking in the backyard that night and not seeing Roy and getting in the car and driving back to the hotel. I couldn't tell you one thing about the ride there or back, though."

"Could you have hit Roy Johnson on Gladestown Road and not remembered it?"

"It's possible. As you can imagine, I've thought about this a lot lately. I think I would remember, but as I said, I couldn't tell you one thing about the ride from Verona and back. So it's possible."

"Anything else?

"No, I don't think so."

"Thanks, Billy."

CHAPTER FORTY-NINE

Kevin called his father on the drive back to St. Albans and told him what happened at the hearing.

"The state attorney who is handling this case knows you."

"Really? What's his name?"

"It's a she. Her name's Jeanette Truluc. Her father's a professor at FSU."

"Oh yeah, Professor Jean Truluc. I gave a few talks to his class years ago. Nice man. Good teacher, from what I observed. It's a small world, isn't it?"

"It sure is."

"Why don't you come out to the ranch tomorrow for lunch?" Tom asked. "We can spend the afternoon hashing everything out."

"What time?"

"Noon is good."

"I'll be there."

Kate's ranch was thirty miles outside of town but it may as well have been a hundred. It seemed as though civilization ended ten miles outside of the city limits, replaced by thick pine forests and open meadows, and from time to time, cattle and horses could be seen in the distance.

The specific directions Kate had given him led him down a long narrow dirt path that opened into one of those deep, wide, luscious green meadows. There, in the middle, nestled between two giant oaks, stood an unimposing, old two-story farmhouse with a tin roof that sloped down like a ski jump and a wrap-around porch that encircled the entire structure. Kevin noticed a barn behind the house, a corral, and a herd of cattle far down the meadow. When he parked in the driveway, Kate was at the front door waiting for him.

"Did you have any trouble finding us?" she asked.

"Nope. The directions were great. How's Tom doing?"

"Come on in and see for yourself."

She led him through a cozy little parlor and into the living room where Tom was sitting on the couch. He looked like he had gained a few pounds and his face had some color from the sun.

"Afternoon," he said while attempting to get up.

Kevin could see the pain on his face. "Stay there," he said.

"I've got to get up anyway. We need to work at the kitchen table where we can spread everything out." Apparently Tom liked to work the same way his son did. After Kevin helped him to his feet, Tom walked on his own to the dining room table. There were some papers piled up already.

"Let me get my things in order while Kate shows you around," Tom told his son as he struggled to sit in the dining room chair.

"He's fine," Kate whispered in Kevin's ear. "He's been so excited all morning waiting for you to get here. This is the best therapy in the world for him. Come on, let me give you a quick tour."

There were three bedrooms on the first floor, one large and

two small. The living room was the center of the house. Kevin was particularly taken with a painting over the couch where Tom had been sitting. It was of an Indian in full war dress mounted on a spotted pony at the edge of a ridge looking out over a valley. The colors were rich and the detail was incredible.

"Beautiful, isn't it?" Tom yelled from the dining room. "It's my favorite."

Kevin looked around after hearing his father's words and noticed that there were several original paintings of the West in general and Indians in particular spread around the first floor of the house.

Kate did not seem interested in showing him the upstairs.

"Just more bedrooms?" he asked.

"Not really," she replied.

"Now you've raised my curiosity. I've got to see what's up there."

Kate led him up the stairs, which opened into one large room. There were a handful of easels there, mostly situated by the windows, and several canvases with scenes in various stages of completion. One was a portrait of an Indian chief.

"Those are your paintings downstairs!"

Kate smiled. She was a pretty woman, and for the first time, maybe because it was the first time he looked closely, Kevin saw a trace of her lineage.

"I grew up out West," Kate told him. "And it has never left me. I'm part Ute Indian on my mother's side, so I love to paint Native Americans and their way of life."

"Is that how you've supported yourself?"

"For the last thirty years."

"So you saw the studio?" Tom asked, beaming when they came downstairs. "She doesn't show it to too many people."

"I kind of forced the issue."

"Nonsense," Kate replied. "I wanted you to see it. Now, what would you like for lunch? I have homemade vegetable soup, ham, turkey, and roast beef."

"I'll help you," Kevin offered.

"No. You and your father have work to do."

Kevin graciously accepted her hospitality. "Then I'll have your homemade soup with a turkey sandwich."

He sat down across from his dad. "So what information have you uncovered that you wanted to share with me?" he asked Tom.

"We can get to that. Tell me a little more about the hearing and your trip to Gladestown."

Kevin went back over the hearing in greater detail and then told Tom about his day on the water with Carlisle Buchanan.

"Carlisle is a walking Everglades encyclopedia. He will be very valuable to us if we come up with an alternative theory as to how this murder occurred."

"That's what I've been working on," Tom said. "And I think I've found the evidence we need."

"Really?"

"Really. Did you know that in 1982, fifty percent of the male population in Gladestown was arrested for drug smuggling?"

"As a matter of fact I did," Kevin said. "I didn't know the percentages but Carlisle told me the story. He told me Roy Johnson was the ringleader."

"Carlisle gave you that information? Have you hired him yet? Because he's the guy you need."

"Not yet, but I'm working on it. Anything else that you found?"

"Roy left a month before the drug bust, but his two lieutenants, Bobby Joe Sellers and Randy Winters, got twenty-year prison terms. It's those draconian federal laws. They never would have gotten that amount of time in state court."

"I knew about those two."

"Did you know who represented them?" Tom asked.

"No. Who?"

"Your favorite drug dealer defense lawyer."

"Bernie?"

"The one and only," Tom continued. "There's more. Randy Winters got out of prison on April fourth of this year, six days before Roy Johnson's disappearance."

"Interesting. What about Sellers?"

"He got out two years ago."

Kate brought the sandwiches and the soup from the kitchen, and they took a break to eat. Kate sat with them.

"Why don't you stay over tonight, Kevin?" Kate offered. "I could saddle some horses after dinner and show you the property."

Kevin looked at his dad, who smiled. "It's the only way to see a ranch."

"Sure," he said. "I'd love to."

After lunch they were back at it.

"So do you have a theory attached to all these facts, Dad, or is this just an interesting story?"

"I do. From the newspaper reports I read, it was speculated that the government had an informant. If Roy Johnson was the informant—and I think we can make an argument that he was and maybe even prove it—then Randy Winters had a motive to kill him when he got out of prison."

"It makes sense in a vacuum," Kevin replied.

"What does that mean?"

"It means it makes sense if we didn't know that Bobby Joe Sellers, for instance, got out two years before. They both would have had the same information and motive, so why didn't Bobby Joe Sellers kill him? And what about the gray car and Billy being in Verona for a week? How do you explain that away?"

"I know, I know," Tom replied. "There are holes in our theory. But at least we have a working theory. You're never going to explain away Billy being in Verona. You just have to put holes in their case and offer your own story."

"What about the reality? Billy was there. I talked to him. He told me he went down there to kill Johnson, but he doesn't think he did. Unfortunately, he was so drunk that he doesn't know for sure."

"I don't know how to answer that. Is it possible that Billy was there and Roy Johnson was killed by someone else? That's an awful big coincidence. Based on everything we know, I don't think you can resolve all the facts and come up with a cohesive theory that explains everything unless there is a big picture that we're not seeing. Why did you decide to talk to Billy anyway?"

"Because Carlisle told me he wouldn't help unless Billy said he was innocent and I believed him. I wanted to know anyway."

"Good for you," Tom said. "You know what else makes sense?"

"What's that, Dad?"

"Roy Johnson as the head of a drug ring and then the CEO of a major corporation. Think about it. It's all about the money for most of those greedy bastards."

Kevin didn't want to get into that conversation. He knew there were a lot of honest men in business, but the number did seem to be shrinking.

"I guess you're right, Dad," he said and let the subject drop.

They took a break after that to let everything sink in.

Kevin knew they would have more conversations before he left. He could not put into words the feeling that he had sitting at that table and bouncing ideas back and forth with his father.

Enjoy the moment, he kept telling himself. *Don't go backward.*

CHAPTER FIFTY

They had beef stew for supper. Kevin wasn't used to home cooking and he devoured every morsel and went back for seconds. While he was eating dessert, Kate went out to the barn and saddled the horses.

They rode out to the end of the pasture to where the cattle were and then over to another pasture where some horses were grazing. After a half hour or so, they came upon a pond and stopped to let the horses drink.

"We should start back soon," Kate said. "You don't want to be riding too much on your first day in the saddle. The fanny gets pretty tender."

"It's beautiful out here," Kevin told her. It was dusk. They were sitting on their horses by the pond, surrounded by tall pines. It was totally silent except for the gobbling of a wild turkey as it ran across the fields about twenty yards in front of them.

"This is my refuge," she told him. "This is where I can be me. The lake house was always that place for your father. I hope he can be happy here."

"He looks happy."

"Oh, he is right now. More than you can ever know. Having you here has lifted his spirits tremendously. I know you have to go back soon to your home and the woman in your life, but you should know you brought great joy to your father by being here."

Kevin did not share his thoughts and feelings with too many people and he probably wouldn't have with Kate if he had spent any time thinking about the situation. But they were sitting there in this pristine spot and Kate had raised the subject of his relationship.

"I don't have a home to go back to, or a woman—just a condo."

"Really?"

"Yeah. I was away less than two weeks when she told me it was over."

"Maybe it wasn't about the length of time you were gone. Maybe it was about other things."

"I think you're right. She said things hadn't been going well for a long time. I hadn't noticed it before she said it."

"Most men never do. Do you see it now?"

"I guess. I think we had different values. We were heading in different directions."

"Then maybe it's a good thing. Time will tell. You'll know it for sure when you meet somebody else."

They turned the horses around and headed for home. As they rode along, Kevin could not help but think that Kate had just shared with him how she and his father came to be together. And she did it in a way that he would totally understand.

CHAPTER FIFTY-ONE

Tom was asleep when they arrived back at the ranch. However, the two men were back to work the next morning at breakfast before Kevin left to return to St. Albans.

"You said something yesterday, Dad, that I've been thinking about. You said Bobby Joe Sellers was released from prison two years ago, right?"

"That's right."

"Do you know the date?"

"I think it was April fourth or fifth. I just remember it was almost exactly two years before Winters got out."

"Wow!" Kevin exclaimed.

"What are you 'wow'-ing about?" Tom asked.

"Carlisle Buchanan's father died two years ago—April twentieth I think he said. I'm not sure of the exact day but it was in April. Rosie told me she thought he was killed."

"Who's Rosie?"

"She runs the local café in Gladestown."

"Boy, you are getting to know the locals. That's good. That's real good."

"Anyway, Carlisle told me his father didn't like Roy Johnson's operation. He thought it was going to ruin Gladestown. I'll bet Scotch Buchanan was the informant and Bobby Joe Sellers killed him when he got out of prison."

"You may be right, Kevin, but that kind of kills our theory, doesn't it?"

"It might kill that theory but we can come up with another one. What would be a reason for Winters to want to kill Roy Johnson other than him being an informant?"

"Money."

"Money works for me," Kevin said.

"So how do we prove Winters killed Roy Johnson for money?"

"One of my former colleagues who still works for Bernie owes me a favor. I could call him and ask him to get me the criminal files on Winters and Sellers. Bernie has a history of being financially involved with his clients. I know this from my own personal experience. Maybe there's something in those files."

"That representation was twenty years ago. Would he even have those files?"

"Oh yeah. Bernie saves everything. He doesn't want something or somebody to come back and haunt him years later. He has clients sign off on everything and he keeps it in his own warehouse."

"Well, son, let's see if we can make his little procedure bite him in the ass."

CHAPTER FIFTY-TWO

Kevin went home to his father's house that afternoon, showing up at the office around two. Jan was at her desk, answering phone calls and doing paperwork.

"You know, your father still gets a lot of phone calls even though he's not taking any new cases."

"Do you filter out the legitimate problems from the nuisance cases?" Kevin asked.

"Oh, yeah. Your father taught me how to do that years ago."

"Well, if you think a case is legitimate, I'll talk to the people."

A smile lit up Jan's face. Maybe she wasn't going to be forced into retirement after all. "I sure will," she said.

He waited until seven that evening to call his friend David Lefter on his cell phone.

David Lefter was one of the nine lawyers who worked for Bernie Stang. David had been a CPA before law school and was on the board of several banks and lending and investment institutions in town. A short, chubby, nervous man with irritable bowel syndrome, David didn't possess the swagger and bravado that the trial lawyers in the office displayed—the kind of personality disorder one needed to be able to walk in any courtroom at a moment's notice and demand to be the center of attention. He was a numbers guy and Bernie's ticket into the world of white-collar crime, which was becoming increasingly more lucrative. David Lefter would have been hard-pressed to even *find* the courthouse.

Kevin had helped David out a couple of times when his bravado got the best of him and he took on litigation cases. One of those involved a bank president's son accused of drug dealing. After David screwed the case up royally, he went to Kevin with his tail between his legs and Kevin bailed him out. "If you ever need anything," David told him at the time, "you can count on me."

David was about to get the call.

"David, this is Kevin."

"Kevin, how are you? I've tried to call you a million times. What Bernie did to you was disgusting. I wanted to quit myself but I didn't have anything else lined up. You ought to answer your cell phone once in a while, you know."

"Yeah, I know. Sorry about that."

"Who are you working for? Why don't we have lunch?"

"I'm up in St. Albans where my father lives."

"Wow, that's drastic. I had heard Bernie didn't want you working here in Miami. He's such a prick."

Kevin was done with the small talk. David was already getting on his nerves. "Listen, David, remember when I did that favor for you?"

"Remember? How could I forget?"

"And you said if I ever needed a favor."

"That's right. I really don't have any extra cash but if you need anything else."

"Turns out I do. I need you to get two old files for me out of storage. The names are Bobby Joe Sellers and Randy Winters."

"That's funny," David remarked.

"What's funny?"

"A person named Randy Winters was in to see Bernie today."

"Really? Do you know what that was about?"

"Haven't a clue. You know they don't tell me anything. I'm the business guy."

"Do you think you can get those files?" Kevin pressed.

"I don't know. Bernie's pretty funny about shit like that."

Kevin knew it. David was so thankful when his ass was in a sling. Now, when the shoe was on the other foot, he was cautious. This was too important to let him off the hook.

"The hell with Bernie. I saved your ass, David, and I need a favor. Are you going to do this for me or not?"

There was a pause on the other line. "What if he goes to look for them? This guy was just in the office."

"Copy them. Put the copies back and he'll never know the difference."

"Okay. I'll see if I can pull them out."

"Be careful."

"I will. Say, one of your old clients has been working here."

"Who?"

"Sal Trivigno. Bernie took over his file after you left and Sal has been working off his fee by painting the place. He comes in to see me every morning, kind of like I used to do with you."

"Did the State ever file a criminal charge?"

"Sal told me the State never filed anything. He said it was because of you, not Bernie. He hates him as much as I do."

CHAPTER FIFTY-THREE

Kevin tried to bring some normalcy to his life by getting into a routine. Every morning after breakfast he dressed and went over to the office and began his day. Two nights a week he went to the ranch and had dinner with his father and Kate. On Tuesday night he stayed over and went for a morning ride before heading back. He was feeling good, although Susan still weighed heavy on his mind, as did Billy.

When he was at the ranch, he and Tom talked nonstop about the case, as they did during their daily telephone calls. Tom was getting much better. His incision was healing and he was getting to the point where he could take short walks around the ranch.

"When I'm feeling a little better," he told Kevin, "we'll have to go out to the lake and do some fishing."

"I'd love that."

Kevin was fielding calls at the office and opening files and working on Tom's two appeals. Without consciously thinking about it, he was laying down his roots.

In Billy's case, he had sent out a subpoena for the financial records of Dynatron. He needed the records so the financial expert that he hired could testify that he or she reviewed the records, that the corporation was defunct, and that all the employees had been fired and lost their pensions and benefits.

That gave twenty thousand other people the same motive as Billy to kill Roy Johnson. There might be other information in there as well that he could use to muddy the case against Billy.

Two weeks after the subpoena went out, he received a call from a lawyer named Kenneth Moss from the U.S. attorney's office.

"Those records you subpoenaed have been seized by the federal government and we're not going to honor your subpoena."

Kevin had dealt with the feds before. They always sounded so arrogant like they had absolute power, which, in most cases, was true. He decided to go on a little fishing expedition with Mr. Moss.

"The corporation is defunct, the CEO is dead, and your criminal case is over. Why do you have or need the records?"

"The criminal cases aren't over. One case was prosecuted."

That was interesting. He needed to keep Mr. Moss talking. Of course, he couldn't ask any direct questions. U.S. attorneys never answered direct questions.

"I don't think you are going to get anywhere with the judge on this unless Roy Johnson was under investigation."

"Well, he was. And so were several other people."

So Roy Johnson was under criminal investigation at the time of his murder. He had to keep Moss talking.

"I think we need to have an evidentiary hearing before the judge on this issue," he told Moss.

"Fine," Moss replied with all the arrogance he could muster. "Set it up. I'll have an agent there to testify."

"I've seen no evidence that Mr. Johnson knew he was under investigation."

"Well, his lawyer sure knew."

"Who was that?"

"Come on, Mr. Wylie, don't play games with me. I've done my homework on you. There's no way you wouldn't know Bernie Stang was representing Roy Johnson."

Kevin almost dropped the phone. Bernie was everywhere in this case.

CHAPTER FIFTY-FOUR

Five weeks after getting out of the hospital, Tom's incision had healed completely and he was feeling well enough to do a little fishing with his son. He and Kate drove up to the lake one Saturday morning to meet Kevin. The two men planned to go out on Tom's little motorboat, something they hadn't done together in almost thirty years.

Kate was happy for them but she was also worried. She hadn't let Tom out of her sight since he came home. Even though he was looking healthier and he was smiling and laughing again, she never forgot for an instant how serious the situation was. She didn't want something to go wrong while he was out in the middle of the lake.

Once again, Kevin had gotten his directions from Kate. The lake house, unlike the ranch, was a little hard to find.

"You turn right on Floyd Lane and go exactly one-half a mile," she told him. "The driveway is on the left. It's hidden and unmarked, but it's right at the half-mile mark."

Kevin went past it twice before he finally saw it, *exactly* at the half-mile mark. It was a long, narrow driveway that needed some tending, as the woods on both sides had almost enveloped it. After a few minutes it opened into a clearing and there stood the lake house. It was a modest, wooden structure, more like a cottage than a house. Kevin could feel his emotions stirring even though he could not specifically remember anything about the place.

The house was on a little hill and the back of it faced the lake. Kate and Tom were already there. Kate was inside straightening up. Tom was down at the dock, loading the fishing poles and tending to the little motorboat. When Kevin saw the dock, a picture came into his mind of a little boy and a dog standing out there, the dog's black-and-white tail wagging constantly.

He went in the house to help Kate. It was clearly a man's place. No frills at all. A couple of Kate's paintings adorned the walls but the rest was all about fishing.

"I can see you don't spend much time here," Kevin said.

"I have over the years, but this is Tom's space. I leave him to it."

There was a question on Kevin's mind he never intended to ask, but it just came out. "Why haven't you and Tom married?"

"Well, he was very fearful of marriage at the start of our relationship, and I was from a different generation. I didn't think we needed a piece of paper to hold us together. As I got older there were times when I wanted to be identified as his wife but I just put it aside. I haven't thought about it in years."

"How about now?"

"Now it's too late, but I have no regrets. Tom and I have something most people don't—a bond that's stronger than any document."

He went down to the dock after that. Tom had everything all set. He wore one of those silly-looking fishing hats with the hooks in them.

"Want a fishing hat?" he asked his son. "I've got an extra one."

"I'll stick with my baseball cap," Kevin told him.

The lake was truly a Florida lake. There were only houses on the west side, so when a person looked out on the lake, one saw nothing but nature. Nature as it looked a hundred, perhaps even a thousand, years ago. Part of the lake was covered with fields of lily pads. Part was hidden under peppergrass that extended out of the water as high as four or five feet. There were corridors through the peppergrass where boats could pass. It was bordered on all sides by tall pines and in the middle were two small islands covered with cedar trees.

The morning mist had not yet lifted as the two men set out. Five minutes after they left the dock, they were gone from sight.

And Kate's fear increased.

They rode about fifteen minutes through the peppergrass until they reached a clearing on the other side. Tom turned the motor off and let the boat just drift as they threw their lines out, hoping to catch a bass or a crappie or a striped perch. Nothing was moving. It was totally serene. A few ducks were floating along, seemingly propelled by the wind. There was a ripple on the surface from time to time, but that was it. The two men were silent for a time as well. It was the nature of fishing. Tom finally broke the silence.

"Reach in that cooler and grab me a beer, will you?"

Kevin just looked at him. "You sure you want to do that?" he asked.

"I'm dying," Tom replied. "Do you want to deprive me of the little pleasures of life? Speaking of which…" He leaned down and reached into his tackle box and pulled out two long, thick cigars. "Care to join me?"

Kevin couldn't help but laugh. He reached into the cooler and took out two beers. He handed his father one and accepted a cigar in return. Tom lit up, then took a sip of his beer.

"Ah, the good life. It's not longevity, son. It's texture. Remember that."

Kevin smiled at the sight of his father enjoying himself on his little boat in this beautiful setting. He decided that this was the snapshot he was going to carry with him for the rest of his life. Then he lit his own cigar.

"So what do we have?" Tom finally asked.

Kevin knew exactly what he was talking about. The trial was only three weeks away.

"We've got the evidentiary hearing on the financial records on Monday. I still don't know what I want to ask this FBI agent. I mean, other than the stuff about everybody losing their jobs, what else is relevant?"

"Think about it," Tom said. "What do you want to prove from this guy? You want to establish that all the employees lost their jobs and their life savings. What was the average loss? How much did the investors lose? That gives a ton of people motive to kill Roy Johnson. Of course, who knows if the judge will let it in or not at trial."

"What else can you think of?" Kevin asked.

"Well, you want to establish that Roy Johnson was under criminal investigation for what he did as CEO of Dynatron and get the date when that investigation started."

"What does that do for us?"

"If they were looking at the company before he left, that feeds into our theory that he bailed out at the right time and took a ton of money. The jury could conclude that's what he did in 1982 and maybe that gave Randy Winters a reason to kill him. It also lets them know what a snake he was. How are you going to get the 1982 stuff in, by the way?"

"I found the name of the FBI agent who headed the investigation. I've subpoenaed him."

"You don't know what he's going to say. Isn't that a little dangerous?"

"Not really. Roy Johnson had to be on their radar back then. That's all I need from him. I'm going to subpoena Sellers and Winters as well."

"How about your man Carlisle, are you keeping in touch with him?"

"No. I really don't want to talk to him too much because at some point I'm going to have to tell him about his father."

"So?"

"So he's one of the main witnesses for the prosecution. Someone might say I'm trying to influence him by feeding him information that's unproven."

"I see. Are you just not going to use him at all?"

"I'll wait until after he testifies."

"It might be too late then."

"Can you think of a better idea?"

Tom removed the cigar from his mouth for a second to take a sip of beer. He had his legs spread out in front of him and his fishing rod resting on his lap. "I guess not," he said.

Once again Kevin marveled at their ability to bounce ideas off each other with such ease. He couldn't keep that to himself. "I wish I had you as a mentor like Ray Blackwell did."

"Well, at least we have the present," Tom said.

Kevin smiled to himself. "I guess you're right. We can't change the past."

"Nor the future," Tom added. "Have you heard from your guy in Bernie's office yet?"

"Not yet. It should be any day now."

"If he comes through for you."

"I think he will."

"How about Billy? Have you talked to him lately?"

"Every day. He's holding up. The kids are doing okay too. I talked to Billy's sister a couple of days ago."

"Good," Tom replied. "You know, this thing about Bernie representing everybody makes me think we're missing something. I can't put my finger on it, though."

CHAPTER FIFTY-FIVE

Judge Thorpe was not happy that Kevin was dragging the federal government into his courtroom.

"Mr. Wylie," he bellowed at 10:00 a.m. on Monday in an empty courtroom—the morning hearings had just ended. "Don't you think your time would be better spent preparing for trial rather than sparring with the federal government? Explain to me why you think the financial records of Dynatron are relevant to your case. I understand why the State would want them. They have to prove that your client was an employee of Dynatron and lost his pension and benefits when Dynatron went belly up. That establishes motive. I get that. I have no idea what you could possibly want with those records."

This was very dangerous territory for Kevin. Judge Thorpe's fuse was already lit. He didn't want the man to explode.

"To be honest with you, Judge, I don't know what's in those records. My job in representing my client is to leave no stone unturned. There may be something in those records that gave somebody else a motive to kill Roy Johnson. For instance, I just learned from Mr. Moss that Roy Johnson was under criminal investigation and that he had an attorney—my old boss, Bernie Stang. Now Bernie would always explore the possibility of a deal, which means Roy Johnson could have testified against other Dynatron employees for a lighter sentence or no sentence at all. That is a pretty good motive to kill somebody. I'd like to find out who those employees were and where they were on the day Roy Johnson was killed."

Kevin had just come up with the theory about Roy Johnson testifying against other corporate officers the night before. It was a weak theory and he didn't plan on using it at trial, although it did provide a reasonable basis for reviewing the financial records.

"What's that got to do with Dynatron's financial records?" the judge asked.

"The information for the possible criminal charges came from the financial records. I didn't know about the criminal stuff until I talked to Mr. Moss. Now I want to ask this agent specific questions about that."

It made some sense even to Judge Thorpe. He looked at Jeanette.

"What does the State have to say?" he asked.

Jeanette Truluc had her own strategy for this hearing. The feds had reluctantly given the State the financial information about Billy, but she did not have a witness to authenticate the information and she wasn't sure she could get a federal agent to testify on the day of trial. Since she had a good working relationship with the FBI field office in Miami and even considered the head of that office, a man named Phil Roberts, a friend, she called Phil for some advice.

"I can get you anything locally, Jeanette, including witnesses. But sometimes *I* can't get information out of north Florida. They don't cooperate even with their own people. It's just the way it is."

Consequently, Jeanette *wanted* the agent to testify. She'd even brought a videographer so she could show the video to the jury.

"Your Honor, we have no objection to an FBI agent testifying about relevant portions of the financial records. I have a videographer here to record that testimony in case we need to use it at trial. Mr. Wylie and I certainly disagree on what's relevant, however."

Judge Thorpe smiled. Being a former federal prosecutor, he understood Jeanette's strategy and he liked it.

"All right. You both make some sense here. I'm going to allow this agent to testify, and Ms. Truluc, you can video it, and I will allow this testimony to be used at trial if the witness is unavailable for any reason. Mr. Wylie, I'm going to give you a lot of leeway here. Ask all your questions. Ms. Truluc, I understand you have objections, but don't make them at this time. I promise you, before this video goes before a jury or before this witness testifies before a jury, all your objections will be heard and decided. Everybody understand?"

All three attorneys, including Mr. Moss, told the judge they understood.

The FBI agent took the stand. He looked like an accountant, small and thin with thick glasses, and in his hand, he had a large black legal binder, which he opened and set before himself.

"Ms. Truluc, why don't you begin the questioning since you plan on using this testimony in your case? It will be less confusing to the jury," the judge suggested.

"Yes, Your Honor," Jeanette replied as she walked to the podium to address the FBI agent.

"Would you state your name for the record, please?"

"Harvey Booth." It was the same man who had told Vern Fleming to go pound salt not so many weeks before.

"And where are you employed, Mr. Booth?"

"I'm an agent with the Federal Bureau of Investigation and I've been so employed for twenty years. I am also a certified public accountant and my responsibilities at the agency include, among other things, reviewing financial records to determine if criminal activity has occurred—mostly money laundering, that kind of thing."

Mr. Booth spoke with confidence and he answered questions that were not even asked, which told Kevin that he had been a professional witness for many years.

"Mr. Booth, do you have in your possession and have you reviewed the financial records of the Dynatron corporation?"

"Yes. When Dynatron announced that it was closing its doors, the United States attorney's office obtained a search warrant and seized all the financial records of the company. They have been in my possession and control ever since."

"Was there a reason why the federal government seized those records?"

"We had reliable information that there were questionable accounting activities going on at Dynatron. To give you just a brief example, very high earnings had been reported and the stock was trading at a very high price just before it totally collapsed. All employees had their pension monies in Dynatron stock as part of a company policy. It was something we had to investigate."

Kevin loved the testimony so far.

Jeanette took Billy's personnel file, which had already been released to her by the government, and handed it to Mr. Booth.

"I have handed you a document that we have marked for identification as State's Exhibit number forty-six and I ask you if you can identify that document."

"Yes. Part of the records we seized were the personnel files of each individual employee to see what that employee had contributed and had earned in the company's pension plan and also to see what other benefits that employee had accrued and then ultimately lost. This document identified as exhibit number forty-six is the personnel file of William Fuller."

"Can you tell us, Mr. Booth, how much Mr. Fuller had in his company pension plan at the time Dynatron closed its doors?"

"Yes, he had nothing in his plan when the company closed its doors. However, three months before that date when Dynatron stock was still trading at a modest level, Mr. Fuller's individual plan was valued at $754,361.67."

"Did he have any other benefits?"

"Yes, he had a premier health insurance plan with major medical coverage and he had vacation and sick leave benefits valued at $37,513."

"What happened to those benefits?"

"He lost them all when Dynatron closed its doors."

"Including the health insurance plan?"

"Yes."

"No further questions."

The judge looked at Kevin. "Your turn, Mr. Wylie."

Kevin walked to the podium. He needed to follow up on Jeanette's questions before heading into his own agenda.

"How many employees did Dynatron have when it closed its doors, Mr. Booth?"

Mr. Booth calmly referred to his black binder for the answer to Kevin's question. "I believe 20,132."

"And what was the average length of employment, do you know?"

"It was approximately twelve years."

"And do you know what the average pension account for all employees was?"

"Not with any definite accuracy, but we have done some models and the best we can come up with is that the average employee lost between three hundred and three hundred twenty thousand dollars in total benefits. That includes pension, health insurance, and sick and annual leave."

"And what did the stockholders lose?"

"Billions."

"There were a lot of angry people out there, weren't there?"

"That is not a calculation I made."

"Let's talk about the criminal investigation. Were you involved in that?"

"Yes."

"And is it accurate that at the time of his death Roy Johnson was under criminal investigation?"

"Yes."

"For what specifically?"

"No indictment had been drawn, but basically, it was for defrauding investors, employees, insider trading—you name it."

"Was an indictment imminent?"

"I'm not sure what you mean by 'imminent.' I can say that it was certain."

"Were there other people at Dynatron who were under investigation?"

"Yes."

"And who were they?"

"There were three vice presidents and the chief accountant. We had already indicted and convicted the chief financial officer."

"Now, isn't it true that when you have multiple defendants like this, you try to work on one or two to get them to turn on the others?"

"Sometimes."

"Mr. Johnson had an attorney, didn't he?"

"Yes."

"And that was Bernie Stang?"

"Yes."

"Do you know if Mr. Stang had any negotiations with the U.S. attorney regarding this matter?"

"No, I don't."

"When did the criminal investigation of Dynatron begin?"

"I can't say for sure. I know we had been looking into the company's finances for about a year."

"Before Roy Johnson left the company?"

"Possibly."

"Were you aware that Mr. Johnson received a severance package of approximately one hundred million dollars when he left the company?"

"Yes. I was."

"When you reviewed all the accounting information for Dynatron were you able to determine where all of the earnings of the company went?"

"No."

"And why not?"

"Dynatron, like most major corporations in the United States, had offshore accounts in the Cayman Islands—tax havens. We could not get at those accounts. We could trace money that went to those accounts but not money that was earned or money that was withdrawn."

"So Roy Johnson could have received more than one hundred million dollars?"

"Possibly."

Kevin had everything he needed. "No further questions, Your Honor."

"The witness can step down," Judge Thorpe announced. Then he looked at Kevin. "Is there anything else you need in those records besides what this witness has testified to?"

"Yes, Your Honor. I'd like all the records. We've just touched the surface here."

"That's what I thought you'd say. I'm going to allow the witness to testify at trial to the extent he has today with all objections preserved, but hear this, Ms. Truluc. I'm going to give Mr. Wylie some leeway before the jury to defend his client.

"Mr. Wylie, I'm going to deny your request for any more records at this time. The government has an interest here because of its ongoing criminal investigation, and frankly, you have not laid any relevancy predicate at all. You have even candidly admitted you are on a fishing expedition. I believe you have what you need to make the defense that you want to make. I'll see you folks in three weeks."

Kevin accompanied the videographer to his office to get a copy of the tape to take home. He wanted his father to see this.

CHAPTER FIFTY-SIX

"It sounds like the judge is going to let you introduce all of this testimony into evidence if you so choose," Tom Wylie told his son, "but where does that get you?"

They were sitting in the living room at the ranch on Tuesday morning, having just watched the tape of Harvey Booth's testimony. Kevin was beginning to think Alex Rivard, Tom's doctor and longtime friend, was a fraud. Tom looked terrific. He was now getting up and down from the couch on his own, and his face, neck, and arms were tan from the frequent walks he was taking. He did not look at all like a man who was dying.

"I've been stewing everything over and over in my brain, trying to come up with a cohesive strategy based on everything we know. Jeanette is going to put on her case, which is going to be very tight and convincing. What do you think is going to happen if you just throw against the wall the fact that Roy Johnson was under criminal investigation and Randy Winters happened to get out of prison a week before Roy Johnson disappeared?"

"The jury is going to think that I'm desperate, which I will be at that point."

"I'm afraid so," Tom said. "Your strongest case will be if your friend comes through and produces those files, and they contain something that indicates Johnson stole some money from Winters and Sellers back in 1982. Then you've got some traction."

"I agree. But David getting those files and those files having the information we need is a long shot to say the least. Do you really think we're sunk without it?"

"Not necessarily. Let's go to your second-strongest argument: that Roy Johnson was the confidential informant."

"That may not be true. The evidence suggests to me that Scotch Buchanan was the confidential informant."

"Why?"

"Because he was killed right after Bobby Joe Sellers got out of prison. We've already talked about this."

"I know. Let's just follow the logic for a minute. You can't make that argument, though, can you?"

"Hell, no. Judge Thorpe is not going to let me speculate that Bobby Joe Sellers killed Scotch Buchanan and therefore Randy Winters probably killed Roy Johnson. He'd tar and feather me right in front of that jury."

"Okay. So stay with the original argument that Roy Johnson was the confidential informant. It's a very strong case because revenge is a powerful motive. If it isn't true, then the State will make your other case for you."

"I'm not sure I'm following you, Dad."

"The State will have to put on some evidence that Roy Johnson was not the confidential informant and that Scotch Buchanan was. That should open the door for you to inquire about both the date Scotch Buchanan died and the date Bobby Joe Sellers got out of prison. Even if they don't, even if you stumble onto it yourself, you should be able to get in the evidence that you need."

"You mean, since I've got the FBI agent subpoenaed, they

might let me ask the questions and find out that Roy wasn't the confidential informant."

"They may let you do that, but I don't think so. I think they'll call him. However it happens, once the evidence is in you can make whatever argument you want in your closing."

"Either way, at least this gives us a chance. It's brilliant."

"We'll see."

CHAPTER FIFTY-SEVEN

Thirty years ago when he first started representing drug dealers and making a boatload of money, Bernie Stang bought several acres of land northwest of Miami near Route 41. The land was dirt cheap back then and Bernie eventually built a warehouse on the site where he stored all his files. Bernie liked to consider himself a hip, modern guy with the latest computer gadgetry. With his files, however, he was old-fashioned, hanging onto every piece of paper.

It fed into his paranoia.

David Lefter felt good about helping Kevin out. Kevin had been a friend—his only friend—who came to his defense when nobody else would. He was scared at first, but eventually, he became comfortable with the idea.

The procedure for looking at old files was rather innocuous. You had to get the key to the warehouse from Bernie's secretary, Mary. And you had to sign a log that she kept, indicating the file you wanted to look at. It all seemed to be based on an honor system.

After working up his courage and identifying one of his old files as a decoy, David went to Mary and signed out the key on a Monday morning. He then drove out to the warehouse, found the two files that Kevin had asked him to get, and removed them. He took the files to a copy place nearby that he had located beforehand, copied them, and returned them to the warehouse within an hour. It was easy, or so he thought.

There was another aspect to the procedure that neither David nor any other attorney who ever worked at Bernie's office knew about. Once David signed the key out, Bernie was notified. Bernie then called the security agency that monitored the hidden cameras at his warehouse and notified them that somebody would be coming and when. The security company was never told the identity of the visitor. Bernie personally left instructions that could not be misinterpreted: He wanted to know what files were looked at and whether any files were removed.

After David's visit to the warehouse, the security agency called Bernie and told him David had taken the files of Bobby Joe Sellers and Randy Winters. The agency did not tell him that David had come back to the warehouse and returned the files after copying them because they did not monitor that event.

Even though he was feeling pretty good about himself after his caper, David was still nervous that something bad was going to happen. Somehow he was going to be discovered. He pulled into the parking lot at work right next to Sal Trivigno's beat-up old pickup truck, which gave him an idea. He took the copied files and put them in the back of the pickup under one of Sal's painting tarpaulins. If any questions were raised about the files that day, his car would be clean *if they came to search it*. If nobody said anything, he'd pick the files up that night after work.

Unfortunately, the plan went awry. Sal happened to be leaving the building as David was coming in. The two men never saw each other and Sal left the premises ten minutes after David had parked his car. When he couldn't find Sal anywhere in the office and subsequently discovered that his pickup was gone from the parking lot, David thought about driving to Sal's home.

You're getting too worked up about nothing, he finally told himself. *The files will keep till the morning.*

David had been married once, many years back. He and his wife had bought a rather large, extravagant home in Coral Gables. Three years later, she left in the middle of the night. Speculation among David's fellow workers at the time was that she left with one of Bernie's rich clients she'd met at the office. Some folks claimed that they had actually observed the flirtation. It was pure speculation, although she had abandoned everything, including the house. David waited three years before filing for dissolution. He got all the marital property in the divorce plus a case of irritable bowel syndrome. Years later, he still lived alone with his illness in the big house.

The night of his caper he was sleeping upstairs in the master bedroom when he heard a noise coming from the floor below. For a moment, he was crippled with fear. Then he remembered his gun. A while ago somebody had told him he needed a gun if he was living alone, so he bought a semiautomatic at a gun show and got a free lesson to boot. He hadn't fired the damn thing since the day he bought it.

He reached into the nightstand and pulled it out. The gun was fully loaded. There was no need to keep it unloaded when he was the only person living in the house. David slowly walked down the stairs. He had an advantage if there really was a burglar because he knew the terrain. He went from room to room, turning the lights on as he entered, ready to shoot. He covered the entire downstairs including the garage (this was a Florida home, there was no basement)—nobody was there. David relaxed. *I'm just a little jumpy because of today,* he told himself.

When he reached the top of the stairs, he was again forced to move quickly, this time making a mad dash for his bedroom and the bathroom. Sitting on the bowl, he wondered why he had been so cool when he thought there was a prowler in the house, only to have to run to the john as soon as the crisis was over. *I need to get rid of this damn disease.*

Suddenly, there was a creak in the hardwood floor in his bedroom. He didn't imagine it. Instinctively, he turned his head toward the sound, looking through the open door into the dark room. There was a figure in the doorway—more sounds—*ping, ping, ping*. Then he felt a throbbing in his head followed by a calm, peaceful feeling like he was floating on air.

They found him the next day sitting on the bowl, slumped over, with three bullets in his brain.

Kevin was just sitting down for lunch at the ranch with his father and Kate when he got the call from Julie, his old secretary at the firm.

"Kevin, it's Julie."

"Hey, Julie. What's up?"

"It's about David," she said rather suddenly. There was an urgency to her voice.

There was only one David she could be referring to. "What about David?"

Julie broke down on the other end of the line. "He's dead, Kevin. David's dead."

"No."

"Yes. He missed a big meeting this morning with Bernie and a client—something he would never do. When David's assistant couldn't get him on his home phone or his cell, she called the police. Apparently he woke up while somebody was burglarizing his house and they shot him three times in the head. I'm sorry I have to be the one to give you such bad news. I know how close you and he were. The funeral is Thursday morning, at ten. I'll e-mail you the details. Is your e-mail still the same?"

"Yeah. Thanks, Julie."

"I'm so sorry, Kevin."

"I know."

"What happened?" Tom asked when Kevin had hung up the phone.

"David Lefter is dead."

"Was he a friend of yours?"

"Yeah. He was the guy who was going to get me copies of the criminal files of Bobby Joe Sellers and Randy Winters."

"Jesus. Do you think there's any connection?" Tom asked.

"There's gotta be, Dad. It's just too coincidental."

"What the hell was in those files?" Tom asked.

Kevin didn't respond. He remembered David sitting in his office, complaining about something or other and all the time squirming like he had Mexican jumping beans in his pants. He had sent this nervous little man to his death.

They ate lunch in silence.

"There is a funeral on Thursday. I'm going to go to it," Kevin finally told his father and Kate as they were clearing the table. "I owe it to David to pay my respects."

"I know how you feel," Tom said. "But keep in mind that whoever killed your friend David might want to kill you as well."

"They have no reason to kill me. I never got the records."

"Do they know that?"

"I don't know."

"That's my point, Kevin."

Kevin knew his father was being the voice of reason but he didn't want to hear reason at this point in time. He had to go to the funeral.

"I'm going," he told his father. "There's no sense discussing it anymore."

Tom Wylie could hear his own voice thirty years before, telling his wife he was riding shotgun with Alex and he didn't care about the consequences. It was something he had to do.

Kevin was just being his father's son.

CHAPTER FIFTY-EIGHT

Kevin left for Miami very early on Wednesday morning. He didn't plan on going to the wake that evening. There would be too many people milling about and he didn't want to run into Bernie. The funeral was a more somber affair and he could leave right after the burial service at the cemetery. He was heading south early so he could stop in Verona and spend some time with Billy.

Billy was still at the county jail. Kevin had called while on his way to let them know he'd like to see his client and they gave the two men a room when he arrived. Billy looked a little thinner but he seemed to be holding up pretty well.

"So, how's it going?" Kevin asked.

"Not too bad. They let me call the kids once a day, which is good."

"I talked to your sister last week. She says they're doing fine."

"For now," Billy said, looking at the floor. "I just don't know what I was thinking—"

"Hold on there," Kevin interrupted. "Remember where you are. This is not the time and place to ruminate about what could have been or what should have been, do you understand?"

"Yeah, it's just that—"

"Let it go, Billy. We've got three weeks until trial. Focus your efforts on making it to that point. Take it day by day."

"Do we have a chance?"

"We have a good chance," Kevin told him. It wasn't a lie, although it wasn't exactly the truth. They had a chance, but not necessarily a good chance. Billy was down, though. Kevin needed to give him some hope so he could get through the trial. If they lost, what he said that day wouldn't matter one way or the other.

When he was an hour out of Miami, he called Susan.

"I read about David's death in the paper this morning. I'm so sorry, Kevin."

"It's very sad. Thank God he wasn't married and didn't have kids. Listen, Susan, let's have dinner."

"Kevin, I've said everything I have to say to you. I know you're feeling bad but that doesn't change anything."

"I know. I just think we should end our relationship with a dinner rather than a cold, impersonal telephone call. Whaddaya say?"

There was a pause on the other end of the line. "All right. But not in South Beach."

There were too many memories in South Beach, he knew. They agreed to meet at an upscale Spanish restaurant in Coral Gables, giving Kevin an opportunity to get to his hotel for a shower and shave beforehand.

He arrived before her, got a table, and waited. Susan came in fifteen minutes later and she looked ravishing in a short, tight black dress. She allowed him to kiss her on the cheek as if they had just met and were on their first date.

"I already ordered some calamari," he told her. "And a bottle of your favorite wine."

She gave him a scolding look.

"What? We're just having a little wine at dinner."

"You know what. I don't want this to get ugly."

"It won't, honey. I promise."

True to his word, dinner was pleasant. Susan talked about her father's business and how well things were going. Kevin talked about the trial.

The little illusion they had created fell apart outside the restaurant when they were saying their good-byes.

"I loved you," Kevin told her as they stood facing each other. "I still do with all my heart." The enormity of never feeling her beside him again, of losing her forever, overwhelmed him.

"Kevin, stop."

"We were going to get married, Susan. How could you just end it so abruptly?"

"I just saw that it wasn't going to work. We're too different. We want different things."

"We could have worked things out. That's what relationships are about—working things out, getting through the hard stuff, never letting go."

She just looked at him. "The truth is, Kevin, I never had you to begin with. You were always somewhere else even when you were here. I knew when you left you weren't coming back. And I knew I couldn't go."

She kissed him softly on the lips. "Good-bye, Kevin."

He watched her all the way to the parking lot until she disappeared inside her silver BMW.

"Good-bye, Susan," he whispered.

CHAPTER FIFTY-NINE

Kevin arrived late to the church for the funeral and sat in the back. He wanted to be there to pay his respects. He'd see everybody later on at the cemetery after the burial service.

Bernie confronted him on the street as they were loading David's coffin into the hearse. "We all go eventually," he said from somewhere behind Kevin. "Some of us quicker than others." Kevin turned to see him standing there with his bodyguard, Vic.

"Hi, Vic. I see you brought Bernie out with you today."

Vic didn't say a word. He just clenched his jaw a little tighter.

"Very funny," Bernie replied. "Although I hear it's a little dangerous to be a comedian these days."

"Is that right?" Kevin asked. "Is this the point where I'm supposed to run away again and hide? And maybe beg for forgiveness?" They were both facing the hearse as they talked.

"Why don't you ride out to the cemetery with Vic and me? We can catch up."

"I'd love to but I was planning to leave right after the service out there."

"Change your plans."

He looked at Bernie. It wasn't a demand as much as it was a request. "Why should I?"

"We need to talk. Mine is the second car behind the hearse," Bernie told him and walked away.

Why not? Kevin thought. *Maybe I'll learn something.*

Bernie had a limo and Kevin slipped into the backseat. The window separating them from Vic was up so they appeared to have privacy in the back.

"Want a drink?" Bernie asked after the car started moving.

"No thanks."

"You've got yourself a pretty high-profile murder case over there in Verona."

"Is that too close for you? I thought you just didn't want me in Miami."

"No, no. Verona is fine. It's just that—" Bernie paused, leaned over, and looked him right in the eye. "You need to stick to the matter at hand and not go digging up carcasses that need to stay buried."

"Is that a threat?"

"I don't make threats. I like to stick with the facts."

"All right, we'll stick to the facts—how do you know I'm digging up old 'carcasses,' as you put it?"

"I know when somebody takes files from my warehouse."

"So you had to kill him?"

"Whoa! Be careful what you say, pal. I didn't kill anybody."

"So you had Vic do it, what's the difference?"

"Vic didn't do it either."

"Look, Bernie, we can argue about who did it from now until doomsday, but you and I both know the reason David was murdered."

"Don't use those files, Kevin."

He thinks I have the files.

"And what if I do?"

"You're playing with fire, Kevin."

"So are you, Bernie."

When they got to the cemetery he opened the door and exited the limo. Vic made a move to get out and follow him, but Bernie stopped him.

"Let him go. This isn't the time."

CHAPTER SIXTY

Kevin stopped at Rosie's on the way back from the funeral. He'd called ahead to make sure Carlisle was there to meet him. Lunch hour was over, the place was empty, and Carlisle and Rosie were playing checkers.

"Carlisle," Kevin said after Rosie went to fix them some gator fritters. She always had to make sure everybody was well fed. "Do you know where Bobby Joe Sellers and Randy Winters are living?"

"No, but I can find out."

"It might be dangerous even asking around."

"I won't ask. I'll just find out. I see them on the water all the time now. It won't be hard."

"I'm going to need to serve them with subpoenas for trial on short notice and it has to be done by a process server. If you can get me their addresses and when they are likely to be home, I'll pay you two hundred dollars."

"Sold."

"You've got to be extremely careful. Don't tell anybody."

"I hear you," Carlisle told him. "You don't have to worry about me."

"I don't want you to do anything out of the ordinary to get their addresses."

"Got it. Hey, you were going to get back to me after you talked to your client and I never heard from you."

There was something about Carlisle that Kevin really liked. Maybe it was his enthusiasm, his honesty, or his love for his dead father—he didn't know. But he felt he owed Carlisle an explanation.

"Yeah, I was. I decided that it's best not to say anything to you before you testify. That way I'm not influencing you in any way. After you testify, we can have a conversation and I'll tell you everything, okay?"

"Sure, but isn't it going to be a little late in the game for me to help you?"

"Yes and no. I've already got a tentative strategy for the trial. However, you know all the players. You know Gladestown and the surrounding waters, and you know the facts better than anybody, including facts that I don't know and don't even know enough to ask about. Once I fill you in on Billy's story and some other things, a picture may emerge for you that I would never see. It could help me with my closing or something."

"All right. I just don't want to spend your money."

"Money doesn't matter, Carlisle. A good man's life is at stake."

As he listened to the words flow from his lips, Kevin realized he had never said them before.

It was a good feeling.

CHAPTER SIXTY-ONE

As usual, Tom and Kate had breakfast on Thursday morning on the front porch of Kate's house.

"I have to confess, Kate, I made a big mistake," Tom told her.

"About what?"

"About this place—living out here. I was always so closed-minded about it, wanting to hang on to my house in the city and the lake house. It's beautiful out here."

Kate just smiled. "Your lake house is beautiful too and you needed your house in the city for your practice. Besides, how would Kevin have found you if you didn't have some sort of presence in town?"

It was Tom's turn to smile. "Has it always been this easy to figure me out?"

"Well, you are a man."

Tom started laughing out loud. "I am that," he said.

Kate became a little concerned. "Take it easy, Tom. You don't need to be laughing that hard."

"Why not? My stitches are all healed. I'm feeling great."

"I don't know. I guess I'm just being overprotective. And by the way, I think our lives have worked out exactly the way they were supposed to."

Tom got out of his chair and knelt down in front of her, kissing her on the lips and then resting his head on her chest.

"It couldn't possibly have been better. You are my love. I don't know why God shined his light so brightly on me."

"Or me," Kate replied with tears in her eyes as she rubbed his shoulders.

Later, she saddled up her Appaloosa and went for a ride alone. Tom used to go with her but no more. He settled for a walk instead. She followed the same path she had taken Kevin on, stopping at the pond to allow her horse to drink, then visiting with the cattle in the meadow beyond. Her morning rides made her feel like every day was a new day to be lived to the fullest. More than ever she needed to live in the present.

She was still taking in the fresh air of a new day when she arrived back at the ranch.

"It was so beautiful out there today," she told Tom from the kitchen as she poured herself a glass of ice water. There was no response.

She walked into the living room to see what he was doing. He wasn't there. She checked the bedroom. No Tom. She rushed from room to room, calling his name. No answer. She started to breathe hard. *Calm down,* she told herself. *He could still be out on his walk.*

Then she checked her watch. She'd been gone an hour. Tom hadn't yet taken more than a half-hour walk. She ran out to the Jeep, jumped in, and started driving. She'd taken a few walks with him. She'd follow those paths first.

Why have I been so nonchalant? she chided herself. *I should know where he is at every moment.*

Kevin couldn't wait to go over everything with his father when he got back to St. Albans. He was up to his eyeballs in something, and he had no idea what it was or how it related to the death of Roy Johnson, if it did at all. As soon as he left Rosie's and headed north he called his father.

Kate answered the phone.

"Hi, Kate, can I speak to my dad?"

"He's not here, Kevin." Her voice was low and crackly. Kevin knew instantly that something was wrong. "He passed out on the road. They took him by ambulance about twenty minutes ago. I'm just getting some things and heading in."

"Is he okay?"

"I don't know." He could hear her voice crack as she said the words.

"Hang in there, Kate," he told her. "I'll be home as soon as I can."

CHAPTER SIXTY-TWO

Tom was lying in bed with his eyes closed when Kevin walked in the hospital room that evening. His IVs were hooked up again and Judge Blackwell was there sitting at his bedside, his head down as if in prayer.

"How is he doing?" Kevin asked.

"Don't know yet," the judge replied. "Alex is supposed to be here any minute."

"Where's Kate?"

"She just went to get some coffee."

Kate showed up a few minutes later with three coffees, anticipating Kevin was going to be there as she had the first time he arrived at the hospital.

"How are you?" Kevin asked her.

"Much better. I'm sorry, when you called earlier I was not in very good shape."

"You had a right to be upset, Kate. I can't imagine what that was like for you."

Kate didn't reply. Not one to dwell on her own feelings, she busied herself handing out the coffees.

They sat nursing their drinks in silence for another twenty minutes or so, nobody in the mood for conversation. Tom remained motionless with his eyes still closed.

Alex broke the stillness with his arrival and replaced it with tense anticipation. He didn't make them wait long, though.

"There is nothing major going on as far as we can tell. We think he passed out because his electrolytes were very low. I'm not exactly sure why. It's not uncommon with cancer patients and I think Tom was doing a little too much. We're going to have to slow him down.

"Right now, we're just going to get him stabilized. He'll be here a few days; then I think he will be able to go home."

"What about the tumors?" Kevin asked.

"We don't know anything new. He's not due for a CAT scan for another six weeks."

Tom never woke up during the entire time Kevin was there.

"Why don't you stay at the house tonight?" Kevin said to Kate when he'd had enough of the hospital room. Ray Blackwell had just left, promising to return in the morning before leaving for Tallahassee.

"Thanks, Kevin. I think I'll just stay here tonight. When Tom gets out of here, though, we're probably going to be staying with you for a while until he stabilizes. I don't want to be too far away from the hospital if this happens again."

Tom stayed three days in the hospital until Alex was assured that he had stabilized and his strength had returned. Then he and Kate moved in with Kevin. They stayed downstairs in Kevin's old childhood bedroom.

"We'll just be here a week or so," Kate said. "Then we'll go back to the ranch."

It didn't matter to Kevin. He enjoyed the company even though he and his dad didn't talk about the case for several days after that.

Kevin spent the majority of his time at the office, working

with Jan. Little by little, things were starting to pick up around there, although he consciously tried to avoid taking on too many new clients before Billy's case was done. After that, win or lose, he'd have plenty to do.

One afternoon Tom just showed up. Jan was ecstatic to see him. He came into the office and sat in one of the client chairs. Kevin was sitting in his father's chair behind the desk.

"You look pretty comfortable back there," he said to his son.

"Just keeping it warm for you, Dad. You look great, by the way."

"Thanks. You never told me what happened down there at the funeral." It was obvious Tom did not want to talk about his health. He was anxious to get back into Billy's case.

"Well, it was very interesting. Bernie thinks I have the files David took from storage."

"Really?"

"Yeah. I have no idea where they are."

"Did you tell Bernie that?"

"Hell, no. I let him think I had them."

"So if he knows the files were taken, he probably had something to do with David's death."

"You'd think so but he swears he didn't."

"He can swear all he wants."

"I've known Bernie for a long time. He's a smart guy, but cautious. Killing David was a stupid move."

"People do stupid things when they're under pressure, Kevin."

"Yeah, you're probably right. Bernie probably had something to do with it but he kept himself at arm's length. I think either Sellers or Winters killed David."

"It stands to reason," Tom said, "if Bernie doesn't want those files to see the light of day, those boys probably don't either. If either Sellers or Winters killed David and they think you have the files, why wouldn't they come after you?"

"I don't think Bernie would allow that, Dad—two lawyers from his firm killed in close proximity in time to each other. Somebody would start connecting the dots."

"So he waits a few weeks and kills you in St. Albans or Verona or Gladestown. The police might think it was connected to the trial but Bernie has very little connection to the trial at this point. I've got a Glock 17 with a clip already in it in the middle drawer of my table in the den upstairs. I'd feel better if you carried it with you."

Kevin remembered that the great tragedy of his life happened because his father was carrying a gun to protect himself.

"I'll think about it," he told Tom. "It's great to have you back. I was starting to get a little confused about things without you to talk to."

"Now if we can only confuse that jury," Tom replied.

CHAPTER SIXTY-THREE

A week before Billy's trial, articles started appearing all over the country with the express purpose of stoking interest in the proceedings. A trial like this could sell a lot of newspapers. Kate saved the clippings, and at Sunday breakfast, before Kevin was to leave for Verona, she, Tom, and Kevin sat at the kitchen table reading some of them. It was July and it was already hot outside at nine o'clock in the morning.

"Here's the only one favorable to Roy Johnson—one out of all the newspapers in the country. It's from the *Washington Times*," Kate said. "It's called 'Alligator Man Killer Deserves Death.'" Since she'd already read the article, Kate went right to the juicy parts.

"'Dynatron was a company that failed but for twenty years it supported thousands of people and thousands of families. Shareholders made millions of dollars. Roy Johnson was responsible for those successes as well.

"'This is a country of laws. There is no more intentional an act than that of vigilante justice. By definition, it is cold, calculated, and brutal. And by law, it is punishable by death.'"

"That would be the *Washington Times*," Tom remarked.

"Taking the side of the businessman no matter what. Read us one that'll pump us up."

"Okay," Kate replied. "Here's one from the *St. Petersburg Times* titled, 'Will Justice Be Served?'" Kate was enjoying herself as she read the excerpts.

"'It has been documented that at least sixteen former employees of Dynatron took their own lives when the company failed. Hundreds more filed for bankruptcy. Divorces followed. Families lost their health insurance. Shareholders lost millions. Roy Johnson wreaked unprecedented havoc in his wake.

"'Our culture has always held in high esteem the gritty, independent American who arises from the shadows to protect not only his own family and property but others as well. Charles Bronson and Clint Eastwood made a living portraying such characters.

"'Many Americans believe that William Fuller should be riding into the sunset rather than going on trial for murder.'"

"Now that's fair and balanced reporting," Kevin said and they all laughed.

"One more," Kate urged. "This is William Frishe from the *New York Times*."

"He's the one who started the whole Alligator Man thing, isn't he?" Tom asked.

"I think so," Kevin replied. He was dressed in shorts and a T-shirt and had his long legs stretched out on another chair. He didn't look like a man about to start a murder trial the next day.

"He's the one," Kate told them, "and that's what the article is about. It's called 'Still the Alligator Man.'" Kate began reading.

"'When I first referenced the "Alligator Man," the belief was that he had been snatched from a deserted road in the Everglades and brought home to the swamps by a fellow alligator. Now we know that he was murdered and probably by one of his own employees who had lost his wife and his best friend and everything he owned at the hands of Roy Johnson. Is Johnson any less the "Alligator Man" because he was murdered by someone whose life he thrashed and ripped asunder? With all due apologies to the alligators, I think not.'"

Kate looked at them, expecting to see smiles on their faces, but their expressions had changed. They had not exchanged a word between them.

"That presents a problem, doesn't it?" Kevin asked his father.

"Yeah," Tom replied. He knew exactly what Kevin was talking about. They were almost thinking as one now.

"Yup. The state attorney is going to read these newspaper articles and work every prospective juror over until she gets a commitment from each one of them that they would convict even if Roy Johnson was a bona fide, actual alligator. And Judge Thorpe is going to be watching you like a hawk, making sure you don't put Roy Johnson on trial."

"He's also got to give me some leeway to defend my client."

"You would think. My advice is that you don't be too obvious about attacking Roy Johnson. By the end of the trial, the jury will know that he was a scumbag."

"What about jurors? Do you have any thoughts about them?" Kevin had his own plan but he wanted to hear from his father.

"You want working people because they will hate Roy Johnson. And you want to make sure they are intelligent enough to follow our strategy, whatever it turns out to be."

Kevin chuckled in a halfhearted way. "This trial would be enjoyable if Billy's life wasn't at stake."

"You know how this works, Kevin. You think about your overall strategy *and* your next question. You start thinking about the endgame and you'll tighten up. I'm going to be right here. You call me if we need to discuss something. I've got my computer ready. You need some research, I'll get it. I'd love nothing more than to be right next to you, son, but that's not going to stop us."

"Right on, Papa." Kevin gave his father a big hug. He hugged Kate too. It was time to go.

CHAPTER SIXTY-FOUR

The courthouse in Verona was a modern-day, white-washed, soulless structure with plenty of parking and places for the press to congregate. Kevin had stayed in a hotel nearby. He'd thought about staying at his condo in Miami, but it was a long commute and he could use those hours for trial preparation. He walked the few blocks to the courthouse, carrying his files on one of those modern-day business hand trucks.

The old courthouse had real character with gargoyles on the corners and nooks and crannies and ghosts. Everything creaked in the old courthouse—the benches, the floors. You were never alone. The souls of slaves and murderers and innocents were everywhere. You could hear and even feel them if you had a mind to pay attention. All that had been bulldozed away, replaced by wide sanitary halls and straight lines.

Kevin arrived early because he had to see Billy before the proceedings began and give him a suit to wear. The presumption of innocence was a true illusion if the defendant walked into the courtroom in prison garb.

The parking lot was fairly empty at that hour and there were few people milling about in front of the courthouse. Kevin knew that would change. The barrage of publicity this case had received in the past week would bring out the gawkers—those who wanted to see or be seen and those who were curious. Probably some death penalty protesters would be there as well, although nobody believed Billy would ever get the death penalty. Even if the jury eventually determined that Billy killed Roy Johnson in cold blood, he had a damn good reason.

Kevin noticed the kiosks across the street as he walked toward the courthouse steps. Every major network was represented with its own little tent, cameras, lights, dozens of minions, and of course, the talking head. This was not a place for network anchors, although they might show up if things got really exciting. This was for the young up-and-comers—beautiful and handsome and smart in a myopic sort of way. They were at the top of their class and knew how to deliver their lines, but couldn't see that they were nothing more than an intricate part of a seamy entertainment show.

Kevin saw it quite clearly. They were here because Roy Johnson had been a captain of industry. They were here because the Alligator Man story had created its own buzz. People killed each other in the inner cities of America every day and it didn't bring out the beautiful people to report on the outcome. There was no titillation there. The networks didn't really give a shit about Billy or his kids or the human tragedy that Roy Johnson had inflicted. They cared about drama and ratings.

Kevin chuckled to himself as he watched them. It was only eight o'clock in the morning but it was already stifling hot—summer in Florida. Some of them were standing in front of their camera, lights blazing, sweating like pigs, as minions wiped their brows every five seconds.

One thing did bother him as he walked up the steps of the courthouse—there was a pool of microphones set up at the top stair in the center. *Why am I so relaxed? Why am I even looking at these idiots? I've got a murder trial that's about to start.*

Maybe it was a carryover from his Sunday morning breakfast with his father and Kate. Maybe it was because Carlisle had come through and both Bobby Joe Sellers and Randy Winters had been served with subpoenas for trial. He'd subpoenaed Bernie too. He wasn't sure what he was going to get out of them, but he had them squirming and that was good enough for now.

He was as serene as he had ever been on an opening day as he walked right past the microphones into the courthouse with his files in tow.

He had prearranged to meet with Billy in a room adjacent to courtroom C, where the trial was going to be held. The guards brought Billy in late as usual. The prison system was run in a military fashion. Everything was on a time clock except when a prisoner had to meet his or her lawyer in court. Then there were always delays.

"How are you doing?" Kevin asked Billy when he finally arrived. The dark patches under Billy's eyes already told him part of the answer.

"Okay, I guess. How about yourself?"

"I'm fine," Kevin told him. "I've got some clothes here for you to put on. We want to look good in front of these prospective jurors." Kevin explained to Billy that the next two or three days were going to be rather boring with individual jurors being brought into the courtroom one at a time and asked pretty much the same questions. "They're all going to be looking at you at some point, Billy, and you'll never know when that is. Consequently, you have to appear interested and focused at all times, understand?"

"Yeah, I understand," Billy replied.

Kevin had brought him a black suit, a white shirt, and a blue striped tie. It was Billy's suit and he fit it well.

Jeanette was already in the courtroom when they entered. She had a black suit on as well. She gave Kevin a cold stare. Kevin turned his head away and focused his attention on Billy.

Judge Thorpe walked in a few minutes later. There was no fanfare since the courtroom was empty, although he did have his robes on.

"Good morning, people. Are we ready to begin this ordeal?"

"The State is ready, Your Honor," Jeanette replied.

"The defendant is ready, Your Honor," Kevin said.

The judge turned to the bailiff. "Is the jury panel ready?"

"Yes, sir," the bailiff answered.

"How many do we have?"

"Fifty to start."

"That will get us going at least. Make sure we have another fifty in reserve."

"Yes, sir."

The judge turned back to the lawyers. "How do you want to handle the questioning?"

"I'd prefer questioning individual jurors," Jeanette told him, which was no surprise to any of them, considering the press coverage of the last week.

The judge looked at Kevin, who had no basis to object.

"I have no objection, Your Honor."

"All right, we'll question jurors one at a time. I've also decided I'm going to sequester this jury. Considering the press coverage already, I don't think they can avoid the media saturation. If you have any objections, state them on the record now."

Neither Jeanette nor Kevin had an objection.

"Last thing before we start bringing jurors in. There's a three-ring circus about to start out there in the street. You folks are seasoned trial lawyers. I don't need to tell you what your ethical obligations are, and I don't think I need to impress upon either of you that this is the proper forum to try your case, not the court of public opinion out there."

Both lawyers assured him that they understood.

"All right, have you had an opportunity to look at the first twenty juror questionnaires?" Each juror had filled out a questionnaire stating their occupation, marital status, whether they'd been a juror before or a participant in a lawsuit—preliminary information for the lawyers.

"Yes, Your Honor," they both answered.

"All right, we'll take a break after the first twenty. Let's bring in our first juror."

Nathan Smith, a middle-aged black man, was the first prospective juror. He was brought in and seated by the bailiff in the juror's box. There was nobody else in the courtroom but Mr. Smith, the lawyers, Billy, the court clerk, the court reporter, the bailiff, two sheriff's deputies standing close enough to Billy that they could grab him if he attempted to escape, and Judge Thorpe.

Jeanette was going to question Mr. Smith first.

Although he agreed in general with his father's opinion that they just needed working people, Kevin had separated those working people into categories. They were stereotypes, he knew, but stereotypes were a good way to begin jury selection. He didn't necessarily want retirees. They tended to be conservative and supportive of the State no matter what the circumstances. Since they were out of the workforce, they didn't identify as strongly with the working person. Women tended to be more emotional, which was good, while men could identify more with the urge to shoot a guy like Roy Johnson, which was better. Blacks had always been screwed by the system so they were more likely to be sympathetic toward Billy. Kevin had that thought in mind as he listened to the answers to Jeanette's questions.

Jeanette had one primary goal during jury selection—tell the jurors Roy Johnson was a bad man and get a commitment from each of them that they would convict the murderer of a bad man, no matter how bad that man was. Nathan Smith was the first test.

"Have you heard about this case, Mr. Smith?"

"Yes, I have."

"And what did you hear?"

"I heard this fellow made a lot of money—millions—and then he left his company, and all those working people lost their jobs and their pensions."

"And what do you know about the defendant?"

"Just that he was one of those working people."

"Knowing what you know, Mr. Smith, do you think you could be a fair and impartial juror in this case?"

"Hell, no," Nathan Smith replied.

"And why is that, Mr. Smith?"

"Because if I was one of those employees, I'd have wanted to shoot the bastard myself. Excuse my language, Your Honor."

"That's quite all right, Mr. Smith," the judge replied.

It went on like that all day with Jeanette searching for the few who said they could be impartial and then testing that statement.

With Eleanor Brown she asked, "You say you can be fair and impartial even if the deceased victim was a bad man—a person who caused people to lose their livelihood and their life savings—why do you say that?"

"Because we have a system of justice. We have courts and judges. If everybody took the law into their own hands, what would we have? Chaos."

For Jeanette, Eleanor Brown was a keeper.

When it was Kevin's turn, he asked the questions he needed the answers to.

"Ms. Brown, you obviously believe in our system of justice, correct?"

"I most certainly do."

"And you believe in our laws?"

"Yes. Absolutely."

"And if the law says that the State of Florida has the burden of proof in a criminal case—and that burden of proof is to the exclusion of every reasonable doubt—will you follow that law?"

"Yes. Absolutely."

"Will you hold the State to its burden?"

"Yes."

"Do you understand that the defendant does not even have to put on a witness to testify?"

"I didn't know that."

"If the State has not met its burden—guilt beyond a reasonable doubt—the defendant does not have to put on a witness. Can you follow the law and find for the defendant, even if he does not put on a single witness?"

"Yes, I can." Eleanor was getting a little fired up.

"Now, the defense anticipates at this point that we may put on some witnesses but the defendant is not going to testify. Did you know, Ms. Brown, that a defendant has a constitutional right not to testify?"

"I think I did. Yes."

"And if the law says that you cannot hold that against him—the fact that he does not take the stand and testify—can you do that?"

"Yes, I can."

"Will you do that?"

"Yes, I will."

Eleanor Brown was a juror Kevin could live with.

As Kevin figured, it took three days. But at the end of the third day, they had twelve jurors and two alternates. Of the twelve, eight were men, four were women. The two alternates were a man and a woman.

The fireworks were about to begin.

Kevin called his father every evening to give him a rundown of the day's events and the jurors that had been selected that day.

"She's really good," he told his father about Jeanette at the end of the first day. "Very thorough. She paints Roy Johnson as the Boston Strangler and then asks each juror if they can convict the person who killed him. When somebody says yes, she tests them to make sure they have a valid reason for their answer."

"I'm sure you're working them over just as thoroughly," Tom said.

CHAPTER SIXTY-FIVE

The crowd outside the courthouse on Thursday morning was much larger than it had been on the previous three days for one important reason: The courtroom was going to be open to spectators that day. They started lining up well before eight. It was a madhouse outside with the crowds and the talking heads and the microphone platform on the courthouse steps.

To her credit, Jeanette avoided the media as much as possible, just like Kevin. Every morning and every evening she appeared before the microphones and gave a terse statement. She avoided answering all but the simplest questions that could be answered with a yes or a no.

Kevin only showed up at the end of the day to say it was a good day, no matter what happened inside. He didn't need to say anything. The newspaper and television reporters had dug up as much dirt on Roy Johnson as could be found and saturated the airwaves and print with the information.

Today, Jeanette wore a wheat-colored linen suit with a tailored white shirt. She softened the no-nonsense look with a colorful silk scarf. Not too bright but pretty enough so the jury would like her. Kevin tried not to notice what she wore and how the soft lines and curves of her body contrasted with the rigid, painful architecture of the courtroom itself. He had to concentrate on what she said and how she said it and the witnesses she called and when she called them. Somewhere there was going to be a weakness—an opening—that he could exploit.

It was the full show inside the packed courtroom on Thursday morning. At the appropriate moment when the doors were closed and everybody was getting a little antsy, the bailiff yelled, "All rise," and everybody stood at attention as Judge Thorpe, dressed in his black robe, lumbered in and took his place at the throne.

"Be seated," he said as he himself sat. He had a thick, meaty voice that befitted his countenance. "Counsel, are we ready to proceed?" he asked the lawyers.

"The State is ready, Your Honor."

"The defendant is ready, Your Honor."

"Before we bring in the jury let me say a few words to our gallery. This is a court of law. It is not a television studio or a sports event. You are allowed to be here because as observers you are an important participant in our judicial process. However, you must remain silent at all times. You must not react in any way to the testimony of witnesses because that could influence the jury. You must not talk among yourselves. If any one of you cannot do this, your privilege to be here will be revoked and you will be removed from the courtroom by a court officer. If you as a group do not follow the rules, you will all be removed. Does everybody understand?"

The gallery nodded almost in unison.

The judge looked at the bailiff. "Bring in the jury," he told him.

A minute later the twelve jurors and two alternates filed into the courtroom and sat at their previously assigned seats in the jury box. When they were all seated, the judge addressed them.

"Ladies and gentlemen, we are now going to begin the formal

phase of the trial. In a moment the lawyers are going to address you in opening statements, where they are going to tell you what they intend to prove or what the evidence will show or not show. After opening statements are made, you will hear from witnesses who will testify under oath from this chair." The judge took a moment to point at a leather chair, immediately to his left but a few feet lower than his dais.

"It is important that you understand that what the lawyers say is not evidence. The only evidence that you can consider is the testimony from the witnesses who appear here and the documentary material that is admitted into evidence. The lawyers may try and put this evidence together for you, but you are the decision makers as to the facts. You are free to accept what they say or not.

"Ms. Truluc, are you ready to proceed?"

Jeanette stood up. "Yes, Your Honor."

She then walked to the podium, which faced the jury, and addressed them. "Good morning, ladies and gentlemen. You all know me from our previous discussions over the last few days. My name is Jeanette Truluc and I represent the people of the State of Florida in this proceeding.

"What I'm going to do this morning in my opening statement is give you an outline and a timeline of what we intend to prove, and I'm going to tell you who the witnesses are and what I expect they will say.

"As you know, the defendant, William Fuller, stands accused of the murder of Roy Johnson on April tenth of this year. You will hear evidence supporting this accusation from a variety of independent sources.

"You will hear sworn testimony from Sylvia Johnson, the victim Roy Johnson's wife, that her husband did not come to bed on the evening of April tenth of this year. He had a habit in the evening of taking a walk down Gladestown Road, which was adjacent to their home. She was usually asleep when he came to bed.

"When she awoke on the morning of April eleventh, he wasn't in bed and it was apparent he had not slept in the bed that night. This had never happened before. She immediately reported his disappearance to Carlisle Buchanan, the sheriff department's auxiliary police officer stationed in Gladestown. She told Officer Buchanan that her husband was wearing black shorts and a white silk shirt on the night he disappeared.

"On April twelfth, Auxiliary Officer Buchanan inspected the waters on both sides of Gladestown Road. He found a large piece of black cloth and the front quarter of a white silk shirt with the pocket still intact, hanging on some mangrove trees in the swamp on the east side of Gladestown Road. Mrs. Johnson identified those two items as similar to the material in her husband's shorts and shirt. On April fifteenth, Officer Buchanan returned to the same area where they had found the clothing, this time with homicide Detective Vern Fleming, and found the deceased victim's wallet with his driver's license and credit cards intact."

It was good strategy on Jeanette's part, Kevin thought, to use a timeline. It gave substance to a circumstantial evidence case and made it appear stronger at the outset. As she continued, Jeanette moved gracefully away from the podium and closer to the jury panel. Kevin saw the eight men's eyes go with her. *Damn! Eight men—what the hell was I thinking?* he said to himself.

"On April twenty-fifth," Jeanette continued with her timeline, "Officer Buchanan learned from a local restaurant owner, Rose Maddon, that a high school boy, Frederick Jenkins, had witnessed a hit-and-run accident on Gladestown Road the night of April tenth. Prior to this time, the assumption was that Johnson may have been the victim of an alligator that snatched him off the road. That same day, Officer Buchanan interviewed Frederick Jenkins, and he confirmed that he had indeed witnessed a hit-and-run on Gladestown Road on the night of April tenth at approximately eleven thirty and he added additional details. The victim was walking on the opposite side of the road back toward town. His back was to the car. The car crossed the road to strike him. Young Mr. Jenkins described the car as an old gray Honda."

Jeanette kept at her timeline.

"On the morning of May second, which was a Monday, George Russo, a bartender at a bar called the Last Stop, which is adjacent to the Verona Inn in Verona, came into the sheriff's office in Gladestown and reported to Officer Buchanan that a man left his bar on the evening of April tenth at approximately eleven in the evening after drinking heavily all night, saying he was going to, quote, 'kill him tonight.' The man drove an old gray Toyota. He had been coming into the bar for a week.

"That same day, homicide Detective Vern Fleming went to the Verona Inn and looked through the registrations for the second week in April. He was looking for anyone who had paid in cash. If you don't have false identification, the only way you can register with a false name is to pay in cash and not show identification. He found a man named Tom Jones. When he looked up Tom Jones's registration card, there was no address or driver's license number on it. Tom Jones was registered at the hotel from April seventh to April eleventh. However, the hotel had a policy of hand recording the license plates of the cars in the parking lot on a daily basis. Detective Fleming got those records for the second week in April and found that an old gray Toyota registered to the defendant, William Fuller, was in the parking lot at the Verona Inn from April seventh through April eleventh. Mr. Fuller was not registered at the hotel."

Jeanette stood to the right of the jurors with her hand on the bar that separated them. She knew exactly what she was doing. Taking them through a timeline was a little tedious. By moving around, she forced them to follow her with their eyes. It was a tactic to keep them focused, although the men didn't need any prodding.

"On May third, Detective Fleming got a copy of William Fuller's picture from the state driver's license bureau, put it in a photo pack with ten other pictures, and presented the photo pack to Mr. Russo the next day, May fourth. Mr. Russo immediately identified Fuller as the man who left his bar on the evening of April tenth and who had been in his bar all week.

"Detective Fleming then proceeded to find out who William Fuller was. Mr. Fuller lived in St. Albans, Florida, a city in northwest Florida, for those who are unfamiliar with it. For twenty years he worked for a company called Dynatron. The deceased victim, Roy Johnson, had been the founder and CEO of Dynatron for twenty years. In 2002, Mr. Johnson left the company, cashing in his stock and receiving a payout exceeding one hundred million dollars. In 2003, the company went bankrupt. Mr. Fuller lost his $750,000 pension plan, his health insurance, and his job. A year later his wife died of leukemia and his best friend, also an employee of Dynatron who lost everything, committed suicide.

"On April first, nine days before Mr. Johnson was murdered, the defendant, William Fuller, and his two children were forced to leave the family home, where he had lived with his wife and where his children had been born, due to foreclosure."

She was back at the podium now.

"I have described to you the State's case. William Fuller had a motive to kill Roy Johnson and the opportunity, and the evidence will show that he did so beyond a reasonable doubt."

Kevin watched the jurors follow her back to her chair with their eyes. It was not a good omen.

Statistically, studies showed that many jurors decide about guilt or innocence early in a case, despite the admonitions of the court to keep an open mind until the conclusion of all the evidence. Jeanette had set out to convince as many jurors as possible to make up their minds before she finished her opening statement and before Kevin had an opportunity to say a word.

Billy leaned over and whispered in Kevin's ear, "Jesus, she's good."

"Yeah," Kevin replied, trying to get his thoughts together.

"Mr. Wylie?" the judge said to Kevin, who immediately stood up.

"Thank you, Your Honor," he said as he approached the podium.

Kevin was a little over six feet tall with blue-gray eyes and thick brown hair. He was dressed in a blue suit that fit his athletic frame well. Like Jeanette, he was not hard on the eyes and he had an easygoing, affable manner in the courtroom. However, he knew affability was not going to cut it today. He had to give this jury something of substance to get their minds back open.

"Good morning, ladies and gentlemen. As you know, I represent Mr. William Fuller, the defendant in this case."

At that moment, as prearranged, Kevin turned to look at Billy and had Billy stand up and look at the jury. *"Try to make eye contact with each juror,"* Kevin had told him earlier. Billy did his best and then sat down as Kevin turned his attention back to the jurors.

"That was a very impressive opening by the prosecutor—

so straight and narrow, with times and dates. Very convincing. Unfortunately, this case, as most things in life, does not slip easily into an airtight package of dates and times and names. For instance, Ms. Truluc told you about William Fuller and his motive. It's the same motive as the twenty thousand other employees of Dynatron who lost everything—not to mention the shareholders, some of whom lost millions—might have had. How many of them drive gray cars that weren't bought last year and might, therefore, be considered old? Where were those twenty thousand other people on the night of April tenth?"

At that moment Jeanette stood up as he hoped she would. It was a weak argument he was making and he needed her help. He needed the jury to think she was trying to stop him from giving them information.

"Objection, Your Honor," Jeanette said. "This is not relevant. Twenty thousand other people are not on trial. Mr. Fuller is."

"Sustained," Judge Thorpe said, as Kevin knew he would.

"Thank you, Your Honor," he said to the judge as if he had won the point. He turned back to the jurors and smiled. It was time to bring up Randy Winters and Bobby Joe Sellers and their connection to Roy Johnson. He had to be very careful since he wasn't sure what that connection was.

"You already heard from counsel for the prosecution that Roy Johnson left his company, Dynatron, a year before it folded and took a hundred million dollars with him. You are also going to hear testimony that Roy Johnson left another place just before the curtain came down, so to speak. In 1982, Roy Johnson lived in Gladestown, Florida. He abruptly left one month before a massive drug bust that netted fifty percent of the male population of that town. The drug bust happened because of a tip from a confidential informant."

Jeanette was on her feet again as Kevin knew she would be.

"Objection, Your Honor. Relevancy."

"Approach," the judge said to the two lawyers who approached the bench out of hearing distance from the jury. The judge went right after Kevin.

"Tell me again what this drug bust in 1982 has to do with this case, Mr. Wylie?" he asked.

"The kingpin of that drug ring, Randy Winters, got out of jail April fourth of this year, less than a week before Roy Johnson was killed. We believe Roy Johnson may have been the confidential informant who caused the drug bust to occur, giving Winters a huge motive for revenge. I have Winters and his attorney, Bernie Stang, and Bobby Joe Sellers, who also received a significant prison sentence in that bust, under subpoena."

The judge just looked at Kevin and smiled. "Are you sure you know what you're doing? Because these jurors are not going to like it if these allegations turn out to be hogwash."

"I understand, Judge. I'm willing to take that risk."

"Well, Mr. Wylie," the judge said, "I knew you were going to come up with something to make this trial interesting. You're an experienced criminal lawyer, so I have to assume you know what you're doing and the danger you are exposing your client to if these allegations are not proven. Having said that, I'm going to overrule the objection and allow you to make the arguments you want to make. Ms. Truluc, I know that I did not give you the opportunity to speak. Would you like to put an objection on the record?"

"Yes, Your Honor. These tactics by Mr. Wylie are not only irrelevant, but I believe they are specifically designed to confuse the jury."

"You may be right, Counselor. Mr. Wylie has already confused me. I'm going to allow him to continue, however."

Kevin walked back to the podium and Jeanette took her seat.

Having gotten the green light from the judge, he tried to create some drama for the jury—a mystery that they could anticipate solving—something to keep their minds open and searching for answers.

"As I said, Roy Johnson left Gladestown a month before a massive drug bust in 1982 and started a major energy company, Dynatron. Where did he get the money to start that company? Was he the confidential informant in that drug bust? And here is some further evidence for you to consider: Randy Winters, whom I have subpoenaed to testify in this case, was arrested by the police in 1982 and spent over twenty years in prison as a result of the confidential informant's tip. He was released from prison on April fourth, 2005, *six days before Roy Johnson was killed*." Kevin spoke in a deep voice to emphasize the last part of that sentence.

He scanned the faces of each juror. They were listening. They weren't necessarily buying, but they were listening. That's all he needed at this point.

"And now let's skip to 2005. You are going to hear from an FBI agent, Harvey Booth, who is going to tell you that Roy Johnson was under criminal investigation at the time of his death, an investigation that began before Johnson left Dynatron.

"So, Roy Johnson left Gladestown in 1982 when the FBI was investigating drug trafficking in that town and just before arrests were made. And he left Dynatron in 2005—with a boatload of money, I might add—when the FBI was investigating both him and his company, and the company went belly-up a year later.

"As I said to you in the beginning of this conversation, this is not a simple narrow case of dates and times involving William Fuller. There was somebody with a much greater motive to kill Roy Johnson than William Fuller and the twenty thousand other employees of Dynatron whose lives were destroyed by Mr. Johnson.

"As I discussed with every one of you during jury selection, the State has the burden to prove its case beyond a reasonable doubt. The defendant has no burden to prove anything. You as jurors, however, need to listen to all the facts, not some narrow, concise, little package of facts that fit into the State's theory of the case, but *all* the facts. If there is a reasonable doubt as to who had the greater motive and opportunity to kill Roy Johnson, then you must acquit Mr. Fuller."

CHAPTER SIXTY-SIX

Kevin stayed in the courtroom over the lunch break and worked. He hardly ever ate during trial days, surviving mostly on snacks.

There were some good things about Jeanette's opening. She laid out her case so well that he had a pretty good idea who was coming and what they were going to say. Although the order of witnesses could change, the first day was probably set with Sylvia Johnson, the grieving widow, as the opening act followed by Carlisle and probably Freddie Jenkins who, potentially, was the most important witness in the case.

Sylvia Johnson was not the typical distressed widow coming into court to testify about the murder of her beloved husband. The jury already knew that she had married a snake and there was at least a hint already that this marriage had been more about money than love. Kevin wanted to cement that point a little more but he had to be careful. She was still a widow, and a beautiful one at that.

Judge Thorpe called the proceedings to order at exactly one thirty. He had given the jury some extra time for lunch since it was the first day of testimony. Sitting in a courtroom all day, listening to lawyers and witnesses and the judge drone on and on, was a difficult task.

"Call your first witness, Ms. Truluc."

"Your Honor, the State calls Sylvia Johnson."

The bailiff left to retrieve the witness from the witness room and returned moments later.

Sylvia Johnson did not disappoint. She wore a black dress extending almost to the tops of her knees. However, it was snug enough to reveal her ample bosom and her firm figure. Her blonde hair was pulled back in a bun, showing the fine features of her face and neck. Kevin once again regretted his decision to pick *eight men* as jurors.

Jeanette took her through her paces, sticking to the facts as she laid them out in her opening. There were a few opportunities for drama, as when Sylvia described waking up and realizing that her husband had not come to bed.

"I almost started to panic right then," she said. "The worst fears go through your mind." Her eyes welled up. Kevin checked the jury. They were listening.

He reminded himself he had to be careful when it was his turn, although he needed to get something.

"Cross-examination, Mr. Wylie?"

"Thank you, Your Honor."

Kevin walked to the podium, which was now facing the witness rather than the jury.

"As I understand your testimony, Mrs. Johnson, you married your husband a little over two years ago, correct?"

"That's correct."

"So that was after he had bailed out of Dynatron and received a hundred-million-dollar golden parachute, correct?"

"It was after he had left the company. I don't know what his severance package was."

"Really?"

"Really."

"You did know he was wealthy, though, didn't you?"

"He was the chief executive officer of a major company. Yes, I knew he was wealthy."

"Had Dynatron gone under before you were married?"

Jeanette was on her feet. "Objection, Your Honor. Relevancy."

"What does this question or any of the other questions you've asked so far have to do with any issue in this case, Mr. Wylie?" the judge asked.

They pranced her in here as the grieving widow. I oughta be able to take a few shots at her, Kevin wanted to say.

"I'll withdraw the question, Your Honor."

"Fine. Let's move along."

Kevin could see this cross-examination was getting him nowhere. The jury had enough information to make its own conclusion about Sylvia Johnson. He decided to let her go.

"I have no further questions, Your Honor."

Jeanette had no follow-up questions.

"Call your next witness," the judge barked. He was getting impatient already.

"The State calls Carlisle Buchanan."

Jeanette started Carlisle's testimony off with his boat ride into the swamp and his initial discovery. She then took him through the second excursion with Vern Fleming and established the chain of custody for the pieces of black cloth and silk shirt and Roy Johnson's wallet found in the swamp. When she had introduced those items into evidence, she had some further questions of "Professor" Buchanan.

"Do you spend a lot of time out on the water, Mr. Buchanan?"

"I'm out most days. Been on the water my whole life."

"In and around Gladestown?"

"Yes, ma'am."

"Have you seen a lot of alligators?"

"Yes, ma'am—hundreds if not thousands."

"Have you ever seen an alligator kill anything?"

"Sure. I've seen dogs get snatched, otters, birds—you name it."

"How about humans?"

"I've never seen it, but I know it happens. More humans are killed by alligators than sharks."

"When an alligator kills an animal, does it kill it for food?"

Kevin was on his feet. "Objection, Your Honor, Ms. Truluc is asking expert testimony from this witness, but she has not established that he is an expert, nor has she tendered him as an expert."

Kevin did not want to make the objection. He had some expert questions of his own to ask Carlisle now that he was a witness. However, he needed to put objections on the record so he would have a basis for appeal in the event Billy was convicted.

Like everybody else, Judge Thorpe seemed to be enjoying Carlisle's testimony. He was resting his head in his right hand, leaning over, listening intently, when Kevin raised his objection.

"Overruled, Mr. Wylie. The witness is testifying from his own experience. You can continue, Ms. Truluc."

Jeanette repeated her question.

"Usually," Carlisle answered. "Like all animals, an alligator will kill if it is threatened as well."

"How does it kill?"

"You mean the method?"

"Yeah."

"It rips and thrashes and tears the limbs apart."

Kevin saw some of the jurors wincing. Jeanette was being very effective with Carlisle.

"Let's say it kills an otter. Does it eat it right there and leave the remains?"

"No. Alligators have what's called gator holes. They take whatever they kill back and store it in the gator hole."

Professor Buchanan went on like that for another hour, telling the jury about the ecosystem of the Everglades and the drought that year and how hungry the gators were. And—over Kevin's strenuous objection—what probably happened to Roy Johnson.

"They probably ripped him limb from limb and stored his remains in dozens of gator holes."

"Would that account for why there are no remains of Roy Johnson?"

"That and the Burmese pythons."

"What are the Burmese pythons?"

"Objection, Your Honor. Again, this is a fact witness, not an expert. Counsel is asking for an expert opinion."

"Overruled."

"There are thousands of pythons in the Everglades now. They swallow things whole. There was a picture in the *Miami Herald* last year of a python that died trying to swallow an alligator whole. Pythons are like vacuum cleaners. If any part of Roy Johnson got away from the gators, a python probably sucked it up. That's why there are no remains."

Jeanette ended her questioning after that statement.

"Cross-examination, Mr. Wylie."

"Thank you, Your Honor." Kevin stood at the podium and looked at Carlisle, who gave him a smile of recognition. Carlisle was one of the few witnesses who was not a prosecution witness or a defense witness. He was there to tell the truth.

"You know the water around Gladestown like the back of your hand, is that correct?"

"I'd say that's accurate."

"Are there other people in Gladestown who have your knowledge of the water and the ecosystem and the alligators?"

"Oh, sure, tons of them. We are a fishing village."

"Do you know Randy Winters?"

"I know who he is."

"You know he was in jail for twenty years for marijuana smuggling?"

"Yes, sir."

"Does he presently live in Gladestown?"

"Yes."

"Is he one of those people who has knowledge of the water, alligators, and how things work out there in the swamp?"

"Definitely. He was a fisherman his whole life. That's why he was such a good smuggler."

"How about Bobby Joe Sellers? Do you know him?"

"Again, I know who he is."

"You know he was in jail for quite a number of years for marijuana smuggling?"

"Yes, sir."

"Does he presently live in Gladestown?"

"Yes."

"Is he one of those people who has knowledge of the water, the alligators, and the swamp?"

"Yes."

"So if Randy Winters or Bobby Joe Sellers hit somebody with an automobile and knocked them into the swamp, they would have the same knowledge about what would happen to that body as you, wouldn't they?"

Jeanette was on her feet before Kevin finished the question. "Objection, Your Honor. This is pure speculation. It has nothing to do with the facts in this case. And it is beyond any expertise this witness has."

"Sustained," Judge Thorpe bellowed as he looked directly at Kevin.

"Your Honor, may I be heard?" Kevin asked.

"No, you may not, Counsel. I have ruled. You can take the issue up with the appellate court, but I will tell you now—stick to questions within the rules of evidence and don't attempt to make a mockery of this courtroom."

Kevin was livid. "May we approach, Your Honor?" he asked politely.

"Come on." Thorpe knew what was coming.

When everybody was there, including the court reporter, Kevin let him have it. "Your Honor, I am moving for a mistrial, and I am requesting that you remove yourself from this case because of your obvious bias and contempt for me. A man is on trial for murder here, and your blatant attack on his lawyer's motivations and competence in front of the jury is highly prejudicial. On the other hand, you let the prosecution treat this man as an expert witness without qualifying him." Kevin wanted to add a few other choice adjectives but he stopped right there.

Judge Thorpe didn't even consider giving Jeanette a chance to say anything. He ripped right back into Kevin.

"The only one digging a hole for your client, Mr. Wylie, is you. You've got so many theories going on in this case you don't even know what they are. I know what you're doing and Ms. Truluc knows what you're doing. You're trying to confuse the jury. You're asking questions you know are objectionable and don't need to be answered. The question creates the confusion. That's unethical, Counsel, and I'm not going to allow it in my courtroom. Your motion for a mistrial is denied as is your motion for me to remove myself. And if you continue in this vein, I'm going to hold you in contempt. Now get back there and start asking proper questions."

If nothing else, Kevin had just established a good appellate record. And his question was out there before the jury.

"I have no further questions, Your Honor," Kevin said when he reached the podium.

"Redirect, Ms. Truluc?"

"No, Your Honor."

"The witness is excused. It's approximately four forty-five so I think we'll call it a day."

The judge instructed the jury about not talking about the case with one another or anybody and not watching the news or reading the paper before he dismissed them to return to their hotel.

CHAPTER SIXTY-SEVEN

The case dominated the evening news in Verona and several cable outlets and was a prominent feature on the major networks as well. The combination of Roy Johnson's status as a captain of industry and possibly an old drug dealer was too sexy to pass up. Then there were the pythons and the potential for a mystery murderer.

It was the perfect storm where news, entertainment, and drama collided.

Everybody in the courtroom, including the press and the jury, knew that Kevin and the judge were not getting along. Although nobody knew what was being said at the sidebar conferences, their personal conflict was additional fodder for the news stations.

Kevin called his father that night to give him a rundown of the day's events. Tom had already seen the news.

"It sounds like you and the judge are going at it hot and heavy," Tom remarked.

"I just asked for a mistrial and for him to get off the case, and he told me I was unethical and threatened to hold me in contempt."

"Wow!" Tom said. "I can't believe I'm missing this. How's Billy holding up?"

"He's doing okay."

"Who's on the stand tomorrow?"

"I think she is going to start the day with Freddie Jenkins."

"You've got to get at him, Kevin. He's the key to their whole case."

"I know, Dad. I know."

CHAPTER SIXTY-EIGHT

The crowd outside was larger on Friday morning and it was abuzz with excitement. Conspiracy and murder lingered in the air with stories of pythons swallowing alligators, fireworks in the courtroom, and marijuana smugglers. No soap opera could measure up to this.

Judge Thorpe had obviously watched the news. He was not a happy man as he stormed into the courtroom at exactly nine o'clock.

"Do we have anything to discuss before we bring the jury in?" he said to the lawyers.

"No, Your Honor," they both replied.

"Bring the jury in," he told the bailiff.

"Call your first witness, Counsel," he told Jeanette as soon as the jurors were seated.

Kevin could tell he was ready to explode at any moment.

"The State calls Frederick Jenkins."

Freddie Jenkins had a jacket and tie on, and he had made an attempt to comb his unruly mop of sandy hair, but none of it had worked. The jacket, a tan corduroy, was too big and the tie was crooked. He looked like a tall, gangly high school kid with a jacket and tie on.

Freddie had taken to heart Carlisle's admonitions to him after their first meeting. He had written down his statement. He had repeated it at the sheriff's office. He had reread it many times since then to the point where he knew it verbatim. Jeanette took him through that statement, asking almost the same questions Carlisle had asked.

When she had gone through his entire testimony, Jeanette produced an easel and several blown-up photos of Gladestown Road. She then had Freddie come down from the stand to explain each picture to the jury as she put it on the easel.

"Now this first picture, State's Exhibit 21A, can you tell the jury what that picture shows?"

"That's Gladestown Road at the spot where I saw the man from the driver's seat in my pickup where I was parked in the Chamber of Commerce parking lot—except it's during the day."

"Who took that picture?"

"I did. You were there with me. It was last Monday, a week ago."

"And on the night of April tenth when you witnessed the man getting hit, as you already testified to, was this the exact position you were in?"

"Yes."

"How far away were you?"

"Twenty or thirty yards."

"Now let's look at 21B." She put another picture on the easel. "Can you tell the jury who took that picture?"

"I did and it's from the same spot as 21A, except it's at night."

"Tell the jury what is in this picture to your knowledge."

Freddie pointed to the middle of the picture. "This light—you can see it covers the road." He was talking directly to the jury and doing a very good job. "That's from car headlights. Ms. Truluc had a car there similar to the one I saw the night of April tenth. The car she had there whose headlights are in this picture was a 1995 gray Toyota Corolla. I even looked at the registration. Now, you can see the car itself over here to the right. It's pretty dark."

"Is that what you saw on the night of April tenth?"

"Well, I saw a similar car and the headlights shone just like what is in this picture."

"What else is in that picture?"

"There's a man with dark black hair over to your left."

Jeanette pulled the easel closer to the jury. Kevin stood and walked over to where the jury was sitting so he could see what they were looking at. The man was clearly visible in the car headlights. He had black hair and a light-colored shirt just as Freddie had testified to earlier.

"He's got a light shirt on too as you all can see," Freddie continued. "And he is walking back toward Gladestown on the left-hand side of the road, facing traffic."

"How did this picture come about?"

"We went out to Gladestown Road at approximately eleven, eleven thirty at night—you, me, and some other people from the sheriff's department. I sat in my pickup where I was on the night of April tenth with a radio that you gave me and I told you down on Gladestown Road where the car was and where the man was. And when everything was in the same position as it was on the night of April tenth, I shot the picture."

"The night this picture was taken, was it any different than the night of April tenth?"

"It was a lot hotter." Some of the jurors smiled as did Jeanette, and a few brave souls in the gallery actually laughed.

"Other than that?"

"No. They both were clear starry nights like most nights in Gladestown."

Jeanette put up State's Exhibit 23C. "Can you tell the jury about this picture?"

"It's a picture I took the same night from the same place, only it shows the car on the left side of the road about to hit the man walking back to town. His back is to the car. The car had come all the way from the right side to the left side of the road."

"Is this what you saw on the night of April tenth?"

"Yes."

"Exactly?"

"Yes."

"No further questions, Your Honor."

"Cross-examination, Mr. Wylie?"

"Yes, Your Honor." Kevin walked to the podium. Jeanette and Freddie had just put on a clinic. Freddie turned out to be a great witness, no doubt with a lot of help from Jeanette. Kevin had to do something to discredit him. Freddie was back in the witness chair.

"Mr. Jenkins, I'm reading the police report here by a Mr. Carlisle Buchanan—do you know who that is?"

"Yes. He's with the sheriff's department. He's the first person who interviewed me."

"He says that a woman named Rosie heard you talking about Roy Johnson's death at her restaurant. Do you know Rosie?"

"Yes."

"Have you been in her restaurant before?"

"Everybody goes to Rosie's. It's the only restaurant in town."

A couple of the jury members chuckled. They liked Freddie.

"It says here in this report that you told some of your friends at Rosie's that you were in the Chamber of Commerce parking lot necking with Becky Yates on the evening of April tenth, is that true?"

"Is what true?"

"Let's take it one at a time. Is it true that you told your friends you were necking with Becky Yates in the Chamber of Commerce parking lot on the evening of April tenth at the time you saw this man being hit by the car?"

"Yeah. That's what I told them."

"Now, is it true that you were actually necking with Becky Yates in the Chamber of Commerce parking lot on the evening of April tenth?

"No. That's not true. Becky wasn't there."

"So you lied to your friends?"

"Well, I wouldn't call it a lie."

"What would you call it, Mr. Jenkins?"

"It was a story. I didn't want my friends to ask me why I didn't do nothing to save the man so I said Becky was there in case they asked. Then I could say she freaked out or something."

"So you told your friends a story that wasn't true."

"Yeah."

"Why did you tell your friends you saw this hit-and-run?"

"Why?"

"Yeah. Why?"

"I don't know."

"Is it because it was all over the news and you wanted them to know you were part of it?"

"I guess so."

"And you made up the story about Becky so you wouldn't look bad when you told them you were there, correct?"

"That's right."

"Did you make up anything else?"

"No."

"You didn't make up a story that you saw something that you really didn't see, did you?"

"No."

"You're sure?"

"Yeah."

"You only made up one story?"

"Yeah."

"Now, Officer Buchanan came to interview you at your high school on that first occasion, correct?"

"Yeah."

"I have his report right here. It says that when he first asked you about the hit-and-run on April tenth, you said you didn't know anything about it. Is that true? Is that what you told Officer Buchanan?"

"Yes. But I told him the truth after Mr. Shay left."

"Who is Mr. Shay?"

"He's the principal."

"And on the day you met with Officer Buchanan, your principal, Mr. Shay, was present, is that correct?"

"He was there for a little bit, but then he left. That's when I told Officer Buchanan the truth."

"So when you said you didn't know anything about the hit-and-run that wasn't the truth, was it?"

"No."

"That was just another story you told."

"Yeah, I guess so."

"You also told Officer Buchanan that Becky called you that night and told you to meet her at the Chamber of Commerce parking lot, is that correct?"

"Yes."

"And then you told him that Becky denied that she ever called you that night, correct?"

"Yeah. She denied it to me."

"And even though Becky denied ever calling you, you insist that she did, correct?"

"Yes."

"That's not just another story?"

"No."

"The car you saw that night—the one you identified in the pictures here as a 1995 Toyota—is it correct you told Officer Buchanan you thought it was a Honda?"

"That's true. I don't know the difference between a Honda and a Toyota. It was a small car and it looked old and gray. It could have been either make."

"Or it could have been a Kia or a Hyundai or any one of a dozen other models?"

"I guess so."

"How do you know the car was gray?"

"At the corner of Gladestown Road, there's a big streetlight. I could see it clearly there."

"Those streetlights give off kind of a yellowy light at night, don't they?"

"Yeah."

"Do you know if you can see color under those streetlights?"

"I'm not sure I know what you mean."

"I mean, do you know if every car no matter what the color looks gray under those streetlights?"

"I don't know. I don't think so."

"You didn't run that experiment the night you were out there taking pictures with the state attorney, did you?"

"No, sir."

"And you don't know who was driving that car?"

"No, sir."

"And you don't know who the person was who was hit on the road that night?"

"No, sir."

"You just know it was a man with dark hair wearing a light shirt."

"Yes, sir."

"No further questions, Your Honor."

"Redirect, Ms. Truluc?"

"Yes, Your Honor. Thank you."

Jeanette walked to the podium. She knew Kevin had taken a huge chunk out of Freddie Jenkins's hide. She also knew that the State's case depended in large part on Freddie's testimony. She had to rehabilitate him.

"How old are you, Mr. Jenkins?"

"Seventeen."

"Your friends call you Freddie, is that right?"

"Yes, ma'am."

"Freddie, I want you to look at the defendant, William Fuller." Freddie looked directly at Billy. "Do you know him?" Jeanette asked.

"No, ma'am."

"Do you have any reason to want to see him convicted of a crime he didn't commit?"

"No, ma'am."

"And you realize your testimony here today could convict him of first-degree murder?"

"Yes, ma'am."

"Do you understand how serious that is?"

"Yes, ma'am."

"Are you here today to impress your friends?"

"No, ma'am."

"Freddie, if you made a mistake, if you really didn't see anything the night of April tenth—now is the time to tell the truth. Do you understand?"

"Yes, ma'am."

"Tell the jury what you actually saw with your own eyes on Gladestown Road the night of April tenth."

"I saw a man walking back to town. I saw a car come from the right side of the road over to the left side and strike the man in the back, knocking him into the swamp."

"Are you sure?"

"Sure as I'm sitting here."

"No further questions, Your Honor."

Kevin wasn't sure all the points he had scored on cross-examination had been wiped away, but it was a damn effective redirect. He only had to look at the jury to see that.

"Call your next witness," Judge Thorpe bellowed.

"The State calls Detective Vern Fleming."

Vern wore a tan summer suit into the courtroom that morning. He knew enough to leave his flyboy shades at home. Jeanette took him through his work at the Verona Inn, where he established that Billy's car, a 2000 gray Toyota Corolla, was in the parking lot from April seventh to the eleventh, although he was not registered at the hotel under his own name. However, there was a Tom Jones who paid in cash and produced no identification.

Vern then told the jury how he got Billy's driver's license picture, put it in a photo pack with ten other pictures, and showed it to the bartender, George Russo. Russo identified Billy immediately. Jeanette had Vern identify the photo pack, introduced it into evidence, and had no more questions. For some reason, she wanted Vern on and off the witness stand very quickly.

Kevin had a few questions on cross-examination.

"Signing a hotel register with an alias is not a crime, is it, Detective Fleming?"

"I don't think so. I'm not sure."

"You've been a cop for many years, correct?"

"Yes."

"Worked a lot of different beats besides homicide, correct?"

"Yes."

"Is it fair to say that people have been signing hotel registers with an alias for years, for a lot of different reasons that might not necessarily be criminal in nature?"

Jeanette was on her feet. "Objection. Relevancy."

"Overruled."

"I'm not so sure that's true anymore. People used to do that when they were having an extramarital affair or something. Now nobody cares. Besides, most hotels only take credit cards."

"It may not be as common but it still happens?"

"If it does, it would be very infrequent."

"And the most obvious alias is John Smith, for example, is that correct?"

"I don't know."

"Is Jones the second most obvious?"

"I don't know that either."

"If you have bad credit and you don't have a credit card, how do you pay for a hotel room?"

"I don't know."

"Wouldn't one way be cash?"

"I suppose."

"You know from your own investigation that William Fuller had credit problems, correct?"

"Yes."

"And he lived in St. Albans and he had two children who lived with him and who he was raising, correct?"

"Yes."

"And your investigation showed that William Fuller, who

had two kids in St. Albans, came to Verona; registered at the Verona Inn as Tom Jones; paid cash; parked his car in the parking lot; and went to the Last Stop, the bar next to the Verona Inn, every night and got drunk, correct?"

"In part."

"Let's stay with that part for now—is there anything criminal in that behavior?"

"No."

"Now, Verona is sixty miles from Gladestown, correct?"

"That's correct."

"And is it correct that the bartender, George Russo, told you that William Fuller left the bar, the Last Stop, which is in Verona right next to the Verona Inn, somewhere around eleven o'clock on the evening of April tenth?"

"That's correct."

"And according to the bartender he'd been doing that for a week—drinking every night and then leaving the bar?"

"That's correct."

"And is it also correct that nobody on the evening of April tenth or at any time ever saw William Fuller in Gladestown?"

"That's not correct. Frederick Jenkins saw his car on Gladestown Road later that evening."

"How much later?"

"Nobody has an accurate timetable. Mr. Jenkins puts it at eleven thirty approximately and Mr. Russo puts it at eleven approximately that he left. So if each one is off ten minutes or so, the times are pretty consistent."

"They are?"

"Yes, in my opinion."

"You just stated a moment ago that Freddie Jenkins saw my client's car on Gladestown Road. That's not correct, is it?"

"Not exactly."

"And to be exact, Freddie Jenkins didn't know if he saw a Toyota or a Honda or some other make or model. Correct?"

"Yes."

"So, Freddie Jenkins, a seventeen-year-old high school student, sees what he describes as a gray car that he saw under a streetlight at night, and that's your basis for concluding that William Fuller was in Gladestown on the night of April tenth and killed Roy Johnson?"

"That and the fact that Fuller had a very strong motive."

"So did a lot of other people. Do you know where they were that night?"

Jeanette was on her feet again. "Objection."

"Sustained."

"Do you know if any of them were within sixty miles of Gladestown at eleven o'clock at night?"

"Objection."

"Sustained." The judge looked directly at Kevin and pointed his right index finger. "Counsel, I'm warning you. I sustained the last question. You should have known better than to ask the same question again."

Kevin stared right back at him. If he was going to make accusations in front of the jury, Kevin was going to respond. "It was a different question, Your Honor."

"No, it wasn't. Now proceed."

Kevin paused for a minute. He had been asking the last few questions rapid-fire, and he wanted to let both the questions and the answers sink in before proceeding.

"After you identified Mr. Fuller as a suspect, did you ever attempt to test his car to see if it was involved in this hit-and-run?"

"Yes, we did."

"When was that?"

"May tenth. It was a Tuesday, I believe."

"And what did you do?"

"We impounded it, took it to the department, and took it apart."

"And what did you find?"

"Nothing."

"You didn't find anything linking this vehicle to the hit-and-run in Gladestown on April tenth, 2005, correct?"

"That's correct."

"No further questions."

"Redirect, Ms. Truluc?"

"Yes, Your Honor. Thank you." Jeanette walked to the podium without any notes.

"Did you expect to find anything when you checked the vehicle out?"

"No. It was a month later. You've got to follow through and check it out but I didn't expect to find any evidence. We may not have found anything if we got the car the next day."

"Why do you say that?"

"If you hit somebody and, say, knock them into the swamp as in this case, there might be nothing on the car to show that—no dent, no clothing, no piece of skin—nothing."

"No further questions, Your Honor."

"Okay. Let's break for lunch at this point," the judge said. It was ten minutes to twelve. "We'll reconvene at one o'clock." After the jurors had filed out, he addressed the lawyers.

"Ms. Truluc, when do you think you'll be finished?"

"I may be done this afternoon, Judge. I've got five witnesses, maybe six, although my questioning to most of them will be short. Mr. Booth, the FBI man, appears by video deposition. I don't know for sure if I'll finish because I don't know how long Mr. Wylie's cross-examination of the other witnesses is going to be."

"Fair enough. If you have some objections to Mr. Wylie's cross of Mr. Booth, you both may want to prepare those at lunchtime and we'll take them up before we show the video of Mr. Booth's deposition to the jury.

"Okay. If Ms. Truluc finishes this afternoon, Mr. Wylie, be prepared to start your case on Monday morning. I'll hear any motions then too. If she doesn't finish today, I still want you to be prepared to start on Monday, Mr. Wylie."

"Yes, Your Honor," Kevin replied.

Sitting in the courtroom eating his Snickers bar after everybody had left for lunch, Kevin wondered about what had happened that morning and what was about to occur. He was somewhat surprised by Jeanette's brief redirect of Vern Fleming, but as he thought about it, he realized that he hadn't really gotten to Vern at all. As for this afternoon, he wondered who the five, *possibly* six witnesses were.

She's going to call the other FBI man, he thought. *She's going to refute the allegation that Roy Johnson was the confidential informant. She's going to open that door.*

CHAPTER SIXTY-NINE

Call your next witness," Judge Thorpe said at approximately five minutes after one.

"The State calls George Russo."

George Russo was a thick man about six feet tall but in good shape overall. He looked like he probably played guard on the football team in high school. The beard he wore when he first spoke with Carlisle and later with Vern was gone. He answered Jeanette's questions directly and without any commentary, but he was clearly nervous. He told Jeanette that he was the bartender at the Last Stop and how this man came in every night and drank heavily during the week before April tenth, 2005.

Kevin initially suspected that they had prepared beforehand. He became sure when they reached that dramatic moment of every criminal trial.

"Do you see the man who came in the bar every night and drank heavily during the week before and including April tenth in this courtroom?"

"I do."

"Can you point him out for the jury?"

George Russo raised his right arm and pointed his finger directly at Billy. "That's him right there. That's the man." It looked like a scene from a movie.

"What time did he leave the bar on April tenth?"

"Around eleven."

"Why do you say that?"

"I don't know why but I remember the news coming on a little bit after he left."

"The eleven o'clock news?"

"Yes."

"So he left before eleven?"

"Yeah, but not too much before. Maybe ten minutes or so."

"What was his condition when he left?"

"He'd had a few but he was coherent."

"Was he friendly?"

"No, he was agitated. I remember just before he left, I was down at that end of the bar serving some customers and I heard him talking to himself. He said something like 'I'm gonna kill him tonight.'"

"Where did he go? Do you know?"

"No, I don't."

"Do you know if he had a car?"

"Yes, he did, a gray Toyota."

"Did you see him get in it that night?"

"I did. Right after he left the bar."

Before finishing up, she took him through his decision to drive over to Gladestown and report Billy's behavior to Officer Carlisle Buchanan.

"When I read that kid's statement in the paper, especially the part about the old gray car, I thought this might be the guy so I drove over and reported it."

"No further questions, Your Honor."

"Cross-examination, Mr. Wylie?"

"Yes, Your Honor."

There was something about George Russo's nervousness that

bothered Kevin. Perhaps he was just nervous because he was in a courtroom speaking in a public setting. Perhaps there was another reason. Kevin was going to try to find out.

"So, Mr. Russo, your testimony is that Mr. Fuller came into your bar every night for a week, correct?"

"Yes."

"And I think you also testified that a lot of your clientele were guests from the hotel, correct?"

"That's correct."

"Ever see any other guests stay for a week and drop in for a drink every night?"

"I'm sure there were, but I don't recall."

"You don't recall. Mr. Fuller is the only person you recall, is that correct?"

"Yes."

"Did you work last night?"

"Yes, but not at the Last Stop."

"I have some records here that show that you worked at the Last Stop from April fifth to May sixth, is that accurate?"

"Sounds about right."

"Do you want to look at the records to make sure?"

"No. That sounds about right."

"So, you didn't see Mr. Fuller come in the bar for a week because you were only employed five days before the event in question, correct?"

"I started work on Tuesday, which was the fifth, so I saw him come in for four straight days. Maybe I should have clarified that."

"And you walked into the sheriff's office in Gladestown on May fourth, correct?

"Sounds right."

"And you voluntarily left your job on May sixth and haven't worked there since, correct?"

"Yes."

"So you came to the Last Stop, let's say, six days before Roy Johnson was killed and left two days after you gave your testimony to the police, correct?"

Jeanette was on her feet. "Objection. Asked and answered."

"Sustained." The judge looked at Kevin. "That's a summary, Mr. Wylie. You'll have your chance for a summary in closing."

"Thank you, Your Honor," Kevin replied. He'd already had enough of Judge Thorpe. However, he would need him when it came to his crucial witnesses. Kevin had a few more questions for George Russo.

"Did Mr. Fuller drive his car into the bar?"

Judge Thorpe glared at Kevin. Jeanette didn't make an objection, though.

"Of course not," Russo replied.

"The parking lot is outside the bar?"

"Yeah, but you can see it."

"And for some reason during your first four days on the job, you had time to not only notice Mr. Fuller and give an accurate description to the police, you noticed what kind of car he was driving, including the color and the make, correct?"

"Yes. It wasn't very busy..."

Kevin cut him off. "No further questions."

Jeanette did not have any follow-up.

"Next witness," Judge Thorpe said before Russo was even out the door.

"The State calls Maria Perez."

The bailiff left the courtroom and returned moments later with a young Mexican woman. After he administered the oath, Maria took the stand. Her English was not very good, and she kept apologizing to Jeanette when she asked Jeanette to repeat certain questions and to the jury when particular jurors asked her to repeat her answers. Eventually, however, they muddled through. Maria was the chambermaid who cleaned Billy's room every day at the Verona Inn. She identified Billy as he sat in the courtroom and she added without prompting from Jeanette that he was a very nice man.

When it came time for cross-examination, Kevin stood up and thanked Maria for coming down and testifying but said he had no questions for her. Maria had no stake in this case at all. She had no reason to be anything but truthful. There was nothing in her testimony that needed to be clarified. As an experienced trial lawyer, Kevin understood there was absolutely no benefit in cross-examining this witness.

The next witness was somewhat of a surprise, but not really. Jeanette needed Becky Yates to establish conclusively for the jury that Freddie was not necking with her on the night of April tenth. There was a downside to her testimony, however, and Kevin immediately brought it out on cross-examination.

"Freddie says you called him to meet you on the night of April tenth. Did you?"

"No."

"Had you been out there at the Chamber of Commerce on other nights?"

"Yeah. We were out there on Friday and Saturday night, the eighth and ninth."

"Around what time?"

"Eleven thirty to twelve thirty maybe."

"Did you call him on those days?"

"I think he called me one night and I called him the other."

"Did you ever talk to Freddie about the night of the tenth?"

"I sure did. He said I called him and I told him I never called him that night."

"Could you have been mistaken?"

"No. It was a Sunday night. I wouldn't call him on a Sunday night."

They did the video of Harvey Booth after that. Jeanette had laid out for the judge all her objections to specific questions and answers. The judge listened to her with a smile on his face. The jury had been removed for this argument. Judge Thorpe ruled immediately after she finished her argument. "As I told you the day Mr. Booth's deposition was taken, Ms. Truluc, I'm inclined to give Mr. Wylie some leeway in defending his client. Whether his strategy is correct or not remains to be seen, but I'm going to let all the testimony in."

The judge told the jury they were to treat the video testimony of Harvey Booth the same as if Harvey were actually in the courtroom testifying.

Everybody watched and listened in rapt silence as Harvey's video testimony was played for the jury. Jeanette got in the information she needed about Billy's retirement account and what he lost. Then it was time for Kevin's cross-examination. He watched the jury carefully: He saw the moment when they sat up in their seats and focused their attention more intently.

"And is it accurate that Roy Johnson at the time of his death was under criminal investigation?"

"Yes."

"For what specifically?"

"No indictment had been drawn, but basically, it was for defrauding investors, employees, insider trading—you name it."

"Was an indictment imminent?"

"I'm not sure what you mean by 'imminent.' I can say that it was certain."

"Mr. Johnson had an attorney, didn't he?"

"Yes."

"And that was Bernie Stang?"

"Yes."

"Do you know if Mr. Stang had any negotiations with the U.S. attorney regarding this matter?"

"No, I don't."

"When did the criminal investigation of Dynatron begin?"

"I can't say for sure. I know we had been looking into the company's finances for about a year."

"Before Roy Johnson left the company?"

"Possibly."

"Were you aware that Mr. Johnson received a severance package of approximately one hundred million dollars when he left the company?"

"Yes. I was."

"When you reviewed all the accounting information for Dynatron, were you able to determine where all of the earnings of the company went?"

"No."

"And why not?"

"Dynatron, like most major corporations in the United States, had offshore accounts in the Cayman Islands. Tax havens. We could not get at those accounts. We could trace money that went to those accounts but not money that was earned or money that was withdrawn."

"So Roy Johnson could have received more than one hundred million dollars?"

"Possibly."

CHAPTER SEVENTY

You could hear a pin drop in the courtroom when Harvey Booth's testimony ended. Kevin knew he had the jury's attention. They were following along like bloodhounds. The question was whether he could produce. They knew now that Roy Johnson had bailed out of his company to the tune of *at least* one hundred million dollars before criminal indictments came down. It was up to Kevin to make the connection—to get them to believe he had done something similar in 1982 and stolen Sellers's and Winters's money, giving Winters the motive to kill him when he got out of prison. That was the battle yet to be waged.

Testimony was not over for the day, however. Nor was the drama.

The next witness was Anne Lyons, Billy's elderly next-door neighbor in St. Albans. Jeanette was going to use her to put the last nail in the coffin, so to speak—to talk about Billy and the kids having to move out of the family home on April first, six days before Billy went to the Verona Inn and nine days before Roy Johnson's murder. Jeanette tried to narrowly tailor the questions to Ms. Lyons, but she was only partially successful. Anne Lyons gave Billy a face, a heart, and a soul, something no other witness had done to that point. Even though Jeanette never asked the question, Anne told the jury about Billy.

"How do you know they foreclosed on Mr. Fuller's house?" Jeanette asked.

"Billy told me himself. He was so strong that day. He had the kids with him. I think he was holding it all in for them. When Laurie died he came to my house and sat on my couch and wept openly. That day they moved out of their home, leaving all those memories behind, had to be almost as tough. But Billy held it all in."

Kevin watched the jury. They were all looking at Billy, who was struggling to keep himself composed as tears streamed down his face.

Jeanette had no further questions and Kevin had no cross-examination.

"It's four thirty, Ms. Truluc. Do you have another witness?" Judge Thorpe asked.

"I do, Your Honor."

"Do you think we can get him on and off in the next hour?"

"I do, Your Honor."

"Then let's proceed."

"The State calls Richard Bothwell."

The moment of truth had arrived. Richard Bothwell was the retired FBI agent who had headed up the task force that busted the drug ring in Gladestown in 1982.

Mr. Bothwell was a tall, slender man probably in his seventies. He swore to tell the truth and took the witness stand.

"Where are you employed, Mr. Bothwell?" Jeanette asked.

"I'm retired."

"Where were you employed?"

"I was a special agent with the FBI for thirty-five years."

"There has been some discussion during this trial about a drug bust in Gladestown, Florida, in 1982—do you know anything about that?"

"Yes, I was in charge of the operation."

"There was statement made here in court that the bust occurred after a tip from a confidential informant. Is that true?"

"Yes."

"There was also a statement made here in court that Roy Johnson, the victim in this murder trial, may have been the confidential informant. Is that true?"

"No. I knew the confidential informant and spoke with him personally. I actually kept up with him over the years. He died two years ago in an unfortunate accident. It was definitely not Roy Johnson."

"No further questions."

Judge Thorpe had that smile on his face again. "Cross-examination, Mr. Wylie?"

"Yes, Your Honor. Thank you, Your Honor. Mr. Rothwell, who was the confidential informant?"

"I can't give that information."

"Why not? You just testified that the person is dead."

"His family is still alive. They could still be harmed or affected in other ways by the fact that he was a government informant."

"Are you saying that somebody could retaliate against them?"

"Yes."

Jeanette was slow to get to her feet but she finally stood up and objected.

"Approach the bench," the judge told the two lawyers.

"What are you doing, Mr. Wylie?" he asked when everybody had arrived.

"I don't trust the government, Judge. I want to know who the confidential informant was so I can check to find out if he was a real person who died two years ago."

"You are taking this way too far, Mr. Wylie. And you're trying my patience."

"Look, Judge, Ms. Truluc brought this man in here and had him testify about the confidential informant. I'm allowed to test his credibility."

Kevin was forceful in his argument. He couldn't afford to lose on this issue.

The judge looked at Jeanette. "He makes a point, Counsel. You did raise this issue. The possibility of the family being affected by this disclosure, while serious, is outweighed by Mr. Wylie's obligation to defend his client and test every witness by vigorous cross-examination."

Yes! Kevin said to himself.

"Your Honor," Jeanette began, "the only reason Mr. Bothwell is here at all is because Mr. Wylie made the claim in his opening statement that Roy Johnson was the confidential informant. The State had to refute that claim.

"There is another reason why the name of the confidential informant should not be disclosed to the jury. The witness's credibility can be tested and satisfied by this disclosure being made to the court in chambers."

"What's this other reason?" the judge asked.

"For the record, Judge, if I reveal the name of the confidential informant to the court at sidebar, am I correct in assuming that I am not opening the door for counsel to use that name for any reason?"

"That's correct, Counsel. You're not opening any doors. Now tell me what this other reason is." Judge Thorpe was getting very impatient with Jeanette.

"I did not know these facts until I actually started preparing for this witness's testimony and for the testimony of Mr. Wylie's witnesses. You could even say that Mr. Wylie brought this to my attention. The confidential informant was a man named Scotch Buchanan, a well-known outdoorsman in these parts—"

"I know who Scotch Buchanan was," the judge interrupted.

"Scotch Buchanan died in an accident on April twentieth in 2003," Jeanette continued. "Bobby Joe Sellers was released from prison on April fifth of 2003. If Mr. Wylie can get that information out to the jury, which I believe he is trying to do, then he can attempt to show a pattern: The informant was killed in 2003 when Sellers got out of prison and Roy Johnson was killed in 2005 when Winters got out of prison.

"Mr. Wylie could not do this directly, Judge, because you would never let him. It's speculation that a jury could buy, but it's pure speculation. He's trying to do it indirectly by forcing me to disclose who the confidential informant was, thus opening the door for this evidence to come in."

Kevin was surprised as he listened to Jeanette's argument. He could not believe she had figured out his and Tom's strategy.

"Is what Ms. Truluc just said true, Mr. Wylie?"

"For the most part, Judge. I did not know for sure whether Roy Johnson or Scotch Buchanan was the confidential informant. However, if it turned out to be Scotch, as it has, then my strategy was exactly as Ms. Truluc laid it out."

A smile broke across Judge Thorpe's face. "What a smart strategy, Mr. Wylie, and it took equal brilliance on your part, Ms. Truluc, to figure it out. The dates themselves are troubling, however. Has anybody looked into Scotch Buchanan's death to determine if it really was an accident, Ms. Truluc?"

"Not that I am aware of, Judge. I certainly will see that it is done in the foreseeable future. However, this is all speculation at this time and it should not be part of this trial."

"I agree. Mr. Wylie, you know that this is not admissible evidence now that Ms. Truluc has made the objection and brought your strategy to light. However, I will tell you this: If your client is convicted and if your speculation about Mr. Sellers and Scotch

Buchanan turns out to be true, that would be newly discovered evidence and a basis for a new trial."

"Come on, Judge," Kevin said. "Once somebody is convicted they are behind the eight ball. Something may be newly discovered evidence but I still would have to show on appeal that it would have made a difference with the jury. You know how appellate courts are ruling these days on that issue. Let me present the evidence now. Let me give my client a fighting chance."

"I'm sorry, Mr. Wylie, I can't help you. The objection is sustained. You cannot inquire into the name of the confidential informant with this witness or any other witness. I know that destroys the defense you stated to this jury in your opening, but you still have other arguments to make. Now, do you have any more questions for this witness?"

"Yes, I do, Your Honor."

"Then you may proceed."

They returned to their respective positions and the judge told the jury that he had sustained the objection. Kevin continued his questions.

"How long had your investigation been going on before you made your bust, Mr. Bothwell?"

"About a year."

"The deceased, Mr. Johnson, was he ever part of your investigation?"

"He was."

"Did you consider him a principal in the drug operation?"

"I did."

"But he was never arrested?"

"No. We could never get anything on him. He left a month before the bust."

"Now, when you busted everybody and found the marijuana, did you uncover any large hidden caches of money?"

"No."

"Who were the ringleaders of the operation who you arrested?"

"Randy Winters and Bobby Joe Sellers."

"And you believe Roy Johnson was a ringleader as well?"

"Yes."

"Did you find any money at Winters's and Sellers's houses?"

"None to speak of."

Jeanette was on her feet again. This line of questioning was going too well for her to sit back and allow it.

"Objection, Your Honor. This is beyond the scope of direct examination."

"Overruled. You brought this witness into court, Ms. Truluc. Continue, Mr. Wylie."

"Did you ever entertain the idea that the money went with Roy Johnson?"

"Oh yeah. He started Dynatron soon after. But we never could trace the money to him."

"Did you ever try to get Winters and Sellers to talk about the money and where it went?"

"Yes, we did."

"Did you try and get them to implicate Roy Johnson?"

"Yes, we did."

"Did you offer lighter sentences for that information?"

"Yes."

"And is it accurate that they never gave you any information about where the money went or whether Roy Johnson was involved in the drug smuggling operation?"

"That's accurate."

"Do you remember who represented Winters and Sellers in their criminal case back then?"

"Of course I do."

"Who was that?"

"Bernie Stang."

"No further questions, Your Honor."

"Follow up, Ms. Truluc?"

Jeanette looked at Richard Bothwell like he was radioactive. She wasn't going near him anymore. "No, Your Honor."

"Do you have any further witnesses?"

"No, Your Honor. Not at this time."

"Okay, let's let our jury go and we can discuss scheduling issues for next week."

After the judge gave his usual instructions to the jury and they had left the room, he turned his attention back to the lawyers. "I take it, Ms. Truluc, that you are ready to rest your case."

"That may be true, Judge. I would like the weekend to think about it."

"Fair enough. Mr. Wylie, you still need to be prepared to start your case on Monday morning at nine o'clock, so get your witnesses notified."

"Yes, Your Honor."

"Anything else we need to take up?"

"No, Your Honor," Kevin replied.

"No, Your Honor," Jeanette replied.

CHAPTER SEVENTY-ONE

The guards gave Kevin a few minutes to talk with Billy after the courtroom was cleared. He was staying at the local jail and they could have talked over there, but this was a lot easier. The guards were like everybody else; once they spent a few days with Billy they liked him.

Kevin gave Billy the most optimistic assessment of their chances that he could.

"We're hanging in there, Billy. This is not over by a long shot."

Kevin called Tom that night to give him a rundown of the day's events.

"I can't believe she sniffed out our strategy."

"It happens," Tom replied. "She's a damn good lawyer. Let's deal with what we have. How do you assess things?"

"Well, I think the jury believed Freddie. I poked a few holes in his credibility and I can make the reasonable doubt argument, but in the end, his testimony combined with George Russo's and the chambermaid's—it's pretty compelling. Nobody doubts Billy was there. Nobody doubts he had a motive to kill Roy Johnson. And nobody doubts he said he was going to kill Roy Johnson.

"On the other hand, there is a lot of sympathy for Billy on that jury and they may believe Roy Johnson took the drug money in 1982. That gives Sellers and Winters a motive for murder. Why Sellers didn't kill Roy Johnson when he got out two years ago presents a problem, but we still have a shot with the evidence as it stands right now.

"The other part of it is I believe Billy. I don't think he killed Roy Johnson. But nothing adds up. It just doesn't make sense. He was there. He had the motive and intent."

"I agree with you," Tom replied. "This one is impossible to figure out if Billy is truly innocent. So what's the strategy going forward?"

"I'm not sure. I've got three snakes subpoenaed to testify. I'm going to make them squirm over the weekend, but in the end, I think I'm better off without them. Unless Jeanette comes up with another surprise on Monday, I may not put on a witness."

"Pore over everything this weekend to make sure you've covered all your bases and then go with your gut instinct. If you don't think you need to call a witness, then don't," Tom said.

"I'm going over to Gladestown tomorrow to talk to Rosie and Carlisle. Maybe one of them can find something to help us."

"Just be careful."

"I will, Dad. I will."

CHAPTER SEVENTY-TWO

Bobby Joe Sellers did not intimidate anyone by his appearance. In his late forties, he was a little wisp of a man standing less than five foot seven and weighing about one hundred thirty-five pounds with long stringy hair and a beard. But he was surprisingly strong for his size. In prison they had called him "Loco" because he was just plain crazy. Nobody would go near him.

Bobby Joe got out of prison in 2003 with only two things on his mind: He wanted to get the son of a bitch who put him in there and he wanted his money. He'd accomplished his first goal but he hadn't gotten the money yet. After two years he was still waiting. Bernie was giving him money in dribs and drabs to live on but that was it. He told Bobby Joe that he had to wait until Randy got out of prison—some kind of a joint account or something—and now Bernie said this little peckerhead lawyer was trying to screw up everything. If they had to testify in this trial, they could lose it all.

The case was front-page news in the major papers on Saturday. The press and the news media focused on the two FBI agents who had testified the previous day and that Roy Johnson was a criminal suspect way back in 1982 and Dynatron may have been financed by drug money.

Kevin worked all day on Saturday at the hotel. He'd had his process servers hand deliver letters to Bernie, Bobby Joe Sellers, and Randy Winters that morning, telling them to be in court promptly at nine o'clock on Monday or face contempt of court charges. He hoped Bernie would make sure the other two showed up. He headed out for Gladestown a little before seven in the evening so he could catch Rosie around closing, when the place was empty, and they could sit alone and chat—over some gator fritters, of course.

Rosie was excited to see him.

"Counselor, I hear you're giving them all they can handle and then some. Come on in and sit down here, and I'll fix you some gator fritters. We need to keep you healthy so Mr. Fuller can go home to his children and not to prison."

"Is that just your sentiment, Rosie?"

"That's the way everybody feels. This place has been packed all week—people coming from all over. And they all want to see Mr. Fuller go home to his children."

"Really?"

"Oh yeah."

The sky had started to darken on the drive over and Kevin had heard the distant rumblings of thunder. A storm was brewing, although he had no idea where it was headed. Storms moved fast in Florida. As he sat with Rosie, the storm hit Gladestown full force—pouring rain, thunder, and lightning. The lights went out almost immediately.

Rosie was perfectly calm. She had candles going in a heartbeat.

"It's times like this that I wish my husband was still around," she told him. "We loved to cuddle in storms."

Kevin was too focused to even picture Rosie and her husband cuddling.

Just then Rosie's cell phone rang. It was Carlisle.

"Who are you there with?" he asked.

"Kevin, the lawyer."

"Are the lights out?"

"Yeah. I think they're out all over town. Are they out at your house?"

Carlisle didn't answer the question. "Rosie, go lock the front door."

"It's already locked. I locked it when the counselor came in. I didn't want anybody disturbing our conversation. Why did you want me to lock it?"

"I was coming in on the boat. I heard Winters over the radio say something about 'the lawyer' being at your place. I think they might try to kill him."

"Come on, Carlisle, you've been watching too many movies."

"Maybe. Is the back door locked?"

"Of course."

"Okay. I'm going to be at the back door in a couple of minutes. I'll knock twice. I want you both to be ready to leave. Do you have candles lit?"

"You know I do." Carlisle and Rosie had been through a few storms together.

"Leave them lit and head for the back door."

There was something about the calm and seriousness in Carlisle's voice that made Rosie stop arguing with him. She hung up the phone.

"Counselor, I want you to follow me into the kitchen," she said.

"Why?" Kevin asked.

"Don't ask questions, just follow me."

By the time they reached the back door in the kitchen, they heard the two knocks. Rosie opened the door. Carlisle was standing there. His car was in the background with the lights out and the motor running. "Both of you get in the backseat," he commanded.

"What's going on?" Kevin asked.

"Get in the car," Carlisle told him. "I'll tell you when we're moving."

"I've got my own car right here," Rosie said.

"Don't argue with me, Rosie," Carlisle told her. It was the way he said it once again that made Rosie walk toward the car without protest.

When they were in the car, Carlisle backed away from the restaurant with the lights still out. He headed down a road behind the restaurant; it could not be seen from the front. After a few minutes, he finally spoke.

"At some point they'll figure you're not coming out," he said.

"Who are they?" Kevin asked.

"Right now, just Bobby Joe Sellers is sitting in his car across the street from Rosie's. I suspect he's waiting for Winters to show up." Carlisle told Kevin about the radio transmission.

"That doesn't necessarily mean they're out to kill me," Kevin said.

"No, it doesn't. Sellers is just sitting across the street from Rosie's in a thunderstorm with his lights out and the car off for no reason. Maybe he likes the sound of the rain."

"How do you know it's Sellers?"

"Because I looked in the car window."

"Without him seeing you?"

Rosie cut in at that point. "Carlisle could be standing behind you and you'd never see him or hear him if he didn't want you to."

"So what do we do now?" Kevin asked.

"We're going to my house," Carlisle replied.

"Not me," Rosie said. "I'm going home."

"When they finally realize you two are not coming out, Rosie, where do you think they're gonna go?"

Rosie didn't answer because she knew the answer.

"Well, if I'm not home, don't you think they're eventually going to go to your house?"

"Maybe. But they're not going to like the reception they receive."

Carlisle's mother, Mary, already had the beds made up when they arrived at her home. Carlisle would not allow any lights on so there was nothing to do but go to bed. Rosie got the guest room while Kevin got Carlisle's room. It was a large room, and against one wall, Carlisle had his fishing rods, a gun rack, and a crossbow with arrows. Kevin studied the crossbow for a minute. It was dark and he couldn't see much. He knew crossbow hunting was a sport for exceptional hunters. He'd had a friend in law school who did it, but he'd never actually seen a crossbow before, although he remembered reading about it in the history of the Middle Ages.

After his survey of the room, Kevin looked for Carlisle from the bedroom door to say good night. He saw him sitting atop a picnic table on the back porch, surveying the landscape with his night vision goggles on, a pistol on the table and a rifle lying across his lap. He looked a lot different than the man who first took him out on the airboat, but Kevin was confident that he was no less efficient. He closed the door and went to bed.

When Randy called saying Bernie wanted the lawyer dead, Bobby Joe was ecstatic.

He parked across the street from Rosie's in the shadows. It was a full-blown thunderstorm. Nobody would see him there. He waited for over an hour for Randy to arrive.

"What's going on?" Randy asked when he jumped in the passenger seat. He'd gotten soaked going from his pickup, which was parked right behind Bobby Joe's car, to the passenger seat. "Man, it's bad out there," he said not waiting for Bobby Joe to answer his first question.

"Nothin's happening here," Bobby Joe told him. "I haven't seen anybody move in an hour."

Randy was the big, burly member of the group but at his core Randy was not a violent man. He was a fisherman who loved the water and happened to become a drug smuggler. He'd initially teamed up with Bobby Joe in that endeavor and now he was lashed to him again, because after twenty years in prison, the only hope he had of a decent life was the money. He would do anything for the money.

Bernie had told both of them they would get their money when the trial was over. Now they were subpoenaed and the possibility of losing everything weighed heavily on the two of them, maybe more on Bobby Joe because he was more emotional.

"This is the perfect time to kill this son of a bitch," Bobby Joe said. "Hell, you couldn't hear a shot two feet away. I'm gonna go check on them."

He was out of the car in a flash. Randy watched him sneak up to the front door of the restaurant, oblivious to the rain, the wind, and the lightning. *Crazy bastard,* Randy thought to himself. *What did they call him in prison, "Loco"? Perfect name.*

Bobby Joe was back minutes later. "They're gone," he said. "The lawyer's car is still out front."

"They probably saw you and slipped out the back door," Randy said.

"Yeah, I thought about that. I went around back. Rosie's car is still there."

"What the fuck is going on?" Randy asked nobody in particular.

They drove to Rosie's house, but there were no cars in the driveway and all the lights were out.

"It's gotta be Carlisle," Randy said. "He knows the two of them. He probably heard my message and went to Rosie's."

"We oughta kill him along with the lawyer. He's crazy anyway. Everybody knows the story of him and that bird. We ought to kill him just for that reason alone."

"You're paranoid, Bobby Joe."

They drove to within two blocks of Carlisle's house. Bobby Joe hit the lights and jumped out of the car. Randy followed him.

They approached the back of the house from the waterside. As they got nearer somebody turned a light on inside, and for a brief moment they could see Carlisle sitting on the back porch with his night vision goggles and his rifle. Randy signaled that they needed to go back to the car.

"That's it for the night," he told Bobby Joe when they got there. "We're going home."

"What are you talking about? There's two of us and only one of him."

"That's Scotch Buchanan's kid and he's got night vision goggles. He'd pick us off like ducks in a shooting gallery."

"We'll go around front."

"Sure. And make it easier for him. He can blow us away as we walk in the front door."

"If we don't get that lawyer, I ain't showin' up in court on Monday. I don't wanna lose that money, but I don't wanna go back to prison either."

"Maybe something else will come up. But we're through for the night."

CHAPTER SEVENTY-THREE

They were all up early the next morning. Rosie insisted on cooking breakfast since Carlisle wouldn't let her go to work.

"You're not opening until the sun comes up, Rosie," he told her.

"But I've got regular customers, Carlisle. You know that."

"You're just going to have to tell them you were sick or something."

She settled for making bacon and eggs for the four of them.

Carlisle drove them down to the restaurant at eight.

"I'm trying to figure out why those guys were after you last night," Carlisle said on the drive over.

"They don't want to testify," Kevin replied.

"They must have something real big to hide."

Kevin was sure they did and whatever it was, it was contained in the files that David Lefter had copied. *Where the hell are those files?* he asked himself.

Everything seemed to be peaceful when they arrived at the restaurant. Kevin's car was still where he left it. Rosie immediately unlocked the front door and made preparations for opening up. Nobody was waiting outside.

"I bet I lost ten customers already," she grumbled.

Even Carlisle laughed.

"You got two beds in your hotel room?" he asked Kevin.

"Yeah. Why?" Kevin replied.

"Because you're going to have a guest tonight."

"Come on, Carlisle, you don't need to do that. I'll be fine."

"I know you will because I'm going to be there."

"What about Rosie? Who's going to watch her?"

"She don't need watching anymore. They were only after her to get to you. You're the prize, Counselor."

Carlisle followed Kevin's car to Verona, and eventually, to his hotel. While Kevin worked, Carlisle slept. He'd been up all night the night before. He awoke around one, and they went out and had lunch.

It was one thirty by the time they arrived at the restaurant, a little diner on a side street a couple of blocks from the hotel. The place was deserted except for the one waitress who covered the counter and the booths. It was a good place to have a private conversation.

"It's time for us to talk, Carlisle," Kevin said.

"I was waiting for you to get around to it. What did Billy tell you about that night?"

"He said he was there. He said he was drunk. But he said he didn't hit anybody on the road, although he couldn't be absolutely sure."

"Is that it?"

"Pretty much. He said that night was actually the fourth night he'd gone over there. He was gradually working his courage up to shoot Johnson. He snuck into the backyard every night undetected. He said Roy went out there every night."

"Do you believe him?" Carlisle asked.

"I do."

Carlisle was trying to process this new information and weigh it against the evidence that he already knew, but Kevin had something else to tell him.

"I have some news about your father's death too," Kevin began.

Carlisle looked puzzled. "What are you talking about?"

"I think your father was murdered by Bobby Joe Sellers."

"What?"

"Your father was the confidential informant who busted the marijuana ring back in 1982. The State has confirmed that to me. Bobby Joe got out of prison on April fifth of 2003. That's too close in time to your father's death to be coincidental. He must have snuck up on your dad."

"No. They knew each other," Carlisle said. "My dad would have invited him aboard the boat. Bobby Joe probably waited until he had the jump on him and hit him over the head with something. Then he must have just shoved him overboard."

Carlisle was clearly agitated by this revelation. He kept running his hands through his hair over and over while staring at the wall. "I was within five feet of him the other night," he finally said to the wall.

"Carlisle, the State is going to get him. I wouldn't be surprised if they detain him for questioning when he shows up for court on Monday."

"If he shows up."

"They'll get him eventually. He's not worth throwing your life away for."

"Maybe." Carlisle was still staring at the wall.

They didn't talk about it anymore after that, although Carlisle stayed with him the rest of the day and that night. It was like his whole being had drifted off to another place.

* * *

The Alligator Man murder had been a topic of discussion on the Sunday morning talk shows with some of the pundits making predictions on the outcome of the trial. They were unanimous in their belief that William Fuller would be convicted, although nobody thought he would get the death penalty.

CHAPTER SEVENTY-FOUR

It was a zoo in front of the courthouse on Monday morning. Barriers were set up to handle the crowds. The talking heads were already broadcasting from their kiosks across the street. Carlisle had walked Kevin over. Although Carlisle left his rifle in the car, Kevin was sure he had a weapon on him somewhere. They were about a block from the courthouse observing the scene.

"They can smell blood in the water," Carlisle said.

"Yeah. Everybody will be in Billy's corner until he gets convicted. Then they'll go home and look for something else to get excited about. The world is crazy."

"I'm with you there. Listen, I'm going to leave now. Walk straight into the courthouse. Don't stop and talk to anybody."

Kevin shook Carlisle's hand. "Thanks," he said. "For everything."

"You've done just as much for me as I've done for you," Carlisle said. "And you've trusted me enough to share with me what your client told you. I didn't fully process it until this morning. I've got a hunch about something—something I remembered. If you can keep this trial going for another day, maybe I'll have some new evidence for you."

Before Kevin had an opportunity to inquire about what that new evidence might possibly be, Carlisle was gone.

The courtroom was full when Kevin finally arrived inside. Some reporters had stopped him at the top of the steps but he had refused to talk to them.

Billy was already there, dressed in the black suit that he had worn the first day. Kevin barely had time to talk to him.

"How are you feeling?" he asked.

"I'm a little nervous. Today's the day, isn't it?"

"Maybe. You never know what the State is going to do."

Just then, the bailiff yelled, "All rise!" and Judge Thorpe entered the courtroom. He must have had a bad weekend with the knee because the limp was more pronounced than normal and his countenance seemed especially malevolent.

"Before we bring the jury in, Ms. Truluc, are you resting your case?"

"No, Your Honor, I have three more witnesses to call."

Kevin was caught totally off guard. *Who the hell is she bringing in now?*

Judge Thorpe did not look happy. "Bring in the jury," he told the bailiff.

When the jurors were seated, the judge looked at Jeanette. "Ms. Truluc, call your next witness."

Jeanette stood up. "The State calls Bobby Joe Sellers."

Jeanette had known about Kevin's intention to call Bobby Joe Sellers, Randy Winters, and Bernie Stang for several days because Bernie had called her boss, Ralph Curtis, and tried to enlist his help in getting the subpoenas quashed. It wasn't hard to size up what was left of Kevin's case: He'd done a good job establishing through the retired FBI agent, Richard Bothwell, that Roy Johnson was probably in on the drug operation and probably used drug money to start Dynatron. If it was Sellers's and Winters's drug money, they had a motive to kill Roy Johnson. Winters got out of prison the same week Johnson was murdered, so he not only had opportunity, but also the timing couldn't have been better for the defense.

Jeanette could choose to ignore those facts or address them in her case. Since Kevin was calling these guys anyway, it was a better strategy for her to get to them first. She had one of the sheriff's men prepared to serve them with her subpoena as they walked in the door on Monday morning.

Kevin saw her strategy immediately. He wanted to kick himself since he had left all three men under subpoena even though he had no intention of calling them.

The bailiff returned empty-handed. "He's not here, Your Honor."

The judge looked at Jeanette. "Was he served?"

"Mr. Wylie had him served, Judge. I was just going to piggyback on that service this morning."

The judge looked at Kevin.

"That's correct, Judge," Kevin replied. "He was served. The affidavit of service is in the court file."

"I'll issue a warrant for his arrest," the judge said. "Call your next witness."

"The State calls Randy Winters."

Randy Winters wore a tan corduroy jacket, black slacks, and a blue open-collar button-down shirt into the courtroom. He was well manicured. Jeanette went through some preliminary questions to establish his prison history. Randy told her he had been in a federal penitentiary for twenty-two years.

"Did you know Roy Johnson back in the eighties before you were convicted?"

"Yeah, I knew him. We weren't close friends or anything, but I knew him."

"Was he part of the drug-smuggling operation?"

"Absolutely not."

"Why do you say 'absolutely not'?"

"Because I knew everybody who was involved and he wasn't."

"We heard testimony from an FBI agent last week that Roy Johnson was a suspect in that drug operation. Do you disagree with that?"

"I don't disagree with it. Everybody was a suspect. They eventually arrested at least half of the men in town. They didn't arrest Roy Johnson because he wasn't involved. He may have been a suspect like everybody else, but he wasn't involved and he was never arrested."

"Did you ever give him any money to hold for you?"

"No."

"Do you know where he got the money to start his company, Dynatron?"

"I assume he had investors like every other businessman who starts a company."

"Did you ever give him any money to invest?"

"No."

"No further questions, Your Honor."

"Cross, Mr. Wylie?"

Kevin stood up. "Yes, Your Honor."

CHAPTER SEVENTY-FIVE

Randy Winters had been a fairly good witness so far, although Kevin suspected that the jury did not believe his story about Roy Johnson not being involved in the drug-smuggling operation. They would have to disbelieve the testimony of an FBI agent to buy that story. Still, Kevin felt he had to go after him.

"Who was your lawyer in your criminal case back in 1982?"

"Bernie Stang."

"Is he still your lawyer?"

"Yes."

"Did you know he was also Roy Johnson's lawyer?"

"No, I didn't."

"Are you testifying that there is absolutely no connection between Bernie Stang representing you, Bobby Joe Sellers, and Roy Johnson?"

"None."

"It's just coincidence. Is that what you are saying?"

"Those are your words, Counselor. I'm saying I don't know how, why, or when Bernie came to represent Roy Johnson. All I know is that he represented me and Bobby Joe. He's a criminal lawyer. That's what he does."

"You got out of prison on April fourth in 2005, is that correct?"

"Yes."

"Where were you at eleven thirty the evening of April tenth?"

"I'm not sure. Probably sleeping. I started fishing right away when I got out. We get up early."

"Was anybody with you when you were sleeping on the night of April tenth?"

"No, I was alone."

Kevin paused a moment before proceeding.

"You testified on direct examination that you knew everybody involved in the drug operation, correct?"

"That's correct."

"Is that because you were running it?"

"Yes."

"How long was it operating for?"

"Several years."

"Can you be more specific?"

"Three years."

"Only three years?"

"Yes."

"It wasn't ten years?"

"No, it wasn't ten years."

"Where is the money you made in that operation?"

"I spent it."

"You didn't maybe squirrel it away in a hidden account in the Cayman Islands with the help of your lawyer, did you?"

Jeanette was on her feet in a heartbeat. "Objection, Your Honor."

"Objection sustained," Judge Thorpe bellowed. Kevin knew there was more to come. "Mr. Wylie, you know better than to ask a question that constitutes nothing more than your own testimony. It does not matter what the answer to that question is. It was intended to plant a seed in the jury's mind without any facts to support it. And I make this statement in front of the jury because, ladies and gentlemen of the jury, I am instructing you to not consider the question. Strike it from your mind as if it was never asked because it is nothing but pure speculation. Mr. Wylie, if you ask another question like that I will hold you in contempt of court."

Kevin waited until the judge was completely finished before firing back. He knew he had to be quick before the judge cut him off. "With all due respect, Your Honor, this jury heard testimony from an FBI agent that Roy Johnson was a principal in the drug operation and that drug money may have been used to finance his company, which had money in offshore accounts in the Cayman Islands. I am in my rights as attorney for the accused to question the credibility of a convicted felon, the man who was running the drug ring, as to where the money really went. I don't have to accept his testimony."

The battle had begun. Everybody—the jurors, the gallery, even some of the court personnel—was frozen, not daring to move. All eyes were on Judge Thorpe.

"Clear the courtroom," the judge yelled at the bailiff. He then turned to the jury, his voice still loud, his anger palpable. "Ladies and gentlemen of the jury, you can take your lunch break now. Come back at one thirty, and remember, do not talk among yourselves." They all nodded like sheep that they wouldn't. It was apparent that they feared for their own lives if they did.

When the courtroom was clear, the judge addressed Kevin. His jaw was clenched and he gritted his teeth as he spoke. "Mr. Wylie, this court demands respect. Lawyers don't talk to judges like you just talked to me in front of that jury. I want the record to be clear that I am giving you this one opportunity to tell me why I should not hold you in contempt."

Kevin was totally calm in stark contrast to the judge. "I apologize to the court if you took offense at my remarks, Judge. They were not meant as a personal attack at all. Before I go further, Judge, could we remove the witness from the courtroom?"

The question made the judge even angrier because he knew Kevin was right. Randy Winters had no business being in the courtroom at that time.

"Remove the witness!" he yelled again at the bailiff.

When Winters was gone, Kevin continued, "I appreciate the court's role in making sure the jury hears only proper evidence and I am well aware of the tactics of asking questions that have no basis in fact. But that is not what I did. I based my question on previous testimony from a government agent. Perhaps you did not recall that testimony when you made your remarks to the jury, Your Honor. What is cross-examination for but to test the credibility of a witness—especially a convicted felon? The State is parading convicted felons in here to support their case."

"Come on, Mr. Wylie," the judge interrupted. He had calmed down somewhat. "You know as well as I do that you had subpoenaed these people and were planning on calling them. Ms. Truluc just beat you to the punch."

"It doesn't matter, Judge. She put these people on. She wants the jury to rely on their testimony."

Jeanette interrupted at that point. "I put them on because you raised them as your straw men. This is a search for justice, and the jury needed to hear from them because you, Mr. Wylie, were using them as your defense."

"And I have no problem with that, but once they get on that stand, they are subject to cross-examination. I don't have to accept what Randy Winters says. I certainly wasn't planning on calling him to establish his honesty and credibility. I was calling him to establish that he was a liar and a cheat and possibly a murderer. And Judge, if I can get back to your issue for the moment: When you attack me and my motives in front of the jury, you are in essence attacking my client and his motives and his credibility. He is on trial for his life. I have to respond as vigorously as I can. That is my obligation."

Kevin had succeeded with his attitude and demeanor in calming the situation down. Judge Thorpe did not respond right away. He may have wanted to hold Kevin in contempt but he had a trial that needed to be completed.

"I'll tell you what I'm going to do, Mr. Wylie. I'm going to hold this matter in abeyance and let this trial continue, and I'm going to go back and read the testimony of the FBI man, Mr. Bothwell, and your question and your response to the court. When this trial is over, I will rule on whether I'm going to hold you in contempt or not. Now do you have any other questions of this witness? If so, I want to know what they are."

"No, Your Honor."

"Okay, you both have a half hour to eat. And let's see if we can avoid World War III this afternoon when Mr. Stang testifies."

CHAPTER SEVENTY-SIX

As usual, Kevin stayed in the courtroom over the lunch break with his candy bar and a bottle of water. He knew Bernie was going to pull something. The man thought Kevin had something on him, something so damning that Bernie had planned to kill Kevin over the past weekend. He could not envision Bernie just walking into the courtroom without a fight. *What the hell is he going to do?* Kevin asked himself. He did not have long to wait.

Promptly at one thirty, Judge Thorpe walked into the courtroom. The gallery was full again. Word got out that things were heating up, and folks were excited.

"Is there anything else we need to discuss before we bring in the jury?" the judge asked.

A tall, rather robust, white-haired gentleman dressed in a white suit with a booming voice rose from the gallery at that moment and addressed the court. "Your Honor, Franklin Rutledge here."

"I know who you are, Mr. Rutledge. And for what reason do you honor us with your presence?"

All the lawyers knew who Franklin Rutledge was and probably most in the gallery did as well. He was one of the most famous criminal lawyers in America.

"Your Honor, I have the distinct privilege of representing my colleague Bernard Stang in the present matter before this court. My client has been subpoenaed by both the State and the defense, and I believe that the State of Florida intends to call my client as a witness this afternoon. I am here to place an objection on the record and to inform the court that my client cannot appear under the circumstances."

"First things first, Mr. Rutledge. Ms. Truluc, do you intend to call Mr. Stang as your next witness?"

"I do, Your Honor."

"Okay. Now, why don't you tell us why your client can't appear and testify, Mr. Rutledge?"

"Your Honor, may I come inside the bar?" Mr. Rutledge spoke the words as if it were blasphemy for a man of his stature to be addressing the court while standing in the gallery. It was fine for a dramatic opening but that scene was over.

"You may," Judge Thorpe told him.

Franklin Rutledge walked down the center aisle and inside the bar, certain that every eye in the courtroom was on him. He stood in the middle of the well between the two lawyers and Billy and in front of Judge Thorpe, who looked down at him from his throne on high.

"Thank you, Your Honor," Rutledge said, sure that the crowd was now hanging on his every word. "My client is a lawyer and not just any lawyer. He happens to have represented the deceased Roy Johnson, and Robert Sellers, and Randall Winters. The attorney-client privilege is one of the most sacred privileges in our society. Indeed, it may be one of the few privileges left to ordinary citizens. It would be a flagrant violation of that privilege if one's lawyer were required to testify in a criminal proceeding about what his client told him."

Judge Thorpe was not impressed with Franklin Rutledge's

theatrics. "Mr. Rutledge, one of Mr. Stang's clients is dead. His communications are no longer protected if he is dead."

"I heartily disagree, Your Honor. The privilege is still there, especially since both Mr. Sellers and Mr. Winters are still alive. If two or even three people are allegedly engaged in an endeavor and one dies, does their attorney have the right to communicate what the deceased said to the detriment of his other clients? I cannot believe that is the law."

Judge Thorpe wasn't sure about that one either. He turned to Jeanette. "What do you say, Ms. Truluc?"

"Well, Your Honor, I'm not interested in privileged communications. I'm interested in whether Mr. Stang represented Roy Johnson back in 1982, whether Mr. Johnson was a suspect in a criminal investigation back then, and whether he knows anything about money being taken by Mr. Johnson to the detriment of Mr. Sellers and Mr. Winters, as the defense suggests."

Franklin Rutledge responded without the judge asking for his opinion. "As you can see very clearly, Your Honor, the second question involves the attorney-client privilege as it relates to Mr. Sellers and Mr. Winters. Your Honor, this is an issue that cannot be debated on a question-by-question basis in front of a jury." Rutledge countered, "We need an evidentiary hearing to determine what questions fall within the privilege and what questions don't. And we need to know the questions before that hearing."

"You are not getting an evidentiary hearing, Mr. Rutledge," Judge Thorpe stated very forcibly. "I've got a jury in the other room that is patiently waiting to hear the rest of this case, make a decision, and go home. I'm not going to make them wait a second longer than we have to."

Judge Thorpe realized that he had not given Kevin an opportunity to weigh in on the matter, even though Kevin didn't seem to be all that anxious to enter the fray.

"Mr. Wylie, do you have anything you want to add?"

"I hate to admit this, Judge, but I'm with Ms. Truluc on this one."

Even the judge smiled at that answer.

All eyes returned to Franklin Rutledge, who paced back and forth in front of the judge's dais.

"I understand the court's dilemma," Rutledge bellowed in his deep southern twang. "Perhaps there is a way to resolve this matter and protect everyone's interests without an evidentiary hearing."

This guy is really good, Kevin thought. *Now he's playing the friend of the court.* Kevin knew that the coming proposal was planned before Franklin Rutledge ever stepped foot in the courtroom. He also knew that Rutledge wouldn't offer it until the judge asked him to.

Judge Thorpe unwittingly played his part. "What is your proposal, Mr. Rutledge?"

"Well, Your Honor, Ms. Truluc could submit written questions, giving myself and Mr. Wylie a copy. Mr. Wylie could then submit his cross-examination questions. I would follow with my objections and submit legal arguments to the court. The court could review the questions, the arguments, and then make a decision. It would be a quick process that would protect the rights of everyone involved and not unduly delay the process."

"And what time frame would you envision?"

"If Ms. Truluc could submit her questions immediately or within the hour and Mr. Wylie could submit his cross-examination by three o'clock this afternoon, we could all file briefs and submit them by eight o'clock tomorrow morning. The court could make a decision and then proceed with the trial."

Kevin could immediately tell by Judge Thorpe's expression that he liked the plan.

"What do you think, Ms. Truluc?" the judge asked.

"I've already stated my objection, Your Honor."

"I assume you are sticking with Ms. Truluc, Mr. Wylie?"

"Yes, sir, and I would add that I told this court I was calling Mr. Stang as a witness in my opening statement. Mr. Stang had his subpoena before that time. This is a last-minute delay tactic. I say we put him on the stand and you deal with the objections as they come up."

Rutledge had a response to that point as well. "There is no way my client could anticipate how this trial was going to proceed and that potential conflicts would arise involving the rights of three of *his* clients. Besides, the method Mr. Wylie suggests would be too confusing for the jury. There would be an objection to every question and then a legal argument. It would be chaotic."

"Your point is well-taken," the judge replied. "A brief delay to resolve this matter is something I can live with and, in the long run, will make the jury's job a little easier. So this is what we're going to do: Ms. Truluc, submit your questions by two thirty this afternoon; Mr. Wylie, submit your cross-examination by four thirty. Briefs will be submitted by eight o'clock in the morning and we will resume the trial at nine. Any questions?"

Nobody had any questions.

"Okay. Let's bring in the jury."

It had been a brilliant move on Bernie's part to bring Rutledge on board. Now Bernie would know for sure that Kevin did not have the files that David Lefter had taken from his warehouse. He could also prepare and explain away every other question that was asked.

CHAPTER SEVENTY-SEVEN

Kevin went back to Billy's cell that afternoon to explain what happened in the courtroom in case Billy was confused. Billy was lying on his cot in his prison skivvies looking a whole lot more relaxed than he did in the courtroom dressed in a suit every day. Kevin decided not to share his thoughts on that subject with Billy, though.

"How's it going?" Billy asked.

"How do you think it's going, Billy?"

"I don't know, Kev. I think you did a good job with Winters today but I don't really know."

"Well, I think we established that Winters was lying about Roy Johnson's involvement in the drug operation. The jury will probably believe the FBI guy, Bothwell, over him," Kevin said, sitting down on the cot with Billy. "The question is whether they think there is a possibility Winters killed Roy Johnson."

"What do you think?"

"I don't know, Billy. I don't know."

Kevin called his dad early in the evening and told him about the day's testimony and the appearance of Franklin Rutledge.

"Well, I don't think you are going to get anything out of Bernie at this point," Tom said. "You're going to the jury with the evidence you have in right now. You've done a fine job, Kevin. You've given Billy a chance. You've put your heart and soul into this case. Nobody could ask more of you."

"I don't know if it is enough, though."

"It will have to be, Kevin. It will have to be."

A few minutes after he hung up with his dad, Kevin received another phone call. It was his old client, Sal Trivigno. His first thought was not to answer, but he changed his mind.

"Hello."

"How's it going, Kev? It's me, Sal."

"It's going fine, Sal. What's up?"

"Listen, I got a problem and I need to see you right away."

"Impossible. I'm in a trial in Verona."

"I'm not sure, Kev, but what I got to see you about may have something to do with that trial."

"What do you mean?"

"I found some files in the back of my truck with the names Sellers and Winters on them. I think they're criminal files."

The files David Lefter took from Bernie's warehouse, Kevin thought. *How the hell did Sal get them?*

"Have you mentioned this to anybody else?"

"Hell, no. I don't do anything without talking to my lawyer first."

"Sal, can you meet me in my hotel room in Verona tonight?"

"I'm already on my way. Just tell me the hotel and your room number."

Kevin gave him directions before hanging up the phone. This could be the breakthrough he needed. He didn't want to get too excited until he saw the files, although there had to be something damaging in there. These were the files that precipitated David Lefter's murder and probably the planned attempt on his own life.

* * *

Sal arrived at seven thirty. Kevin was pacing the room when finally there was a knock on the door.

"Sorry I'm late," Sal said when Kevin opened the door.

Kevin rushed Sal into the room and practically grabbed the files out of his hands. Without saying a word, he started going through the documents. It didn't take him long to find the reason Bernie would have killed to get them back. There was a memorandum in there evidencing a meeting between Bernie, Roy Johnson, Bobby Joe Sellers, and Randy Winters a month before the drug bust in 1982. Everybody had signed the document except Roy Johnson. Evidently they knew the feds were closing in. Bernie recommended ceasing all operations. Roy Johnson was with him, but Bobby Joe and Randy wanted to complete their last big score. It was agreed that Roy would take his share and leave. Bernie would put Bobby Joe's and Randy's money in a joint account requiring two signatures in the Cayman Islands.

Why would Bernie prepare and sign a document incriminating his clients and himself? Maybe he needed something to remind these guys of the deal in case they did go to prison. Maybe he needed some leverage to ensure that they didn't kill him down the road. Sellers and Winters would have insisted he sign it as well as themselves and Bernie probably felt the document was safe in his storage facility. Roy Johnson almost certainly refused to put his name on the paper.

It was all speculation, but it was the best Kevin could come up with. The reasons for the memorandum didn't matter, though. The only thing that mattered was its existence.

So Bernie was a part of the operation all along. No big surprise there.

"Sal, how did you get these files?" Kevin asked.

"Nice of you to finally notice I was in the room," Sal replied.

"I'm sorry, Sal. I've just got a lot on my mind. Where did you get these files?"

"Yesterday I picked up the tarp in the back of my truck and found them lying under it."

"Do you have any idea how they got there?"

"Not really, but I've been thinking about it nonstop. The day David was killed I left Bernie's office early. David's car was parked next to mine. I remembered that the next day when I read about him being killed and all. I never went back to Bernie's office after that. He wasn't paying me anyway. So when I found those files in my truck, I figured David must have put them there. It's the only thing I can think of. That's why I called you."

"You did good, Sal. And David probably put the files in your truck because he didn't want anybody to know he had them. Listen, I've got to go through this stuff in great detail before tomorrow morning, so I've got to cut this short. I want you to go home and forget you ever saw these files. Understand?"

"Don't worry about that. I don't want to end up like David."

Kevin walked him to the door. "How's the wife and kids? Everything okay?"

"Yeah. I've got a job with a steady paycheck. Things are good."

"Good. I'll give you a call when this is all over."

"Good luck, Kev."

"Thanks, Sal."

After Sal left, Kevin pored over the files.

As he thought about how he was going to present this new evidence the next day, his euphoria started to turn to despair. The files that he had were copies. He had told David to take the originals and put the copies back, but David, not being a trial lawyer and not understanding the all-important evidentiary difference between originals and copies, kept the copies and put the originals back.

I won't get this memo into evidence, he told himself. *Bernie will deny ever seeing it and deny the event ever happened. Sellers and Winters will do the same if given the chance. The judge knows how false documents can be made: You snip signatures, paste them on a piece of paper, cover the lines with Wite-Out, copy the manufactured document, and you've got what looks like a perfect copy.* No, without corroboration, he wasn't getting this memo admitted into evidence no matter how hard he tried.

On the other hand, Bernie had killed David Lefter over these files. Bernie had sent someone to try to kill him. *Bernie thinks that I have the original files!*

What do I do with all this?

There was more.

While the memo was incriminating for other reasons, if produced, it would eliminate the last defense that they had—that Sellers and Winters killed Roy Johnson because he took their money. This memo established that Roy Johnson took *his* money and everybody agreed to it.

After running everything over and over in his head, he knew there was only one decision to make. He couldn't use the memo at trial. If he tried, he would fail and Bernie would destroy the original. After the trial, he could turn the document over to the State and they could get a search warrant for Bernie's warehouse and get the original, but it wasn't going to help Billy.

Another person's image was floating around in his brain as well—David Lefter. David had lost his life getting the documents. *I can't let David's efforts amount to nothing,* Kevin told himself. *I have to get the original of this memo.*

CHAPTER SEVENTY-EIGHT

It was always nice out on the water. Sure, it was still hot but not as muggy. The air had room to circulate. There was a breeze at night. Rainy days were a delightful change. Summer storms were great. Watching the lightning wake up the sky, hearing the crack of thunder, revealing the sea in all its glory, was a sight no human being should miss. But a steady diet of anything could get boring. He had a woman with him now. He'd had somebody pay her for a week. She'd been good for him and he'd decided to keep her on for another week. She loved the boat, loved all the toys. They made her happy and then she made him happy. It was a sixty footer and it was loaded. He could have afforded better but he didn't want to get too ostentatious, didn't want to stand out.

He'd be bored with her in another week, though, and he'd have to get another woman. Or maybe he could find some other amusement. Money let you do anything you wanted.

They'd just had sex and she was sleeping down below while he walked the deck. It was his evening ritual: walk the deck, drink a little wine, gaze at the stars, and contemplate the vastness of the universe. This night was clear but it was moonless. The stars, the vast painted ceiling of the heavens, were there to behold, but the ocean, dark and foreboding, could only be heard, not seen.

He especially liked these moonless nights when he could only see a few feet beyond the boat. He liked to imagine what was lurking in the blackness—creatures of the sea, maybe, that only came out on nights like this. The thought made his walk more interesting, although he didn't believe any of it. He was a practical man at his core.

On his second tour around the deck, while stealing a glance up at the Big Dipper, something or maybe someone—he couldn't be sure—grabbed his neck and shoulder and pulled hard. He felt his feet slip out from under him as he plunged over the side into the black sea. It happened so fast he had no time to react yet it seemed like it was all occurring in slow motion. He was in the air for what felt like minutes before he abruptly hit the water.

There was a loud splash but nobody heard it. His girl was fast asleep. He descended quickly before his instincts kicked in and he righted himself and headed for the surface. Whatever it was, human or animal, grabbed him again, though, and held him under. He struggled mightily for a time but the force was too strong. Eventually he was calm. He could feel nothing.

CHAPTER SEVENTY-NINE

Sheriff Cousins had just finished his breakfast and was about to leave the house to go to the office. His wife, Marge, walked him to the door as she always did. It was their little ritual. He would kiss her good-bye at the doorstep and she would watch him walk to his car and then she would wave as he drove off.

"Have a good day, honey. Hurry home," Marge said after she kissed him good-bye.

"I'll be home for lunch," he told her before he turned and headed for the car.

"What's that behind you?" she asked.

"Where?"

"Right side sticking out of the bushes. It looks blue."

It was blue. It was a long blue duffel bag. Sheriff Cousins pulled it from the bushes. It was heavy and there were holes cut in the sides. He unzipped it as Marge watched from a safe distance.

What she saw made her scream and run back into the house.

Frank Cousins was inclined to follow her to make sure she was okay but his duty came first. There was a man's body in the blue bag, his wrists and feet bound with rope. The face looked vaguely familiar. Sheriff Cousins put his two fingers on the carotid artery to check for a pulse. To his surprise, the man was still alive. He called 911.

"This is Sheriff Frank Cousins. I need an ambulance at my house immediately—2217 Corona Boulevard."

After the ambulance and a squad car had arrived, when he had done everything he needed to do, Sheriff Cousins went back in the house to make sure Marge was okay.

CHAPTER EIGHTY

It was overcast on Tuesday morning and it seemed to set a tone outside the courthouse. The crowds weren't there. There were people milling about, but the afternoon off and the weather seemed to have curbed the enthusiasm. Even the kiosks were silent, the bright lights off. As he walked up the steps, Kevin knew that all would change once the verdict was in. People would gather again for an hour or so and the news would carry the story all night long. However, by ten o'clock the next morning after the morning shows, no matter what the verdict, the saga of Billy and his kids would be forgotten, replaced by some new tragedy.

When the lawyers were at their stations and the clock struck nine, the bailiff announced, "All rise," and Judge Thorpe limped into the courtroom. There was still a full gallery of spectators.

"Are we ready to proceed?" he asked. Both lawyers assured him that they were. Franklin Rutledge was there as well, standing behind Jeanette. "Okay, it is my understanding that we have one witness, Mr. Bernie Stang; then the prosecution is going to rest. Is that accurate, Ms. Truluc?"

"Yes, Your Honor."

"And Mr. Wylie, you are not putting on any witnesses, is that correct?"

"That's correct, Your Honor."

"All right, here is my ruling about what you can ask Mr. Stang and what is off-limits. I've read all the memos. I believe the testimony should be limited.

"Ms. Truluc, you can ask if Mr. Stang represented Winters and Sellers in 1982. You can also ask if he represented Mr. Johnson back then. You can ask if Mr. Johnson, to Mr. Stang's knowledge, was part of that criminal investigation back then. You can ask if Mr. Stang was aware that Mr. Johnson took any money belonging to Winters and Sellers when he left Gladestown in 1982. And you can obviously ask if Mr. Stang represented Mr. Johnson when he was being investigated for criminal activity related to his company Dynatron and when that representation began.

"I believe this inquiry covers the defenses raised by Mr. Wylie on behalf of his client while protecting the attorney-client privilege of all parties. Any questions?"

Nobody had any questions. Kevin stole a glance at Franklin Rutledge. He was smiling triumphantly.

"Bring in the jury."

When the jurors were seated, Judge Thorpe addressed Jeanette: "Call your next witness, Ms. Truluc."

"The State calls Bernie Stang."

Bernie looked regal as he walked into the courtroom in his tailor-made black suit and black tie. He had that air of confidence about him that bordered on arrogance. Jeanette first took him through his credentials as a lawyer, establishing that he had been a criminal lawyer for approximately thirty years.

"Did you represent Robert Sellers for trafficking in marijuana back in 1982?"

"Yes."

"Did you represent Randall Winters for the same offense?"

"Yes."

"Did you represent Roy Johnson back in 1982?"

"No."

"Did you know Roy Johnson back then?"

"No."

"To your knowledge, did Roy Johnson ever take any money belonging to Winters or Sellers back in 1982?"

"To my knowledge, no."

"Would you have been in a position to know?"

"I believe so."

"And you represented Roy Johnson in 2004 regarding a criminal investigation of his company Dynatron, correct?"

"Yes."

"Can you tell the jury the dates of that representation?"

"I really can't without my files. I believe it was a period of about six months. And Mr. Johnson was never indicted for anything."

"No further questions, Your Honor."

"Mr. Wylie, cross?"

"Yes, Your Honor."

Kevin walked to the podium. He just stood there for a moment watching Bernie, who was squirming. It was subtle, but Kevin could see the fear. After Franklin Rutledge's best efforts and the judge's ruling, Bernie knew that Kevin could still spring that memorandum on him. He could call it rebuttal evidence.

Kevin was tempted. He could abandon his rational analysis and try for the dramatic finish by producing the memo and attempting to wrap it around Bernie's neck, or he could let Bernie have this little victory and retreat to fight again another day.

Kevin smiled and winked at Bernie with his right eye so the jury couldn't see. Bernie took that as a message and relaxed. Kevin finished the charade.

"Mr. Stang, you said that you were in a position to know back in 1982 whether Roy Johnson took any money belonging to Mr. Sellers or Mr. Winters, correct?"

"Yes."

"Were you taking care of their money back then?"

"Absolutely not."

"No further questions, Your Honor."

Bernie had a smile on his face as he walked out of the courtroom.

The judge looked at Jeanette. "Ms. Truluc?"

"The State rests, Your Honor."

The judge directed his attention toward Kevin, who stood. "The defense rests, Your Honor."

"Okay, we'll take a half-hour break. I'll hear any motions the parties have to make. Then we'll come back for closing arguments. Court is adjourned."

When the jury left, Kevin made his perfunctory motion for acquittal, which the judge denied.

Jeanette's closing argument was pretty much the same as her opening. She took the jurors back.

"You've heard a lot of testimony in recent days about what happened twenty-three years ago. This case is about what happened on April tenth, 2005. The evidence presented in this courtroom has shown that on that date, William Fuller intentionally killed Roy Johnson."

She started with Roy's wife reporting the event to Carlisle and Carlisle roaming the swamp and finding pieces of Roy Johnson's clothing and his wallet. Then she took them through Freddie Jenkins's testimony, taking the photos Freddie identified and putting each one on an easel before the jurors. George Russo was next, followed by Maria Perez, the chambermaid who identified Billy as having stayed at the Verona Inn for a week.

"After George Russo and Ms. Perez came forth, Detective Vern Fleming did the police work. He went through the guest registrations and compared them to the license numbers of cars in the parking lot of the Verona Inn. A Mr. Tom Jones, an obvious alias, stayed at the inn and paid cash the same days and nights that Mr. Fuller was identified there by two eyewitnesses. An old gray Toyota registered to William Fuller was identified in the parking lot on those days as well, leaving no doubt that William Fuller stayed in the Verona Inn for a week before the murder. He went to the Last Stop bar on the night of the murder saying he was 'going to kill him tonight' and drove to Gladestown and ran Roy Johnson down."

Jeanette then shifted gears to talk about Billy's motive. "William Fuller lost everything because of Roy Johnson: his job, his retirement savings worth three-quarters of a million dollars, his health insurance, his best friend who committed suicide, and ultimately, his wife, who died of leukemia. The straw that broke the camel's back occurred on April first when Mr. Fuller and his children were forced to move out of the family home. Six days later, Mr. Fuller was in Verona plotting Roy Johnson's murder.

"Motive and opportunity, ladies and gentlemen, it is all right there for you as plain as day beyond the shadow of any reasonable doubt. Yes, it is a sad case. Yes, Roy Johnson was not a good man. However, that is not something you or I can consider. This is a country of laws. The rule of law is our foundation. If you find that the facts I have just discussed with you are true—and I do not believe you can find otherwise—then your obligation under the law as jurors is to come back with a verdict of guilty."

It was a very effective closing. All Kevin needed to do was look into the eyes of the jurors to see that.

"Mr. Wylie?"

"Thank you, Your Honor." Kevin walked to the podium that was now facing the jurors.

"I told you at the start of this trial that the State was going to attempt to condense this case into a narrow set of facts that seemed to fit nicely together. And I asked you, every one of you, if you would indeed follow the law and keep your minds open until all the evidence was in and all the arguments were concluded—and you assured me that you would. And then I asked you if you would hold the State to its burden under the law to prove guilt to the exclusion of every reasonable doubt—and you told me you would. And I told you that, under the law, I did not have to put on any evidence on behalf of my client—and you told me you understood.

"So let's look at the evidence with that law in mind and let's start first with the very simple set of facts that the State wants to limit this case to. The State's whole case rests on the testimony of a seventeen-year-old boy named Freddie Jenkins. There is no dispute that if William Fuller chose to go to the Verona Inn on his own, away from his family and friends for a week, he had the absolute right to do so. Freddie Jenkins is the glue that binds the State's case together.

"Freddie Jenkins could not identify the man walking on Gladestown Road the night of April tenth. He could not identify the man driving the old gray car that night. He didn't know if the car was a Honda or a Toyota or some other model of car. And he didn't even know if it was gray. You may recall my asking him if every car doesn't look gray under a yellow streetlight.

"There were other problems with Freddie Jenkins and his testimony: He admitted he lied to his friends and told them that his girlfriend, Becky Yates, was with him that night. He admitted that he initially denied being on Gladestown Road the night of April tenth when Carlisle Buchanan first asked the question.

He also said he was at the Chamber of Commerce parking lot that night because Becky called him. Becky testified that she never called him. That's three lies by this young man. Are you going to base a murder conviction on his testimony?

"Now the State describes April first, the date William Fuller and his children moved out of the family home, as the 'straw that broke the camel's back.' Why? Obviously because of the date—the close proximity in time to the murder. Let's hold that thought for the moment.

"You will recall the testimony of Richard Bothwell, a retired FBI agent called by the State. Mr. Bothwell ran the criminal investigation that culminated with the arrests of Bobby Joe Sellers and Randy Winters in 1982. He testified under oath that he believed that Roy Johnson was a principal in that drug operation, that Johnson left a month before the drug bust, and that he believed Johnson used drug money to start his company, Dynatron. One of the reasons he believed that is because neither Winters nor Sellers had any money on their person or anywhere else when they were busted.

"You also heard from Harvey Booth, another FBI agent, that Roy Johnson was under criminal investigation for his role as CEO of Dynatron. You all remember what he did there—he left before the company went under *and he took all the money*.

"Here is where we get to another date—April fourth, 2005. That's the day Randy Winters got out of prison after twenty-two years. If Roy Johnson was part of the drug operation back in 1982 and if he left a month before the drug busts and took the money *as he did with Dynatron*, nobody had a greater motive to kill him than Randy Winters.

"You saw Randy Winters in this courtroom. He was the man who ran the drug-smuggling operation. He had both motive and opportunity since he lived in Gladestown. So Winters got out of prison"—Kevin paused for a moment—"on April fourth, 2005, and then he killed Roy Johnson.

"I don't have to prove anything to you. I simply have to point out to you that there is a reasonable doubt. You heard one of the State's witnesses, Anne Lyons, Mr. Fuller's neighbor, tell you a little bit about him—how he cried when his wife died and yet how stoic he was for his children the day they moved out of the family home. He was one of twenty thousand people who lost everything at the hands of Roy Johnson. Can you find that he was Roy Johnson's murderer because of this flimsy motive shared by so many and the fact that he was in Verona some sixty miles away from Gladestown for a week—when you have this homegrown criminal with both a greater motive and a greater opportunity?

"I can't answer that question for you, but I trust that you will make the right decision."

CHAPTER EIGHTY-ONE

It took less than an hour for Judge Thorpe to instruct the jury on the law. When he was finished, they retired to deliberate. It was not yet one o'clock in the afternoon.

Kevin took his Snickers bar and his water to the jail and hung around with Billy in his jail cell, waiting for the verdict.

"I think you did a great job, Kev. No matter how this turns out, I want you to know how much I appreciate what you and Tom did for me."

"Well, let's hope we can send you back home so you can raise those kids."

"They're almost raised. They just need a few more years—those formative years. I was a little older when I lost my dad. Your father filled that void for me."

"Well, Billy, I'm going to live in St. Albans and Kate is still there, along with your sister. No matter what happens, we'll take care of those kids and make sure they get plenty of guidance."

Billy smiled. "It's kinda like what goes around, comes around."

* * *

They were only out three hours. Kevin got the call at the jail.

"It's time, Billy. The jury's got a verdict."

Billy started to shake a little as he stood up. "I'm glad you came back with me and I'm glad we had that conversation. My mind is at ease no matter what happens."

It was all very formal when they arrived at the courtroom. The gallery was full. The reporters and the runners for the television stations were gathered in the back of the room ready to bolt out and either broadcast or file their stories immediately upon the announcement of the verdict. The judge waited until everybody was seated before addressing the bailiff.

"It is my understanding that the jury has a verdict?"

"Yes, Your Honor."

"Bring them in."

As the jurors filed in, Kevin tried to glean something from their faces and their body movements. Nobody made eye contact with him. When they were seated, the judge asked for the foreperson. One of the women stood. Kevin didn't know if that was good or bad. He could see them clearly now. Two of the women had been crying. Some of the men were visibly agitated, holding their arms, rubbing their hands. This had been hard on them, that was clear.

"Have you reached a verdict?" the judge asked.

"Yes, Your Honor, we have."

"Would you hand the verdict form to the bailiff?"

The bailiff took the verdict form from the woman and handed it to the judge, who read it.

"The defendant will rise."

Both Billy and Kevin stood up.

"Madam Clerk, will you publish the verdict?" the judge asked as he handed the verdict form back to the bailiff, who handed it to the clerk.

"In the case of State of Florida versus William Fuller, defendant, we, the jury, find the defendant William Fuller *guilty* of murder in the first degree."

For a second or two it seemed that everybody held their breath in a silent collective sigh. Then all hell broke loose. Reporters raced for the door. The gallery exhaled and everybody started talking all at once. By the time Judge Thorpe reached for his gavel, the situation was already out of hand.

"Order in the court! Order in the court!" the judge yelled at the top of his lungs, all the while banging his gavel. The bailiffs dispersed into the gallery, telling people to sit down or they would be removed. Gradually the situation started to die down.

Kevin put his arm around Billy as soon as the clerk read the verdict. He instinctively felt Billy starting to fall. Billy didn't say anything, he just kind of let go. Kevin eased him into his chair.

"Don't worry, Billy," he said. "This is just the beginning. We've got several reasons to appeal and we can get a new trial."

Billy wasn't listening. It was like the events all around him were happening in a world he was no longer part of. He was in a cocoon and Laurie was beside him now. He could feel her hand inside his. He turned to look at her and she smiled at him. Then, as quickly as she came, she began to fade away.

"What about the kids?" Billy asked her, but she was already gone.

"The kids will be fine," Kevin told him. "Your sister and I will take care of them until we get you out of jail."

The sound of Kevin's voice told him he was back among the living. He longed for that other place, though—the place where Laurie was.

"Mr. Wylie," Judge Thorpe interrupted them.

"Yes, Your Honor."

"Do you want the jury polled?"

"Yes, Your Honor."

One by one, the judge started asking each juror the same question: "Juror number one, is this your verdict?"

"Yes, Your Honor."

"Juror number two, is this your verdict?"

"Yes, Your Honor."

Before he reached juror number five, someone started banging loudly on the courtroom door, which one of the bailiffs had locked after the verdict had been entered and the chaos and the reporters had been ushered out.

The judge stopped the proceedings and addressed the bailiff at the back of the courtroom.

"Open those doors and see who's causing that commotion."

The bailiff went to the door and opened it. Sheriff Cousins entered the courtroom accompanied by two uniformed police officers. They each had a hand on the arm of a handcuffed man. Sheriff Cousins led the way as they proceeded to walk up the middle aisle.

"Sheriff, you'd better have a pretty good reason for interrupting these proceedings," Judge Thorpe said.

"I do, Judge," Sheriff Cousins replied.

"And that reason is?" the judge asked, anger still in his voice.

The sheriff took the handcuffed man from the two deputies and walked with him inside the bar so that he and the man were situated in front of the lawyers' tables, looking up at the judge.

"Judge, I'd like you to meet Mr. Roy Johnson."

The commotion started again, only this time there were fewer people. The press had already vacated the premises, thinking they already had the story.

"Clear the courtroom!" the judge yelled to the bailiffs, who immediately started ushering people out. It took a good fifteen minutes to empty the place.

"Everybody be seated," the judge said after the courtroom had been vacated. Only the lawyers, the jury, and the court personnel were left, along with Billy, the deputies guarding him, the sheriff, his two deputies, and Roy Johnson.

Kevin looked at Billy, who still appeared to be in shock. He put his left hand on Billy's right forearm. He was a little bit shaky himself. He looked over at Jeanette, who held her head down, shaking it from side to side.

"Sheriff, are you absolutely sure of this?" the judge finally asked.

"Yes, Judge. We identified him through photographs and we checked his fingerprints with the FBI database. There is no doubt about it."

"How did this happen?"

"I found him practically on my doorstep this morning, Judge. He was in a blue body bag and he had been drugged. I have no idea how he got there."

"We will discuss this in greater detail at a later date. For now," he said, raising his right index finger and pointing it at Roy Johnson, "get this man out of my sight."

After the sheriff and his deputies walked out of the courtroom with Roy Johnson in tow, the judge addressed Kevin.

"Mr. Wylie, do you have a motion to make?"

"I do, Your Honor. I move to vacate the verdict entered against my client."

"Any objection, Ms. Truluc?"

"No, Your Honor. The State joins in the motion."

"So ordered."

The judge next turned his attention to the jurors.

"Ladies and gentlemen, you have witnessed something in this

courtroom today that I have never seen before in my many years in practice and on the bench, and probably will never see again. It shows you that even when the evidence appears to be overwhelming, you can never be absolutely sure of a person's guilt or innocence.

"I just dismissed your verdict against Mr. Fuller because he is innocent. I am going to release him to go home in a matter of moments.

"I thank you for your service. This is part of your duty as citizens and you have done it well. I know that you will take this experience with you for the rest of your lives. It will hopefully imbue you with a healthy skepticism about all things that seem certain.

"You can go home now."

The jurors stood up and filed out of the courtroom. A few of them, including the two women who had been crying, stole a sympathetic glance toward Billy on their way out.

It was now the lawyers' turn.

"Ms. Truluc and Mr. Wylie, you both conducted yourself as true professionals in this courtroom. Things got heated from time to time but you made sure it never got personal.

"Mr. Wylie, I must say that you surprised me with your tenacity. You never let go. You were prepared to go to jail for your client. You knew there was another story. You didn't know what it was, but you kept picking and probing and prodding until the dam burst wide open. I don't know how, but I believe that what happened in this courtroom today is a direct result of your efforts."

The judge then looked at Billy.

"Mr. Fuller, the State of Florida owes you an apology. I have based my entire career on the belief in the judicial process. I have known for a long time that it is an imperfect system, but the events of today have given me greater insight into that fact. You are free to go home to your children."

The judge tapped his gavel lightly. "Case dismissed!" he said and stood up and limped out of the courtroom.

Jeanette immediately came over to Kevin. "I apologize for putting you and your client through this," she said. "And for what it's worth, I'm with the judge on this one. You did a great job for your client."

"It wasn't me," Kevin replied, shaking her outstretched hand.

"I beg to differ," she said.

"I need to talk to you about something very important in the near future," Kevin said. "I have to go to St. Albans for a few days to see my father. After that, I can come back."

Jeanette looked at her watch. "I'm catching the six o'clock flight to Tallahassee and I'll be there for a few days. If it can't wait, I can meet you in St. Albans or Tallahassee tomorrow or the next day."

"I'm leaving tomorrow morning so I won't get to St. Albans until the early afternoon."

"You've got my cell phone number. Give me a call."

Kevin had an idea right at that moment. "Do you think there are any seats left on that Tallahassee flight?"

"There usually are. Why, are you thinking of flying back tonight?"

"No. I've got a carload of stuff to transport, but I know Billy wants to get home to his kids. You wouldn't have a problem being on the same plane with him, would you?"

"Absolutely not."

She turned to Billy, who was standing a few feet away from them. He had just finished shaking hands with his guards and was talking to them while Kevin and Jeanette were conversing.

"Congratulations, Mr. Fuller. I wish you all the best in the future and I'm sorry for the terrible inconvenience we caused you."

"You were only doing your job," Billy said to her. "And you did it very well."

CHAPTER EIGHTY-TWO

The circus was still going on outside in the street when Billy and Kevin emerged from the courthouse. The talking heads were delivering the news of the stunning events inside the courtroom, along with their expert commentary, to the rest of America. Everything stopped when they saw Kevin and Billy. They all rushed to the top of the courthouse steps, jockeying for position in front of the microphones, hoping to get that all-important first interview.

Kevin stepped up to the microphones with Billy at his side.

"Justice comes in many forms," he said. "Today it came in the form of a lightning bolt from heaven. My client is both relieved and gratified that justice has prevailed. Now he simply wants to go home and be with his children."

Having said his piece, Kevin grabbed Billy by the arm and together they muscled their way through the crowd.

"I'm going to try and get you on the plane to Tallahassee tonight, Billy," he told him when they were in the car. "I'll pick up your stuff at the jail later tonight and bring it home with me."

Jeanette was correct. There were seats available. Billy called his sister's house and talked to the kids. They were going to pick him up at the airport. Billy was beaming when he got off the phone.

"They're so excited," he told Kevin.

It was time for Kevin to leave. The two men had not yet acknowledged what had happened between them.

"You saved my life," Billy told Kevin as he hugged him.

"Few people get a second chance like you're getting, Billy. Make the most of it."

"I will, Kevin. I absolutely will."

Kevin did not call his father until after he left the airport. He wanted to be totally alone when he told Tom about the events that had transpired earlier in the day. By the time he made the call, however, Tom knew most of it.

"We weren't even close in our analysis," Tom said.

"That's true. But we peeled the layers back and uncovered enough facts for this to happen."

"You did that, son."

"We were a team, Dad. A good team."

He picked up Billy's stuff at the jail and headed for Gladestown, calling Rosie on the way to let her know he was coming.

They had a quiet dinner that night after Rosie closed down. Just the three of them—Rosie, Carlisle, and Kevin. Rosie served broiled fresh red snapper with mashed potatoes and green beans.

"Okay, Carlisle," Kevin said when the meal was on the table and they were just starting to eat. "Tell us how you figured this out."

Carlisle smiled sheepishly. "Well, it all really came together from our last conversation, Kevin, when you told me that Billy had been at Roy Johnson's house four nights in a row observing him in his backyard. I did that once—went in the backyard. Roy's bodyguards were all over me, so I knew Billy couldn't have gone back there four times undetected.

"Then when I was in Roy's backyard in my mind, down by the docks looking at the yachts, I saw it."

"Saw what?" Kevin asked.

"The Sea Ray."

"Will you talk straight, Carlisle," Rosie said as she buttered a piece of bread. "'Cause I'm not following you."

"I go out to the Dry Tortugas every week to fish. I saw a sixty-foot Sea Ray out there for a month. I don't know why I was attracted to it. Maybe Scotch was leading me there. Anyway, I never saw anybody on it and I knew I had seen it somewhere before. I just couldn't remember until I went back to that dock in my mind.

"I still didn't put it all together until I recalled that Sylvia was the one who first suggested that I look for her husband in the swamp. Then I knew it was a setup."

"Old Roy Johnson wanted her to get close to you," Rosie said. "So she could feed you information and find out what you were doing in the investigation. He didn't plan on his wife getting under the sheets with you, Carlisle. I think she decided that part all on her own."

Kevin and Rosie laughed while Carlisle looked a little embarrassed.

"So how did you get him?" Kevin asked.

"I just went out there, parked my boat a little ways away, waited for nightfall, and rowed over in my dinghy. It was perfect because it was a moonless night. I anchored right beside the boat, put my night goggles on, and waited for the rat to come out."

"Ha!" Kevin exclaimed. "You are something else, Carlisle."

"And for your heroic actions," Rosie added, "you're going to get some of my famous homemade cheesecake tonight."

Carlisle beamed at her words, as if nothing, no accolade of any kind, could have made him any happier than a piece of Rosie's cheesecake.

CHAPTER EIGHTY-THREE

Kevin got up at five the next morning and headed out for St. Albans. He wanted to get home early enough to see his father and Kate and meet with Jeanette. He didn't want one extra day to pass before he put that memo in her hands. Jeanette was the person to give it to since she was intimately aware of all the players and would understand its significance.

When he was thirty miles outside of St. Albans, he called his father. Kate answered Tom's cell phone.

"Where's my dad?" he asked.

"He's in the hospital. He can't come to the phone right now."

"When did this happen? I just talked to him last night."

"Three days ago."

"Three days ago?"

"Yes. He didn't want you to know. He thought it would distract you from what you were doing."

"How bad is he?"

"He's in a lot of pain and he hasn't been sleeping much."

"He seemed fine when I talked to him." Kevin wasn't questioning Kate's veracity. He was just having a hard time processing the information.

"He pumped himself up for your conversations," Kate said. "He knew you were relying on him."

"What does Alex say?"

"Alex is in Africa for a month on one of those medical missionary trips. He didn't want to leave, but Tom insisted. His partner has taken over Tom's care. He's competent, but the personal touch is not there. The guy is a little arrogant, to tell you the truth."

Kevin had never heard Kate say a bad word about anybody since he'd met her. This was bad, very bad.

"I'll be there in a half hour."

Kate was standing outside the door of Tom's room when he arrived. Her physical condition told him all he needed to know. There were black circles around her eyes, which looked almost hollow. Her shoulders slumped. She looked totally exhausted and there were tears in her eyes.

She tried to straighten up when she saw Kevin. "He's sleeping. They put him on an IV when we got here because he was so dehydrated. The nurse says he'll look a lot better tomorrow."

"What happened?" Kevin asked, still a little in shock.

"He just stopped eating. I kept telling him he had to eat even if he wasn't hungry, but he couldn't do it. Every time he ate something it came right back up a few hours later. Then he stopped drinking and I knew I had to get him into the hospital.

"I'm sorry I didn't call you three days ago, Kevin, but you know your dad well enough now."

"I understand, Kate. Now, do me a favor. I'll sit with him. You go back to the house and go to bed. You'll want to be well rested when he wakes up tomorrow."

"Okay," she said. She had no resistance left.

He almost forgot to call Jeanette. It was a little after nine when he remembered.

"I'm sorry that I didn't call you earlier," he told her when she answered the phone, "but I got tied up here at the hospital."

"Are you okay?" Jeanette asked.

"It's not me. It's my father."

"Is he okay?"

"I don't think so. I haven't talked to the doctor yet, though."

"We can put this meeting off for as long as you like."

"No, we can't. I have to meet with you. It's extremely important."

"How about lunch tomorrow?" she suggested. "I've got some business in St. Albans. I'll come to you."

"Are you sure?"

"I'm sure. I'll call you when I get to town. Let's plan on noon."

"Okay."

CHAPTER EIGHTY-FOUR

The nurse was right. The IV did perk up Tom somewhat. Kate was at the hospital at seven the next morning and he was already awake, smiling and talking up a storm, although he looked like a ghost.

"Kevin's here," Kate told him.

"Good," Tom said, becoming emotional all of a sudden. It was so unlike him. "It's been great having him here, Kate, and I have you to thank for it because I never would have made that call."

"I know."

"God certainly works in strange ways, doesn't he?"

Kate just looked at him.

"What?" he asked.

"Is that you, Tom Wylie, talking about God?"

"I've always thought there was a God. I mean, people like you don't just show up to rescue people like me without there being some kind of divine plan."

Kate leaned over and gently kissed him on the forehead before putting her hands on his cheeks and looking into his eyes.

"I think you're right. I think there has always been a divine plan at work here."

* * *

Ray Blackwell was in to visit later that morning when Kate and Kevin were both there. He brought an old friend.

"You remember Eddie O'Brien, don't you, Tom?"

"Of course, how could I forget one of the world's worst fishermen? How are you, Eddie?"

"Fair to middling, Tom. How about yourself?"

"Couldn't be better. I'm just in here for a few days for sympathy purposes. Kate won't give me any attention otherwise."

Kevin was somewhat surprised by the repartee since Eddie O'Brien was wearing the clerical garb of a Catholic priest, complete with collar.

"Kate, good to see you," Eddie said as he hugged Kate.

"Eddie, this is my son, Kevin," Tom said.

Eddie O'Brien shook hands with Kevin. "Nice to meet you, Kevin. I'm not usually so informal but your dad, Ray, Kate, and I have shared a glass or two over the years."

"Or three," Ray Blackwell added.

They stayed for almost two hours, sharing stories about fishing and the social events that went along with it. Kevin watched his father. He really had picked up during the visit. Billy arrived in the middle of it all and everybody congratulated him on his victory. Then Tom started to nod off and they knew it was time to go.

"Eddie," Tom said after all the good-byes were said and Father O'Brien was about to leave the room.

"Yes, Tom."

"When the time comes, will you say a few words for me?"

"It will be a privilege, Tom."

CHAPTER EIGHTY-FIVE

Jeanette called Kevin as he was leaving the hospital. They made arrangements to meet at a local restaurant. She was already there sitting at a table when he arrived. Her hair was down and she was dressed in jeans and a T-shirt, a much different look than her courtroom appearance. She seemed so relaxed and casual.

They each ordered a sandwich and a drink.

"So, what is it that you wanted to talk to me about?" Jeanette asked when the waitress left with their order.

Kevin took Bernie's memo from his jacket pocket and handed it to her. Jeanette read it once, then read it again.

"So Bernie did represent Roy Johnson back in 1982 and he was handling the money."

"Seems like it."

"How long have you had this?" she asked.

"I got it Monday night."

"So you had it in your possession when Bernie was on the stand? Why didn't you ask him about it?"

"That memo is a copy."

"So?"

"So, I don't have the original. If I asked Bernie about this memo, he would have just claimed it was a fraud."

"It's hard to believe you sat on this."

"I couldn't get it into evidence and it wouldn't help my case so there was no decision to make, really."

"I'm not questioning your analysis. I think it's accurate. It just took great self-discipline not to at least give it a shot."

Kevin told her about David Lefter. How he had asked David to get the files from the warehouse. How David was murdered soon after that. And how Sal had found the copies in the back of his truck.

"I don't want David Lefter's efforts to have been in vain."

The waitress came with their orders and they took a break to concentrate on their meal. Kevin wanted Jeanette to have a minute or two to absorb what he had said.

"I don't know what you want from me, Kevin. I have the same problem with a copy of this memo. I'm not going to be able to use it."

Kevin looked at her and smiled. She was right where he wanted her to be.

"Just hear me out," he said. "I asked David to go to the warehouse and take the originals, copy them, and put the copies back. He did everything I asked, except he put the originals back."

"So?"

"So, at David's funeral, Bernie threatened me. Said if I tried to use the files, I would regret it. Somebody must have seen David take the originals and told Bernie. He killed David because he thought David had the originals. He threatened me because he thought I had the originals. When I had him on the stand the other day, he was squirming. He *still* thought I had the originals. I winked at him to try and let him think that his threats had worked, that I had them but I was not going to use them.

"If I had tried to get the copy of the memo into evidence, Bernie would have known I didn't have the originals. He would have gone looking for it and destroyed it."

"Where are the original files?"

"I think they're still in the warehouse where David put them."

"And you want me to get a search warrant and get them?"

"Exactly. This memo implicates Bernie Stang in money laundering, conspiracy, and racketeering and also establishes that Bernie and Randy Winters committed perjury. It is also the reason David Lefter was killed."

"Okay, okay. I'll need an affidavit from you about what you've told me."

Kevin reached into his jacket pocket and pulled out some papers and what looked like canceled checks. "Here is your affidavit."

"You came prepared. What are the canceled checks for?"

"They're my old payroll checks. They all have Bernie's signature on them, just in case your handwriting expert needs some samples."

"You think of everything."

"I try."

"My friend Phil Roberts runs the FBI office in Miami. He will jump on this, I can assure you. He'd love nothing better than to put Bernie behind bars. He knows Bernie will get wind of this soon enough. I'll need to get a U.S. attorney to draw a federal warrant but that's not a problem. If we can get the search warrant Monday morning, Phil will be in that warehouse Monday afternoon."

"Thanks, Jeanette."

"Don't thank me. I'm just doing my job."

CHAPTER EIGHTY-SIX

The next day, Friday, Tom didn't wake up until almost noon, and when he did, he was very lethargic. Dr. Blake Patterson came in to see him while Kate was out running some errands. Kevin was there by himself. The doctor smiled at Kevin but didn't introduce himself. He briefly glanced at Tom, who was sleeping, as he read Tom's chart, but that was it. He never touched him, never even felt his pulse.

This is the guy that Kate doesn't like, Kevin thought, *and with good reason.* He followed Dr. Patterson out into the hallway.

"Doc, can I have a word with you?"

Blake Patterson continued to walk as he talked to Kevin. "I'm in a bit of a hurry. I have rounds to make. What's on your mind?"

"Can you stop for a minute?"

Dr. Patterson stopped but he was perturbed. He was a tall, good-looking guy with brown hair and blue eyes and manicured nails.

"I can't waste my time on terminal patients," he said. "I can give you a minute."

"What did you say?"

"You heard me. What's your question?"

Kevin stepped closer to the doctor, so he was in Blake Patterson's space.

"I don't know who the hell you think you are, but that's my father lying in there. Don't talk to me like that."

The good doctor was flustered for a moment until his arrogance returned.

"I don't appreciate being threatened," he said. "I could have you removed from this hospital."

"I don't give a rat's ass what you appreciate, Doc. I'll do more than threaten you if you don't talk to me in a civil manner about my father's condition."

Apparently Dr. Patterson decided it might be good for his own personal health to just answer the question. "We don't know for sure. We haven't taken a CAT scan. His vital signs are fluctuating, though, which tells us his tumors are growing. He's a very sick man."

"That wasn't too hard, was it? You actually sounded like you cared. You should try it more often."

Tom was still sluggish on Saturday morning, although he picked up somewhat later in the day when visitors started coming. How they knew to come was anybody's guess, but they came in a steady stream both that day and on Sunday. There were lawyers Tom had worked with and tried cases against, judges, clients, and old friends. Ray Blackwell came late in the day on both days. Billy was there as well in the afternoon.

Kevin watched in amazement as his father tried to greet everybody and pretend that things were going well. The visitors would pretend too. They'd talk and laugh about people and cases and things that they had shared with each other over the years. Then they'd say good-bye and promise to see each other soon.

It was in the hallway that Kevin would see the tears in their eyes and the shake in their heads and shoulders as they walked away. One of them was a lawyer he knew from Miami.

"Hi, Jack. Thanks for coming."

"I'd have been here sooner, Kevin, if I'd known," Jack Tobin said. "Your dad is so special to me. I'm sure you know that he represented me when I was charged with murder. He took my case only because it was the right thing to do—and he saved my life. I love the man."

A large black man was standing next to Jack. Kevin did not recognize him. The black man stuck his hand out.

"I'm Henry Wilson."

Kevin shook his hand. He remembered the name. "I feel like I know you, Henry," Kevin said. "I've read so much about you and Jack."

Henry could see that Kevin was a little confused about his connection to Kevin's father.

"I read about your dad's work with the civil rights movement when I was in prison," Henry said. "So I visited him when I got out and we became fast friends. I was the one who asked your dad to represent Jack."

Kevin did not know what to say; he was both surprised and overwhelmed.

Kate and Kevin took turns staying overnight. They didn't want to leave Tom alone. Hospice was brought in on Monday and they started giving him morphine for the pain that was becoming noticeably worse.

Each morning, Kate gave him a sponge bath. She had to be careful because his skin was so sensitive. Kevin just watched. The morning ritual was an act of love between them.

On Tuesday morning Tom called his son close to his bedside. He could only talk in a whisper now.

"I want to go home," he told him.

"Okay, Dad," Kevin replied and turned to Kate. "Will you

get the car and meet me out front?" Kate practically flew out of the room.

Kevin took the IVs out of his father's arm, unhooked all the other monitoring devices, and took his father in his arms. He was shocked at how light he was.

As he started for the door, a nurse walked in. "Where are you going?" she demanded in her most authoritative tone.

"We're leaving," Kevin replied as he walked past her.

By the time he entered the hallway two orderlies were walking toward them, followed by Dr. Patterson himself.

Dr. Patterson repeated the nurse's question. "Where do you think you're going?"

"We're going home," Kevin replied as he continued walking.

"You can't do that," the doctor told him. "This man is not authorized to leave the hospital."

Kevin just kept walking, holding his father close. "Who's going to stop me, Doc? You? And them?" He looked at the orderlies who were already retreating. They weren't getting in the way of this crazy man.

"You're killing him," Dr. Patterson said.

Kevin kept going. "He wants to die at home and that's where we're going."

Kate was right outside the front door when he arrived. Security personnel were on their way. Kate opened the back passenger side door, and Kevin and Tom slipped in as she took off, letting the speed of her exit close the door. As they drove, Kevin looked down at his father. Tom's eyes were closed but he had a wry smile on his face.

At the house, Kevin placed him in his bed. Kate pulled the shades down because the sunlight hurt his eyes. Together they took care of him, washing him and wiping him like a mother would a newborn baby and feeding him morphine when he appeared to be in pain. Tom was in and out of consciousness now. He could hardly speak.

On one occasion, he tapped Kevin on the cheek like he'd always done when Kevin was a boy. On another occasion, he gestured to Kate to come near. He put his hand on his heart. "*Mi amore*," he whispered. Kate pressed both her hands to her own heart before kissing him softly on the lips.

On Wednesday morning, sunshine had already started creeping through the crevices in the blinds. Kate was sitting at his bedside while Kevin was in the chair by the bookcase. Tom's favorite album *Stardust* was playing and Willie Nelson was singing "Someone to Watch over Me." Kevin simply had a feeling like a whisk of air blowing by, but not exactly—something he would never in his life be able to describe in words.

"I think he's gone," he whispered to Kate.

"I know," she replied.

They sat there in silence for the next hour or so, both of them lost in their own thoughts about the soul that had left and the body that remained behind.

CHAPTER EIGHTY-SEVEN

Jeanette called him on Wednesday afternoon.

"We got the search warrant yesterday. They're executing it today," she told him.

Kevin's mind was somewhere else but he did acknowledge the good news. "That's great. Will you let me know what they find?"

"Sure. I'll give you a call either later today or tomorrow. How's your dad?"

Kevin couldn't get the words out right away. There was an awkward silence before he could finally speak.

"He died this morning."

"Oh, Kevin, I'm so sorry. We don't have to talk about this now."

"No, no, it's fine. I need to keep my mind occupied."

Another pause. "Listen," Jeanette finally said. "I'm going to be in St. Albans tomorrow afternoon on business. Would you like to have an early dinner tomorrow night?"

"Sure."

They met at seven the next night at a quaint little Italian restaurant on the outskirts of town. Jeanette wore a white summer dress.

"You look very pretty tonight," he told her.

"Thank you," she said.

They had some wine and both ordered pasta for dinner.

Jeanette could see the weariness on his face. It had been a difficult trial, and now this. She felt badly for him. They certainly had their differences along the way, but they had been through a war together and she had come to respect him as a person. Perhaps the evening could be a brief respite for him. Besides, she had some good news.

"I'm curious," Kevin told her. "And I hope this isn't too personal. Why does a prosecutor from Verona have so much business in St. Albans?"

Jeanette smiled. "Good question. I gave my notice at work. My parents are getting too old and I need to be closer to them. Maybe not in the same town but St. Albans is close enough. I've been looking for office space."

"Are you going to open your own shop?"

"Yes. Nothing fancy. I'd like to be a sole practitioner doing a general practice, mostly civil litigation, maybe a little criminal. I don't want to go from being a prosecutor to being a defense attorney—no offense."

"None taken. I agree with you. I plan on doing pretty much the same thing."

"Really? You're opening your own shop in Miami?"

"I'm not going back to Miami. I'm taking over my father's practice here in St. Albans."

"Are you serious?"

"Dead serious. And I've got some vacant office space if you're interested."

It was Jeanette's turn to smile as she sipped her red wine. It was from Australia, full-bodied and dry.

"I'll think about it," she said. "Now I've got some other really good news for you."

"What's that?"

Just then the waiter brought their entrees. They took a few moments to assist him in retrieving empty plates and setting down the new ones. Then Jeanette answered his question.

"The FBI went to Bernie's warehouse to execute the search warrant and they found the original files just as you surmised they would. They've got the original memo with everybody's signature on it."

"That's great. Have they made any arrests?"

"They picked Randy Winters up for questioning and he's started to talk. I guess when they mentioned that humane little cocktail they give to you on death row up there in Starke penitentiary, Randy decided to tell them everything he knew."

"And you made me wait all night for this?"

"We were enjoying ourselves."

"Okay, tell me the story."

"Well, I guess Roy Johnson had these bodyguards who were ex-CIA guys or something like that. You already know this next part: Your client was down in Gladestown for several days, driving to Roy Johnson's house every night around eleven, staking him out. The bodyguards saw him the first night. They wanted to shoot him but Roy stopped them. He called Bernie and that's when they got the idea they might be able to use him.

"Roy was going to be indicted, there was no doubt about it," Jeanette continued. "And they were going to make an example of him. Give him a stiff criminal penalty so it would look like the courts and the system meted out justice equally. Anyway, that's where your client came in.

"They weren't sure how they were going to use him, but they followed Billy to Verona that first night and they had a guy in a position to watch him."

"George Russo?" Kevin interrupted.

"Yeah. You were mostly right about him. It was coincidence that he just started the week before Johnson disappeared. However, after the bodyguards followed Billy back to the Last Stop where he got a nightcap before going to bed, they gave George Russo a little incentive to go to work for them. He monitored Billy's comings and goings. He called them on the Sunday night that Johnson disappeared to tell them Billy had left the bar. After Johnson's men made him go to the police with his story, he quit the bar, thinking he could just disappear. But they found him and brought him back for the trial. He hasn't been seen since.

"They knew all about Freddie and Becky up there in the parking lot. Those two had been going there for months. They only needed one eyewitness for the setup, so on the night of the murder, they had their own 'Becky' call Freddie and tell him to meet her. Freddie was sitting there, his eyes glued to the road, looking for Becky, when the murder occurred."

"Wow, this was quite an operation."

"Oh, I'm not done yet," Jeanette said. "Roy Johnson had noticed one of the illegals from the migrant camp walking on Gladestown Road in the evening almost as regularly as he did, and the man was always drunk. He was the last piece of the puzzle. They set their 'murder' plan in motion as soon as he left the migrant camp that night. They put Freddie in place in the parking lot and then one of the security guards drove a car that looked just like Billy's right down Gladestown Road, knocking the poor bastard into the swamp. Freddie had a bird's-eye view. By the time Billy showed up—about fifteen minutes later—it was all over. Freddie had already gone home.

"The next morning Sylvia Johnson reported her husband missing and gave a description to Carlisle of the exact clothing the migrant worker was wearing. Of course, the worker wore a white T-shirt and cheap shorts and Sylvia had to upgrade those clothes, but it was the colors that were important. Freddie couldn't see the quality of the clothing, only the colors."

"So the gators really did eat somebody?"

"No. They couldn't take a chance that any part of the body would be found. Winters and Sellers were hiding in a small boat in the swamp. They pulled what was left of the body out after Freddie drove home. It's buried a hundred miles out in the Gulf somewhere, anchored down by concrete blocks.

"Winters and Sellers planted the pieces of Johnson's clothing. They were counting on Sylvia Johnson to get Carlisle to search the swamp. They put the piece of black cloth in an obvious spot where they knew Carlisle would see it. Once he found the clothing, they went back and planted the wallet."

"How did they know Billy wasn't going to shoot Johnson on one of those earlier days?" Kevin asked.

"They didn't. There was no risk of Johnson getting shot if that's what you're asking. Winters said there was a sniper on Billy every step of the way. If he made any move that remotely looked like he was going to shoot Johnson, he'd have been dead."

"Wow!"

"Yeah. And the plan would have worked if it hadn't been for whoever it was who found Johnson and brought him back."

"You don't know who it was?"

"Nobody knows. The feds figure it had to be somebody very strong, who knew the water like the back of his hand, and who could move as silently as an Indian. Do you know anybody like that?"

She had a smile on her face when she asked the question, like she knew something but she wasn't telling.

Kevin returned the smile. "Haven't a clue," he told her.

"That's what I thought you'd say. I guess the identity of that person will just have to remain a mystery."

"Did Winters say who killed David Lefter?" Kevin asked.

"Yeah. He said Sellers did it at Bernie's direction. He said Sellers killed Scotch Buchanan too."

"Where's Bernie?"

"I don't know. They haven't picked him up yet."

"And Sellers? Did they find him?"

"Nope. There are literally hundreds of islands south of Gladestown. Winters says he's out there somewhere. I don't think we'll ever see him again."

CHAPTER EIGHTY-EIGHT

It seemed like the entire city of St. Albans was at the wake the following Thursday night. Kevin was there with Kate greeting people as they came. It was a difficult transition for him but he had no choice. The people came from all walks of life. One of them was a distinguished-looking, elderly black man with white hair who walked with the aid of a cane. Kate knew him. She gave him a hug and he asked her to introduce him to Kevin.

"This is Reginald Porter, Kevin. He's an old friend your dad represented years ago."

The name sounded vaguely familiar but Kevin couldn't place it.

"I read about your trial down there in Verona. You're just like your daddy," Reginald Porter said. "You don't give up." At one time that statement would have made him bristle. Now Kevin felt proud.

"He represented me when nobody would. They said I raped a white woman. They were gonna kill me sure as I'm standing here now." The old man pulled up his right shirtsleeve revealing his bare arm.

"I wanted you to see the hair on my arm stand straight up when I say the name Tom Wylie."

Kevin looked at the man's forearm, and sure enough, the hairs on his arm were standing straight up.

"That was over forty years ago, but it still happens," he said, his face stone-cold serious. "His dying won't change that. Your daddy was some kind of man, son. Some kind of man."

Ray Blackwell came by as Kevin was finishing his conversation with Reginald Porter. "I don't think your father would be all that crazy about people making such a fuss over him. What do you think?"

"Oh, I think he'd say he didn't like it. Then he'd start looking around taking mental notes of who didn't show up."

Ray Blackwell started laughing. "You're absolutely right. You got to know him pretty damn well in that short time, didn't you?"

"Maybe better than anybody I've ever known. You were right, Judge. I stayed, we got to the truth, and my time with my dad truly changed my life."

"He was one of a kind," the judge said. "And I loved him dearly."

Kevin was surprised when Jeanette arrived with an elderly man. He spotted her as she walked in the door and wondered why she was there. He found out soon enough.

"Kevin, this is my father, Jean Truluc."

"Pleased to meet you, Mr. Truluc. Thank you for coming."

"Hello, Kevin. I asked Jeanette to drive me here because I needed to come to pay my respects and I wanted to tell you personally how much I admired your father. He was a giant in the civil rights movement in Florida."

"Thank you, sir."

Jeanette wore a black dress with a gold necklace and cross and her hair was down. She looked magnificent.

Kevin introduced Mr. Truluc and Jeanette to Kate.

"It is so very nice to meet both of you," Kate said. "And Mr.

Truluc, you should know that Tom had so much respect for you and the work you are doing at the university."

Mr. Truluc smiled. "Thank you for saying that."

"That special someone has arrived, hasn't she?" Kate said to Kevin as Jeanette and her father walked toward the casket to pay their respects.

"What are you talking about?" Kevin asked.

"I saw the way you two looked at each other."

Kevin laughed. "I think you're misinterpreting things. We just got done throwing darts at each other in court."

"I don't think so. I'm part Indian, you know. I can see and feel what's not always visible to the naked eye."

"I noticed," he told her. "How did you know Dad was gone?"

"I felt him come to me."

"Maybe that's what I felt too. We're the only family that we have now."

"Yes, we are," Kate said as she hugged him. "And I want some grandbabies—not right away, but someday."

The funeral was the next morning at eleven o'clock. Kevin was surprised once again when he saw Jeanette standing in the vestibule. He walked over to her.

"My father wanted to come," she explained, "but my mother is very sick. I told him I would represent the family."

Father Eddie O'Brien conducted the funeral service and he gave a memorable sermon, cracking the crowd up with stories of his antics with Tom and Kate and "an unnamed supreme court justice."

Ray Blackwell, Kevin, and Kate laughed along in the first row.

Eddie O'Brien finished on a slightly somber note.

"I believe our task in life, simply put, is to pick up our cross, for we all have crosses to bear, and to carry it on that long journey through life, and along the way to find God within ourselves. Tom was not what one would call a religious man, but he was honest and humble and real. He loved his fellow man and he showed it by his deeds. Sometimes, reaching out for others can cause your own journey to be more difficult. And so it was with Tom. He never complained, though. And, at the end, when you saw him with Kate and Kevin, and felt the love among them, and when you look around this church at so many friends touched by this man in some way, you know that Tom's journey to God was complete."

Kevin looked across the main aisle of the church and saw Jack Tobin sitting on the other side with Henry Wilson. Both men had their hands over their faces, trying to shield the world from their feelings.

Sitting in that pew, watching those two men, and listening to Father O'Brien's words, Kevin finally understood. By coming back to St. Albans to confront his dad, he'd found out who his father was, and in the process, he'd found himself. That gut-wrenching pain he felt in the courtroom when Billy's life was on the line was the pain of living and caring for other people. It was his father's legacy to him.

CHAPTER EIGHTY-NINE

Jeanette had accrued several weeks of vacation time and she decided to take some of it after giving her notice. That prompted Kevin to leave work every day at two and make the short trip to Tallahassee to see her. They went jogging or bicycle riding or caught a movie and generally got to know each other in a setting other than a courtroom. Like the other parts of his life that had recently become so clear, Kevin started to see Jeanette as the woman for him. He didn't know if she felt the same way.

A couple of weeks later, on a Friday, Kevin got his answer. He took the whole day off and picked her up at ten. They went out for coffee, then for a long run in the park. It was still hot and they were both sweating profusely when they were done. Following their usual routine, they went back to the house to shower.

Jeanette's father had taken her mother to Jacksonville for some tests at the Mayo Clinic that morning so Jeanette set him up in the shower in her room.

"I'll use my parents' shower," she told him.

She must have changed her mind about the arrangement because halfway through Kevin's shower she joined him. There was no need for an explanation; she just put her arms around him and kissed him softly on the lips.

Later, after they made love and lay together on her bed, she shared her plans with him.

"I think I'll take that office space you have for rent in St. Albans."

Kevin sat up in the bed, a huge smile on his face. "Don't you want to know how much?" he asked playfully.

"When people are *simpatico*, they don't let minor obstacles like rent get in the way of their decisions," she told him.

They both laughed and put their arms around each other and hugged and kissed and for the moment were happier than two people had a right to be.

The next day they drove down to St. Albans together. Kevin showed Jeanette around the office and introduced her to his father's secretary, Jan, who was now his secretary.

"Jeanette is going to be working with us," Kevin told Jan.

After the office, they went to the house and continued the tour.

"This fireplace is beautiful," Jeanette said as they passed through the living room.

"You know, there's plenty of room here," he told her.

She looked at him and smiled. "I can see that there is," she said. "We're already moving pretty fast. We need to get to know each other a little better before we move in together, don't you think?"

Kevin kissed her softly. "I guess you're right," he said. "I'll just have to wait."

When they went upstairs, he showed her his father's den.

"Certainly enough pictures of you," Jeanette remarked. Then she eyed the drawer in the middle of the table.

"This is like the old kitchen tables with the drawer in the middle for the silverware," she said, opening the drawer. That's when she saw the Glock and picked it up.

"Be careful with that," Kevin said. "It's loaded. My father wanted me to carry it after David Lefter was killed, but I refused."

"He gave you good advice," Jeanette told him. "This is the exact model that I have."

"Oh, the one you use at the pistol range when you hit the target ten out of ten times?"

"That's the one."

"Boy, you gave me a message that day. Keep my distance."

Jeanette smiled as she hugged him. "I didn't know you very well then, honey."

They spent that night together in the upstairs bedroom. After they made love, Jeanette rested her head on Kevin's chest and fell asleep. He had never felt more peaceful and content than he was at that moment.

The next morning he rose early and bounded downstairs. He wanted to surprise her with breakfast in bed. A little after eight, when the bacon was cooked and the home fries were almost done, as he was about to put the eggs on, there was a knock on the front door.

Kevin started to open the door, wondering who could be calling so early. Suddenly there was a shove from the other side, and Bernie and Vic were in the room before Kevin knew what had happened.

"Good morning, Counselor," Bernie said. "Vic and I were just in the neighborhood and thought we'd pay you a visit and thank you for setting the feds on us."

Vic pulled out a gun from underneath his coat.

Kevin knew what was coming now. He backed away from the door into the living room.

"So even at this late date, Bernie, you're having Vic do your dirty work," Kevin said. "Vic, are you going to hold his pecker for him when you're both in the joint?"

Vic raised his pistol, but Bernie stopped him with his arm.

"I'm not going anywhere, kid," Bernie replied. "I got the best lawyer in the country. Remember?"

"Oh, you're going, Bernie, and you know it. Why else would you be here?"

Bernie smiled and pulled out his own gun, a small Beretta type.

"You got me on that one, kid. That's why I'm gonna personally blow you away for what you did."

Jeanette was in the light stages of sleep when she heard the voices downstairs. One of them was clearly Kevin's. Another sounded vaguely familiar. She got up from the bed and walked toward the landing, which looked down on the living room. She saw Kevin come into view, followed by Bernie Stang and another man. Then she saw the gun in the other man's hand. That woke her up.

Jeanette retreated quickly but quietly to the den and grabbed the Glock from the middle drawer. By the time she got back to the landing, Bernie was raising his arm to fire point-blank at Kevin. There was no time for conversation. There was only one move to make and she had to do it instantly.

She fired the Glock several times. Even though Jeanette had all that training at the gun range, it was a lot harder aiming at a human being. Most of the shots missed their mark. Only one caught Bernie in the right arm, but it was sufficient to knock him down and force him to drop his gun. As soon as the shots were fired, however, Vic turned in her direction and pointed his gun directly at her. Kevin saw the move. He was on Vic before he could get a shot off, pile-driving him into the far wall. Vic's head hit the wall so hard he was unconscious at impact. Kevin picked Vic's gun up off the floor and aimed it at Bernie, as he took his cell phone from his pocket and cradled it in his left hand and called 911.

"This is so unlike you, Bernie," Kevin said to his old boss after he had given the 911 operator all the necessary information. "You usually play it smart. I expected you to be out of the country by now."

Bernie was conscious but not moving. Blood was pouring from his right arm and he was clutching it trying to stem the flow. Kevin kicked his gun far enough away so he couldn't get at it. Jeanette had descended from upstairs almost in a daze. The Glock was still in her hand, although it was pointed at the floor. Her right arm hung listlessly by her side as she stood by Kevin.

"I couldn't get out." Bernie almost whispered the words in a voice that seemed to be gasping for air. "All the airports and marinas were under surveillance. Had to head north. Have a friend in Pensacola with a plane."

Kevin was surprised that Bernie had actually answered him. It had been a stupid move for him to make this stop, a move fueled by anger and a lust for revenge. Maybe he just needed to try to explain it away.

"But you couldn't just drive by here, could you? You had to stop."

Bernie didn't answer.

Vic was starting to wake up, but Kevin could hear the sirens in the background. In a few minutes it would be all over. He put his left arm around Jeanette, and they both took a few steps back so they were far enough away from both men in case one of them tried to make a move.

A few seconds later, there were several hard raps on the front door. Kevin laid his gun on the coffee table. He gently removed the gun from Jeanette's hand and placed it on the table next to his. She had not said a word since firing the first shot and still appeared to be in a trance.

"The door's open," Kevin yelled and the cops burst in the room, their guns held high.

EPILOGUE

Bobby Joe was born on the water. His father had been a fisherman, as had his father before him. Bobby Joe felt safe on the water. He knew every twist and turn in the Everglades, Florida Bay, and the Gulf waters. That's why he'd been such a good smuggler.

After prison, he felt strange around people even in his hometown of Gladestown. People made him jumpy and out of sorts. Consequently, he liked to stay at one of the out islands, where he had built a little cabin during his smuggling days. Nobody knew about this place, not even Randy. That's where he went when he got his subpoena.

On one of his trips to town while he was pulling into the dock, someone told him about Roy Johnson's resurrection. He lit out like a man who'd literally seen a ghost, although Bobby Joe knew all along that Roy Johnson was alive.

After that, he got his supplies up the coast where nobody knew him. He could slip in and out unobserved. He could even pick up the paper and follow the stories about Roy Johnson.

Bobby Joe wasn't one to make decisions quickly. He knew he could never live in the States again. Even if he changed the places he slipped in and out of, he knew he would be discovered eventually. He had to go south, deep into the Caribbean.

In the meantime, before he moved on, Bobby Joe spent his days and nights drinking beer, sipping a little whiskey, smoking pot, and listening to nature's evening serenade. The world was his oyster. Fuck people. He didn't need people.

One night, when he'd had all the beer and whiskey he could drink and he'd just finished a monster joint, Bobby Joe heard an outboard motor in the distance. Although he was drunk and stoned, Bobby Joe instantly leaped up from his chair like a Florida panther and doused the small fire he had going in the fireplace. Silently, he crept through the woods to the tree line to see the boat. Boats sometimes motored by during the day, but almost never at night. *Who the fuck is it?* Bobby Joe asked himself, his hands shaking slightly. *And did they see the light from the fire?*

Carlisle was puttering along as slowly and as silently as he could, his eyes looking out on the water and the islands as he passed. There were too many places for him to stop and explore each one. He had to pick them at random and keep a close track. It had become an obsession, an every night affair for him. Bobby Joe was out there somewhere and Carlisle was going to find him no matter how long it took. He wasn't sure what he was going to do with Bobby Joe when he found him. *I know what Scotch would do,* he told himself. *But I'm not Scotch.*

Bobby Joe's fate would have to wait until that day of reckoning.

Bobby Joe saw the Grady-White pass in the distance. He didn't recognize the boat or who was on it. If he had, he would have turned stone cold. His little skiff was hidden well. Nobody could find it, except maybe somebody who knew the water and the area as well as he did. A thought passed through Bobby Joe's fuzzy brain for a second, and then it was gone. Bobby Joe started to relax as the sound of the boat's motor faded into the night. He took a swig from his whiskey bottle as he leaned back against an old pine.

They'll never find me, he thought. His ignorance was blissful.

In the distance, Carlisle saw a great blue heron headed in the opposite direction. Unable to tell in the dark if it was Scotch or not, he decided to turn the boat around and follow it. It would probably seem a foolish decision to most people, but not Carlisle.

He wants me to go back, Carlisle thought. *He must think I'm close.*

ACKNOWLEDGMENTS

My greatest joy has always been my family, and I have been blessed in that regard.

My three children, John, Justin and Sarah, are my anchors. We have always been there for each other. John's wife, Bethany; Justin's wife, Becky; my children's mother, Liz Grant; my five grandchildren, Gabrielle, Hannah, Jack, Grace, and Owen; and my great granddaughter, Lilly, make up the rest of my inner circle. The next band of that circle is my brothers and sisters: John, Mary, Mike, Kate, and Patricia and their significant others, Marge, Tony, Linda, Bill, and John. You form a unique bond when you grow up in a railroad flat in New York City with your mother and father and five brothers and sisters. My siblings have always kept my feet firmly planted on the ground. I also have an extended family of aunts, uncles, cousins, nieces and nephews, in-laws, close friends, as well as three godchildren, Ariel, Madison and Nathaniel, and two great godchildren, Annalyse and Juliette, whom I love dearly.

I'm thrilled to have a new publishing home at Center Street, and I'm grateful to the publisher, Rolf Zettersten, and my editor, Kate Hartson, for their enthusiasm for my work. Kate's advice and expertise have been invaluable to me throughout my career.

Kate is the reason I am a published author. She has been my mentor from the very beginning. Kate's assistant, Lauren Rohrig, has been a joy to work with and has provided some valuable contributions to the editing of this book. I would also like to thank Andrea Glickson, director of marketing, and Shanon Stowe, publicity director, and I'm excited to be working with the Hachette sales team, especially my good friend Karen Torres.

Thank you to the staff at Center Street for the outstanding layout and cover design of this book, and especially to designer Tina Taylor.

Larry Kirshbaum, my agent on my first two books, has always given me tremendous support. Emily Hill has taught me, and is still teaching me, how to promote my books on the Internet. My friend Patty Hall provided me with some key insights and suggestions at various places in the book.

In fact, I owe a large debt of gratitude to many friends who have read my work and provided me with their honest analyses and opinions. I am tempted not to name names because I'm concerned that I might forget someone. But, having filed that disclaimer, I'm going to give it a shot: Dottie Willits, Kay Tyler, Robert "Pops" Bella, Peter and Linda Keciorius, Diane Whitehead, Dave Walsh, Lindy Walsh, Lynn and Anthony Dennehy, Caitlin Herrity, Gary and Dawn Conboy, Gray and Bobbie Gibbs, Teresa Carlton, Linda Beth Carlton, Kerrie Beach, Cathy Curry, Dee Lawrence, Ron DeFilippo, Urban Patterson, Stephen Fogarty, Brian Harrington, Paul Hitchens, Nick Marzuk, and Richard Wolfe.